A SARA...

WARRIORS
OF THE GALAXY

GARRY J. PETERSON
BOOK THREE OF THE *STARGATE EARTH SERIES*

Robert D. Reed Publishers • Bandon, OR

Robert D. Reed Publishers
P.O. Box 1992
Bandon, OR 97411
Phone: 541-347-9882; Fax: -9883
E-mail: 4bobreed@msn.com
Website: www.rdrpublishers.com

Editor: Cleone Reed
Cover Designer: Pam Cresswell
Book Designer: Amy Cole

Soft Cover: 978-1-944297-88-6
EBook: 978-1-944297-89-3

Library of Congress Control Number: 2020952235

Designed and Formatted in the United States of America

DEDICATION

This book series is dedicated to the four people who have enabled me to take my writing dreams and aspirations to a much more professional level and turn my creative capability into writing products that make me feel proud to be an author.

To my wife, *Vaune,* for keeping me grounded, as I am the perpetual, out-of-control optimist that always finds sunshine in the clouds and believes that only those who risk, are free.

To my dad, *Pete,* for sharing his views on extraterrestrials, weather phenomenon, and the fourth dimension – time. He also inspired me to become a more curious and observant person.

To my daughter, *Sarah*, in a reverse mentoring role, for encouraging me to take uncomfortable risks and to seek answers and solutions that are often beyond our typical reach.

To my good friend and mentor, *Dr. Harry Bury,* for giving me the perseverance and guidance to seek spiritual perspectives for my future *worldview* and inspire others to join me on my journey.

ACKNOWLEDGMENTS

My interest and passion for all things concerning humanity's past, present, and future is grounded in the speculative truth that the past is inaccessible, the present is disruptive, and the future is simply unknown.

Reading and research are at the heart of my science fiction storylines and plot points, and my own life stories help to frame the generational dynamics within my writing.

The following authors have had a significant impact on my writing authenticity:

- David Hatcher Childress, author of *Technology of the Gods*.

- Giorgio A. Tsoukalos, author of *Gods or Ancient Aliens?*

- Eric von Däniken, author of *Chariot of the Gods*.

- Mike Bara, author of *Dark Mission: The Secret History of NASA*.

- The following authors have added to my reading enjoyment and writing growth:

- Clive Cussler

- Tom Clancy

- Stephen Hawking

- M. D. Cooper

Many thanks to Mark Terry, writer and author, for his guidance and continued support to enable me to make my dream of an epic science fiction series come true.

Warm and heartfelt thanks to my wonderful publishers, Cleone and Robert D. Reed, for having faith in me and my stories and providing the encouragement to stay focused.

To my incredible book cover designer, Pam Cresswell, my sincere gratitude for taking my conceptual cover ideas and transforming them into truly spectacular visual images.

To book designer and formatter, Amy Cole, many thanks for making my book a lovely piece of literature to see and read.

Proofreading by the Hyper-Speller at www.wordrefiner.com

And, to transform warrior princess **Sara Steele** into a beautiful and intimidating heroine, with amazing attire and images to match her beauty and her strength, I am truly grateful and humble for the support of the following artists:

- Design by Kate Knuvelder

- www.kateknuvelder.weebly.com

- Photography by Christopher Alberto, Dancing Lonewolf Photography

- www.simple2cphoto.com

- Videography by Mahmoud Awad Hussein

- www.bay.today

- Make-up by Claudette Hernandez

CONTENTS

PRELUDE

The existence of alien life on planet Earth has been discussed and argued for centuries. Ancient alien theories are now well-established and fiercely debated. The complex issues of "are there or aren't there... were there or weren't there" cannot be answered in a simple *yes* or *no*.

The only real choice we have is to gather the facts and existing evidence and draw our own conclusions. Be it documentation, artifacts, "research technology," or mathematical commonality, the number of believers grows as the facts become harder to disprove.

In book one, *Shattered Truth*, ancient alien hunter Pete Stevenson was the family generational pioneer in the search for the truth that was out there. In what could only be called a "bittersweet" journey, Pete found such evidence, including encounters with friendly temporal aliens, and he paid the ultimate price with his life.

Pete's son Mike was charged with carrying on his dad's mission to distinguish "informed speculation" from "irrefutable fact." After starting out as an unwilling participant in Pete's ancient alien hunting, Mike uncovered many significant facts and hard evidence that changed his thinking from renouncement to acceptance.

Mike's daughter Sara had an intense need to either prove or disprove Grandad Pete's alien theories; and as her vision became clear, she established and directed the Extraterrestrial Research Team, or ETRT, and her similarly-wired associates became our world's best shot at understanding alien presence and even determining planet Earth's survival.

In *Shattered Truth*, Sara's team was introduced to the same friendly temporal aliens that her grandad had met, but this time the alien encounters prevailed in real, life-and-death circumstances. Sara had been given the ultimate gift of alien friends and their resources and the penultimate truth that she was Earth's Chosen One.

In book two, *Alien Disruption*, Sara Steele became the absolute leader of a multi-talented and intensely focused group of determined disruptors: fighting crime, tyranny, secret societies, suppressed technology, climate change, and even evil aliens. Having been physically rebuilt and now possessing superhuman strength, Sara's capabilities were taken to the limit.

The most dynamic storyline in *Alien Disruption* became the intense, mutually beneficial and effective relationship between Sara and the benevolent, female alien leader, Echo, as well as Sara's strong physical, mental, and emotional bond with alien warrior, Pulse.

In this third book in the series, *Warriors of the Galaxy*, Sara undergoes an additional physical and mental transformation into the Warrior Princess persona needed to combat evil aliens while working closely with Echo, Pulse, and the elite alien forces they command.

Humor, storytelling, and the several flawed, but well-intentioned characters give the reader a sense that this story is as much about people, family, and what we all struggle with day after day, as it is about science fiction.

The ending of *Warriors of the Galaxy* will provide a multi-faceted cliffhanger that will tie books one, two, four, and five seamlessly into the *Stargate Earth* series.

I am the eye in the sky
Looking at you
I can read your mind…
I am the maker of rules
Dealing with fools
I can cheat you blind…
And I don't need to see any more
To know that
I can read your mind…
I can read your mind…

Song – **"Eye in the Sky"**
Songwriters: **Alan Parsons**
and **Eric Norman Wolfson**

✦ ✦ ✦

Science is not only compatible with spirituality;
it is a profound source of spirituality.

It is far better to grasp the universe as it really is
than to persist in delusion,
however satisfying and reassuring.
*~ **Carl Sagan***

EVERY GENERATION HAS A LEGEND...

Sara didn't start out expecting to change the world. She inherited it from her dad and grandad, but she didn't expect it. For much of her early years, Sara thought her family was pretty weird, and there seemed to be plenty of evidence to prove it.

Her late grandfather, Pete Stevenson, maybe the weirdest of all, was an automotive engineer whose hobby was trying to chase down proof of aliens and time travel all over the world.

Incidents through the years seemed to suggest that Grandad had, indeed, come across compelling evidence that alien presence was real. *Informed speculation* regarding alien presence had now become *irrefutable fact.*

For the longest time Sara didn't think she'd inherited the weirdness gene, *but boy, was she wrong.*

Now, Sara Steele has become the Warrior Princess and, together with a strong team of outliers and overachievers, enters an unknown future built on a disruptive present following an inaccessible past.

TRIBUTE TO MY DAD...

As I was writing this third book in my five-book series, I thought back to what inspired me originally to write even book one – it was my dad. He was the reason I began putting thoughts and words together that distinguished *informed speculation* from *irrefutable fact*.

Book one, **Shattered Truth**, was a difficult book to write due to the heavy research that was required to build the foundation for the five-book series. My dad always said, "If it's worth doing…it's worth doing right." He also said that you only have one chance to make a good "first impression", so I knew that first book needed to be the best it could be.

As the second book, **Alien Disruption**, was coming together, I used some of my dad's humorous side to add a little fun into the dialogue and banter between and among the humans and aliens. Because I chose to focus on the character development and growth of my main characters, I titled each chapter in both of the first two books from an individual character's point of view, which also helped in my character development.

In this third book, **Warriors of the Galaxy**, I have each chapter titled with the plot point that the chapter is addressing. I remember Dad saying that whenever you write anything, write it from the reader's perspective… and so I have. I am literally writing each book from a reader's sense of enjoyment and participation.

In **Warriors of the Galaxy,** you will also find that I have focused on relationships in a much more detailed and relevant manner. Friendships, alliances, conflicts, and even intimate personal relationships will likely jump out at you. As the human-to-human and alien-to-human interactions progress, strong physical chemistry is apparent, with pleasurable results.

I hope you enjoy my latest Sara Steele adventure in this five-book series, **Stargate Earth,** and in mid-2021, book four will be out. **Battlestar Earth** will be the final reckoning for humanity and will involve the characters in the book you are about to read.

Late in 2021 will come the fifth and final installment of this epic series, **Journey to Earth 2.**

Just thinking out loud… what questions may be raised in **Journey to Earth 2** that will require another glimpse into the parallel universes… far, far away?

Thanks Dad!

Enjoy!

CAST OF CHARACTERS

HUMANITY

Sara Steele – Warrior Princess and the granddaughter in the family with extremely high levels of curiosity and risk-taking, who becomes the conduit from the established worldview of the past to the ever-changing future reality and the *touchstone* for the newly created *world order*. Sara leads the Extraterrestrial Research Team, or ETRT.

Mike Stevenson – Sara's dad and the son of Pete Stevenson, a pragmatic and fact-based decision maker, who also follows his dad's conviction, but with significantly more care and methodical approach. He had visions and dreams of the future, which both fascinate and terrorize him.

Michaela Marx – the astrophysicist team member who has the brains and drive to add energy and connectivity to all things scientific in their quest for uncovering the alien truths. A strikingly beautiful woman, she easily intimidates all who make her acquaintance.

Scott Woods – the ultimate visionary with strong beliefs in what Sara and her team are undertaking, and with the financial, political, and social means to fund the team's mission and needs. He will drive mission implementation with all the resources required by the ETRT.

Cameron Sullivan – the American President and high-level enabler whose position and vast international experience allow him to obtain key information and cut through red tape when needed. He takes on the high-level decision-making responsibilities from an often-skeptical leadership base and proves out the theory that you can teach an old dog new tricks.

Samantha Worthington – the Vice President and former American astronaut with ties to criminal groups and has formed a liaison with an evil alien culture.

It quickly becomes apparent that she has her own personal agenda… not in sync with the investigative team or the needs of humanity.

Doctor Matthew Palmer – the founder and CEO of the leading-edge secretive lab that is doing research and development on metahuman, IT, AI, and hologram technologies. Responsible for rebuilding the wounded Sara Steele, his relationship with Sara gets fairly complicated.

Commander RJ Baker – the son of FBI operative Robert Baker and a key member of the ETRT and the Project Zeus Mission to explore the galactic universe. It soon becomes clear that his involvement with Sara's ETRT alliance with the friendly aliens, and the critical Zeus Mission, has a very significant impact.

METAHUMANS

Elonis – the metahuman with developing social and self-awareness skills that becomes a close friend and ally to Sara. Elonis has the celestial knowledge and technical information database that the research team needs and is a valued friend to the entire ETRT team.

Valos the metahuman with vast skills in matter acceleration, energy transfer, and quantum communication. Her assimilation skills prove invaluable.

Torin – the metahuman skilled in metallic applications, structural dynamics, and epigenetics. Her analytical skills meld facts quickly and succinctly.

BENEVOLENT ALIENS - THE ARRANS AND GREYS

Echo – the Arrans' commander and leader who is the benevolent provider of future alien knowledge and tools that are so badly needed in the Earth's current battles and struggles to survive. Her contribution to the understanding of critical issues and blending of both human cultures and alien cultures provides insight for key implementation needs.

Pulse – the Arrans' ultimate warrior and second in command of the alien force who revealed himself in the last chapter of book two and who seems to have a telepathic bond with Sara. A combination of strength, character, experience and warmth gives an added personal upside in his relationship with Sara.

Laser – Echo's operations director

Spirit – Arrans' link to the soul and spirituality

Peace – The calming influence for the Arrans race

Vibe – Echo's vibration and magnetic guru

Vigor – The Arrans' energy guru

Aeon – The androgynous leader of the Greys alien race

Ava – The advanced AI with superior quantum communication skills

Eva – The advanced AI with X-ray vision and supersonic hearing

Ivan – The advanced AI with extreme telepathic extraction technique

MALEVOLENT ALIENS - THE DRACS AND THE DENON

Vipor – The Dracs' leader from their warrior caste

Serp – The Dracs' second in command from their intellectual caste

Derk – The Denons' leader who took the Earthly name Scorpio

Singe – The Denons' second in command

1

EARTH, THIS IS MARS...
WE HAVE A PROBLEM!

It is 2027. From the red planet, Mars, comes an emergency communication into NASA's Mission Control's most remote location.

"This is Command Major Thomas Shilling, Viking Four outpost commander, calling from Mars Base Delta. Do you read?"

Moments later, given a very short transmission delay, a response was given.

"Yes, Commander Shilling, this is Richard Monteville, Mission Control, Alaska. We are on a secured, quantum, communication link. What is your emergency?"

Another momentary pause...

"Our three satellite towers have experienced a tremendous wave of destructive, magnetic pulse... an incredible and powerful surge. All three communication towers have been badly damaged and at least nine astronauts have been killed."

Two loud *bangs* were heard, and a noticeably shaken Commander Shilling continued hurriedly.

"This magnetic wave came from the far side of our galaxy and with no discernable warning. With no significant weapons defense systems, we had no time to respond or engage in any countermeasures whatsoever."

An extremely concerned Richard Monteville asked, "What is the situation right now, Major Shilling?"

"The wave has passed, but it is heading towards Earth. Please be warned that, based on its current speed, and your magnetic attraction, it will impact the Earth in about one hundred and seventy days."

"What is your current damage assessment, Commander?"

A slightly longer pause ensued.

"The wave has greatly damaged our power sources and we are evaluating just how long we can go with back-up generation. We are unsure just how severe the damage has been."

Thinking quickly, "Commander Shilling, is your antimatter micro- reactor functioning?"

"Hold on… I am checking into that right now. The loud *explosions* that you may have heard were coming from the reactor bunker."

Monteville motioned for several of his staff to patch in.

One staffer asked, "Is your microreactor operating?"

"Negative. As you know, we have had this outpost here for over thirty years, and we have never had any magnetic pulse of any significant magnitude affect our infrastructure. It was at least ten thousand times more powerful than any previous wave… and no warning."

Another crashing sound is heard.

Monteville at Mission Control is confronted with a major telecommunications problem… the signal is rapidly weakening.

"Command Major Shilling, our communication with you is getting weaker and is breaking up."

"Yes, here too. This magnetic wave resembled an atomic blast in its scope and disruption capability."

"So, both quantum communication and interspace transportation are impacted, Commander?"

No response…

"Commander, both quantum communication and interspace transportation are affected?"

"Yes. The cosmic web and the associated star connections are being fried. Interstellar movement among any species, human or alien, is now impossible. Any galactic travel right now would have catastrophic consequences!"

Total silence from the Mars base for several minutes.

A very frightened Commander Shilling responds, but with a very low voice, "All primary power is gone. Survivors are in bunkers. We are likely doomed."

Monteville, with his staff focused on the transmission line, asked, "Can you hear me, Major Tom?"

Waiting a few seconds, Mission Control's Richard Monteville again pleaded… "Can you hear me, Major Tom?"

That was the last transmission from the Viking 4 outpost.

Richard Monteville looked up from his communication monitor, realizing the magnitude of what just happened, and placed a code RED to President Cameron Sullivan.

"Alaska calling. Mars outpost is gone. Survivors unlikely. Destructive magnetic wave in route to Earth. ETA is one hundred and sixty-eight days."

2

BACK TO THE FUTURE

It's November, 2026, and Sara Steele had just returned from a debriefing with the U.S. President, Cameron Sullivan, following a game-changing meeting with the World Council in Dubai, which was intended to be an exposé of all things weird and sinister that was confronting the world at that time, and her team had been focused on for many months.

Sara was preparing to present the results of that Dubai meeting to the entire Extraterrestrial Research Team, known as the ETRT, the following morning. As always, Sara Steele's plate was full and would likely get much fuller.

Exiting the airport limousine, she gathered her luggage and computer case, as well as the secretive notes from POTUS, walked through the main door of her firm's high-tech office in Palo Alto, California, and was greeted by the friendly face of the night security guard.

"Hi Sara, great to have you back home again."

"Thanks Bill, I'm happy to finally be home."

"Everyone is excited to hear about your meeting."

"Which one?"

Bill smiled at Sara's humor, given her two game-changing meetings in the last week, as he unlocked the elevator to the top floor.

As managing director over a group of nearly two hundred exceptionally talented researchers and scientists at *Blue Horizon*, a subsidiary of *Sky Force PLLC*, she would be quite busy with the significant and alien-impacted presentation.

She took the elevator to the top floor and gathered her notes from both meetings. She began to formulate her talking points and an outline for the Dubai presentation and couldn't wait to begin.

Entering her glass-walled office with alien artifacts and memorabilia from her Grandad Pete Stevenson scattered throughout, Sara threw her signature, white chore jacket and blue blazer over a nearby guest chair, slipped on her comfy denim jacket, and logged on to her desk computer.

It was 8:30 pm and she was already back to the grind after an intense meeting with the President following a very long flight from Dubai and realized that this night would be a long one of organizing thoughts and preparing her presentation.

Michaela Marx, the highly respected senior member of the team, preeminent astrophysicist and Sara's dearest friend, entered her office. Sara looked up and smiled at the fiercest combination of brains and beauty on the planet.

"Welcome back, Sara. How was your D.C. trip?"

Sara quickly walked over to Michaela and they hugged, both realizing the enormity of what lay ahead.

"The meeting with President Sullivan was brutal, but the D.C. flight was good. I needed that time to think about our Dubai event. How are you? Relaxed and recovered from the Dubai spectacle? And how is everyone here?"

"I'm fine," Michaela responded with a warm smile. "That return flight on Nancy's plane was very exhilarating and so reflective... I'm just so proud of all that the team has accomplished. The entire ETRT team is extremely anxious to hear from you tomorrow... on both Dubai and the POTUS meeting. Anything I can give them in advance?"

"Sure can," a grinning Sara added. "My thanks for all their hard work and sacrifice. It made me realize how lucky I am to have such a great team to work with. Can I make you a drink? Got a bottle of Dubai's finest vodka. I was just about to make a vodka raspberry cocktail and would love to share it."

Michaela replied inquisitively, "I'll get a couple glasses. Sara, I don't remember them serving alcohol there."

"In Dubai, only non-Muslims can drink, so hotels and restaurants serve the best drinks for their clients. This cocktail is so smooth."

Sara poured them each a drink in their weird and wonderful space- capsule glasses, sat back in her chair and toasted Michaela. "Did anything leak back here as far as our meeting went... any info at all?"

"No, not really. Seemed a lot more hushed than everyone thought. They expected at least a blow-by-blow report of all the agenda issues. The lack of feedback meant to them that there was much to keep confidential."

"Over the top comes to mind," Sara uttered with an impatient sigh.

"Can't wait to share..."

Sara walked over to her purse, zipped it open to a small compartment, and pulled a tiny flash drive from the inside. There was also one of her prized possessions, a small, framed picture of her with her father Mike and her grandfather Pete at a Christmas party that was so nice and so "yesterday."

With drink in hand, she motioned Michaela over to her desk, paused for a moment, and inserted the flash drive into her computer. After she entered the password barcode from her E-watch, the video booted.

"This is the full video of the final day's meeting with the World Council and the rather surprising ending that we were all involved in. It's already encrypted. This info is not to be shared with anyone for the time being."

Michaela nodded in agreement.

At that time, Sara received several text messages and a request for a video chat with her boss and the founder and CEO of *Sky Force PLLC*, Scott Woods.

"Give me about ten minutes to take care of these admin issues and we can get started, Michaela. I really need to touch base with Scott."

"No problem, Sara. I'll just open my activity log and get primed for the next couple of days."

About twenty minutes later, Sara returned and continued with her re-cap, "President Sullivan is formulating a strategic plan going forward, and we need to select what and how we release this info. You might want to refresh your drink before you get started… this is absorbing stuff, even having been there and seen that?"

"Sure. A topped-off refill would be fine."

Michaela freshened her drink and walked over to the computer and started the video, which was nearly an hour long. Sara left her to view the meeting video and walked over to a conference table that held several alien artifacts and related material, well organized and documented, serving as a reminder of the alien age that they were now in.

She stopped to gaze at a *carved wooden bird* found in Saqqara, one of Egypt's oldest burial grounds, and was one of her grandad's prized, alien artifact possessions. How he came into possession of such a rare and valuable artifact was still a question for another day.

The papyrus inscription of *I want to fly* from the funeral tomb where it was found was haunting, for sure. This bird had eyes and a nose and wings, but the wings were not typical bird wings.

But it was her dad, Mike Stevenson, who viewed this carving as more of a modern aerodynamic design and fully two thousand years before man's first flight. Mike was the inspiration for getting a team together to build a scale model five times its size, adding a rear stabilizing rudder that appeared to be broken off of this carving.

When tested by legitimate experts, it flew like one of today's highly developed gliders. In fact, it was a design that was used today. This was an uncontested evaluation and became a seminal moment in the search for the alien unknown.

Sara glanced at Michaela, who was still transfixed watching the video and seemed to be mesmerized by what she was seeing, even though it was firmly etched in her mind as a remarkable game-changer.

"The best part is that amazing ending and Echo's gift."

"Roger that, Sara."

Sara then sat down in front of one specific item, her grandad's log book. Opening it and turning the pages, she once again looked over to a very engaged Michaela.

"Remember when we found Grandad's log up at the cabin?"

"Of course. I'll never forget the rush… the absolute rush."

"Well, little did we know at that time that Grandad and his cabin would be the keystones to unlocking the secrets of the cosmos and change the course of our lives forever."

With that comment, Sara thought back to the event that began that incredible journey and put her grandad on the path to establishing the truth about alien presence on Earth.

It all started in Grandad Pete's cabin in the woods, but it was a bittersweet remembrance, to be sure. Even though the alien adventure began at that cabin in the woods, and the ETRT was created because of that cabin's contents, the sadness of the attack on that cabin would haunt Sara Steele forever.

Her husband, Paul, the kind and gentle Paul, was killed in that cabin attack!

3

ALIEN ENCOUNTER
OF THE BEST KIND

Sara glanced over to Michaela and uttered, "Let me know when you get to the end… I'd like to watch it again."

"Will do. This encounter with the alien Arrans race was right out of a science fiction movie."

Sara thought for a moment and added, "To paraphrase author, Tom Clancy, 'the difference between reality and fiction… is that fiction needs to make sense.' I guess this is our new reality."

Sara stood up, gazed out the window into the calm and serene night, and thought to herself just how quickly life as she knew it had changed. She knew very well that she would be entering a time in her life that was going to be both exciting and demanding.

Moments later, Michaela spoke up, "Okay. At the exciting part… hell, they're all exciting."

Smiling, Sara walked over to the video as Michaela pulled over another chair.

Together, they relived the change of worldview unlike anything ever imagined and watched Sara's words and actions once again.

"World Council members, I am sorry to alarm you, but an attack is in process and we have taken immediate action. Mister Shipley, seated in the front row, has a timer to a detonation warhead for a missile about to be launched from a satellite in the sky above us."

There was silence from some attendees and gasps from others as Sara spoke, paused, and spoke again, *"I will explain everything soon, but for now, you need to listen… and listen closely."*

From the video, Sara had gotten the attention of nearly everyone in the audience.

"It was this terrorist leader's intention to launch the missile, excuse himself from the meeting, and be far away before the missile struck, killing everyone here."

Loud screams could be heard from many in the audience. The others were waiting for Sara's next words, *"It was also his intention to place blame for this massacre directly on me and my ETRT team, as a selfish act of a radical suicide bomber."*

A voice from the third row could easily be heard, *"Miss Steele, why should we believe you and this outrageous story?"*

"Because, the missile has already been launched from that satellite. It is set to impact our location in twelve minutes and thirty seconds."

With that dramatic disclosure getting everyone's attention, Sara firmly continued, *"Be calm, please be calm. Everyone will be fine. Please, stay calm."*

Slowly, the attendees were gaining comfort from Sara's demeanor and her conviction. As the assembly room got manageably quiet, Sara explained, *"My friend, Elonis, is a metahuman and has been by my side for the last two years. We have been introduced to a culture of benevolent aliens that are here now helping mankind and have been here literally for centuries."*

Still, the chamber was fairly quiet.

Sara went on, *"These friendly aliens were the ones who destroyed the nuclear missiles in route to two targets in the United States last month."*

The man with the earlier question interrupted, *"But, the missile? What about the damn missile about to strike us?"*

"Let me introduce you to my alien friend, Echo, who will answer that question for you."

With that announcement, Commander Echo appeared, dressed in what appeared to be a full battle uniform, smiled at Sara, and spoke, *"We are the Arrans, from another universe, another galaxy and another time, and have been on this earth in some form for tens of thousands of years."*

With some members still in late stages of a physical suspension that was necessary to secure the alleged bomber, Shipley, each person's cognitive capacity was slowly being regained.

Now, as each person's full mobility was restored, they were able to understand everything that was occurring since the Arrans-induced time-slip.

Echo appeared to be a high-ranking alien leader, a tall female in a bright-blue uniform with a black cape and a belt-mounted sheath that carried an impressive light sabre. She spoke to the audience with a decidedly soft and confident, speaking voice, *"Our present location is an exoplanet one hundred ten light-years away in the constellation you call Leo."*

With an assured sigh, Echo continued, *"We have major colonies today in what you refer to as the Trappist One System, where seven planets exist."*

Waiting for a response, and when none came, she went on, *"We began as observers, and throughout your history, we have tried to help mankind many times, but not always successful. We will not harm you."*

The entire chamber was quiet and subdued, trying to understand the words and gauge the intentions of this alien leader.

"But the missile? What about the damn missile?" The same concerned man asked again.

Echo responded in a soft and reassuring voice, *"If each of you will look out the ceiling skylights, or any of the right-side windows, you will be able to see the incoming missile."*

The attendees moved to where each could get a glimpse of the approaching missile as Echo paused and then spoke, *"We will eliminate that missile in… eight seconds; seven, six, five, four, three, two, one… gone."*

A bright flash of a bluish-white haze took over the entire sky. What could be observed as a rapidly moving rocket or missile was moving very quickly towards them one moment and then, in a flash, it was gone with no apparent effects of debris, radiation, or even any noise of any kind.

A respectful applause and much relief followed Echo's words and the destruction of the missile.

"You owe your gratitude to this young group of humans, who with tremendous courage and conviction, were able to take the clues of the past and put this puzzle of our involvement together."

Sara was moved by her mentor's words.

"We would have preferred to remain behind the scenes, as we have been for centuries. The ultimate survival of this planet brought us to this day and time."

✦ ✦ ✦

Now, the dramatic scope of the sudden alien presence was revealed for the first time. Several aliens appeared, in the formation of a triangle, and all in different colored uniforms, apparently representing individual teams or special skills, or maybe even different locations.

Sara could now see the Arrans' Dubai contingent of Pulse, Laser, Spirit, and Peace among the *elite force* aliens commanded by Echo.

The conference attendees, mostly frightened and overwhelmed, could see that the aliens amongst them had an almost uncanny resemblance to the humans, except for being taller, with smaller ears, somewhat elongated skulls, and slightly longer extremities.

The entire auditorium became peaceful… it was as if they were in a church, or chapel or some religious or spiritual arena. They were here, yet they were somewhere else!

Laser removed the three people, viewed likely as terrorists, from the World Council leadership committee, in addition to Stewart Shipley, and contained them near Sara and Elonis, per instructions from Echo.

Many in the audience tried unsuccessfully to text or phone others. There would be no outside communication.

Echo began her explanation, *"The three people we now have were the principal leaders in this terrorist plot, along with the human that Sara and Elonis had contained. He was the leader of a large conspiracy to destroy significant portions of the world's infrastructure and replace it with a radical, socio-political structure."*

Frenzied movement and chatter were now being replaced by awe and bewilderment.

"It was also their intention to suppress significant, advanced technology development worldwide. I will address that issue soon. An example of this hidden technology was that highly sophisticated missile that we destroyed."

The alien leader sensed a calming of the audience and continued, *"My Earth name is Echo and when you thought you were alone, you were not. It was my team that disrupted the recent attack on the two American cities, knowing the devastating consequences."*

A very relieved Sara gazed at Michaela in the audience and smiled.

"We must leave you soon as we have many other planets, with cultures and societies in need, in other galaxies in our universe. As difficult as this may be for you to understand… we are humans from the very distant future."

With that comment, Sara realized that a whole new can of worms had been opened.

"We are you, with evolution that takes millions of years. We have God in our hearts and minds and share your spiritual values. We are likely closer to God than you, not physically, but spiritually."

Sara, Michaela, Elonis, Pulse, and Echo joined hands in a gesture of unity and strength.

"We will leave behind several capsules that will explain much of our involvement over the past centuries and also provide the technology that will help to navigate the changing world that is now upon you."

This announcement was one that Sara had not expected.

"And we strongly recommend that you form a coalition between this young, self-less group of believers and the World Council. These perpetrators of destruction are identified and appear before you. But others exist."

Pausing, Echo continued, *"Recognize these people as bad people that will cause you harm. We will be taking these four involved in this attack with us."*

There was no pushback from anyone.

"You will need to identify and stop those who still remain amongst you. After this message from us today, and the capsules left behind, that should be easier."

Echo glanced over to Sara before she added one last piece of wisdom, *"You have in your society what is called the Law of Polarity."*

Pausing, Echo continued. *"That Law states that everything that exists has an equal and exact opposite. That is, anything that comes into existence will have the manifest opposite come into existence."*

This recurring theme was not lost on Sara as Echo continued, *"Humans cannot experience sadness without having an idea about happiness. Light cannot be experienced as such if you do not know what darkness is. And you cannot experience bad or evil without understanding good and righteous."*

Sara, reading her thoughts from Echo, knew what Echo was about to say, *"This Law of Polarity applies directly to alien civilizations, too… there will be good and bad."*

As the capsules were being arranged and identified, Echo moved over to the capsules and explained to the entire audience, *"These are the eight capsules that will provide you with the tools and capability that you will need to learn, refine, and implement significant technological change. The team led by Sara Steele will be in charge of implementation. There will be no negotiation of that edict."*

After a brief pause…

"Let the world know that Sara Steele and the ETRT have our support and will be the sole drivers for this technology.

Echo's voice grew louder, *"What we are giving you… we can take away."*

Sara was humbled by Echo's faith in Sara and the ETRT.

"What we are providing you with are seeds, not pills. These capsules are not magic wands and will not be immediately implementable. They will require your best minds and your absolute patience to reach the final results that will then be extremely beneficial."

At this point Michaela could be seen taking notes.

"As I have said before, your current Artificial Intelligence, Information Technology, and general scientific technology will enable you to develop and master the knowledge

that is here. In our minds, your greatest threats will come from humankind itself, from within, and not natural disasters."

After a long pause for all to absorb what was just said, Sara spoke on the video, *"Echo, we are deeply indebted to you, not only for your involvement today, but for all that you have done for mankind in the past. Why are you revealing yourselves now, and with these amazing gifts?"*

Sara knew the answer, of course, but needed all those assembled to hear it as well.

"We have helped civilizations before, but those not nearly as advanced as yours. With the Mayans and Egyptians, we had to provide the tools and technology that wasn't available to them back then. As I have said, you have the technology and just need to further develop that technology."

Sara was hanging on Echo's every word…

"These capsules are not simple solutions and will still require much time to master. They must be developed, monitored, and controlled by only those people who have the greater good of mankind as their mission."

With the transformational work done, the alien visitors waited for a small cylindrical tube that was descending, to open.

Echo took a deep breath and spoke, *"Goodbye and we implore you take these lessons learned to heart. We do not plan to be back soon, as there are over five thousand planets in this solar system, and it is our obligation to help other civilizations as much as we can."*

The alien Pulse sensed Sara's surprise and let her know that they, Pulse and Sara, were now linked. He softly spoke the word "forever" and Sara smiled at him.

Echo smiled and continued *"Nearly every star in your night sky has at least one planet in its orbit. And it was not our choice to reveal our presence, but the attacks on your world gave us no option. For Planet Earth, this is the end of the beginning.*

"We ask you to always seek the greater good, and we do expect that you will make the most of your second chance… with the technology that we provided to you today."

Echo raised her hands into the air, in a majestic and inviting sort of way and finished, *"Do what's right, do it together with people you respect and trust, and do it to the best of your abilities."*

In an instant, Echo, her close and apparent, second-in-command, Pulse, and the remaining Arrans' team were gone via the small spacecraft, as quickly as they appeared. As they departed, the large and intimidating alien Pulse looked over to Sara and *telepathically* communicated.

<Goodbye, Warrior Princess… Until we meet again.>

4
INITIAL GAME PLAN

"It's still numbing to think that we... hell, the whole world, experienced such a spectacular and game-changing event."

"Absolutely, Sara." Looking up at Sara with a next-step thought, "By the way, have you and POTUS set up a meeting with American and world leaders to show them that video? 'Cause, the world, technically, doesn't know what the heck occurred in Dubai."

"I just talked briefly to Cameron on a secured line following our last brief visit, Michaela, and he is frantically trying to assemble a small cadre of people who he can trust for our latest *alien reveal*. I can't imagine what a struggle it is today to truly trust your colleagues."

"Ya want another vodka raspberry cocktail?" Sara winked."

"Number three... why not!"

Sara poured her dear friend another drink, reigniting a fond memory of her trip to Dubai, and the two friends toasted.

Michaela added confidently, "At least we don't have that respect problem with the ETRT. What a great team of dedicated and trustworthy professionals."

"Yep." Sara then continued, "I do have a short list of 'got to do' priorities. Interested?"

"Let it rip, Sara. Great to be back in the game."

Michaela kicked off her tan leather boots. A strikingly beautiful woman, Michaela was tall, with a dark complexion and an infectious smile. Normally a serious person, Michaela could be as sexy as a runway model, if the evening called for it. Today she was wearing a cropped military jacket, in taupe with black trim.

With that exchange, Sara removed her denim jacket, rolled up her shirt sleeves and gazed at her "*I Am the Storm*" arm tattoo, and flipped her projector E-watch to the only whiteboard in her office that wasn't jam-packed with notes and various urgent matters.

Michaela asked, "Would you rather wait until we have our core group here?"

"Nope. You and I are gonna be driving this from humanity's perspective, so no time like the present."

"Excuse me… humanity's perspective?"

Sara paused a moment and then said, "Echo and I shared many thoughts as the Dubai meeting was ending. Actually, they were her thoughts; I was just listening."

Michaela grinned and gave Sara a "thumbs up."

"Things are going to get quite busy, Michaela, and I know for a fact, that an alliance with our alien friends is of utmost urgency and importance."

Michaela began to speak, but stopped to let Sara continue.

"Let's just look at our 'short list' for now."

Michaela gazed up at the whiteboard as Sara projected her "short list."

1. *Strategically reveal contents of the Dubai video as required.*
2. *Assemble ETRT and de-brief selectively.*
3. *Determine rollout plan for the eight alien capsules from Echo.*
4. *Determine rollout plan for Sara's eight capsules provided by Pulse.*
5. *Meet with the Grandad Pete hologram to "catch up" with developing needs.*
6. *Project Zeus.*

Michaela chimed in immediately, "Where the hell did number four come from?"

"I'll get to it shortly. It was another gift from Echo that Pulse delivered just to me."

"Okay," Michaela nodded, "number one is now in Cameron's lap."

"Yep," Sara agreed, "he's got the ball on this one."

"I'll set up an ETRT meeting as soon as you're ready, okay?"

"Yes, Michaela. Just give me a day or two to prepare."

Michaela, with an impatient sigh, "I guess numbers three and four are the heart of the issues and will certainly require some incredible planning, analysis, and eventual implementation."

"For sure, Michaela. They're like the outliers… just waiting for our best effort. Damn it, this is going to be a challenge."

Sara paused and held up her hand. Michaela knew that Sara was receiving an incoming telepathic thought from someone.

<We need to talk soon.>

<Of course, Echo. What is so important?>

<Will forward you my agenda.>

About thirty seconds passed as Echo sent a fairly detailed agenda through her thoughts to Sara, and Sara looked drawn and pale.

"Michaela, we'll pick up on the last couple issues later. That was Echo."

"Echo? Already? So soon? Can I ask what she said?"

With her gaze flicking back and forth from her office window to the whiteboard, Sara muttered, "Echo wants to meet with me very soon."

"To discuss what, Sara?"

Pausing again momentarily, Sara responded softly, "Take a deep breath."

Holding up her hands as if to say. *"What's next,"* Michaela nodded, "Ready."

Now it was Sara's time for a short, reflective pause…

"The impending mass extinction of human life on Earth."

5

NEW MILLENNIUM
URGENCY

With that devastating comment barely digested, Sara rose from her chair and Michaela could see that her friend was visibly shaken. Trying to find words to break into Sara's concentration, Michaela simply muttered, "Mass extinction doesn't leave anything to the imagination."

Michaela glanced from the whiteboard to Sara and offered, "We can discuss this urgent issue and the last couple issues on your list later."

"No. Let me tell you the overview of what Echo said and why. Yes, the issues list can wait a bit."

Grasping her drink on the table and finishing it quickly, Sara provided an explanation of Echo's remarks, "Apparently, our Earth has experienced five extinctions of plant and animal life over its history. Volcanoes, earthquakes, floods, and of course the mass extinction of all prehistoric life with a meteor striking Earth sixty-six million years ago are well documented."

"Of course," a now much more serious Michaela added.

"Echo has always feared, I'm told, that mankind's disregard of the environment and lack of focus would one day lead to Earth's demise."

"Gotta say, I'm totally in agreement there," Michaela scowled.

"Exponential climate change results have advanced the brutal timeline, I guess," Sara concluded.

"Sara, this is, of course, quite serious. Why didn't she mention this to you in Dubai? I mean, it wasn't like it'll wait till later."

"Apparently, there is a new and dangerous variable that will have a significant impact on our ability to address climate change and global threats."

"Any idea what Echo meant by this?"

"Her last words to me were chilling."

"There are powerful worlds... evil worlds... out there that we cannot see."

6

NEW MILLENNIUM
IMPORTANCE

The very next day, as Sara was trying to process the message from Echo, she received a call from Mara Wallace, chief aide to President Sullivan.

"Hi Sara, it's Mara. How are you doing?"

"Oh, you know, same old end-of-the-world stuff. And you?"

Chuckling, Mara advised, "The President is ready to meet with you and to follow up on the last meeting and call you two had."

"Great, Mara. When?"

"He said he could have a plane sent to pick you up tomorrow afternoon. You would have dinner tomorrow night with him and have the meeting on the following day, Wednesday. Does that work?"

"Of course. Sure. Anyone else at the meeting?"

"Yes. He will send you an encrypted message with the proposed attendees to make sure you are okay with his selections."

Sara was very pleased that POTUS would think so highly of her contribution.

"Thanks, Mara. What time tomorrow?"

"The car will pick up at one o'clock pm, your time. You and the President will then have dinner on Air Force Two in route to Washington."

"Gee," Sara thought. *"Special treatment."*

"Mara?"

"Yes, Sara."

"Why not Air Force One, may I ask?"

"The President wants to keep his departure off of the daily news cycle."

Call ended.

✦ ✦ ✦

Meanwhile, close metahuman friend of Sara and ETRT member, Elonis, was contacted by Echo, as Elonis often was, to set up the *mass extinction* meeting with Sara. Walking into Sara's office, Elonis was her usual "to-the-point."

Sara turned to greet Elonis as her trusted associate spoke, "Sara, Echo has indicated that she needs to talk with you soon, as you know."

"Yes, Elonis, I'm aware of her sense of urgency."

Sara pulled up her E-Watch meeting agenda and asked, "When?"

Elonis, aware of the Washington meeting in just two days, answered swiftly, "This Friday, two days after your meeting with POTUS."

Startled at the intense schedule, but not entirely surprised, Sara asked crisply, "Okay, Friday is fine. Where? My place or the office?"

"Neither."

Sensing an 'aha moment', Sara responded. "Okay, Elonis, where?"

"Pulse will pick you up."

"Pulse? What the hell?"

A very puzzled Sara stared at Elonis as her metahuman friend advised, "You will be meeting Echo on her Starship Destiny on their base on the far side of the Moon!"

7

ETRT PRIORITIES

As Elonis departed, Sara grabbed a couple cocktail napkins and wiped the sweat from her face. She was beginning to feel overwhelmed.

She glanced at the blood pressure monitoring device on a lower shelf that she used weekly and thought, *"Hell, I already know it's high… so why bother!"*

She pulled up the current personnel list on her handheld device and looked at the short list of the strongest people who could tackle the critical issues that needed to be established and action plans developed.

Feeling a bit discouraged by her *short list*, she *texted* Michaela.

> "Hi M. What cha doin'?"
> "Research. The usual."
> "U got some time right now?"
> "Sure, Sara. Give me 5."

With that, Sara began to jot down some meeting notes. She then glanced at two of her favorite photos: one with former husband Paul on a hike they took in Colorado, and one with Doctor Matt Palmer, her current boyfriend and literally the man that rebuilt her after the cabin explosion nearly claimed her life. She had nothing but good recollections of their memorable sailing cruise prior to Dubai.

"These were the best of times," she thought lovingly.

Sara looked up and could see a smiling Michaela coming through the door.

"My, you are in a good mood. Must have been some sexy research, eh?"

"Funny, Sara. Nope, just excited to get started on our next, great challenge. Can only imagine where future roads will lead."

"Got that right, Michaela."

Sara opened the liquor cabinet and smirked, "How about a stiff one to get us going?"

"Why not? What cha got in mind?" Michaela also thought, "*This lady didn't drink quite this often before Dubai.*"

"Remember those 'Between the Sheets' drinks that I mentioned a while back?"

"Yep. Don't remember what was in them."

"Well, light rum, brandy, triple sec, lemon juice, and lemon garnish."

"You have all that stuff here?"

"Sadly, Michaela, I do."

Both women laughed as Sara pulled out two martini glasses.

"Shaken… not stirred!"

"Sara, you're the best… and I just love your ability to get the mood lifted."

"*If only she knew,*" Sara thought somewhat distractedly.

"Sara, isn't this the drink that you and Matt had on your unbelievable sailing trip?"

"Yep. It was. Still enjoy 'em."

As Sara took a couple minutes to fix and pour two drinks, she knew that it was Michaela's presence that got her creative juices going.

Sara also realized that whatever and wherever the journey took her and the ETRT, Michaela Marx was going to be at her side. The brutal murder of her very close friend Kat, at the hands of terrorists, bonded Sara to Michaela, and Sara was sure that the feelings and admiration were mutual.

"Cheers, my friend."

"Cheers, Sara."

✦ ✦ ✦

"So, Sara, where do you want to begin?"

"First, the last two issues from last time we met included my meeting with the amazing Grandad Pete hologram for 'God knows what' might ensue."

"I hear you, girl."

"Yeah, Michaela, the fact that Matt and Jeremiah could create a fully cognizant hologram of my murdered grandfather still freaks me out."

"Well, the idea that your grandfather had the vision to do what he called a laboratory *brain dump*, speaks volumes of the kind of man Pete Stevenson was."

"You know, Michaela, it is fate… it's gotta be fate that has driven all of this crazy shit happening to us today."

"Not gonna argue that point one bit!"

"And Project Zeus. I haven't given you any explanation of Project Zeus, right?"

"Affirmative, '*I Am the Storm*' lady."

"Okay. Sorry, Michaela. And I don't regret getting the tattoo. It'll make sense one day."

Taking a deep breath, Sara nodded, "All right, fine. Here goes."

"When you and Echo were talking to the attendees of the Dubai meeting…"

Michaela interrupted Sara, "My God, what an incredible opportunity that was. I remember it like it happened yesterday."

"Whoa, girl. Relax. There will be much more of that to come, I assure you."

Michaela smiled as Sara continued excitedly, "As Echo was talking, she was also telepathically communicating with me concerning the future needs here on Earth."

"That alien lady is definitely one helluva multi-tasker, Sara."

"Hell yes." Sara grinned. "She wants us to begin thinking about designing and building intergalactic spacecrafts for both offensive and defensive needs."

"Damn, that sounds ominous."

"Yeah, Michaela, but it is 'so' Echo. She is thinking long-term."

"Not surprised," replied a smiling Michaela.

Sara continued with two of her devices opened. "We named the program Zeus after a strange dream I've had several times… a progressive dream; and suffice it to say, we have nothing more than a sexy name at this time."

"Got it. Likely a discussion issue for you and Echo when you meet."

"Yep. For fricking sure, Michaela. Plus, I gotta get Scott involved in this Zeus project ASAP. Not only does he run *Sky Force PLLC*, but, as you know, his side business is funding commercial space flight aboard his intergalactic spacecrafts."

"Definitely, Sara, and with his new *Galactic Voyager* starship prototype nearing completion, he needs a new challenge."

"Damn straight, Michaela."

Both ladies chuckled.

✦ ✦ ✦

"So, Michaela, we have a short but dynamic list of issues that we need to start some detailed project and planning status."

Michaela was ready for recording and note-taking.

Sara added confidently, "They include Zeus, of course, the video of Echo's presentation to world leaders, the eight capsules that were Echo's gift to mankind, the meeting results from the Pete hologram, and the eight capsules that Pulse gave to me."

"What the hell, girlfriend! When were ya gonna tell me about the second eight capsules?"

"Michaela, as if our plate isn't already full, Pulse provided me with eight, highly confidential, technically advanced capsules, he deemed for 'my eyes only,' which are likely far more critical to Earth's salvation than Echo's eight capsules for the world."

"Salvation? Seriously?"

"Well, maybe *salvation* is a little strong… but maybe not."

"Great answer, Sara," Michaela muttered, amused by her friend's candor.

"Hell, Michaela, I'm the aliens' damn *dipsty dumpster* with all this stuff and it's not what I wanted."

"Whoa girl. Sorry. That's why you have me."

A nodding Sara responded, "And I couldn't do any of this without you, dear friend."

They clanked their nearly empty martini glasses as Sara poured two more drinks and emptied the shaker.

"So, here are the eight capsules that Pulse detailed for me as you spoke with Echo."

Sara projected the descriptions of the eight confidential capsules on her whiteboard, as Michaela brought out her laptop for follow- up research needs.

Capsule 1 will provide the entire plans and list of materials needed for ter-raforming Mars, a technique that we have used for thousands of years. Earth's technology will be able to use massive reflectors and mirrored devices to bring heat and light to Mars over a three-to-five-year period, rather than tens of thou-sands of years.

Capsule 2 will give you a blueprint for taking the Artificial Intelligence that will be in the ongoing-development stage from Echo's Capsule 6 to the very essence of General Artificial Intelligence or Super AI where androids will per-form any of mankind's needs in a socially responsible manner.

Capsule 3 will enable you to understand and positively adjust significant weather patterns around the world. It will also enable you to control space weather and geo-magnetic energy, which will become a source of opportunity for climate management, or for dangerous consequences, if managed poorly.

Capsule 4 will teach you how to levitate and use various anti-gravity or negative gravity methods to your advantage, especially when colonizing other planets, by developing the upward forces necessary to cancel out the weight of the object so the object does not fall or rise, but can be steered.

Capsule 5 will enable you to travel back and forth through time, using a four-dimensional fabric called space-time. Forward time travel is relatively easy, because it is based on speed. Backward time travel is risky, because it alters disease, catastrophes and mortality. Reverse time travel was responsible for many of the major worldwide plagues and epidemics.

Capsule 6 will address quantum teleportation, which is our proven process of transmitting atoms or molecular combinations in their exact state, from one location to another using state-of-the-art communication and sharing quantum entanglement between the sending and receiving location.

Capsule 7 will enable you to perform superluminal spacecraft propulsion, also known here on Earth as warp speed, traveling at speeds greater than the speed of light by many orders of magnitude. Today, we can travel from Earth to the Andromeda Galaxy in less than twenty minutes.

Capsule 8 will give you a blueprint for how you can defend your planet, if or when the time comes to do so, with much of the technology that was just presented, a strong mastering of Full Artificial General Intelligence, accelerated evolving technologies, and the use of antimatter microreactors.

As Michaela tried to process the enormity of this data, Sara added her assumption, **"It is Capsule number eight that will likely require a focus on Project Zeus."**

8
VIEW AT 30,000 FEET

The following day, as Sara was awaiting the limo to take her to Air Force Two, Michaela called, "Ya gotta minute? I know you're headed for a mundane dinner with the Pres!"

"Cute. Damn, you're almost as funny as Connor."

"Hey, Sara, even I know the value of humor in this disruptive world."

"Disruptive is spot-on, Michaela."

"Sara, I've been going over our rather massive *to-do* list and we obviously don't have nearly enough firepower to address our critical priorities."

"No shit, smarty pants. What cha thinking?"

"Miss *smarty pants* has aligned critical issues versus our current skill set versus deficiencies in our capability… personnel, I mean."

"Cool, Michaela."

"I have a three-dimensional model I will send to you soon that you can review and critique and compare to whatever POTUS has in terms of military or science professionals to throw into the mix."

"Hot damn, girl, you are good!" Sara thought intuitively, *"My one… plus her one… equals about ten people."*

With that exchange completed, the front doorbell rang. Sara folded up her devices, disconnected her electronics, and answered the door. She opened the door, and a huge smile broke out.

"Lieutenant Baker. It's you!"

"Yes, Miss Steele, it is your favorite FBI agent, I hope, with your chariot awaiting."

Sara gave Lieutenant Robert Baker, a tall, impressive bodyguard-type with broad shoulders and a warm manner, a huge hug and tears were clearly visible. Lieutenant Baker was one of her Grandad Pete's best friends and allies.

"What are you doing here? Are you my driver?"

"No, I am not your driver, but still assigned by President Sullivan as your attaché and security chief. You and I just haven't had a chance to discuss my role yet, given the Dubai priorities."

"Wish Grandad was here to see this. It would make him so happy."

With that remark, she was thinking ahead to the hologram of her grandad and bringing *hologram Pete* up to date on current issues.

"I loved that man… your Grandad Pete. He was way ahead of his time."

Lieutenant Baker secured Sara's luggage as Sara zipped her computer case closed and grabbed her light jacket. They walked together to the car.

Once inside the limo, they brought each other up to speed with goings-on and the short trip to the airport and Air Force Two began.

✦ ✦ ✦

As Sara strolled over to Air Force Two, she was still excited to have Lieutenant Baker escorting her.

"So, I'll see you on my return trip?"

"Nope. I'm going with you, thanks to the President."

Sara was delighted with that news, but she didn't inquire as to why he was staying. All would come out soon enough…

She thought reticently… *"Just capture the moment and the issue at hand."*

President Sullivan met them at the top of the Jetway and was all smiles.

"Great to see two of my favorite people."

He shook the hand of Lieutenant Baker and gave Sara a gentle hug.

"Welcome aboard."

Sara crisply replied, "So nice to be here and it is an honor for me to have this opportunity, Cameron."

Lieutenant Baker was a bit surprised by their relationship, and a first-name basis. He knew he was in rare air… or would be soon.

✦ ✦ ✦

Once in the air, drinks were provided and Sara enjoyed a glass of Cameron's selected red wine, Kathryn Hall Cabernet Napa, 2018. Lieutenant Baker had a soft drink.

Dinner was truly exceptional and reflected Cameron's healthy dining preferences. A crisp and very green spinach salad with firm cherry tomatoes was followed with grilled sea bass with grape salsa. A fabulous blueberry sorbet ended a terrific meal.

The President was an intimidating presence himself, an athletic-type and former Navy Seal with an impressive list of enemies *killed* and *captured*. Following dinner, they moved to the conference room with only Sara and Lieutenant Baker attending.

"So, let's get down to business. Let's discuss what we will present tomorrow and to whom, okay?"

"Yes, of course," Sara nodded appreciatively.

At that moment, an aide brought in a carafe of the remainder of the dinner Cabernet.

"Serve yourself," the President advised.

Lieutenant Baker poured a glass for Sara as the President declined.

"Sara, I'd like you to present the Dubai video to a small group of handpicked senior leadership attendees and afterwards allow some open discussion. Does that work for you?"

"Yes. Who will be there?"

"Sara, I have approached two distinguished, former military commanders with the sole purpose of securing a trusted cadre of military leaders, and two senior members of Congress, both members of my New Liberty Party, and a small number of scientific and NASA confidants.

"One of the military leaders, General James Patrick, is now the commanding officer of the Pacific Fleet. He was involved in three major American military conflicts: Gulf War of 1990–1991, the War in Afghanistan that began in 2001, and the Iraq War of 2003–2011.

"Patrick has seen combat and recon efforts around the globe and was the liaison to three former presidents and was well recognized as a man with a heart of gold and a will of steel. He relished combat and was known around his subordinates as a true patriot and selfless leader, and commanding the Pacific Fleet was his life-long dream.

"The other is a renowned military expert, General William P. Grant, who possessed recognized negotiation and recon skills and a photographic memory. Whenever a historian was writing a book or seeking information from the past, Bill was the guy to talk to, or even better, listen to. In fact, he is credited with finally bringing North and South Korea together in a complete denuclearization of the peninsula."

Cameron continued with clearly one of his most trustworthy additions, "I am also very pleased to include my National Security Director, Donald L. Meacham, who I trust and respect as much as anyone on this planet."

Cameron interjected himself into the mix, "As a former Navy SEAL, I was the actual person that infiltrated the ISIS headquarters disguised as an FBI informant, and my involvement was directly credited with stopping the well-armed ISIS contingent from carrying out what would possibly have been their most hideous post-9/11 attack ever. My role is now an active one."

The current president was an extremely worthy adversary and a known risk-taker, but more importantly, now a very good friend of Sara and the ETRT.

"I have also contacted subject matter expert in General Artificial Intelligence and long-time friend, Dr. Emil Griffith, who is a well-respected, Ivy League, Eco-political visionary and paranormal theorist, with the intention to bring him up to speed quickly with our alien encounter and get another set of eyes to look into both our present data and to get his extrapolated predictions."

Sara was getting extremely relaxed and excited as she could see that Cameron had been busy putting his *dream team* together.

"The two senior congressmen I spoke of head up the Intelligence and Foreign Affairs Committees. So, they make a great combination of expertise and trust. Oh, and there is one more addition. Bob?"

"Thanks Cameron," Lieutenant Baker responded. "Sara, my son is Commander RJ Baker, currently assigned to the U.S. Space Force as Operations Director. He is a graduate, with honors, of the Air Force Academy and holds a PhD in Celestial Mechanics."

"Excuse me, Lieutenant Baker, but I don't recognize that curriculum… never heard of it."

"That's not surprising, Sara. It is a discipline that is in its infancy, compared to traditional physics and astronomy disciplines."

"I see. Brief explanation?"

"Sure. Celestial mechanics is a branch of astronomy that deals with the motions and counter-motions of objects in outer space. Currently, celestial mechanics applies principles of physics to astronomical objects, such as stars, planets, and exoplanets, to produce ephemeris data."

"Oh my gosh. How cool and how relevant."

"Indeed, Sara. In his doctorate research, RJ studied Kepler, Isaac Newton, Lagrange, Newcomb, and Einstein. His thesis expanded the little-known knowledge of classical mechanics to the entire galaxy as we know it."

As Sara smiled, Lieutenant Baker continued proudly, "I believe the title of his thesis is '*Celestial Mechanics and Dynamical Astronomy applied to the current Galactic Universe.*' I think I have that right."

Sara high-fived her friend and added, "I am so impressed."

Lieutenant Baker added a remarkable piece of info for Sara to digest, "You know, Sara, you and my son actually have a common interest, I believe."

"I have never met your son. What link is that?"

"RJ was one of the space anomaly experts that was brought in to evaluate an in-space astronaut accident that baffled the aerospace community."

"Really." Sara was puzzled. "Which incident was it?"

"It was an incident that is far from resolved to this day."

Sarah was listening for the critical detail from Lieutenant Baker.

"Astronaut Samantha Worthington's cracked helmet and her unlikely survival."

9

CALM BEFORE THE VIDEO STORM

With yet another startling revelation, Sara could sense a most bittersweet journey about to begin. On the one hand, her life and her responsibilities were never clearer nor more intense.

But, with the team that Cameron was assembling, in tandem with the ETRT, Sara was becoming very optimistic that together they could weather any storm. She also knew that she didn't know what she didn't know.

Cameron broke the silence, sensing that Sara was extremely reticent concerning that last remark.

"So, we good with this proposed team, Sara?"

Glancing back over to Cameron, Sara nodded affirmatively.

"Any more additions that you see, Sara?"

"Not at this time, Cameron. Michaela has put together a personnel list of some immediate technical needs, but I haven't seen it yet. From purely a leadership perspective, this list of yours is quite impressive."

Cameron smiled and closed his notepad.

Sara looked over to Lieutenant Baker and excitedly said, "I am very anxious to meet your son. It would appear that he will play a very significant role going forward."

"He's a great guy… smart and curious as hell."

"I like him already. I love curious people," a smiling Sara quipped.

✦ ✦ ✦

Cameron suggested that the three of them return to the lounge and handle any personnel matters that they had for the duration of the flight.

Sara called Michaela and gave her a brief wrap of the Cameron meeting, "So, Sara, you okay with the team that Cameron has assembled?"

"For now, Michaela, yes. I'll meet them tomorrow and let you know what I think. So far, so good."

"By the way, I sent you the cube with the technical needs we have from my perspective. I know you haven't opened it yet, but when you do let me know what you think."

"Will do, Michaela. I'm sure it will be quite comprehensive. Thanks in advance."

"Oh, and Scott says he'd like to talk with you."

"Really? Any idea what about?"

"Nope."

Scott Woods was the founder and CEO of Sara's company, *Blue Horizon*, and without the help of Scott and his wife, Amanda, none of this alien investigative progress would have been made. He was also deeply committed to his current passion... building an inter-galactic commercial spacecraft.

It took a few minutes to get the call to Scott placed, but Sara was eager to catch up with the philanthropist that enabled Sara and the ETRT to reach the lofty heights that now form the baseline for further alien research.

"Hi Scott. It's Sara. What's up?"

"Hi Sara. Thanks for calling. I know you're busy with POTUS right now, so I'll be brief."

"I hope it's nothing serious."

"Well, it's about Amanda. She is still suffering from her terrorist abduction and the trauma of a life-threatening experience."

"I'm sure she is, Scott. She is lucky to be alive."

"And she would not be alive if it wasn't for those remarkable ETRT professionals. Dear God, such good and talented people."

"Thanks, Scott," Sara said proudly.

"So, she is now in therapy and will no longer be able to function as our CFO... at least for now. If anything changes, I'll let you know."

"Sorry to hear that. Tell Amanda that the team wishes her well."

"Will do, Sara."

"Scott, can I ask you a business question?"

"Of course." Scott thought, "*With Sara, it is always business...*"

"I'd really like to get an update on your newest aerospace venture with the Galactic Voyager suborbital spacecraft. Suborbital spaceflights for space tourists are gonna be exciting."

"Yes. We have both the mother ship and the rocket-powered and point-to-point, three-thousand-mile-per-hour spaceplane approved and ready to go."

"That's super-great news, Scott."

"Yes. Yes, it is. But that's not why you are asking, right?"

"Right, Scott. The ETRT may need to do some R&D work, along with the U.S. military, on a fleet of weaponized starships for 'way down the road' stuff."

"Your boss wasn't born yesterday… way down the road could also mean 'how fast can we do it,' eh?"

"Yeah, you'd be right!"

"I will definitely be looking forward to that conversation, Sara."

"Great. Me too. Talk later."

"Sure, Sara. Be safe and look forward to seeing you soon."

Sara then placed a call to her dad, Mike Stevenson, and gave him as much info as the current situation would allow.

Sara took a moment to gather her thoughts before connecting on the call, "Hi Dad. How are you and Mom?"

A very relieved dad said, "We're fine, Sara. It's good to hear your voice. You still aboard Air Force Two headed to D.C.? Mara Wallace gave us the update, as usual."

"Yep. Going to meet a leadership team that Cameron has assembled, and I will present the Dubai video for the first time outside of the ETRT."

"Nancy is still thrilled that she was able to help."

"Dad, we couldn't have done it without your friend's great generosity. The ETRT is still drooling over her magnificent plane. It was the perfect ending to that Dubai visit, and it allowed us to fly 'under the radar' for secrecy concerns."

Pausing a moment, Sara asked, "Is Mom there?"

"She's taking a bath. Want me to get her?"

"No. Not now. I don't have a lot of time."

"Understand, Sara… so when are Mom and I going to see you?"

"Unfortunately, I have a couple really huge meetings coming up, so it won't be soon. As soon as I get a break, we can at least video-chat."

"I'll tell Mom. That would be great."

"Gotta go Dad. Love you."

"Love you too. Good luck with your meeting tomorrow."

As Sara ended her call with her dad, a troubling thought entered her mind.

"Given my global notoriety being exposed tomorrow, how safe are my parents at home in rural Ohio?"

10

STEERING
COMMITTEE FORMED

Sara arrived at the White House at 8:00 am the following morning, being escorted by Lieutenant Robert Baker, and she was very happy and proud at that particular moment.

The two of them were led to the Situation Room, a conference and intelligence management center in the basement of the West Wing of the White House. It is run by the National Security Council staff and is equipped with secure and advanced communications.

For this meeting, only President Sullivan's aforementioned attendees would have access. The silence around that meeting on this particular morning was unusual. On a typical meeting day, you would hear chatter in volumes until the President entered.

As the attendees took their seats, President Sullivan greeted the esteemed group, "Good morning to you all. Let this be recorded as the first meeting of the preliminary task force to determine if a robust steering committee is necessary and inevitable."

The President waited for everyone to get settled. Sara was perusing the group of older, white and most definitely established Washingtonians.

"I would like to introduce Miss Sara Steele of the Palo Alto-based *Blue Horizon,* a high-tech research firm conducting alien awareness investigations, in addition to their more notable traditional work. Sara is the Managing Director and leads the Extraterrestrial Research Team, known as the ETRT."

Dressed in a conservative, gray business suit with a white shirt, a small, silver pendant, and black flats, the blonde beauty with upswept hair struck an image of a serious businesswoman, which was her intention.

"Thank you, Mister President, and thank you all for attending this morning. As the president indicated, my Palo Alto team now has the study of extraterrestrials on our front burner, given the recent events in Dubai."

Pausing, Sara continued directly, "Let's go around the room with intros, okay? A brief summary of backgrounds and relevant skill sets would be fine."

POTUS kind of cringed, given the fact that these big-ego guys were now being told to become accountable by this young, blonde woman to see if they "make the cut".

"Hello Sara. I am General William P. Grant, not yet retired, and I have most recently finalized the denuclearization of the North and South Korean peninsula. My military specialty and experience are in recon skills and counterterrorism. I am happy to meet you."

"Thank you, General Grant."

"Hi Sara. I am General James Patrick, and I am currently the commanding officer of the Pacific Fleet. My battle experiences include the Gulf War of 1990 to 1992, the War in Afghanistan that began in 2001 and is still a major conflict, and the Iraq War of 2003 to 2012. Likewise, it is good to meet you."

President Sullivan interrupted the meeting with a clarification, "It has always been the case to separate partisan politics from our military leadership and mission. But both General Grant and General Patrick are members of my New Liberty Party, as our need and their will has coincided."

Sara smiled at that explanation.

"Hello Sara. I am Donald L. Meacham, and I am the National Security Director. My career has included stints as foreign ambassador and liaison to twelve countries over the last twenty-five years. I was also the lead prosecutor in the Hilton espionage case that brought down that governor's mafia empire."

"Sara, I am Doctor Emil Griffith, and I chair the Ivy League Eco-Political Vision Board, and I am, admittedly, a paranormal theorist. One of my skills is to take scientific data and extrapolate that data into predictive equations and correlated likelihoods of otherwise debunked theories. I do not discount the probability that alien life exists elsewhere in our universe."

"Hello, my name is Frank Polansky, and I am the Chairman of the Senate Intelligence Committee, and my expertise is in gathering and evaluating domestic and foreign intel, and keeping the President informed through his daily PDB. I have an international staff numbering in the thousands."

"Hello, Miss Steele. I am Ernesto Suarez, and I am the Senate Foreign Affairs Committee Chairman. Our teams dig deeply into the more mundane and often overlooked data that often has a serious impact on our national security. One of my outside interests includes the Manhattan Project of the 1940s that involved many countries getting involved in wartime-weapons development. I am a big fan of your ETRT."

"And I am Lieutenant Robert Baker and an attaché to Miss Steele."

Cameron made a personnel announcement before presenting the morning agenda, "Absent from today's session is Bob's son, Commander RJ Baker, now with the U.S. Space Force. As you may know, he is at the Kennedy Space Center working on upgrades to ISS2 and will likely join us at our next meeting.

"You all know about the incredible Dubai incident in October and although the details presented were sketchy, and the PDB's were seriously redacted, you will soon see in its entirety the amazing events that will change our world as we know it. Be prepared for a game changer unlike anything any of us could ever imagine.

"Sara, please proceed."

"Thank you, Mr. President."

Sara got everyone's attention with her next remark, **"Thank you all for what you are about to commit to."**

11
DÉJÀ VU

Sara began the Dubai video with the thwarted missile attack arranged by the former G-12 member and World Council co-chair, Stewart Shipley. It seemed that the viewing audience was distracted or preoccupied… the video would surely change that!

As the video played, the entire committee was becoming more transfixed on every twist and turn of the missile attack and Echo's dramatic entrance and destruction of the incoming missile warhead.

The eight capsules clearly became the top takeaway from the video, after the acknowledgement that benevolent aliens literally *saved the day.*

As the capsules were being arranged and identified, the alien commander, Echo, moved over to the capsules and explained to the entire audience, *"Here are eight capsules that will provide you with the tools and capability that you will need to learn, refine, and implement significant technological change."*

Echo then demanded, *"The team led by Sara Steele will be in charge of implementation. There will be no negotiation of that edict."*

After a brief pause…

"Let the world know that Sara Steele and the ETRT have our support and will be the sole drivers for this technology."

Echo abruptly ordered, *"What we are giving you… we can take away."*

Sara was visibly overwhelmed but very pleased to hear Echo's complete trust and confidence in her and her team… again.

The entire body of Dubai attendees surrounded the capsules as Echo spoke.

*"**Capsule 1** will show you how to desalinate the oceans and provide fresh water to serve the world's growing population. It will also begin to allow the rising sea levels to be prevented or reversed. This will combat global warming as the polar ice caps will not rebuild themselves.*

*"**Capsule 2** will explain how you can ionize the atmosphere to significantly reduce destructive hurricanes and tropical storms when they reach their biggest threat.*

It will also demonstrate how to bring water from even a dry atmosphere to use to fight the immense wildfires.

"Capsule 3 will show you how to use the vast resources on your planet to produce enough food to eliminate hunger and starvation, even in the most underdeveloped countries. As you will see, agriculture is driven by solar and wind energy, not by the ever-depleting coal and oil assets.

"Capsule 4 will allow you to gather the correct ingredients to manufacture the necessary drugs to cure many of mankind's diseases and eliminate famines totally around the world. It will also substantially reduce worldwide medical costs for drugs and services.

"Capsule 5 will enable you to create the strongest metal known in our universe, from materials on this planet, such as platinum, aluminum, and iron and from meteors that you will be able to capture. This material can be used for a variety of industries and can be liquefied for other applications.

"Capsule 6 will provide you with a process, including several fundamental scientific breakthroughs, to take your current weak AI technology and create a path for machines to successfully perform any intellectual task that a human being can and possess full consciousness.

"Capsule 7 will provide tools to better understand human DNA and how to identify and wash elements of DNA. It is common knowledge that human DNA was designed and manipulated by extraterrestrials, and research on the human genome is already verifying that fact.

"Capsule 8 will rapidly accelerate worldwide solutions to global warming. In the nearly ten years of the Greta Thunberg climate change improvement target of 1200 points in levels of achievement, your Earth is still below 500 points. Your planet is dying because of this problem.

"What we are providing you with are seeds, not pills. These capsules are not magic wands and will not be immediately implementable."

Echo paused, *"They will require your best minds and your absolute patience to reach the final results that will consequently be extremely beneficial."*

At this point Michaela Marx could be seen taking notes.

"As I have said before, your current Artificial Intelligence, Information Technology, and general scientific technology will enable you to develop and master the knowledge that is here. In our minds, your greatest threats will come from humankind itself, from within, and not natural disasters.

"Absolute power corrupts absolutely. And fear and power will no longer drive society, economies, and governments… technology will!"

After a long pause for all to absorb what Echo had just said, Sara spoke, *"Echo, we are deeply indebted to you, not only for your involvement today, but for all that you have done for mankind in the past. Why are you revealing yourselves now, and with these amazing gifts?"*

Sara knew the answer, of course, but needed all those assembled to hear it as well.

"We have helped civilizations before, but those not nearly as advanced as yours. With the Mayans and Egyptians, we had to provide the tools and technology that wasn't available to them back then.

"As I have said, you have the technology and just need to further develop that technology.

"These capsules are not simple solutions and will require much time to master. They must be developed, monitored and controlled by only those people that have the greater good of mankind as their mission."

After another brief pause, Echo went on, *"At one point we had to step in and remove the Mayans from Earth and relocate their civilization to another planet, as infighting and internal strife was becoming their downfall."*

Echo appeared to sense a mixture of fear and hope among the attendees.

"Although the entire world and human race was suspended in time during this ordeal, we have blocked all memory of our engagement from the minds of the world's population. Only the people assembled in this auditorium are aware of us and what took place today."

Sara could see confusion and consternation in the eyes of many present.

"To reveal to the world all that you have seen today would result in mass panic, hysteria, and even the likely demise of religions as you know them. Sara, her team, and these members of the World Council will be the ones that must take today's events and put significant change initiatives in place and soon."

Pausing, Echo attempted to close her remarks, *"It is the proper choice, again, given the fear and chaos that our presence here on Earth would involve, that this selected group will become the torch bearers.*

"The greater the misery... the greater the peace. You will come out of these latest events stronger and more determined than ever before."

Sara paused the video to allow for this info to sink in and concluded with the end of the video and the aliens' departure.

With the capsule presentation finished, the alien visitors waited for a small, cylindrical tube that was descending to open.

Echo walked over to her team before turning to the still-stunned audience.

"Goodbye and we implore you take these lessons learned to heart. We will not be back, as there are over five thousand planets in this solar system, and it is our obligation to help other civilizations as much as we can."

Echo raised her voice slightly and proclaimed, *"Nearly every star in your night sky has at least one planet in its orbit. It was not our choice to reveal our presence, but the attacks on your world gave us no option. For planet Earth, this is the end of the beginning.*

"We ask you to always seek the greater good, and we do expect that you will make the most of your second chance… with the technology that we provided to you today."

Echo raised her hands into the air, in a majestic and inviting sort of way and finished with words that actually "echoed" through the chamber, *"Do what's right, do it together with people you respect and trust, and do it to the best of your abilities."*

In an instant, Echo, her close and apparent, second-in-command, Pulse, and the remaining aliens were gone via the small spacecraft, as quickly as they appeared.

✦ ✦ ✦

As Cameron surveyed the now subdued and quiet group of powerful leaders, their demeanor was quite the opposite of what an onlooker might expect. They were now fully aware of what just happened and, more importantly, what the worldview of the new millennium might look like.

Sara approached the president with her suggestion of next steps, wanting to get some immediate perspectives.

"Let's just go around the room and have everyone describe their first reaction to the Dubai video," Cameron advised intently.

The group mostly nodded in agreement.

The President added, "And thanks to Sara Steele for today, as well as for her courage and tenacity back there in Dubai."

General James Patrick spoke first, "Thank you, Sara, for your bravery and for today's breathtaking video. It certainly captures our dire position both as a country and as a world in peril and indicates our immediate needs. I will review this information for our next meeting regarding plans and accountabilities from my perspective."

An excited Doctor Emil Griffith offered his first impression, "This revelation absolutely solidifies the thinking of many people in my circle of professional contacts and gives me incredible motivation to take my eco-political visions and paranormal teaching to an actual, real-world cultural fact."

Glancing at Sara, General William P. Grant nodded in agreement. "This is the glue that ties so much of age-old speculation regarding the history of mankind from the early beginning and the literal evolution of our species, in my mind, to irrefutable truth, and I can't thank Sara Steele and her brave team enough. We have a tremendous amount of work ahead of us."

A somber Intelligence Committee Chairman Frank Polansky was slightly less enthusiastic. "Well, this evidence is compelling, but I will need to analyze this data before I get on board. But, for now, I'm leaning toward buy-in and will have these issues become our agency's top priority, for sure."

Foreign Affairs Committee Chairman Ernesto Suarez took a very proactive posture and even set a planning portal in place. "This startling truth takes on a truly global perspective and I would suggest that President Sullivan look into an effort similar to the Manhattan Project of the 1940's and assess the joint development worldwide leadership regarding the implementation of these capsules."

"I think that is a helluva suggestion, Ernie, and I will take it under review."

Donald Meacham, the National Security Director, had been jotting down notes as everyone spoke. He then gave his opinion, "As was previously said, many thanks to Sara and her ETRT for the incredible passion and commitment to take this foundation of unknown and unbelievable data to where we are today, at a fork in the road that can be either annihilation or salvation."

Pausing a moment, Meacham continued, "We need to build a strong and capable force, at many levels in implementation going forward, and I see one of my jobs will be the vetting process of everyone in our orbit…" Meacham flicked a gaze at Sara and smiled.

"With the consequences of failure so extreme, we must have very capable people whom we trust, respect, and can count on going forward."

President Sullivan pointed a finger at Meacham and gave a "thumbs up."

Lieutenant Robert Baker offered his expertise, "You know, I have had experiences in my career that have touched nearly every segment of the knowledge and experience of the leadership cadre present today. I see myself as an integral facilitator of what will surely be a plethora of required actions going forward."

"The quarterback, eh Bob?"

"Exactly, Cameron. And with my son's added Space Force capabilities, we should be able to get a great plan underway and implement it as rapidly as possible."

A much more relaxed Sara simply uttered, "Thank you… thank all of you."

Cameron announced abruptly, "This will conclude today's session. You will all receive encrypted docs after you leave here today. We will reconvene soon. You will all need to study this material and be prepared to develop a game plan when we meet next time… place and time TBD."

"With no further comments, Sara, do you have any last words?"

Sara took a moment to realize that this revered group of leaders were all men. Not one female was chosen. She was mentally comparing them to her powerful alien leader friend, Commander Echo of the Arrans race.

"Thanks again for your commitment and contribution going forward. Please keep this thought in mind…"

"It is far better to grasp the universe as it really is than to persist in delusion, however satisfying and reassuring."

12

RE-ENERGIZE?

Sara had only been back from the D.C. trip for a few hours when she realized that she had many text messages and voice messages to return. She had been expecting Elonis to contact her with arrangements for the meeting with Echo, but that was not one of them.

While she waited, she went into her master bedroom and began to draw a warm bath. Disrobing, she poured some *Goddess of Sex Glitter Bath Salt* product that Michaela had given her. She loved the fragrance, and glitter seemed so apropos, if not immediately perceived as uncomfortable.

"Glitter, Michaela, really?" Sara thought skeptically.

She looked at her body in the mirror and began to caress herself both sexually and in an examination of the rebuilt arms and legs that now defined her.

Slipping into her warm bath, now nicely mellowed with dissolved and intoxicatingly fragrant bath salt, she placed her head on her bathtub pillow to relax.

Sara was now able to disconnect, at least for this short time, and give herself pleasure. She caressed her breasts and felt the warmth between her legs as thoughts of days and months gone by… filled her head.

Occasionally adding warm water to her bath, Sara enjoyed this alone time. She remembered her grandad saying, "There is a big difference between loneliness and solitude… I need solitude."

"Amen, Grandad," Sara thought softly.

So, after her bath, she polished her nails in a bright lipstick red. Often she would use black as an alternative… depending on her mood.

Sara slipped into some loose-fitting clothes and headed out to her comfy back yard, to put a nice salmon steak on the grill and noted all the people she needed to respond to.

She fixed herself a Three Olives Grape Vodka and Seven-up cocktail, positioned the wood plank needed to grill the salmon, put two ears of corn on the other side of the grill, and began her phone calls.

"Hi Michaela, it's me. How ya doing?"

"Fine, Sara. How was your meeting?"

"Okay." Sara laughed. "Mostly older white guys. Don't see any passion or urgent purpose being shown… at least not initially."

"Not surprised. Did you review my personnel list?"

"Yep. Great start. Thanks. Let me get a couple things done; maybe we can meet later this   week."

"That'll be great. I'll be ready when you are."

"Oh, and thanks for those bath salts… they were dreamy."

"You are quite welcome, Sara."

"Fine. Night, Michaela."

"Good night, Sara."

Next up were her parents. She checked on the grill progress and gave them a call.

After several phone rings, Christine Stevenson finally picked up.

"Hi Mom."

Christine was thrilled to hear from her daughter.

"Hi Honey. It's been a long time. You okay?"

"Sure. Just had a meeting at the White House. Did Dad tell you about it?"

"Yes, he did. How exciting!"

"Is Dad there?"

"No. He's putting away his kayak and has his telescope out back by the river. Some star-watching or something. When are you coming out?"

"As I told Dad, I have several loose ends to tie up; maybe in a few weeks, okay?"

"Okay. How are you and Doctor Palmer doing? We haven't heard much from you about him since Dubai. We really like him."

"Well, Matt has a lot on his plate at the lab, and I have been kind of busy too."

"I hear you. What cha doing right now?"

"Grilling some salmon. Maybe talk again in a few days."

"Sure, Honey. I'll let you go. Stay safe. Love you."

"Love you too, Mom."

Sara hung up, turned toward the grill and removed the salmon and corn and tried to enjoy her dinner, given the myriad of events taking place in her life. She just needed to relax and try to unwind.

As she finished eating, she returned about a half dozen text messages and looked up to the sky, wondering what constellation her dad was focused on tonight.

She fixed another Grape Vodka and Seven-Up cocktail, and with fresh ice cubes rattling in her glass, Doctor Palmer called.

"Oh, shit," Sara thought. *"I should be the one making this call."*

"Hey, how'd your trip go? Good meeting?"

"Hi Matt. Yeah, pretty good for a preliminary, get-to-know- everybody exercise. How are you and Miah doing?"

"We're fine. Wondering when you will be coming out to do that session with 'Pete.' Jeremiah will need a little time to get all the hologram updates loaded."

"Well, I have one more commitment to take care of…"

Sara was not in the mood to tell her current boyfriend Matt about the Echo meeting just yet.

"Give me a few days, okay?"

"Sure, Sara. Was hoping you and I could get some quiet time together, too. I miss you."

Sara wasn't even in a mood for this, but instead of blowing off her on-again, off-again boyfriend, she softened a bit.

"Matt, there is nothing that I want to do more than spend some quiet time with my favorite guy. Just let me get some loose ends tied up first, okay?"

"Of course. We're ready here when you are."

"Thanks for being so understanding."

"Love you, Babe. Be safe."

"Love you, Matt."

Sara sat back in her big soft chair with drink in hand. She closed her eyes and began a mini-meditation. It was so nice to have peace and quiet and put all the alien stuff on the back burner for a while… so nice!

Everything was quiet… until it wasn't.

Out of the evening sky appeared a ghostly figure moving ever so closely to Sara. Her heart rate quickened, and she took a deep breath. "What the hell!" she stammered. "Who's there?"

It was Pulse!

13

FLY ME TO THE MOON

"**P**ulse. What the hell are you doing here? You scared the crap out of me."

"Sorry to frighten you. I was trying not to."

"So, walking slowly and quietly in the dark wouldn't frighten me?"

"Oops, I guess you're right. Again, I'm sorry."

Now more relaxed, Sara inquired, "Why are you here? Since Dubai, I didn't think I'd see you anytime soon. Is something wrong?"

Pulse eased closer to Sara and she gave him a hug. She could see that he was in full flight gear… uniform, shoes, gloves, and all. That was kind of odd.

He was tall, even for the alien Arrans race. About six feet and ten inches in height, with the typical elongated skull, long arms, large eyes, and small ears, dressed in that flight suit with his broad shoulders, he looked like a character right out of *central casting*.

Pulse was dressed in a scarlet-red flight suit with gray epaulets. This time, he also was wearing a black cape. Sara had not seen the cape before.

"So, is something wrong? I'm happy to see you, Pulse, but when we parted it seemed like there would be a time for me and us to digest the sixteen capsules, before there was any need to meet."

"True, Sara. But Echo has summoned you for an urgent talk."

"I'm aware of that. She even said that we would meet on her starship, not here."

"That's right. On her starship."

"And?"

"And, I will be taking you there."

Sara was mentally switching between the quiet night alone and serene dinner, to another ohmigod.

"Okay, Pulse. When?"

"Now."

"Now! Are you shitting me? I can't go now. I'm preparing to meet with the ETRT in a couple days to start our planning and implementation work regarding the capsules."

"Echo is aware of that and feels you can manage both."

"I'm glad she has such faith in me... damn it!"

Pulse smiled and thought, "*Echo and Sara Steele are my two, favorite people... both females.*"

Sara chugged the remainder of her drink, sighed, and sat back down on her soft and cushy chair. This was definitely not what she expected.

"Echo wants to meet now?"

"Yes. Tonight."

"Where, Pulse?"

"On her starship, the Destiny."

"And where exactly is the Starship Destiny?"

"On the Moon; the far side of the Moon."

Turning her head up in the direction of the Moon, Sara uttered in disbelief, "The distance from the Earth to the Moon, Pulse, is 240,000 miles!"

"Actually, Miss Steele, it is 238,950 miles to our base camp there."

"Pulse. It's at least a three-day trip."

"Not for my star runner. It's 'parked' about five hundred feet from here."

"Details, please."

"Sure. My star runner, the Galactic Falcon, is equipped to travel at a moderate warp speed, which will get us there in minutes, or a more recreational speed of about fifty thousand miles per hour."

"Falcon? Seriously?"

"Sara, you know I'm a big fan. Gather your things... let's go... I mean, if it's okay, let's go."

✦ ✦ ✦

Sara closed her grill and went back into her house. She calmly put all of her cooking materials away, quickly cleaned off her dishes, and turned off the kitchen appliances.

She channeled all of her remote devices to default to her main, encrypted tablet, pulled a light jacket out of her hall closet, locked all the doors, hit the bathroom for a couple items, and met Pulse back on the patio.

She also left a voice mail incoming message indicating that she would be unavailable for a couple days... a bit of a retreat.

"I'm ready. Show me your Falcon."

Pulse led her through her back yard a few hundred feet and stopped.

"I don't see your star runner. What's up?"

A smiling Pulse raised his left arm and hand and Sara could see a large metallic device on his wrist. He pointed in a general direction and waited for Sara to follow his arm's direction. A light click could be heard, and in an instant, the Star Runner Galactic Falcon appeared.

Sara snapped, "Holy crap, it was cloaked!"

"Yes. Impressed?"

"Hell yeah. Show me aboard."

Pulse led Sara to a slowly opening, descending stairway. As they stopped prior to entry, a smiling Sara said, "All right... why the hell not?"

Pulse took Sara by the hand, and as they began the short walk onto the spacecraft, Sara nodded, approvingly, and Pulse could sense her acceptance and delight.

As they stopped momentarily, Sara turned to Pulse, embraced him warmly and with a quick kiss on the cheek, added enthusiastically, **"Fly me to the Moon."**

14

COSMIC JOURNEY

As Pulse followed Sara up the few steps to his spacecraft, he couldn't help but think of those words from Sara: Fly me to the Moon.

So deeply involved in the assimilation of all things earthly for many years, Pulse recalled that the song "Fly Me to the Moon" was recorded in 1964 by both Doris Day and Frank Sinatra. Young Sara Steele, however, would likely not know that.

"Pulse, your Falcon is amazing."

Making a left turn at what appeared to be a galley and gazing at the cockpit of Pulse's spacecraft, she was fascinated by how simple the design was and how uncomplicated the hardware looked… and it smelled nice!

It resembled a larger version of the cockpit of a current jet aircraft, but it wasn't much bigger than her office. All touchscreen digital; no analog dials anywhere.

"Let me show you around. You see our flight screen and the seats for two navigators, with four passenger seats behind. The windshield, or viewport, is covered now, as part of our cloaking; but when it opens, it is relatively small."

Sara was in awe of her new surroundings. Pulse continued proudly.

"The rear of the craft is mostly for communication equipment. All luggage, personal gear, and any objects to be transported, are stowed below."

Pulse opened a hatch to reveal the large cargo hold. Sara placed her belongings there.

"The Falcon is sixty-five feet long, about twenty-four feet wide, and as you can see, it has relatively short wings, as they are used primarily for radar, communication and environmental analysis."

"It is amazing. How much cargo does it hold?"

"The payload capacity is about thirty thousand pounds. The crew capacity is six in the control cockpit and twenty aft. I can show you the rear of the craft once we are underway."

"Can't wait."

"Please, be seated." Pulse handed Sara a small jumpsuit with a pair of silky-smooth gloves and motioned for Sara to take the seat on the right. She slipped into the suit and sat down. There was a bar between the two seats and the touchscreen.

"Now, look at the touchscreen." Sara glanced in that direction. "Now, with the special gloves, touch the upper-right corner icon."

Sara slid her gloves on, touched the icon, and the entire screen was lit. Many more icons appeared.

"What did I just do?"

"You basically touched our version of earth GPS and the *home* feature. We are now locked into a mostly hands-free journey to the Moon."

"That was easy. What next?"

"From here, you need to decide what speed you want for the journey. The lower left icon is our version of warp speed. Once we are properly elevated in altitude, the trip will be rapid… less than five minutes to Moon orbit."

"Holy cow!"

The lower right icon is the slowest pace, about forty-seven thousand miles per hour. At that rate, it will take us about five hours plus the landing time."

Sara was beyond words.

"So, Sara, what is your pleasure?"

"The slow boat, for sure."

"Great. I'll take it from here."

◆ ◆ ◆

As Pulse buckled them in their seats, he touched the screen and the cabin lights dimmed. The craft ascended vertically to about three hundred feet and was still. Pulse looked at Sara and showed her which screen icon to engage next.

Taking his lead, Sara touched the only three-dimensional dial on the screen and the craft moved quickly and steadily in both a vertical and angular direction.

"Holy crap!" Sara was literally in another world.

As the Galactic Falcon moved effortlessly and at a fairly low altitude, Sara had many questions.

"Why so low?"

"Just until we get out of visual and radar range. Then we will begin our cruising speed."

"Why don't I feel the motion?"

"There is an energy casing that surrounds all of our vessels that permits the spacecraft to almost always be in a state of equilibrium. We do much interstellar travel. This is for comfort and to protect all contents, people, and cargo."

"What is that smell?"

"Do you like it?"

"Yes. It's very soothing and serene. I love it."

"There is a story here."

Pulse was anxious to tell this particular story.

"Many years ago, I was able to sneak aboard one of Virgin Galactic's early flights on their Space Ship Two vehicle, the VSS Unity, as part of my assimilation."

"Pulse, where is this going?"

"Patience, dear Sara. I know it's difficult for you." Pulse chuckled.

Following an impatient sigh from Sara, Pulse continued.

"The flight was nothing special, as it was old technology to me. But what I was totally impressed with was the beautiful aroma in the cabin."

"Say what?"

"The cabin lighting was warm and comfortable. You're sitting in that ambient lighting now."

Sara was getting so relaxed.

"And, that smell was sage, used to 'burn off' odor and mixed smells. I loved it and now all of our vessels... starships, star runners, warships, and recon ships all use both the lighting and the sage."

"You are full of surprises... wonderful surprises."

Sara had a quick thought, "*Warships?*"

"Thank you... I love to surprise you."

"One more question. The glyph on your flight suit is also on the outside of your ship and in a couple locations here in sight. It has three abstract rings, from large to mid-size to small. Can you explain?"

"Yes. You are very observant. The outer ring describes our world in the multiverse. It marks the territory that we claim as our Sovereign Nation. No other alien culture would dare cross into our domain."

Sara was forming a visual in her mind.

"The middle ring is fluid. It indicates the location in the Solar System that is our present venture. In this case, Earth."

Pausing a few seconds, Pulse concluded his description, "The inner circle defines our craft as battle, recon, or simply transportation. The Galactic Falcon is the latter."

"I love it, Pulse. You know you are so special to me... I enjoy spending time with you."

With that heartfelt comment putting the controlling alien Pulse in a relaxed mood, he turned to Sara, bent over her, and with the long fingers of his right hand, he slowly moved them to caress and stroke Sara's neck and blonde hair.

With his left hand, he gently held Sara's head and parted her flowing locks in a most kind and sensitive manner.

Sara hadn't expected this affection but did not resist.

After a short, but warm kiss, Pulse lifted his head and smiled at Sara in a warm and genuine manner.

Sara leaned aggressively into the arms of Pulse and they engaged in a long and passionate kiss.

Pulse reached over and turned the cabin lighting off.

15

LUNAR DESTINATION

Pulse led Sara to a long couch that appeared to be in a staging area of some kind.

While holding her hand, he motioned toward the couch. "Lay down."

"Pulse!"

"Relax, Sara. I just want to help relieve some tension. My big hands are good for a lot of things… I'll show you."

Sara smiled and laid on her back, assuming a relaxed position.

"Now, Sara, turn over."

Sara turned over on her stomach. Pulse took her arms and extended them past her head, and gently pulled her feet apart about six inches.

"Are you relaxed, Sara?"

"Yes. Yes, Pulse, I am so relaxed."

For the next twenty minutes, Pulse gave his guest the most marvelous massage, in her words, that a spaceship passenger could ever expect. He had hot-stone feel, he had cold-stone feel, he had all of the right stones… he was definitely the man in charge and Sara was devouring the attention.

Even the lighting and marvelous scent in the room was remarkable to Sara, and certainly something that she had not expected. In a very short period of time, Pulse had put Sara in a mental state that she hadn't experienced since her childhood.

With cabin lights dimmed, Pulse left his guest to enjoy the serenity of the moment and returned to the cockpit. Pulse smiled. Sara smiled. Good things come in small packages.

✦ ✦ ✦

They were now two hours into the flight, and all was calm and on schedule. Sara joined Pulse after about forty-five minutes of quiet time.

"Sara, would you like one of my favorite drinks, the Cosmic Cosmo?"

"Sure. On top of being a wonderful masseuse, you are likely a helluva bartender. What's in yours?"

"I started with the usual ingredients in a drink called a Kamikaze: vodka, sugar, and lime. I swap out the sugary syrup with my favorite European triple sec for a touch of citrus and a splash of cranberry for tartness."

Sara was enjoying herself so much she almost lost sight of the fact that the pending meeting with Echo would be as serious as any she has had during this journey.

"Be right back, Sara."

As Sara waited for Pulse to make the short round trip from mini-bar to the cockpit, a million things were going through her mind. At the top of those things was how safe and secure she felt in the arms and presence of her large alien friend… And, those big hands!

Pulse returned and uttered, "Okeydokey."

"Hey, Pulse. That's our slang."

Both smiled and touched glasses in an appreciative toast. It was apparent to Sara that Pulse had an interest in her sexually, and if given the chance, the massage was likely a foreplay by her alien friend.

Sara was already thinking of how she would respond, as she was getting aroused just looking and talking with Pulse while her eyes scanned her male friend's physical form, from head to toe… pausing in the middle.

Pulse leaned over to give Sara a kiss, and she responded with her arms embracing his broad shoulders. Pulse stood up, lifted Sara to his height, and she responded by slowly wrapping her legs around his hips.

They enjoyed a heavenly and long-lasting kiss, as Sara could feel Pulse's manhood beneath her. She was getting wet with anticipation and rocked her body on his as they enjoyed the close and intimate contact.

Her mind and body raced in tandem anticipation. She was extremely aroused and felt his arousal as well.

Then suddenly, Pulse pushed Sara away and set her in her chair. He immediately became quite serious and all focus on their physical closeness was gone… his manhood shrinking.

"What's the matter, Pulse? What's wrong? I don't want you to stop!"

"Nothing's wrong, Sara. I'm sorry. Echo just sent me a thought asking what our ETA is."

"So, tell her."

"Sara. This is Echo. She absolutely knows our ETA. She just wants us to hurry it up and stay on point with our journey."

A somewhat frustrated Sara smiled, totally getting where the amazing Echo was coming from. Echo meant to break up the party... whatever that happened to be.

"Timing... it's always the damn timing," she thought disappointedly.

"Buckle up, Sara."

Sara tightened her shoulder and belt straps, with thoughts of what would have likely happened if not for Echo's intrusion.

"Warp speed in five, four, three, two, one."

In an instant, Sara did feel the motion this time and could see in the cockpit viewport what appeared to be a lightning-fast journey through a portal resembling a kind of *black hole*.

✦ ✦ ✦

Minutes later, the spacecraft's velocity slowed, and Sara could see the star runner circling from a fairly bright side of the lunar surface to a much darker appearance. Hence, the dark side of the Moon.

At this time, Pulse had taken over manual controls of the craft, presumably to circle and land.

"Much different sight than anything you've seen from an aircraft, right?"

"Yes, Pulse, it is. I'm at a loss for words."

Pulse cut his speed further, as a greenish haze became quite noticeable.

"What just happened?"

"We create our own atmosphere when we need to visualize. Echo will explain."

Pulse began a soft glide into a colored path entirely visible to Sara. As he gently glided into the approach, he swerved a bit. Sara found that to be strange,

"Now, what just happened?"

"Children playing with what you would call drones. Sometimes they get into the flight paths."

"Seriously?"

"Yep. Kids will be kids."

Sara was beginning to make out the silhouette of a very large city, and on the left was a gigantic, saucer-like craft. Pulse indicated that it was Echo's Starship Destiny. Many buildings dotted the lunar landscape, and Sara could see people and transportation devices moving about quickly.

On the right was a landing pad, not a runway, but several hanger-type structures were present, indicating a vast array of spacecrafts were housed there.

As the ship slowed its forward speed and began to hover as it slowly descended onto the pad, Sara's thoughts were of a fantasy place in the back of her mind,

"I'm not in Kansas anymore!"

16

EMERALD MOON SHADOW

As the door opened and the stairs descended, Sara could see Echo standing on the pad, smiling and happy to see her earthly friend.

Echo greeted Sara with a warm, loving hug and winked at Pulse.

"Welcome to the Moon. How was your flight?"

"Indescribable. A dream. A beautiful dream comes true. Thank you so much for bringing me into your home, and for making me feel like family."

Echo smiled and responded, "You are as much our family as one can be."

"Pulse, gather Sara's things as we head over to Destiny."

Sara was in a monstrous bubble, as she could see from the emerald-green haze thousands of feet above.

"Echo, I can breathe easily and gravity is like on Earth. And the green…"

As they walked, Echo gave her human friend the overview that both puzzled and amazed Sara, "The bubble, obviously, is artificial. We created it hundreds of years ago as we took this star as our primary basecamp and local training facility in your Solar System."

Sara thought, *"Hundreds of years… training facility?"*

Echo continued with her description, "The green haze was selected as it was the primary color given off by the basalt rock here on the Moon. We contained it… Pulse, what word am I looking for?"

"We *canned* it for a perpetual color for our artificial atmosphere."

"Thank you, Pulse."

At that time, a small, open, passenger hovercraft arrived and stopped in front of the three people.

"That's our ride to my Starship Destiny. Jump in."

Within five minutes they were at the base of a massive spacecraft. Sara likened it to a large *flying saucer* that she saw in science fiction films many times.

As they exited the hovercraft at the base of the ship, two large doors opened into what appeared to be an elevator.

"We'll head up top to the Operations Command Center," Echo announced.

"We would call it the bridge on a large navy ship," uttered Sara.

"Yes, you would. Next to our Command Center is our version of your *war room*. That is where we will be meeting."

With the elevator doors closed, Sara turned to look out the glass window at a breathtaking sight of unimaginable landscape and buildings. Pulse pushed an *up* button as Sara was speechless.

"This vertical speed of this lift will take your breath away, Sara. We have three hundred and fifty floors to the top, which is our Command Center."

Sara looked at Pulse, looked at the floor indicator pad on the elevator and once again looked out of the open window.

"Ohmigod, we are going to the top floor!"

17

PRELUDE

As the three exited the elevator on the Command Center floor, Sara could see many people moving about. As Echo was leaving the elevator, most people stopped to acknowledge Echo's presence, and they all seemed to nod affectionately or reverently at their powerful female leader.

Echo was typically tall, about six feet, four inches in height, and wore her usual blue uniform with orange epaulets. Her facial features were drawn and pale compared to Pulse, but her look was stern and serious. Echo physically moved in a way that spoke of command, control, and purpose.

Sara looked on attentively and respectfully. Echo smiled as she walked.

Echo had her signature Battlestar hilt, but with a new sabre, as Sara now owned the Sabre Destiny, given to her as a gift from Echo.

As she reached the Command Center, Echo introduced Sara to the flight staff assembled, "This is Sara Steele, our chosen one and a true warrior who has demonstrated her strength and perseverance with many difficult encounters on Earth."

Sara was feeling proud and special. Many in the Command Center smiled approvingly at their earthly guest.

"Sara, this starship is both a *Magellan Voyager* of your explorer history, and home to thousands of our people. For many, this is the only world they have known."

Sara was moved, humbled, and enlightened by Echo's words.

"There are powerful worlds that we cannot see… there are powerful worlds that we need to find… there are powerful worlds that could end your world."

Echo's not-so-subtle words had Sara now getting extremely focused.

"I am about to provide you, Sara, with what your team calls a data dump. This will be the view from, how do you describe it Pulse, one point two million feet."

Pulse tried to explain to Echo that the analogy from Sara's world is *the view at 30,000 feet*. Echo quickly computed that numerical analogy times 240,000 miles.

However, Sara understood the point. It was Echo's *big picture* that was about to be presented.

✦ ✦ ✦

They moved to the large conference room adjacent to the Command Center. As they were all sitting down, two members of Echo's leadership team, Laser and Spirit, joined them. Sara flicked a smiling gaze in their direction.

"Hi Laser. Hi Spirit. It is so good to see you."

Laser, dressed in a green uniform with black epaulets, spoke first, "It is good to see you, Sara, especially here at our home. Welcome."

"A little less stressful than Dubai, right Sara?"

"You are correct, Spirit."

Unlike her personality, Spirit looked a bit menacing, with her black uniform, shiny black boots, silver epaulets, and a silver hilt with a short sabre sheathed.

"Alter ego?" Sara thought.

As a series of three-dimensional screens began to appear on two sides of the room, Echo began, "We are gathered together to provide Sara with as much information and data as we can, as she and her teams process the issues at hand. We will first present the issues.

"As you know, our species, today called the Arrans, are from an exoplanet that is one hundred and ten light-years away in the constellation you call Leo. We have major colonies in what you call the Trappist One system, which is on the inner edge of the habitable zone.

"In earlier times, we were simply like you… Earthly humans. Today a select group of us are physically on Earth with this basecamp on the Moon."

Sara was getting a rapid education on general alien evolution.

"As I have said to you before, we strive to be *vraiment très bon*, or a *really good* alien culture. We have been the monitors of this galaxy for millions of years, but have only reached a greater presence since the beginning of the First Millennium, as the evolution of humankind and the universe as you know it, has progressed.

"For lack of a better description, we are the evolution of man. Sara, we are 'you' in the future."

Echo continued as Sara listened intently, "Sara, your galaxy has many alien cultures, both good and bad, and I will give you as much information as you can absorb to help you understand."

"Go ahead, Echo, I'm ready."

"We have often spoken of the Law of Polarity," Echo continued.

"In this case, alien cultures consist of both the good and the bad.

"The malevolent spirits that you would see as the direct opposites to angels, are the Denon. They have evolved from human souls that have endured extensive torture in Hell by Alastair and similarly driven alien cultures. In this process, they have become corrupted, extremely evil, and, in addition, very powerful.

"And they usually require a human vessel to walk and function on Earth, and can morph into recognizable human forms. Death and destruction are always in their path. Your Earthly terrorist groups would be ideal hosts for their mission on Earth."

Sara was thinking about the possible correlation to the New World Order terrorist group that likely took her grandad's life.

"The humanoid beings with reptilian features are the Dracs. The males are driven by whims and their own pleasures and have shapeshifting ability. The females have a chameleon ability and are more reserved and controlled than the males.

"The ruling elite council of this species refers to themselves as Devonian, a reference to a geological period.

"The Dracs originated in the Alpha Draconis star system, which is only two hundred fifteen light years away, and was formerly the Polestar."

Sara understood and, rather than offering her knowledge to a highly evolved alien, simply had a reinforcing thought.

"A Polestar is a bright star closely aligned to the axis of rotation of an astronomical object and is used for navigation since it stays in the same place. It holds still in the sky while the entire northern sky moves around it."

Pausing a moment, Echo continued, "The Dracs have two main castes; one is a dangerous warrior caste, eight to ten feet tall, six hundred to one thousand pounds, and are super-psychic and very fast.

"The second caste is the highly advanced and intelligent race that has thousands of biological offspring here on Earth. They are indistinguishable from humans."

"They are here now, right?"

"Yes Sara, Dracs are here, were here and will likely continue to be here."

"Echo, what about the *Greys,* or who we call the Reticulans race? They are every bit as real as the ones we are exposing."

"You are correct, Pulse, and you raise a good question."

"Sara, the *Greys* are diminutive humanoid beings and have been around Earth long enough to become the stereotypical, extraterrestrial alien. Inasmuch as they are a food source for some alien cultures, and have Martian roots, they are very real."

Pulse interjected his initial observation. "Sara, the *Greys* are what is often depicted on the Sci-Fi Channel as a typical extraterrestrial."

Echo nodded, smiling, "Thank you, Pulse, for your relevancy."

Sara formed a mental picture of the gray stereotypical alien seen in so many TV shows and movies, and thought, *"They are real!"*

Echo glanced at both Sara and Pulse and added, "The leader of the *Greys* here on Earth is Aeon, a friend of ours and one that you will soon meet."

"Echo, this is incredible information, but you have already given me much of this info when we first met."

"I did. I wanted to refresh your memory for what we are about to face."

"Something new or some new info is now in play?"

"Yes, Sara."

"Echo, your voice carries a much stronger inflection… and seriousness."

"You have remarkable intuition."

"Then, Echo, what is this conversation leading into?"

"The reason I brought you here tonight… the reason we can't wait any longer."

All looked directly at Echo, knowing full well what was coming.

"Sara, Earth is likely facing a mass extinction from two very different catastrophes."

18

EARTH'S SIXTH MASS EXTINCTION

Sara heard words that sent a chill down her spine. She could see that Echo had a prepared graph.

"Sara, the five major mass extinctions on planet Earth are listed on my screen:

1. *Ordovician – Silurian, 440 million years ago, 85% of all species lost.*
2. *Devonian, 375 million years ago, 75% of all species lost.*
3. *Permian – Triassic 250 million years ago, 96% of all species lost.*
4. *Triassic – Jurassic 200 million years ago, 80% of all species lost.*
5. *Cretaceous – Tertiary, 66 million years ago, 76% of all species lost.*

"Sara, your eco-system and world economy are collapsing, as we have discussed in the past.

"There are water shortages and mass starvation."

Sara was recalling Echo's negative worldview remarks from their initial meeting as Echo continued emphatically.

"The world is experiencing mass extinctions unlike anything since the dinosaur era.

"Global warming and the burning of fossil fuels is continuing without proper leadership to stop it.

"The devastating Covid-19 pandemic exposed global infrastructure deficiencies unimaginable prior to the outbreak of the novel coronavirus.

"We estimate that by the year 2050, all fish in the oceans will be gone and coral reefs will have been destroyed.

"It is highly likely that by the year 2100, Sara, Earth will have become uninhabitable, by today's standards.

"Your civilization, as part of the galaxy, is on an unchecked path to its end."

Pulse was getting somewhat annoyed at Echo's persistence, given Sara was part of the solution and not part of the problem.

Echo read Pulse's thoughts, acknowledged him, but continued, "Your culture lacks the necessary consciousness and spirituality. It is what your scholars call 'the law of correspondence,' as above... so below."

Sara was becoming upset, unable to respond to the facts and observations presented by Echo.

"The reality that you see on your Earth today is a collection of what is going on within the economic and social systems of worldwide countries today."

Seeing a very pensive Sara, Pulse advised softly, "Sara, this is why we came to your Earth... to provide guidance and problem-solving skills that could pivot away from Earth's demise and re-boot humanity to change behavior and literally save the planet."

"Sara," Echo snapped, "that was our long-term plan. Hence the capsules."

"So, Echo, what has changed? This is all information that could have been discussed before today."

"Sara, we believe the reptilian Dracs are making preparations to mount an attack on Earth."

"How? Why? When, Echo?"

"Signals sent from Earth many years ago gave away your position and technology... your scientists inadvertently led them here. Pete Stevenson would recall the when and how. The why is all about Earth's critical minerals and vast resources."

Sara, sensing a tip-of-the-iceberg moment, asked a strategic question.

"What was the tipping point? Why didn't we have this discussion while we were in Dubai?"

"Sara, a potential extinction level event has recently changed everything and now requires our total and complete focus... that is the combined focus of the Arrans and all of humanity."

Sara waited as the *bottom line* was obviously coming...

"The Dracs launched a destructive magnetic wave several days ago that has already destroyed a joint Earthly venture outpost on Mars."

Sara winced.

"It will impact the Earth in one hundred and fifty-six days!"

19

SPACE CLOCK IS TICKING

With that jaw-dropping news, Sara went from discouraged to petrified. "Echo, what are you talking about and where did it come from? And why?"

"Sara, we have established quantum teleportation of galactic information for hundreds of years, and have strategically set up space 'buoys' throughout the solar system to serve as *early warning* devices for any activity or alien behavior that was outside of predetermined algorithms."

Sara understood that simple explanation… but was still immensely impressed.

"This wave possibly originated beyond your solar system and this event qualified as significantly outside the normalcy and quiet of space."

Pulse added harshly, "There have been Galactic Alliances, albeit loosely constructed ones, which have precluded these events from happening in your Solar System. Now, it seems, any rogue advancement must be viewed as hostile."

With that comment from Pulse, the alien leader Echo held up her hand as if to summon someone into the meeting room.

As the door opened, Sara could see a thinner alien version of Pulse, likely about six feet two inches in height, but not with the athletic build of Pulse.

Each of these Arrans had a common trait, not lost on Sara… they seemed to manage a smile, regardless of the situation.

Wearing the signature, scarlet-red-and-gray uniform of Pulse, Sara assumed that this alien was a member of Pulse's elite force team.

He entered, acknowledged Echo with a slight wave and spoke, "Hello, Sara Steele. I am Vibe, a member of Pulse's Special Operations Unit."

"Hello Vibe. It's nice to meet you. I imagine you are here to explain this magnetic wave."

"Yes. My special skills include vibration and zero-point energy fields, but my primary expertise lies in cryptochromes and molecular signal transduction under near-zero magnetic fields."

Both Echo and Pulse managed smiles, knowing what a true technology expert Vibe was and how relevant he would be in dealing with this latest calamity.

Echo asked crisply, "Vibe, simply speaking, what is the current situation?"

"A destructive magnetic wave was launched, likely from beyond the Andromeda Galaxy, which reached Mars three days ago and likely destroyed any life or infrastructure on Mars, with Earth on its trajectory for impact in one hundred and fifty-five days from today."

"Vibe, can you explain this wave for me?"

"Sure, Sara. A transient, electromagnetic disturbance, or electromagnetic pulse or EMP. They are usually radiated, magnetic or electric fields, generally disruptive or damaging to electronic equipment."

Echo chimed in, "Unfortunately, tell Sara what you told me."

"Of course, Echo. We had believed that weapons of global destruction had been developed by an evil alien culture… and now we have our proof."

"Which alien race, Echo?"

"Likely the Dracs, Sara."

"Oh God!" Sara was shaken with this news.

Echo sadly advised as she gazed at a distraught Sara Steele, **"The Dracs have now likely set their sights on Target Earth!"**

20

CRITICAL SUCCESS FACTORS

With that revelation, another chart dropped down from Echo's many screens and had the letters CSF and today's date. Sara had a feeling that she was going to get a lecture uncannily resembling ones from the past.

"As you can see, Sara, we must now focus on what I call *Critical Success Factors* if we are going to be ready for this monumental challenge.

"Thanks, Vibe, for your input."

"You are quite welcome, Echo."

"Critical Success Factors, Sara, are essentially the major elements for an organization or project to complete their mission."

Sara nodded as Echo continued, "Our CSF's right now are two-fold."

"One, we must now confront a dangerous enemy who is poised to destroy humanity as you and I know it. For now, allegedly.

"Two, we must still be cognizant of our first goal, and that was to help mankind avoid mass extinction."

Sara was thinking… *"I would love to have my dad, the ultimate management guru, here to see what was unfolding on… on the far side of the Moon!"*

"If the CSF's are the 'big picture,' the activities within them are called KSF's or Key Success Factors."

Sara immediately thought, *"Been there… seen that… thanks Dad."*

"Echo, my dad lectured about similar operating principles throughout his career. I swear you two are using the same playbook."

"We are well aware of Mike Stevenson's management capabilities and how much knowledge he got from dad and your grandfather, Pete Stevenson. There are many reasons why the Stevenson family held an attraction for us."

"Thank you, Echo." Sara knew a compliment when she heard one.

A sub-screen appeared with further KSF details:

1. *Planning*
2. *Teams*
3. *Processes*
4. *Tools*
5. *Communication*
6. *Execution*

"Planning will require clear roles and responsibilities for everyone involved in any project. Accountability will be the threads woven throughout the planning and implementation process.

"Cross-functional teams with requisite team skills, competencies, and experience will be of the utmost importance."

Sara was absorbing a Management 101 course from an alien. Why not?

"Innovative and high-tech processes with solid infrastructures will be demanded.

"Tools for problem solving and military defense will be crucial.

"Communication, competence, and cooperation will be vital within and among so many human factions and alien cultures."

One big, scary word crossed Sara's mind. *Cooperation.*

"We will work together with you to build this foundation to successfully reach our mission on both fronts."

"What's this 'you' shit?" Sara thought somewhat confused.

Sara was as focused as she had ever been in her life.

Echo had but one overwhelming takeaway to throw Sara's way.

"And what is the end result of accomplishing these critical and difficult activities?"

Sara seemed to hear Echo's next word before it was spoken.

"Survival of humanity."

21

INITIAL STRATEGY

R ealizing that she had just delivered a huge data-dump on her human friend, Sara, Echo called for a short break, "Let's adjourn to my office, where some refreshments are waiting."

Sara was pleased at the timing of the much-needed respite.

Vibe excused himself, leaving Echo, Pulse, and Sara to meet in Echo's office. Pulse indicated that he needed a few minutes and then would join them.

Echo motioned in the direction of what she called a Relaxation Room, or as Sara would describe it, a restroom, for Sara and her to use. Both women were noticeably quiet. As the two women entered the Relaxation Room, the other females in the room slowly exited, as if on cue. Sara thought that was strange.

"So, you and Pulse got a chance to get to know each other during your flight?"

"Yes, Echo. Pulse is a tremendous person... so strong and so knowledgeable."

Echo carefully added her perspective, "Sometimes Pulse doesn't know the difference between doing things right and doing the right things right. But, I agree, Pulse is a unique and cherished asset."

As they moved from the Relaxation Room down a long hallway, Echo grasped Sara's hand, stopped, turned and held Sara close to her.

"It's a lot to take in, Sara." Echo smiled and paused momentarily, as the two moved on toward Echo's office.

"I'm not sure what I expected today, Echo, but nothing like this from many perspectives."

"I understand. When the urgent pushes out the important... how do you make time for the important?"

"Gosh," Sara thought. *"That is my dad's tag line!"*

Echo picked up on Sara's thought and just smiled.

"Echo, it is clear to me that people here trust you, respect you, and listen attentively to all that you say."

"Thank you, Sara. That trust and respect is earned."

They had now arrived at Echo's office and Sara was surprised at how small it was. On a ship of this vast size, Sara thought the office of the *Big Kahuna* would be big as well.

Reading Sara's thoughts. "It is all I need, and I spend most of my time managing by walking around and listening to my people."

At that moment, Pulse arrived with two Cosmic Cosmos for himself and Sara and a glass of fizzy water for Echo.

"Cheers," he said, as all three took their glasses and toasted.

Sara was experiencing a kind of "family moment."

They all sat around a clutter-free small, rectangular table and Echo began.

Echo touched a device on her wrist and a hazy, two-dimensional white board appeared in front of them. It was blank.

"Sara, this is what I believe you should plan to do as soon as you return home."

Magically appearing on the board were specific bullet points in a to-do list, cascading down in order as a really neat graphic effect:

1. *Meet with the President's steering committee and address my eight capsules.*
2. *Create an agenda, a person in charge, and regular meeting dates and places.*
3. *Fill in the personnel holes at the ETRT and set up a plan going forward.*
4. *Establish a trusted cadre of blended talent to address your eight capsules.*
5. *Find out where each current member of the New World Order is imprisoned.*
6. *Gather data that will support my/our theory of the Earth's impending mass extinction.*
7. *Focus heavily on maximizing security, firewalls, and tracking technologies.*
8. *Meet with hologram Pete as soon as possible for his perspective of the future.*

Pulse, using his recall and making a little, lighthearted reprieve, "Just like that old, late-night, TV guy's Top Ten list, only different."

Echo grimaced. She seemed to be annoyed at Pulse's humorous side, but deep down appreciated his *life balance* objective in today's disruptive universe.

Smiling at Pulse's failed attempt to lighten the moment, Sara interjects, "Echo, this is a lot to take in. I will need so much help from so many people."

"My Sara, humanity has always looked at evolution as evolving competition… the survival of the fittest. It was detailed in that context by Darwinian Theory.

"You will need to look and drive evolution in a much different way."

"And what way is that, Echo?"

"The evolution of cooperation. The survival of the collective."

22

BACK TO REALITY

Sara tried to understand Echo's rhetoric regarding Darwin's Theory of Evolution, assuming there was much more to this symbolism than just a statement. Echo planted seeds... constantly. It is as if she had a continuing puzzle that needed to be solved.

And bullet point number five. When did that even become a *thing* of importance?

"Echo, can you explain bullet point number five? It just seems out of sync with the others?"

"It is for now. I have my intuition running swiftly on this issue and I just need some data. That's all. Can you do that for me?"

"Of course, Echo. That will be an easy one."

"Good. Now for your trip home. I don't want your loved ones to worry that you are not currently available."

With that, Pulse jumped in excitedly, eager to help.

"I'll get the Falcon cranked up."

"That won't be necessary. You'll be staying here. Vibe will fire up his star runner and take our guest home."

Pulse didn't comment. You just don't question Echo.

"If you will excuse me for a few minutes, you two can say your goodbyes. Oh, I almost forgot something."

Echo reached into her office desk drawer and pulled out a small, but intricate, wrist device that she gave to Sara.

"This is both a tool and a weapon. Put it on your wrist."

Sara did just that.

"Vibe will explain its function, but it will not be yours to use until you are properly trained."

"Trained?" Sara was puzzled.

"Yes. Later. Now, I must go."

Echo walked out of her office, leaving Sara and Pulse to wrap up any loose ends. They talked for a few minutes, gave each other big hugs, and were sadly finishing their conversation when Echo and Vibe returned.

"Sara, I have loaded everything we talked about into this small thumb drive with about five hundred and twelve terabytes. As you will find, there is significant back story and research data contained here, along with some very important implementation details for all sixteen of the capsules."

Echo handed Sara a dime-size device that magnetically attached itself to Sara's E-watch.

Smiling, Sara hugged Echo and thanked her for everything. Sara gave Pulse a brief hug as Vibe and Echo had a quiet couple of words.

Sara and Vibe headed to the elevator, went down to the first floor and an awaiting hovercraft, and then sped off to, apparently, Vibe's star runner.

✦ ✦ ✦

As they approached the pad where many spacecrafts were lined up, Sara was getting excited about the trip home. As the hovercraft came to a stop in front of Vibe's star runner, Sara made out a similar, but slightly different glyph.

"Vibe, this is your ship?"

"Yes, it is. It is the same design as all of the star runners in the fleet."

"I see. What is the name of yours?"

"Mirage."

"*How cool,*" Sara thought. She knew there was a story here and she was excited to hear it.

Vibe took Sara's belongings on board, and they settled into the usual seats in front of the touchscreen dash.

"Right-upper-corner icon, Vibe?"

"Yes. But this time, tap it twice; that'll set the course for your home on Earth."

Sara tapped the icon twice and found how comfortable she was getting with this new transportation.

"Miss Steele."

"Yes, Vibe."

"Speed. What's your pleasure?"

"Vibe, the slow, scenic route, if you please."

With that, the craft began its usual ascent and trajectory. No drones this late at night. Sara smiled.

As they accelerated from emerald green to black sky, Sara looked over to Vibe and winked. "I bet Echo wanted us to use this time to talk 'shop,' as we say."

"Affirmative."

"And the oncoming magnetic wave was number one on her list, right?"

"Negative. The wave would be number two."

Sara was startled, given the dire consequences of a destructive magnetic wave striking Earth in just five short months.

"Well, Vibe, that is your strength, right?"

"Yes, Sara, of course. I am very knowledgeable in that discipline, as you have heard."

Sara paused a moment before muttering, "Very well. What is it that you and I need to discuss for the next several hours?"

Gazing back at Sara, Vibe answered crisply and enthusiastically, "The magnetic wave will get much attention, but for now, you and I need to discuss another major military defense objective that will need to be scoped and scaled…"

"*Scoped and scaled,*" Sara thought, "*WTF!*"

"What is this major military defense objective, Vibe?"

"Future Project Zeus."

23

BACK FROM THE FUTURE

Sara and Vibe spent hours talking about the developing secret program called Project Zeus, as they headed back to Earth and Sara's home.

Sara continued to be impressed with the incredible talent and resolve of Echo's unique management team. Having grown up around the skills and knowledge of her dad and grandad, this was truly *next level* stuff.

"Sara," Vibe said as he handed a small chip to Sara, "this is my contact info, both for general and confidential communication. Never hesitate to call me, okay?"

"Yes, Vibe, of course. Thank you."

As Vibe escorted Sara from his heavily cloaked Star Runner Mirage, Sara noticed that she had only been gone about fifteen hours.

"So, Vibe, how did you come up with the name Mirage?"

"Sara, you are one of the most perceptive humans we have ever encountered. Take a wild guess."

"Well, my first thought is that you are also the cloaking genius of the tribe. Am I close?"

"Yep. Very good. My designs are used throughout the fleet and have never been compromised."

"One day, Vibe, I would like to hear how you managed to accomplish such a feat."

"Of course, Sara. Someday, likely soon, I will show you."

"And thank you, Vibe, for the 'heads-up' warning about the need to focus on Project Zeus. Our military, as far as I know, does not have recon starships and battle starships in their fleet."

"I believe that they have plans, but that is all. We will soon be faced with the need to demonstrate to global leadership how critical a Federation Starfleet will become... once we separate the good guys from the bad guys."

Smiling, Sara replied, "I'll add it to my lengthy 'to-do' list, Vibe."

"Yes. Of course. Goodbye, Sara Steele."

"Goodbye, Vibe."

Vibe quickly walked away, and Sara was left to contemplate a literal plethora of amazing events.

She turned her E-watch on for messages, and had a few, but not as many as she thought she would have.

She walked into the house, threw her light jacket on a chair in the kitchen, and made herself a cup of whipped Dalgona coffee with oat milk and a pinch of cinnamon. She fixed herself a fruit plate and some bran cereal and tried to relax and think.

As she ate her light breakfast... or lunch... or dinner... she had lost track of time, she gazed at the voice and text messages that she had. Matt and Michela had called. Her dad also called, but that could wait.

Mara Wallace left her a message that President Sullivan would like to talk later in the day. That was timely, she thought.

Walking into her office with coffee in hand, she felt that she needed to do what she called a *bubble meditation*. That was an analytic technique from Eastern cultures that had worked for her in the past.

She removed her clothes and tossed them in the corner of the room... now in bare feet and with just her bra and panties, it was time to relax. Sara sat back in her comfy leather chair.

With her eyes closed, she would think about a problem that she was trying to solve and separate it from everything else by placing it in a large, clear bubble. This would usually help her isolate the problem from existing emotions and solve it logically.

Sara tried and tried..., but wasn't successful. Just too many problems. *"I don't need solitude. I need an army,"* she thought.

So, she pulled up Echo's top-eight list to review, analyze and make notes.

1. *Meet with the President's steering committee and address my eight capsules.*
    "I will discuss with Cameron when we talk later today regarding the wave."

2. *Select a person in charge, an agenda, and regular meeting dates and places.*
"Similar to the ETRT program."

3. *Fill in the personnel holes at the ETRT and set up a plan going forward.*
"I need to further review Michaela's input and get cracking on this."

4. *Establish a trusted cadre of blended talent to address your eight capsules.*
"This is so important. It won't be easy. Will needs lots of help here."

5. *Find out where each member of the New World Order is imprisoned.*
"Clueless, for now."

6. *Gather data that will support my/our theory of the Earth's Mass Extinction.*
"Michaela et al."

7. *Focus heavily on maximizing security, firewalls, and tracking technologies.*
"Must get with Scott and Matt, and soon."

8. *Meet with Pete as soon as possible for his perspective of the future.*
"Bittersweet but oh so important. Very soon."

As Sara was about to tee up the rather nebulous data from Vibe on Project Zeus, so currently obscure that it never made Echo's short list, Sara's phone rang.

Looking down at the number, it was coming from Matt's lab, but it was neither Matt nor Jeremiah's extension.

It was not restricted, per the phone's extensive incoming security and spam filters, so Sara answered the phone.

"Hello. This is Sara."

"Hello, Sara Bear. It's your grandad!"

24

INCEPTION OR
DECEPTION

At that moment, Sara thought she was lost in a maze.

"Grandad?"

"Yes, Sara. Don't be frightened. It is your favorite hologram."

"All right… not frightened. But this is nuts!"

"Sara, Echo has been giving me intel data on what you and your team have been doing. That should not be a surprise. You know that Pulse has been my enabler for a while now."

"Yes. Of course. I just didn't think you were 'in the loop' with all the stuff that's going on."

"Not only in the loop, Sara… I am a big part of the loop!"

"Go ahead, Grandad."

"You are aware of quantum teleportation of info and data points?"

"Yes."

"And you are now quite aware of hologram technology developed by Matt's team and now shared with the Arrans race."

"Say what?"

"Sorry, Sara. Matt's team doesn't know they are sharing it with the Arrans."

"Yeah, Grandad," a bit puzzled, "I guess not."

"We need to talk soon regarding the magnetic wave. Can you get out here soon, Sara?"

"Why can't we just talk tonight?"

"Well, I need to physically transfer some energy and cognitive capability to you as you begin this important journey."

Sara was confused. "I'm not exactly sure what you mean."

"I need to create a mental portal from my visionary experiences in the future into your current 'hard science' data set."

"Put this into mathematics for me, Grandad."

"Of course. Echo wants to create an exponential growth model, whereby my thoughts or sightings of the future bundle with your actual events going forward into the future. Meat on the bone, so to speak."

"Okay. Got it… I think. Unless something else comes up, I should be able to get out there within the next few days."

"That would be good."

"Right now, I need to talk to POTUS."

"Later, Sara Bear."

"Love you, Grandad."

After they hung up, Sara realized that Pete was not Pete… just a hologram.

She sent a text message to Mara Wallace to please set up the call with the president.

✦ ✦ ✦

About ninety minutes later, Mara was in contact with President Sullivan, and Sara and Cameron began their talk.

"So, how was your meeting with Echo?"

"It was cosmic, Cameron."

"That's funny. Where did you meet?"

"Cameron, I can't get into any detail here right now… not until I'm sure I still have a secure line. I promise I will have lots to tell you when we meet."

"Fair enough, Sara. Did Echo mention the magnetic wave?"

"Yes, she did. I assume your intel has had some kind of acknowledgment?"

"We heard from our Mission Control post in Alaska that a power burst had taken out a joint colony on Mars."

Sara thought, *A fricking joint colony on Mars? Does this shit get any weirder?*

"I'll be in my office tomorrow, Cameron, and it will be much more secure than here."

"Of course."

"In fact, Cameron, I have some background info about that incoming event that we will need to discuss further tomorrow. It can't wait."

"I'll have Mara clear my schedule for us, okay?"

"Yes. Fine. Thanks."

"Sara, this steering committee is in the inception stage and we need to get it right, both in terms of members and key issues."

"Couldn't agree more, Cameron."

"I am suggesting a meeting at Camp David the week after next. Too soon or too far out?"

"No. Not at all. Sooner is better, but I don't want to spread our exceptional, but limited, resources too far. I need to get the ETRT staffed and up and running, and I'm sure you have significant vetting in place right now."

"What would be your main agenda items for our Camp David meeting, Sara?"

"The relevance and role of Echo and the Arrans, the development and implementation of the eight alien capsules, an overall long-term strategic plan, and multiple areas of communication, both here in the U.S. and abroad. Yours, Cameron?"

"Well, I'll be looking at leadership and accountability and making sure that trust is a given. We'll need to map our journey carefully with milestones and contingency plans."

"For sure, Cameron. There is one more thing that Echo needs."

"Go ahead."

"She wants to know the physical prison locations for every member of Scorpio's New World Order and key terrorist leaders behind bars."

"Why, Sara?"

"She didn't say. But it is odd, and Echo doesn't do anything vague or that isn't purposeful."

"Any opinion at all, Sara?"

"Whatever it is… it can't be good!"

25

ETRT NEW FOCUS

Early next morning, Sara was in her Palo Alto office with a to-do list that was as big and unmanageable as any she had ever faced. She was looking at all of her devices to see what she had done and what she had yet to do.

Sara Steele was feeling overwhelmed… again.

As she was consolidating and categorizing her priorities, Michaela walked into her office, gave her a huge hug, and comically asked, "So, '*I am the Storm*' warrior, what's new?"

"Funny… but kind of true. When are we meeting with the ETRT?"

"Looking at her watch, Michaela said, "In about forty-five minutes."

"Enough time to take a walk outside and talk. You won't believe where I was yesterday. I wish I could put some of this stuff in the 'bucket' of fiction, but it's all true."

The two friends strolled through the busy office building quickly, trying to avoid anyone that would take up precious time, and grabbed a bench outside near a soothing waterfall.

Sara proceeded to give Michaela the blow-by-blow account of her trip to the Moon and back, sans the Pulse episodes, which would basically take up all their talking time, and briefly what the short-term needs were agreed to going forward with Echo and the Arrans.

"Oh my God," snapped Michaela, listening to Sara's recollection of Echo's summation. "We really are Carl Sagan's pale blue dot."

"Yeah, but that pale blue dot is going to be the intersection of many different interstellar cultures, all with self-serving agendas. And right now, we don't have a clue as to what we are facing and what countermeasures we will need."

"And, Sara, that epicenter is obviously right here and right now."

Sara paused and summarized, "This time it was more about the destination being the problem than the journey. Echo touched on so many crucial issues, even I was overwhelmed."

"So, what do we do with our meeting this morning?"

"Michaela, I believe we need to be open and honest. There is no time for posturing to figure out the next move or two. I'm gonna assume we have a well-vetted group and let's go forward."

"Agreed, Sara."

"So, my friend, which ETRT members will be here today?"

Sara received several text messages as she spoke. Michaela could see the angst in Sara's mood swing.

"Connor, Justin, Elonis, Jacqui, Summar, and our newest member, Tiffany, with the epigenetics and quantum physics knowledge."

"Yeah, I read her bio and resume. She is a helluva addition. I have been very anxious to meet her."

"Oh, and Jeremiah is here as well, for both today's meeting and, I guess, to travel with you this afternoon to see the hologram of Pete at Matt's lab. He didn't give me much detail on your trip."

"Yes. I'm glad Miah is here for both needs."

"Sara, do you need any help with prep or the presentation?"

"No, Michaela, I have had time to lay out a plan. However, we are now faced with both short-term and long-term planning needs."

"This will be the first major meeting of the core of the ETRT in quite a while, Sara. Without a firm agenda, do you have a theme or meeting title to get everyone's attention and focus?"

"Yep, I certainly do."

"I'm all ears."

Pausing a moment, Sara blurted, **"Humanity's potential mass extinction!"**

26

DISRUPTION IN DUBAI

With those words, Sara and Michaela returned to Sara's office, gathered their devices and presentation materials and headed to the main ETRT conference room where a very anxious, but otherwise subdued, team ETRT waited.

As they entered the meeting room, a round of light, but respectful cheers greeted Sara, as the team welcomed her back and was eager to hear the latest news and to get their assignments.

"Hello, all. It's great to see you and super great to get back to work."

Leaning over to Tiffany, the ETRT's newest member, Sara gave her a gentle hug and nodded, "Hi Tiffany, I'm Sara and I am so happy to have you on board. Welcome to the incredible ETRT."

"The thrill and privilege are all mine, Miss Steele."

"Oh, gosh, please call me Sara."

"Yes, Sara."

"And Tiffany?"

"Yes, Sara?"

"Just as an FYI, everything that you are about to hear from me is one hundred percent true. Crazy weird, but true. Got it?"

"Yes," Tiffany replied with a sense of foreboding anxiety.

Tiffany, a short, thin young lady with a perfectly tailored, chestnut-brown business suit with matching shoes, looked a bit uneasy as she tried to force a smile. Her dark eyebrows, dark glasses, and light-colored lipstick gave her a serious and studious look.

Arriving late was Connor, a lanky, bone-faced man with hair the color and texture of straw. Connor was the ETRT's technical genius and self-proclaimed team comedian.

"Sorry guys, I went to a trampoline center and was thrown out by a bouncer!"

"Really? Again?" was the crisp response by Justin, an African-American and the quintessential code master, wearing his usual, black turtleneck sweater and round, wire-rimmed glasses.

Smiling was Matt's CTO, Jeremiah, who waved at Sara as she laughed at Connor's joke.

Rounding out the team was Jacqui, the team's extraordinary detail person, and metahuman Elonis, one of Sara's biggest assets.

As everyone filled their water glasses and prepared their devices for note taking, Sara began, "Team, this will be a meeting unlike any other. I have some incredible news and announcements, and I'm not going to sugarcoat or defer any of the extraordinary events, as we need to be completely open, honest, and transparent."

Sara had everyone's attention.

"First, did everyone see the Dubai video?"

All hands were raised, including Tiffany's hand.

"Well, at the time, we were told by Echo that the attendees at the conference would be able to remember the entire situation. That was not the case."

Even Michaela was surprised by that statement.

"As it turned out, Echo erased everyone's memory, except for this team in Dubai. So, we have the daunting responsibility to present the video to world leaders as authentic and not fabricated."

Pausing as the team recognized an info setback that wasn't expected, Sara continued, "I'm going to do a bit of a data dump for now. Jeremiah and I must leave this afternoon for his Utah lab, but Michaela and Elonis will do the requisite 'deep dive' on the forthcoming issues immediately. Okay?"

The ETRT was accustomed to Michaela and Elonis *subbing* for Sara.

"I met with Echo, the commander of the alien race, the Arrans, yesterday on her Starship Destiny, way out in space. Several of the topics today come from that meeting."

The room was fairly quiet, but the team members knew another *tip-of-the-iceberg* was about to be shown.

"I was introduced to other members of Echo's cadre, and they have some incredible resources. Her leadership team is awesome, and her elite forces are so well-skilled. I have never been in the presence of such accomplished people regarding technology, our galaxy, AI, and GAI.

"Echo explained that there are three other alien cultures positioned on Earth right now. Two, the Dracs and the Denon, are evil and dangerous."

Pausing, "But one culture, known as the *Greys*, are, mostly, helpful and friendly."

Several hands went up.

"Not yet, guys. Those details will come later. An urgent issue has been brought to the forefront and is now critical for us."

The mood in the room grew even more serious, as the team members knew that Sara was likely preparing for a jaw-dropping announcement.

"Echo presented two devastating scenarios of mass extinction here on Earth, which is more about when, and not if."

27

ENCAPSULATED DRAMA

Sara didn't want to create panic, and this group of outliers were not the panicking kind, but she could see that their usual calm and collected demeanor was now being tested.

"One scenario is likely due to the intentions of these evil aliens, and the other is the man-made destruction of our planet if we don't fix what ails 'mother earth' with serious solutions right now.

"You saw from the video, Echo provided humanity with eight critical capsules. If you look at your handheld devices, those eight are now listed."

Sara watched as Connor downloaded the descriptions of the capsules for the team to understand:

Capsule 1 will show you how to desalinate the oceans and provide fresh water to serve the world's growing population. It will also begin to allow the rising sea levels rise to be prevented or reversed. This will combat global warming as the polar ice caps will not rebuild themselves.

Sara advised, "This capsule aligns very well with groundbreaking work that is already underway. We should be able to create exponential acceleration of that work with this capsule.

Capsule 2 will explain how you can ionize the atmosphere to significantly reduce destructive hurricanes and tropical storms when they reach their biggest threat. It will also demonstrate how to bring water from even a dry atmosphere to use to fight the immense wildfires.

Michaela offered an opinion, "I believe that much of this solution-set resides in preparing atmospheric seeding, similar to what we now see in the Saharan dust storms that significantly reduce hurricane development.

Capsule 3 will show you how to use the vast resources on your planet to produce enough food to eliminate hunger and starvation, even in the most underdeveloped countries. As you will see, agriculture is driven by solar and wind energy, not by the ever-depleting coal and oil assets.

For this capsule, Jacqui chipped in, "I have seen major data sets that attack hunger and food production from many disconnected, yet relevant perspectives. I have always thought that hunger was a result of worldwide greed and would like to stay on top of this one."

Capsule 4 will allow you to gather the correct ingredients to manufacture the necessary drugs to cure many of mankind's diseases and eliminate famines totally around the world. It will also substantially reduce worldwide medical costs for drugs and service.

Sara interjected, "Michaela and I have created a 'short list' of scientists and physicians who will be part of a global consolidation of subject matter expertise. This one will rock!"

Capsule 5 will enable you to create the strongest metal known in our universe, from materials on this planet, such as platinum, aluminum, iron, and from meteors that you will be able to capture. This material can be used for a variety of industries and can be liquefied for other applications.

Sara was excited to address this capsule, "I have contacted my dad, Mike Stevenson, who has expertise and contacts to 'head up' the ETRT's contribution to whatever the POTUS committee comes up with."

Capsule 6 will provide you with a process, including several fundamental scientific breakthroughs, to take your current weak AI technology and create a path for machines to successfully perform any intellectual task that a human being can and possess full consciousness.

Sara uttered, "I have told you of my exposure to the Arrans' incredible AI technology and will assume that Connor and Justin will assist POTUS on this one."

"Abso-tively," a smirking Connor offers.

A confused Tiffany is told that it was a Connor word, combining absolutely with positively.

"Oh," Tiffany replied. "I get it. Cool."

Capsule 7 will provide tools to better understand human DNA and how to identify and wash elements of DNA. It is common knowledge that human DNA was designed and manipulated by extraterrestrials, and research on the human genome is already verifying that fact.

"I can't wait to help on this one," Michaela winks.

Capsule 8 will rapidly accelerate worldwide solutions to global warming. In the nearly ten years of the Greta Thunberg climate change improvement target of 1200 points in levels of achievement, your Earth is still below 500 points. Your planet is dying because of this problem.

"This is a huge platform," Sara snapped. "We will all be working on this one, with Michaela and her team driving our contribution with the POTUS committee."

Jeremiah asked, "We hear you mention this POTUS committee. In your opinion, will it be strong enough to tackle these issues?"

"That is a great question, Miah. I would say that the jury is still out on this one. I will monitor closely and let you guys know what I think and if we need to get involved."

"Now," Sara muttered pointedly, "as remarkable as these 'gifts' are concerned, they are not the priority of the ETRT. As you know, I am working with POTUS and we are assembling both a leadership team and an implementation committee to take these tools and find a way to develop and use them, and sooner, rather than later."

The ETRT members looked skeptical, at best.

"These capsules are currently in the possession of President Sullivan."

Michaela added some assurance, "I have been provided significant details on these eight capsules and will be sharing that info with you all very soon."

"Thanks, Michaela. Now, for the eight capsules that you saw in the video presented by Pulse, and meant solely for execution by the ETRT, these are our number one priority."

Connor begins a second download:

Capsule 1 *will provide the entire plans and materials needed for terraforming Mars, a technique that we have used for thousands of years. Earth's technology will be able to use massive reflectors and mirrored devices to bring heat and light to Mars over a three-to- five-year period, rather than tens of thousands of years.*

Sara advised, "From what I have seen, this is a technology that the Arrans have utilized before."

Capsule 2 *will give you a blueprint for taking the Artificial Intelligence that will be in the ongoing-development stage from Echo's Capsule 6 to the very essence of General Artificial Intelligence or Super AI where androids will perform any of mankind's needs in a socially responsible manner.*

Sara stopped the presentation. "I have heard that Echo has several super-AI metahumans that are absolutely indistinguishable from humans and possess massive computing capability."

Capsule 3 will enable you to understand and positively adjust significant weather patterns around the world. It will also enable you to control space weather and geo-magnetic energy, which will become a source of opportunity for climate management, or for dangerous consequences, if managed poorly.

Michaela added her thoughts, "I have begun to research this capsule and will admit that it is a huge stretch, given our present capabilities."

Capsule 4 will teach you how to levitate and use various anti-gravity or negative gravity methods to your advantage, especially when colonizing other planets, by developing the upward forces necessary to cancel out the weight of the object so the object does not fall or rise, but can be steered.

Connor chimed in, "I already have some basic theories and fundamental, fact-based incidents that I am extremely 'geeked' on. So, this not only makes sense, but could be closer than you might think."

Capsule 5 will enable you to travel back and forth through time, using a four-dimensional fabric called space-time. Forward time travel is relatively easy, because it is based on speed. Backward time travel is risky, because it alters disease, catastrophes, and mortality. Reverse time travel was responsible for many of the major worldwide plagues and epidemics.

Tiffany responded, "This actually falls within the scope and scale of some of my current research and will be an issue that I would love to be considered for."

Sara smiled affirmatively.

Capsule 6 will address quantum teleportation, which is our proven process of transmitting, atoms or molecular combinations, in their exact state, from one location to another using state-of-the-art communication and sharing quantum entanglement between the sending and receiving location.

Sara offered her opinion, "I have seen how the Arrans focus on interstellar communications and have confidence that we will benefit soon from their guidance."

Capsule 7 will enable you to perform superluminal spacecraft propulsion, also known here on Earth as warp speed, traveling at speeds greater than the speed of light by many orders of magnitude. Today, we can travel from Earth to the Andromeda Galaxy in twenty minutes.

Sara advised, "I have been on an Arrans spacecraft that has demonstrated warp speed that allows travel from the Earth to the Moon in mere minutes."

Capsule 8 will give you a blueprint for how you can defend your planet, if or when the time came to do so, with much of the technology that was just presented, a strong mastering of Full Artificial General Intelligence, accelerated evolving technologies and the use of antimatter microreactors.

Again, Sara added to the description, "We have already begun discussing a plan to design, build, and test physical spacecrafts with truly innovative AI technology to drive implementation."

As the ETRT members tried to digest the magnitude presented by these eight capsules, Sara planned to shock the team with even more startling news.

"These eight capsules are currently in Utah and we will begin our work on these as soon as possible. Elonis and Michaela will advise the ETRT regarding timing and assignments soon.

"All right. That does it for now. But I'll leave you with one last sobering revelation presented by Echo last night."

The entire team held their collective breath.

Sara glanced at her friend Michaela and announced the inexplicable, **"An extremely dangerous magnetic wave with a catastrophic power surge has been launched in the direction of Earth, and it will impact us in about a hundred and fifty-four days!"**

28

BACK TO THE FUTURE

With that announcement, Sara and Jeremiah headed to Scott's plane for the trip to the Utah lab and the meeting with the hologram of Pete, leaving Michaela and Elonis to fill in the many blanks from Sara's presentation.

Ken Darragh, Scott's pilot, had the plane ready to go when Sara and Jeremiah arrived.

"Hi Ken," Sara said, smiling.

"Hi Sara and hi, Miah. Good to see you both. Y'all ready to go?"

"Yep Ken," Sara said excitedly. "Very anxious to get out to the lab and get Matt's update on all things weird."

"Funny, but likely true," quipped Ken.

As they walked up the Jetway to enter the plane, a young woman with her hair in a bun, dressed in a pilot's uniform, greeted them.

"Hello, I am Cara Mia Miles, your co-pilot today. Welcome aboard."

"Hi Cara Mia, I'm Sara and this is Jeremiah." They both shook hands with the newly added flight associate.

"Cara Mia is a beautiful name."

"Thanks, Sara."

"Is there a story there?"

"Well, Sara, actually there is."

As the two passengers got situated in their seats, Miss Miles explained, "My grandparents picked the name. I was told it was from a movie or song back in the 1960's."

"It is a beautiful name."

"Thanks, Jeremiah. I love it, too."

Once airborne, Sara knew that they had time to discuss several issues regarding the Pete hologram and the implications brought out by Echo.

Sara decided to keep the conversation focused entirely on the hologram and not muddy the cosmic arena with too much info gained in the last 48 hours.

She also received a text message from Mara Wallace that the Camp David meeting had been scheduled.

✦ ✦ ✦

As their plane landed in Utah, Matt greeted them. Sara and Matt embraced, both sensing a strong degree of relief which nearly always defined their relationship.

"Hi Miah, good ETRT meeting?"

"For sure, Matt. Not your average bunch of overachievers, for sure."

As they drove to the lab, Sara gave Matt the big picture view of the last couple of days, including the devastating magnetic wave headed to Earth.

Matt listened attentively to Sara's update and offered his opinion, "Well, again, we have a new number-one priority. Par for the course. Damn."

Matt brought Sara up to speed on the work being done with Pete and his current state… as advanced as it was.

"Sara, Pete had his consciousness uploaded to a digital bank for perpetuity. That was his original desire and our original premise."

"Yes, Matt, but it also provided Pete a digital afterlife following his death, and I don't believe that ever entered his beautiful mind."

"I'm sure it did not," Matt responded.

Jeremiah was anxious to throw in his two cents, "What I find remarkable is that Pete could not have had any idea that he would become a keystone in any alien alliance with humanity."

"Well," Sara added excitedly, "I think I can enlighten you both during our meeting today, as I have just become aware of an incident many years ago that opened up a literal Pandora's Box. It was the unintended consequence of people trying to do good and what researchers do as part of their wiring."

Jeremiah interjected some news, "We added some technical aspects into our continuing research into virtual and augmented reality that could provide a useful glimpse into the future."

"Sara, you know that VR is a complete immersion experience that shuts out the physical world and AR overlays virtual objects on the real-world environment."

"Yes, of course," Sara answered.

"Well," Jeremiah continued, "we have now created an enhanced mixed reality, which we call EMR, which can take digital images of future thoughts, dreams, and possibly Pete's future prognostications, and anchor virtual objects into the real world."

"Holy cow!" Sara was putting two and two together thinking of the value of EMR with the Pete hologram.

As the three walked through the main lab into Jeremiah's recently updated holo-display lab, Sara smiled at the new name above the entrance that Miah had picked:

SUPER ARTIFICIAL INTELLIGENCE

"Sorry, guys," Jeremiah added, "but I get chills every time I walk into that room."

Sara quickly replied, "No need to apologize, Miah. I think it's very apropos."

Sara thought humorously, *It could be worse... like **Super Holographic Information Technology!**"

With that, they walked into the lab where super-techy Tyreek had booted the hologram of Pete for their arrival.

"Hi Tyreek."

"Hi Sara. Good flight?"

"Yes, thanks. Ya got Grandad ready to go?"

"I'm ready, Sara," Pete, gazing at Sara, responded softly. "It's good to see you."

"It is so good to see you, Grandad. I missed you."

"Yes, much as happened since we last met, and Echo says you need my data on the magnetic wave."

"Yes, Grandad, we have a ticking time bomb of sorts and only a couple months to figure out a countermeasure."

With that comment, Jeremiah grabbed a device from a corner shelf and handed it to Sara.

"Okay, Miah. What's this?"

"I told you about our work with the enhanced mixed reality, or EMR."

"Yes."

"Well, this device, a smaller size version of a VR headset, is the latest iteration of our EMR."

Matt chimed in, "It is fairly sophisticated, and Tyreek and Miah get all the credit for its rapid development."

Jeremiah put the device on Sara's head and adjusted it for fit. Next, he guided a floating version of the device onto Pete's head. Jeremiah then glanced over to Tyreek to be sure the two devices were in sync.

Moments later, Sara spoke in amazement, "I am beginning to visually see everything that Echo and Vibe described to me as if I am there right now. It is a bit hazy, but it is clearing up now... so realistic."

Pete uttered his perspective, "And I am looking into the virtual archives of my awareness to search for the origin and dynamics of the wave."

Several quiet minutes followed before Sara had a joyous outburst.

"I see it. I can actually see it. I know roughly where it came from in the solar system, and I have a complete signal transduction of the event... and galactic coordinates integrated into the real-time continuum."

Matt and Jeremiah looked at each other and were aghast. What did Sara just say and how could she have even thought of those words?

Taking off her headset, Sara calmly said, "I have downloaded the transmission into my E-watch and will take it back to the office for review and action planning with Echo. Thank you, Grandad."

His virtual headset disappearing, Pete nodded, "So glad I could help."

Matt and Jeremiah were stunned... excited... but stunned.

Sara noticed the amazement on the faces of Matt and Jeremiah, given her grasp of knowledge that was unexpected.

"Sorry, guys. I received a hands-on class in *Signal Transduction* from an Arrans' IT guru named Vibe."

This meeting with Pete was crucial, for so many reasons, but Sara just couldn't help jumping right back in with her *question of the day.*

"Grandad, do you recall back in 2000 in California being part of the *Messaging Extraterrestrial Intelligence,* or METI?"

"Yes, I do."

"In October, 2002, a radio signal was launched toward the Luyten's Star, some twelve light-years away."

"Yes, Sara. "And in 2002, a *Fast Radio Burst,* or FRB, was received with an alarming Morse code type of repeating a message that could not have been random."

Sara asked, "Are you aware of what that incident has led to?"

"Yes, Sara, I am well aware now that the extraterrestrial research efforts back in the early 2000's, as innocent as they seemed to be, would have a terrible downside."

Sara's mind was flooded with thoughts and second-guessing. She looked at the hologram of her wonderful grandfather, Pete, and reached the same conclusion that Pete had reached…

"It enabled an evil alien civilization to find us by tracing those signals back to Earth."

29

MAD MATT

Matt was unhappy with Sara for repeatedly withholding vital info from him. As they left the lab, Matt confronted Sara with his displeasure.

"First, it was the knowledge of Echo, Pulse, and the entire Arrans presence on Earth, and now, the mere suggestion that our hologram is the key to unlocking the future... why keep me in the fricking dark?"

"Dammit, Matt, I'm sorry. It wasn't intentional... just that with so much going on, and not knowing what, if any, danger you, Jeremiah, and Tyreek could be in, I just thought it best to keep you out of it."

"Danger? What possible danger in telling your boyfriend what the hell is going on? I am the one who literally re-built you. Don't I deserve that much, at least?"

"Give me credit for thinking this out."

"What are you getting at, Sara?"

"Echo has confided in me that there are other alien species on Earth, and they are evil and a significant threat."

"Whoa... I'm listening."

"I am at the center of all things cosmic right now and considered a key person with all the actual data and strategic direction in my grasp. Anyone... and I mean anyone close to me is vulnerable. You are certainly at the top of the list, along with my parents."

Giving Sara a hug, Matt said, "Okay. I see. I do see what you mean and I'm sorry."

"I'm sorry, too, Matt. Let's put this complicated past behind and focus on what the hell we're gonna do going forward."

"Sounds good. Dinner tonight with my girl?"

"For sure. Looking forward to it."

✦ ✦ ✦

With that, they went back to Matt's house to freshen up for dinner. Matt opened a bottle of his and her favorite wines, a Caymus Cabernet, as he began to fix a fine seafood dinner for himself and his lovely Sara.

"Cheers, Sara."

"Cheers, Matt. Sorry about earlier… Will make up for it tonight."

"Looking forward, Sara. Why don't you jump in the shower while I get our dinner going?"

"Can do. Thanks. Be back in a few…"

While Sara was in the shower, Matt put an appetizer together, a shrimp ceviche, and began the baked salmon with creamy coconut-ginger sauce over coconut-ginger rice.

He glanced over to a Key lime pie that had been ordered and would be a great ending to a great meal.

He thought to himself, *"All of Sara's favorites."*

Moments later, Sara emerged from her shower wearing only one of Matt's dress shirts and nothing more.

Sara approached Matt and gave him a huge hug and a long, luscious kiss. Matt was already thinking ahead to post-dinner intimacy as he continued their embrace.

Following dinner, Matt surprisingly came up behind Sara, picked her up and walked her into his bedroom. His athletic body resembled a hard-as-nails wrestler's physique, rather than a prominent physician and surgeon.

The mirror over the dresser framed their image as Matt pushed aside the collar of her shirt and nibbled the sweet spot where her shoulder curved into her neck.

Sara thought, *"This is my Matt… soft, sensitive, and giving."*

She shuddered as he slowly, deliberately caressed her body. Laying her on her back, he unbuttoned her shirt buttons, slowly removed the shirt and ran his left hand gently over her breasts, kneading her firm nipples.

As he moved his right hand onto her back… her lower back and below, he felt her shudder, encouraging him to do more. As he cupped her breasts and backside, Sara pulled him down for a lasting kiss.

Her tongue swept through his mouth while her lips pressed firmly and wet as she murmured, giving Matt the signal that her sighing sounds of pleasure brought his manhood out firmly and readily.

She wrapped her legs around Matt's torso, encouraging him to continue his attentions. He felt her muscles momentarily tense, then felt a ripple of response from Sara pulling her thighs tightly into his warm body. She was warm, hungry, and moist.

Sara thought impatiently, *"Please go all the way!"*

Gradually, her limbs grew slack, her hold on him relaxed, as he moved his body onto hers. Matt took his time making a trail of kisses up and down her neck, her chest, and torso, as Sara widened her legs so Matt could get better positioned for penetration.

"Now Matt," she whispered softly.

Within minutes, they were two intimate lovers who had waited far too long to resume their physical relationship. Matt thought of the first time he saw the lovely but damaged Sara, and Sara thought of their wonderful time sailing and loving on the high seas.

Sara was radiated from head to toe, as her dam burst open with delight. They reached a point of simultaneous climax that brought back wonderful memories of past love making.

Matt paused and looked her straight in the eye to let her know that he was always there for her and would never let her down or disappoint her… not here or anywhere.

He ran his hands through Sara's gold locks and kissed her forehead, her cheeks, and her lips.

"I love you, Sara."

Sara paused a moment before responding.

"I love you too, Matt."

"You are my everything, Sara."

Matt smiled as Sara added one more comment, **"Matt, you are the only 'man' in my life!"**

30

COMIC STORM

With only two days to catch her breath concerning the incredible meeting with the hologram of Pete, and a wonderful reunion and sex with Matt, Sara had to prepare for a crucial meeting with POTUS and the steering committee, now named by the committee as Operation Cosmic Storm.

Sara thought, sarcastically, about that name, *"Why not call it Danger: Evil Aliens Are Coming!"*

After Sara's determined and persistent efforts, Michaela Marx was added to the committee; and the two of them were headed to Camp David for the follow-up meeting to the first meeting only a couple weeks ago.

"So, Sara, how was your evening with Matt? I'm sure you had a lot to 'catch up' on."

Sara slowly responded, "It was another one of those bittersweet evenings. I so much enjoyed spending time with that marvelous man, but I am so preoccupied that even the sex... the good sex, was kind of a diversion."

"Could there also be a little 'Pulse diversion,' Sara?"

"Don't go there... please. I'm conflicted with the big guy, for sure, but Matt and Pulse are two extremely different people."

Michaela let Sara go on...

"They are both 'tens,' with such great attributes, but I feel so safe and secure around Pulse, and you know as well as I do, this damn alien environment that we find ourselves immersed in, is anything but calm and quiet!"

"Gotcha, girl. Let's focus on today's meeting."

"Yes, Michaela, that would be wise."

"You mentioned before that you were a bit apprehensive about all the 'old white guys' on the President's committee. I can understand the energy and passion characteristics being an issue, but they do have experience, Sara."

"Yes, of course."

Sara thought for a moment before her follow up.

"I will be looking for a 'take charge' guy among them. My hope is that one of these 'old, experienced' guys will have the balls to get himself immersed in the 'deep dive details' of carrying out the incredibly hard work that will be required."

Sara and Michaela were the first to arrive, keeping to Sara's dad Mike's constant reminder that *early is on time; on time is late*. They waited in the vestibule of the conference center as members of the committee began filing in.

Michaela was texting as Sara was pulling her meeting materials together. As a tall, dark, and handsome military man entered the vestibule, Michaela poked Sara and whispered into her ear.

"What a hunk! Damn, but he is the hottest guy I think I've ever seen. Wonder what job he has around here?"

Sara just smiled, as all would be revealed soon.

Director Meacham approached the two ladies and asked crisply, "I hope we are ready for this. Hi, I'm Donald Meacham, the National Security Director."

"Hello, I'm Michaela Marx, astrophysicist and ETRT Senior Program Manager. It's nice to meet you."

"Hi Sara."

"Hi Director Meacham. And yes, we are armed and ready to go."

The three of them entered the main conference hall as others began filing in. Refreshments were in abundance, so they each grabbed a drink and some finger food and took their seats.

President Sullivan entered the room with six of the committee members around him, chatting incessantly and fairly loudly. He approached Sara and Michaela.

Giving Sara a gentle hug, the president smiled and said, "Hello Sara. It's great to see you again and I'm hopeful we can have a productive meeting today."

"I agree, Mister President," setting first name aside for now, "and we will do our best."

"Hello, Michaela, welcome aboard. We are so happy to have your expertise and counsel here to keep us on track and focused."

"Thank you, Mister President. I will do my best."

POTUS took a seat at the end of the oval conference table and the members quietly and respectfully took their seats.

At the far end of the table was Lieutenant Robert Baker, who smiled at both Sara and Michaela.

President Sullivan spoke, "Greetings to all. Glad we were all able to meet so quickly." Noting an empty chair, Cameron muttered, "Bob, is RJ here?"

"Yes, Mister President, he is. Sorry for the delay. He had an emergency call from the JPL. He'll be here momentarily."

Michaela was pissed. *"One guy holding up such an austere group!"*

Sara passed around her meeting agenda and introduced Michaela, "We have a new addition to the team. Everyone, this is the actual Michaela Marx that I have been telling you about and whose actions are well documented in all of the briefings you have received."

"Thanks, Sara. It's great to be here with you. I am anxious to participate in any way possible."

At that moment, in walked that hunk of a military man, looking every bit as dashing as the image Michaela had of him in the vestibule.

"Hello everyone. I am Commander RJ Baker, Operations Director of the U.S. Space Force. I apologize for my tardiness, as we had a Code Three issue at the Jet Propulsion Lab."

The President immediately chimed in, "No need to apologize, Commander Baker, we are happy to have you on board."

Michaela went gaga over this newly identified person and whispered to Sara, "Holy shit... and smart, too!"

Sara smiled and could see Commander Baker gazing at Michaela, looking as striking as ever in her favorite, mauve leather jacket, but this time with a little, reddish blush noticeable on her smiling face.

Sara sized up the situation and thought devilishly of what was going to become a likely event.

"You don't need a crystal ball to see this one coming..."

31

COSMIC STORM

POTUS began the meeting, "Per Sara's agenda, we will go around the room and get each member's pre-work assignments from the classified data of our first meeting and strategy for the eight alien capsules discussed at that meeting. I'd like to hold the general discussion until we are done with the first pass."

Each member was assembling their report-outs as President Sullivan continued, "Let's start with General Patrick. Jim?"

"Thanks, Cam. My work with the Pacific Fleet and foreign military conflicts gives me a good perspective for the type of personnel we will need for the capsule analysis and implementation. I have pulled out several critical success factors and have begun the vetting process for individuals that we will need to recruit."

"Good start, Jim," Cameron replied. "General Grant?"

"I have looked at the capsules from a baseline perspective; in other words, where will we be coming from on these capsule journeys and what will it require from us in terms of innovation and technology to build a bridge from that past to the capsule's end game."

Sara and Michaela both smiled. This was a proactive perspective.

"Bill, that makes great sense." Cameron was pleased. "Doctor Griffith, what do you have for us?"

"Cameron, I have looked at the capsules from the technical perspective of our AI and DNA capabilities, and we are lacking the talent right now to get a good, sound plan together. I have contacted both academia and corporate brainpower, in pure confidence, to see what resources are available to me and for us. I'm optimistic."

"Great. Next up is our Intel Committee Chair, Frank Polansky. Frank?"

"Well, I'm not quite up to speed yet, I must confess. I still have my team going over the evidence, much as we do in preparation of the President's PDB. Just looking to assure legitimacy."

An annoyed Sara whispered to Michaela, "The President's Daily Briefing. Seriously"

"Well, Frank, please expedite."

"Yes sir. Will do."

"Ernie, you're up."

"As Foreign Affairs Chair, I had two immediate tasks. The first was within my communication expertise. I have begun the process to secure all incoming and outgoing comm and devise the best way to bundle our global and space interaction. I will, of course, be working closely with the ETRT and Doctor Baker."

Michaela thought, *"Doctor Baker? Are you kidding? He has a PhD?"*

Sara, Michaela, and Commander Baker flicked smiling glances toward Mr. Suarez. Then, Michaela cast a rather sheepish glance to RJ, who made immediate eye contact.

Michaela had another thought, *"I'd better focus, or I'll likely embarrass myself soon."*

Ernesto continued, "I have also taken the lead regarding a Manhattan Project option, by creating a short list... a very short list, of international leaders that may need to become active participants."

"Excellent, Ernie. Great work." The President was quite pleased, as were Sara and Michaela.

POTUS looked at the next seated gentleman, the National Security Director Donald Meacham, who responded to the President's head nod.

"As I have mentioned before, we need to build a strong and capable force at all levels of our... let's say, pyramid. The planning will become important and the implementation will become absolutely critical. So, my main role will be the vetting process, and I already have a multi-layered process locked and loaded."

POTUS commented, "Thanks, Don. And, as always, you are likely way ahead of the curve. Lieutenant Baker?"

"Thanks, Mister President. As my assignment is to be the facilitator here, I am ready and able to begin compiling all of our data into accurate, concise, and manageable components. I will be your data dump-master going forward."

Even his son, RJ, smiled at the lighter tone from his usually serious father.

Also enjoying the remark, POTUS turned to Commander Baker.

"We know you're just getting on board here, Commander, but do you have any opinion or thoughts?"

"Thank you, Mr. President. I will wait until we wrap, if that's okay with the committee. I want to digest the next session of accountability and assignments."

"That'll work. Sara and Michaela, anything to add?"

Sara simply replied, "No, not at this time. We would also like to see where we go with the next round focusing on the pending roll-out of the eight capsules' implementation."

✦ ✦ ✦

At that point in the meeting, President Sullivan called for a 45-minute break for everyone to catch up on their regular obligations.

As they all rose to take care of business or enjoy some refreshments, Commander Baker walked over to Sara and Michaela.

"Hello, Sara, I'm RJ Baker. Pleased to finally meet the leader of the pact."

"The pleasure is all mine. Love to have you join our group of outliers and overachievers."

RJ laughed and stretched out his hand to Michaela. "Hello. Now that you know who I am, with whom do I have the pleasure?"

"Hi… I'm Michaela. I'm with the ETRT."

There was an awkward pause.

"I knew that, Michaela. What is your role with the ETRT?"

"I'm the space lady. Actually, the astrophysicist that works on space stuff."

Sara was dumbfounded. How could her trusted friend, the most knowledgeable, competent, and articulate person on the planet, come up with a *duh*.

Lieutenant Robert Baker then approached the three people talking and saved the day for the clearly love-struck Michaela.

"Hi guys. Getting acquainted?"

"Yep, Dad. These ladies are truly amazing. I couldn't be happier than to be right here, right now."

Michaela just wanted to *get small*.

Noting the need to get away, Sara muttered, "Would you please excuse us? We need to take care of a few things."

Both men nodded.

Once inside the ladies' room, Sara quipped, "Well, you really did impress him, eh?"

"I'm sorry, Sara. I haven't felt like that or been as feeble as that since… I don't know when. RJ Baker is one awesome dude. Smart, handsome, and single… looking at his ring finger."

"Earth to Michaela. Come on back."

32

COMMITTEE STORM

They both chuckled as they walked back into the conference room, with Michaela glancing sheepishly at RJ Baker as the Commander was sitting down.

Sara couldn't help but notice that Michaela's blouse was revealing a bit more cleavage coming out of the lady's rest room.

President Sullivan spoke, "Okay. Good start. Now let's address the actual eight capsules from the officer-in-charge perspective. Each will need an OIC and point of contact."

Sara, Michaela, and RJ, the resident outliers, were ready.

"Capsule number one addresses the ocean desalinization. Who all will be working on this?"

Three men raised their hands and Cameron asked, "Who will be the point of contact?"

General Grant responded, "I will, Cam, and the three of us also have taken on capsule number three regarding the development of food production capabilities."

"Great. How about capsule two, the focus on hurricanes and tropical storms. Ionizing the atmosphere sure sounds challenging."

An unlikely hand was raised by Intelligence Committee Chair, Frank Polansky. "I'll take this one on. Should be able to discern between fact and fiction here. I do have a couple associates, including the Secretary of the Interior, who will welcome this task."

"Thanks, Frank. Appreciate your stance here."

Commander RJ Baker interjected his thoughts, "I would like to be included in this project, as I have a lot of experience with the science of ionization."

"Fine. Thanks, Commander."

"I would like to help, too."

"Certainly, Michaela. That would be great."

A smiling Cameron looked down at his agenda.

Sara thought, "*Well, no surprise. I certainly saw that one coming with my wired-up girlfriend.*"

"Very well. We are at capsule number four, addressing the ramped-up manufacturing of drugs to combat mankind's diseases and eliminate world-wide famine."

Donald Meacham chimed in, "I see the need to carefully recruit health and science experts here, and since I will be deeply engrossed in vetting, I can certainly take a parallel course and staff this need as well."

"Outstanding, Don." The President was very happy with his National Security Director.

"Capsule five dealing with the creation of a super-metal sounds intriguing. Any takers?"

"Yes, Cam," General Patrick advised. "I've lived a life of metal-to-metal incidents everywhere, and often not strong enough. I know a couple metallurgical nerds that will be easy recruited."

"I bet you do, Jim. Thanks. I think I've already heard from the team member willing to take on capsules six and seven."

"That's correct, Cam," Doctor Emil Griffith announced. "AI and DNA studies really 'float my boat.' Can't wait to get a small team assembled."

"With Jim's bucket spoken for, we have only capsule number eight, the climate change initiative that has been a polarizing issue for decades."

After a brief pause, Foreign Affairs Committee Chairman Ernesto Suarez offered his services.

"I can see how this critical issue will need strong alliances created globally, and I believe I can drive this initiative with a laser focus. As you know, I have already spoken on the Greta Thunberg warnings and I am one of her strongest advocates."

Again, Commander RJ Baker spoke, "And I will be happy to assist you, Chairman Suarez. I live and work in this ever-changing climate of ours."

And again, Michaela, glancing at Commander Baker, offered her opinion, "Count me in, too. Climate change has been one of the ETRT issues that I have championed."

Sara leaned in and whispered to Michaela, "You surely aren't playing 'hard to get.' You okay?"

Michaela just smiled as the President continued.

"Well, that concludes the initial accountability portion of today's meeting. Does everyone have their updated breakout team rosters?"

No one raised their hand, so each committee member was apparently prepared for the next session.

"Before we adjourn to our respective breakout rooms to start our deep dives on these capsules and discuss joint functional team development, does anyone have anything to add?"

Following a very short pause, Commander RJ Baker spoke out, "Yes, I do, Mr. President. I applaud you and your team's commitment and mission, and your reaction to these alien 'gifts' is commendable."

"Please, Commander Baker, give us your thoughts."

Sara and Michaela were both paying close attention to the Commander's next words.

"Your mission has good intention... but, in my opinion, your implementation lacks passion!"

33

GALAXIES FAR...
FAR AWAY

The Commander's words showered the room with cold water, and even Sara and Michaela were puzzled at the rather harsh assessment.

RJ, realizing his words came as a surprise, added some clarification, "Maybe 'intention and passion' are not exactly what I meant to say, but *reactive* and *proactive* is what I am alluding to."

President Sullivan asked crisply, "We are listening, Commander; please explain."

"I believe we need to immediately take the gifts from the Arrans race and energize them in a purely proactive manner."

Sensing the opportunity to clarify further, RJ continued, "I suggest we gather data from a number of exploratory missions and working with the ETRT's current database, and, hopefully, the Arrans' expertise, consolidate and optimize what we know as fact."

Commander Baker now had everyone's attention.

"The Arrans give us seeds, as they described them. We need to become much more aggressive with what we are now in possession of and pursue all relatable facts and known science and actually test theories as we progress out of this path of innovation."

Michaela and Sara went from puzzled to ecstatic with his recommendation.

Doctor Griffith nodded and added his thoughts, "I get it. I totally am on board with this observation. We must now do cost/benefit analyses, correlation studies, simulations and regression analyses, and truly energize these capsules with 'what we know' and 'what we don't yet know.' We simply can't wait for Echo and the Arrans to tell us what to do next."

"Exactly," Commander Baker said.

Sara offered an ETRT analogy, "Yes, this is how the ETRT has been wired. Call it reverse engineering or starting at the end and working back; we have had our shares of setbacks, but without those 'lessons learned,' we would have never gotten to where we are today and, possibly, this Camp David meeting may have never happened."

President Sullivan advised, "I never did think of this as a necessary ingredient to success, but now I clearly do. Commander, what is your 'big picture' of what we need to do now?"

"There are galaxies far, far away, and we have had numerous research vessels gathering data for what seems to be forever. Look at Voyagers two, three, and four and other exploratory crafts.

"Consider the five-hundred-meter aperture spherical radio telescope, known as FAST. It has an extra-galactic range that has already discovered a black hole about thirty times larger than the Sun."

"But that kind of info is really not relevant to these eight capsules, Commander," Chairman Frank Polansky said.

"No, Mr. Chairman, it is a bad comp to use. My point is that we have tremendous data collection and analytic capability that we need to align with the development of the eight capsules."

Lieutenant Baker wanted to defend his son… but held his thoughts.

Michaela, doing last-minute research on her handheld device, anxiously responded, "With a post-doctoral-astrophysics fellowship myself, and somewhat familiar with Commander Baker's paper on *Celestial Mechanics and Dynamical Astronomy applied to the current Galactic Universe*, I totally agree with the Commander on taking a proactive stance."

Sara winked at Michaela as her friend continued, "He is not advocating complex guiding principles, only validation and verification elements."

Now, Commander Baker was noticeably impressed.

"I guess you can now say that our linear path has gone exponential, eh, Commander?"

"Yes, Mr. President. Sorry to muddy the waters a bit. That was not my intention."

"No need to apologize, Commander. Can't believe that we were so smug in thinking that old tricks could solve new problems. Where to from here?"

As Sara and Michaela smiled and recognized what a giant leap had just been witnessed, Commander Baker followed up, "I will work with the proper Federal Agencies and the ETRT to begin the review process of all exploratory ventures, if that's okay with this committee. I'll work with my dad as the facilitator to make sure whatever we do is essential, accurate, and timely."

✦ ✦ ✦

Following that detour provided by Commander Baker, the committee headed for lunch followed by the afternoon breakout sessions to start the deep dive on building the foundation for the eight capsules.

Sara and Michaela wanted to spend some time with Commander Baker, but he was apparently called to a critical conference call with the Jet Propulsion Laboratory that they discovered later concerned cyber terror at that facility.

On his way back from that call, the two women met him.

"Thanks for that support from both of you."

"You are quite welcome, Commander Baker," Sara noted.

"Please, ladies, call me RJ."

"And please don't call us ladies," joked Michaela.

"Hey, I'm impressed that you knew of my thesis paper, Michaela. Not many people do."

"Well, I pride myself on being 'up to date' with emerging technology and innovative thinking."

Sara, having watched her friend nervously researching Commander Baker on her handheld device during the meeting, almost laughed out loud, as Michaela continued, "I would love to hear more about your work and your current mission with Space Force. Sounds right in my wheelhouse."

"Would love to do that and catch up with all that the ETRT has in play. Dinner sometime soon?"

"I'd like that," Michaela answered softly.

"RJ, you looked a little preoccupied with that conference call. Everything okay? Anything we can help with?"

"No, Sara, I don't think so. We have a possible cyber terror hacking incident at the JPL and it's troubling."

"I think we can help."

"How, Sara?"

"As Michaela will agree, we have two certified cyber geniuses back in Palo Alto. What they have done for us and for the military is absolutely amazing."

"Well, then, all the more reason for me to get out there. Let me clear some time posthaste and I will make it happen. Thanks."

✦ ✦ ✦

President Sullivan joined an already assembled committee in the conference room for the final session of the day.

"It looks like we made some good progress with our breakout sessions. I could see smoke coming through the doors."

Some laughter could be heard from a tired and somewhat drained group.

For the next 45 minutes, each self-appointed committee member who took on a capsule or two gave a report-out as to the status of the breakout sessions and next steps.

Lieutenant Robert Baker recapped, "We have made a great deal of progress today, and I will be summarizing and confidentially distributing notes and issues for our next meeting. As with a PDB, you will get daily updates and any to-do items that meet consensus guidelines. Any questions?"

"Thanks, Bob. I have two administrative items to report on before we adjourn." Scribbling on his note pad, the President continued, "One will be short and one, well, not so much."

Having just spoken to Cameron, both Sara and Michaela knew what was coming.

"First, as a request from Echo, the Arrans Commander, we have all the New World Order and spin-off groups' bad guys corralled at our Supermax prison in Florence, Colorado.

"As you know, Supermax is a facility for the worst of the-worst criminals who pose an extremely serious threat to both national and global security. Nearly twenty prisoners are now in uniform confinement there."

Donald Meacham added, "We do not yet know why Echo had requested this to be done, but Sara Steele says it must be done and it was."

"Thanks to both of you," Sara added, and provided follow up.

"I have known Echo for several months now, dating back before Dubai, and she doesn't do anything without a purpose… usually a very critical purpose. I will keep you posted."

President Sullivan glanced at the door as a new figure walked in.

"With that understood, please welcome our highest-ranking military officer, and current Chairman of the Joint Chiefs of Staff, General Arthur van Buuren, with an important announcement."

Everyone knew General van Buuren, as his legacy had been the cornerstone for everything good to great with the U.S. military. The recipient of numerous awards both in peacetime and in war, he was a living, breathing legend. His being here was truly remarkable… and was a sign.

"Thanks, Cam, and it is so nice to be here, but I'm afraid that I am not bringing good news today."

That comment turned what was a very positive meeting into an air of concern and apprehension.

"I'll get to the point. You all are aware that an alleged magnetic wave was in route to Earth, and until now we were not in a position to comment."

Tension was high, as all in the room knew of the allegations. Only Sara and Michaela were coming from a position of fact, thanks to Echo.

"We are now in complete validation of the following, and there is zero doubt of a disturbing truth."

General van Buuren paused.

"A catastrophic magnetic wave is in route to our planet and this power surge will impact us in one hundred and fifty-two days!"

34

WAVE OF DESTRUCTION

Gentleman van Buuren motioned to Sara and said, "The joint Chiefs have been in contact with Miss Steele and her ETRT concerning this dangerous problem and I'll let her take it from here."

With that lead, Sara stepped over to a podium in the corner of the room and opened the new discussion.

"Thank you, General van Buuren. Yes, President Sullivan put us in touch with the military on this magnetic wave issue and we have had many discussions and consultations. I will give you the 'big picture' as the ETRT and I see it."

Sara projected a timeline on a large whiteboard to her left and used that as a speaking frame of reference.

"About two weeks ago, Mission Control, Alaska, received a dire emergency broadcast on a secure, quantum communication link from the Voyager Four outpost on Mars, as you know. As you also know, a powerful magnetic wave destroyed that outpost in a matter of seconds.

"What we didn't know at that time was the origin of the power surge and the destructive capability as it would impact Earth in less than one hundred and sixty days."

Sara pointed her laser at the relationship between Mars and Earth and a sketch of the wave. "I was made aware of those issues about ten days ago by the Commander of the Arrans race, Echo, and her leadership team."

Sara gazed over to POTUS who nodded in the affirmative for her to disclose the meeting site.

"I met Echo on her starship, called Destiny, on the far side of the Moon, and she vividly described the Mars attack and gave me a calculated estimate of the damage that such a power surge would have on us."

Noting several hands raised, Sara simply said, "I will take questions once I have finished presenting what we know as of now."

POTUS thought, *"Cold showers, all around!"*

After a couple-second pause, she continued, "The Mars outpost experienced what they called an explosion, and it seemed to grow stronger as it passed, but it was really what is called a matter-antimatter reaction. Echo gave me an E-drive that Michaela has analyzed, and I'll have her take it from here."

Commander Baker was excited to see and hear about the problem and was anticipating some root-cause explanation from Michaela.

Moving in front of the whiteboard, Michaela took Sara's laser pointer and continued, "With speed increasing, I assumed that the wave was an incredibly powerful energy source creating magnetic pulses, like cosmic rays, that grew stronger as they would radiate towards Earth, while destroying all life in the solar system."

Commander Baker quickly interjected his opinion, "But cosmic rays do not grow stronger as they travel. Sources of any kinds of particles of radiation decrease in intensity as they radiate away from a source. They fall off in proportion to the distance squared, getting quite a bit weaker."

Michaela was impressed and Sara was just amazed with both of them, as Michaela continued.

"Yes, Commander Baker, and that would mean that if these bursts were to kill millions of people on Earth, they would certainly have wiped out all living beings at their source."

Doctor Griffith offered his thinking, "I see an Echo 'aha moment' coming, eh Miss Steele?"

"Yes, that's correct. The Arrans believe that a highly sophisticated matter-antimatter engine was used by an evil alien race, whom the Arrans are familiar with, and that machine was capable of sending out waves of destructive energy that continually grew stronger as it radiated towards Earth causing repetitive chain reactions that would destroy all life in the solar system."

General James Patrick didn't waste any time to get his question out, "So, what are we going to do about it?"

Sara crisply replied, "We need to find the source and somehow evaluate the destructive potential of the surge."

"And how to stop it," Commander Baker offered.

"Yes, and we have a plan. I should say Echo has a plan that we will be involved in."

"We are listening, Sara," the President said.

"Echo has a destroyer spacecraft in her fleet, and we will attempt to penetrate the wave in route to its source. The Arrans have a powerful telescope that will be engaged in space and will replace any U.S. satellites or telescopes that were likely destroyed by the wave."

"What will the telescope do, Sara?" asked Donald Meacham.

"It is designed to seek abnormal, or artificial, heat sources at the point of origin of the surge. Then, they have a quantum teleportation device that can transform energy from the surge source into matter, like a 3-D printer, that will allow us to replicate the matter-antimatter machine to determine how to destroy it at the source."

General van Buuren was jotting down notes and couldn't wait to ask a couple questions.

"Sara, what can you tell us about the alleged evil alien race responsible for this that Echo referred to?"

"It was likely the work of a species of reptilian humanoids called the Dracs, and they have been a part of our world for centuries."

The President, making a small gesture of humor to the dire news, offered an observation, "Well, that is a helluva sidebar, eh?"

Michaela offered her own comic relief, "Sara is our puzzle master."

"Sara, did you say you were going on this mission as well?"

"Yes, General van Buuren."

And when are you leaving?"

"In two days."

Doctor Griffith interjected a question that was likely on everyone's mind, "And how will that spacecraft survive an encounter with an incoming powerful and destructive magnetic wave?"

Sara was prepared for that question, "They will fabricate a small open-ended wormhole, which will serve as a tear in the wave, and pass through that wormhole to the calm and quiet of the other side of the wave."

Note taking stopped as everyone was transfixed on Sara's explanation.

"And, they will be fractionated light-years beyond today, and therefore closer to the source of the surge."

Stunned and silent, they were waiting for one more point from Sara.

"They will set up a powerful telescope focused on that enormous heat source and pinpoint its origin."

General Patrick snapped, "They can do all that?"

"Oh, hell yes!"

35

ALTERED STATE?

The next morning, Sara and Michaela were discussing the meeting at Camp David. Michaela was preoccupied with her RJ Baker encounter and Sara took note.

"It's not often that you get off of your serious track as you did while flying back from Camp David. Penny for your thoughts."

"RJ Baker is an awesome talent, seemingly a very nice guy, and handsome as all get out. Given we are both single, of course I'd be interested. It was embarrassing how we met, but I think I recovered nicely, don't you?"

"Michaela, you're a rock star at ETRT and everyone knows it. Now Commander Baker knows it too."

Hesitating a moment, Sara added, "RJ is a hunk and you're as sexy as hell. I think that physical chemistry will prevail."

Sara checked her handheld device and continued, "We are on our way to Tiffany's house this morning for a breakfast meeting and I am unclear as to why. We can discuss yesterday's session with the committee later. But first, what's up with breakfast at Tiffany's?"

"Well, all I know is she has something of vital interest to share with both of us and says it is urgent."

"Michaela, we can handle this in the office. Why at her house?"

"Apparently, Tiffany has a monthly meeting with friends, who share a different agenda than we do, and she wants to introduce us to the group and their work."

"Their work on what, Michaela?"

"Haven't a clue. This shouldn't take long, though."

Sara had a feeling that this morning's impromptu meeting would be a waste of their time.

As they drove to Tiffany's house, Sara got a call from Commander Baker. As she could see who it was, she put his call on speaker,

"It's Sara, RJ. Nice to hear from you."

"Good morning, Sara. Am I interrupting anything calling right now?"

"Nope. In the car headed to a meeting with an associate."

Michaela was all ears…

"I won't keep you long. If you're driving, I don't want to distract you."

"It's fine. What's up?"

"First, I want to thank you for all your help and for the pre-work you sent me. It made it much easier for me to contribute given the info you sent."

"No problem. Glad it was helpful."

"I hope my out-of-the-box ranting didn't upset or embarrass you or Michaela."

"RJ, out-of-the-box is what we do. It's our specialty."

"Figured as much. By the way, when you see Michaela, tell her I enjoyed meeting her and was impressed with her solid contribution. She is a very smart lady."

"Will do, RJ. Why don't you tell her yourself?"

Michaela was holding her breath.

"Well I'm kinda busy right now. Maybe later when things slow down at the JPL. I do want to spend time with her on a purely business basis."

Sara could see Michaela frown.

"Plus, I now have a list of agenda items for yesterday's meeting of the 'Operation Cosmic Storm' committee."

Sara scowled a bit and replied,

"Not sure where that committee name came from; certainly, not from me. It's something from a superhero movie script."

Michaela smiled as RJ could be heard laughing.

"Sara, that's not what I called you about. I'll be brief as I now have an incoming call."

"Go ahead, RJ."

"Do you recall that astronaut incident concerning a spacewalk accident and a cracked helmet? My dad gave me the background on it and indicated that you had inquired about technical explanations from him."

Sara didn't recall talking to Lieutenant Baker, but did have questions for Mike, her dad.

"Why, yes, I do recall the incident. The astronaut was lucky to survive, and no verifiable cause for the accident was ever determined."

"Well, I was involved in the study of that incident, and I am still looking into it, being the curious soul that I am."

"I like curious," Sara muttered.

"I have evidence that is irrefutable and quite disturbing."
"Go ahead… please."

"Astronaut Samantha Worthington's DNA prior to that mission doesn't match her DNA today. It appears to have been altered!"

36

BREAKFAST AT
TIFFANY'S

As RJ said goodbye and hung up, Sara and Michaela pulled into Tiffany's driveway and both were aghast.

"What the hell did we just hear, Michaela? If that didn't come from a reliable source, I would never believe it."

"Sara, you have had your share of suspicions with VP Worthington ever since you met with her husband after the incident in space. Suffice it to say, Pandora's Box is now wide open."

"For sure, Michaela."

As they both exited the car and walked up to the front door, they had almost forgotten why they were there, given RJ's startling revelation.

Tiffany greeted them at the front door, with a hoodie on. The meticulously dressed and perfectly accessorized team member Tiffany was wearing a hoodie and flip flops. Alter ego?

"Come on in. How was your meeting yesterday?"

A somewhat surprised Sara, looking at Tiffany's casual dress, replied, "Fine. Obviously, more work to do. You have a lovely townhouse, Tiffany. Thanks for inviting us over."

"Glad you could make it."

Tiffany led the ladies into the kitchen where a breakfast buffet was set up and several people were sitting around a dining table enjoying their food.

"Everyone, please say 'hello' to my colleagues, Sara Steele and Michaela Marx."

Smiles with high-fives and thumbs up from seven total strangers were a surreal mix of professionalism and some grass-roots setting.

Tiffany had the seven breakfast guests introduce themselves and then Tiffany did some casual explaining for why they were all there.

"This is our *Power of Eight* group. We meet once a month with an agenda that is very simple. It's all about the *power of group intention* harnessing the energies of a small group to heal others, our lives, and making the world a better place."

Michaela added curiously, "I have heard of small groups of people tapping into extraordinary human capacity for sharing and healing, using the miraculous power of group intention having a boomerang effect."

"Yes," Tiffany advised proudly, "Crystal here blew out her knee playing tennis and was in such pain that she became addicted to painkillers."

Crystal responded on cue, "After only two months with this group, I am pain-free and totally off of meds."

"Hi, I'm Dan. I had severe multiple sclerosis and was confined to a wheelchair about nine months ago."

With that comment, Dan rose from his chair and bounced a couple times with no help whatsoever.

"Gee whiz," offered Sara incredulously. "That is remarkable."

Tiffany took the opportunity to get the visit with her colleagues back on point.

"Well, that's our story and we're sticking to it.'

Soft laughter from her group was heard as Tiffany took her segue from calming interaction to an astonishing fact.

"If you guys would excuse us, I need to meet with my colleagues for a few minutes. Ladies, please grab a plate with some food. You may need some nourishment."

"Okay, no mixed message there," Sara whispered to Michaela.

Taking Tiffany's suggestion, Sara and Michaela filled plates with some fruit and sweet rolls and followed Tiffany into her office… and oh, what an office.

Walking into her office, it reminded Sara of a mini-Palo Alto lab. "This is awesome, Tiffany."

There were six computer screens, an apparent three-dimensional holographic table, a telescopic port, and one oddly present stark mirror with no reasonable need to be inside such a high-tech office or lab.

"I see you looking at my projection-type, holographic, three-dimensional display."

"Well, yes… of course," answered a puzzled Michaela.

"Due to the limited spatial-temporal resolution of display devices, dynamic, holographic, three-dimensional displays suffer from a critical trade-off between the display size and the visual angle."

Michaela was in awe.

"And, I am working on that problem," Tiffany added.

"So, Tiff, what's the result you are looking for in this research?"

"Well, Sara, this is just a hobby for now. I am, as you know, a Type A that needs a bunch of stuff happening, and this is just one thing."

"Endgame, Tiff?"

"Oh yes, sorry. My endgame is to adopt holographic, three-dimensional displays in industrial applications; namely, digital signage, smart-glasses, and head-mounted displays. Cool, eh?"

"For sure," Sara said. "I have a couple people in Utah that we need to introduce you to."

"Amen to that," Michaela added, smiling.

"Okay, thanks, but that's not why I asked you here."

"Holy cow, there's more?" Sara was surprised with all that this visit was revealing.

"Oh yeah. Look at this."

Tiffany pulled up a timeline on a two-dimensional version of her hologram, with the title, *Darwin's Theory of Evolution*.

"If you look at this timeline that goes back as far as five hundred thousand years, which is likely the oldest known evidence for anatomically modern humans, we have been able to find skull fossils from 'then' until 'now,' thanks to extremely hard work by many paleoanthropologists."

Michaela was getting goosebumps, thinking where this might be going.

"Actually, in Ethiopia, a cranium was found that dated back to almost three and a half million years ago, but that isn't relevant here. What is relevant is what I found… or what was not found."

Sara could hardly wait.

"Human skull remains have been found fairly regularly throughout the world. But, over the past several centuries, our more recent past, there was a period of about two hundred thousand years where no human skull remains were found."

This was news to Michaela.

"If you look at the last skull found prior to that time frame and compare it to the first skull found after that time frame, one huge difference can be seen. The 'new' skull is noticeably elongated from the 'old' skull. No discernable evolution whatsoever."

Tiffany held up a finger with an additional thought, "This is what is fascinating. In my very basic research, the brain size in the elongated skull seems to be noticeably larger than the brain size just two hundred thousand years earlier."

Pausing briefly, Michaela jumped in with her preliminary conclusion, **"Someone or something intentionally interfered with evolution!"**

37

WAR OF THE WORDS

Driving back to the office, Sara and Michaela were still amazed by what was experienced at Tiffany's home… both the Power of Eight process and results, as well as the Darwinian disconnect that Tiffany had implied.

Michaela spoke first, "I am blown away!"

"No shit, Michaela. That woman is extraordinary and so damn focused."

"I am extremely fascinated by Tiffany's expose on evolution," Michaela added.

"Me too. That was remarkable research and one helluva segue for further studies."

Michaela wryly concluded, "I will figure out a way to fit this into either my ETRT role or my '*operation cosmic storm*' agenda, Sara, due to its incredible implication."

"Funny. Let's just drop the 'cosmic storm' work references for now. We both know this is going to likely be a rollout between the ETRT and the Arrans… although I could be wrong, given RJ's involvement."

"Yeah, Sara, I want to see what RJ and Lieutenant Baker can do to get some discernable traction going."

"We just need to make nice with the snail's pace coming out of that committee right now."

"I agree, Sara. And with the addition of RJ's help outside that committee, we should be able to move our agenda with the other eight capsules along quickly."

"Yep. By the way, has RJ contacted you lately? Either work stuff or personal stuff?"

"No, damn it. I hope I didn't come across as too bold and assertive."

"I'm no shrink, Michaela, but you should never apologize for being yourself. He may have been a bit intimidated by a beautiful and smart woman. He wouldn't be the first."

"Thanks," Michaela said as she cocked her head and ran her fingers through her dark and flowing hair.

With that brief exchange, Michaela was feeling somewhat relieved. Sara received a text message from Mara Wallace, chief aide to President Sullivan.

"Oh boy," Sara thought. *"What now."*

"Good morning, Sara. It's Mara Wallace."

"Hi, Mara. What's up?"

"The President has an urgent need to speak to you. Is now a good time?"

"Of course."

"Okay, hold on and we'll go to our joint-secured line."

"Thanks. Will do."

"POTUS wants to talk. This can't be good," Sara said anxiously.

Moments later, President Sullivan called, "Good morning, Sara. How are you doing this morning?"

"Good, Cam, thanks. What's up?"

"Well, nothing that you want to hear and certainly nothing that I expected to be bringing up, and that's for sure."

"Crap. Let me have it."

Michaela was scowling at Sara's words, knowing her friend was pissed.

"I am getting pushback right now in chamber with my Congressional meeting from a number of committee members as well as several staffers that are now getting involved in the planning and execution of the capsules, as well as other alien issues."

"Can't say I'm surprised, Cam. Can you give me a couple examples?"

"Of course. Some of this is political." Pausing, "Most of this is political. Our party, the New Liberty Party, was created to become the voice of reason between the well-established conservative and liberal parties."

"Man, I'm already lost, Cam."

"Sorry. I just need for you to understand how politics and science don't mix well, and the concerns coming from various people within our mission may be driven by the politics, and not the science or, should I say, especially the alien science."

"Bingo," Sara snapped. "Even I should have seen that coming. Again, examples Cam?"

"Yes. Intel Chairman Polansky strongly believes that the Dubai video was either created or altered. There wasn't any debris field from the alleged armed-rocket destruction."

"He was right about the debris field. Echo's strike cleaned the debris immediately."

With an impatient sigh, Sara asked, "What next?"

"There has been early concern about the capability to ionize the atmosphere to a degree necessary to destroy hurricanes, and eliminating hunger seems to be a pipe dream for several experts in the field."

"Guess we'll just need to find better experts," Sara added cynically. "Please continue."

"Climate change and global warming issues are a political nightmare, still, and it is likely we will need to pull this one away from any party activity."

Michaela was getting even more annoyed.

"General Patrick is seeing some roadblocks going up with key people in just the pre-work needed to begin the legitimate process of capsule development."

POTUS could be heard sighing and clearing his throat.

"We are also in a sensitive position, trying to reach certain international leaders, given that we can't truly reveal the entire extent of the project. That is an issue that Don had brought up and it is now my issue to solve."

Sara was taking mental notes as Cameron continued, "The last major issue is a big one."

"So, only one more?" Sara said sarcastically.

"Your explanation of how the aliens planned to tear a hole in the magnetic wave and magically drive their ship through was met by disbelief from several people who heard you. Some don't even think the power surge is that much of a concern."

"Well, I guess we have but one option."

"What is that option, Sara?"

"I will contact Echo and have her consider an alien show-and-tell!"

38

SHOWTIME!

Sara immediately contacted Echo with her follow-up to Cameron's summation, "Echo, can we delay our trip into the wave by a few days to meet with the leaders of the United States in their Congressional Assembly Hall?"

An annoyed Echo responded, "When, Sara?"

"Unless we can do it right now, it'll have to wait until the end of the week."

Echo went from annoyed to angry, but not surprised, after hearing of the pushbacks.

"Tell the President that we can have the meeting right now!"

"Right now, Echo? Really?"

"Yes. I'll assemble my team, along with you, and we'll settle this bullshit matter once and for all!"

Sara was aghast. *"Echo swore!"*

◆ ◆ ◆

Sara relayed her message from Echo to Mara Wallace, who told POTUS of Echo's intention.

"Thank you, Mara. This will be good. Any idea on when we should expect our cosmic visitors?"

"I'm not sure, Mister President, but I would expect that it would be soon."

"Okay. I'll get the chamber ready."

"Madame Speaker, could I call a thirty-minute recess and have a word with you?"

House Speaker Elinor Gifford complied.

"What do you need, Cameron?"

"I just got word from Sara Steele that she and the alien commander, Echo, are in route to our chamber as we speak."

"Now? How? And, for what purpose, Cam?"

"Not sure, but I think we're gonna get a heavy dose of some 'in-your-face' alien reality."

"Cam, some sort of explanation or demonstration?"

"Damn right. I'm sure that Commander Echo is pissed with the skepticism, finger-pointing, and slow pace of our work with the capsules, and she has a plan to kick-start our reluctant politicians."

"How are they traveling, Cam?"

"Traveling is not how you would describe their transportation mode... they will likely be teleporting, Madame Speaker."

"Oh my!"

"Yes, Madame Speaker, I think we are in for an 'alien reality show,' bar none!"

"Can't wait, Cam. The floor will be yours."

"No, Madame Speaker... it will be hers!"

✦ ✦ ✦

As Speaker of the House Gifford was calling the recessed group to order, she gave POTUS the floor.

"Members of Congress, we will be joined soon by Miss Sara Steele, whom you know and heads up the ETRT, and the leader of the Arrans race, Commander Echo."

A mixed bag of responses could be heard.

"We really don't have time for this, Cameron," an annoyed Frank Polansky replied. "We have much more pressing issues to address today."

"I understand your concern, Frank, but given our somewhat slow start to the rollout of the capsule project and the committee members' concerns brought out today, Echo and Miss Steele will be here to address those issues."

"Why should we have to wait on these people... our time is very valuable!"

"Chairman Polansky, with all due respect," Cameron scowled, "knowing who we are dealing with, I don't think we have long to wait."

Almost as if on cue, Echo and Sara materialized from a bluish haze on the chamber floor, representing a *first impression teleportation*.

Anyone who did not think that today would be a game-changer would be rudely awakened.

Speaker Gifford gestured to President Sullivan, who took over the introduction, "May I present Miss Sara Steele and Supreme Arrans Commander Echo."

"Hello, I am Sara Steele, Managing Director of the ETRT division of *Blue Horizon* in Palo Alto. Many in this room know me and I am pleased to be here, especially under these urgent times."

Looking up at Echo, Sara continued, "Please welcome the Arrans Commander, Echo."

Echo has on her battle attire: full uniform, hilt, battle saber, black cape, and she now was wearing a black cross necklace trimmed in silver. Sara had never seen the cross before. In fact, Sara had never seen her mentor dressed in full battle gear. Echo was intimidating.

"Hello, I am Echo of the Arrans race and we are temporal aliens and literally the human race from the future. Our advanced species has been on this planet and within your galaxy for thousands of years."

All the small talk from earlier turned to stone-cold silence.

"We are from an exoplanet in the constellation you call Leo, and we have another home in the Trappist One region in the constellation you call Aquarius."

President Sullivan nodded in a totally transparent sign of agreement.

Echo began with a scathing lecture, "The universe that we are all a part of is fourteen billion years old and life has evolved here on Earth for a very long time."

Echo paused, as she wasn't seeing total attention from her audience.

"It is inexcusably egocentric for any of you to conclude that you are alone in the universe."

Echo paused and then described the alien threat from the Dracs.

"We now have conclusive evidence, from the destructive magnetic wave heading towards Earth, and the fact that this is not a natural occurrence, that an evil and formidable alien species has likely targeted Earth for their own cultural survival needs."

Even Sara was overwhelmed with that doom-and-gloom scenario.

"This alien nemesis, the Dracs, are a warrior species from the Alpha-Draconis star system, and found Earth when a well-meaning group of scientists tried to make contact with alien life forms many years ago."

Sara was now putting two and two together.

"My intention today is not to give you a galactic alien history lesson, but to prepare you for what your humanity likes to call the 'New Normal'."

Sara had never heard Echo so domineering and forceful.

When she was finished, Sara telepathically asked Echo…

<Will you bring up the Denon species as well?>

<No, Sara. Not here. At the President's committee.>

Sara quickly approached the President and told him that Echo would attend the small meeting at Camp David later to discuss issues that are for the committee only.

Echo was noticeably agitated and snapped back at the assembled politicians, "I have just telepathically asked Pulse, my second in command, to join us."

With that statement, a tall figure with broad shoulders and strong build, in a scarlet and gray uniform, was beginning to materialize on the chamber floor, directly in front of the hundreds of very focused congressional attendees.

Within a few seconds, seven-foot-tall Pulse was fully intact, hands on his hips. Photo op? Damn straight!

39

GREATEST SHOW ON EARTH

"**I** am Pulse, of the Arrans race, and I am pleased to be here."

Cell phones and note-taking were abandoned, given this alien's dramatic entrance.

"I was summoned by our leader, Commander Echo, whom you now know, while carrying my duties at our base camp on the far side of the Moon."

"Thank you, Pulse, for getting here so quickly."

Sara thought, *"Humor from Echo just doesn't happen that often."*

Echo then gave a very serious revelation, "The Covid-19 virus that your world has been struggling against for many years was brought here from the future by humanoids from the Alpha-Draconis star system, who we call Dracs, the evil alien race that I spoke about earlier."

Everything about the meeting and that day's agenda had immediately flipped.

Echo continued in a commanding voice, "The reason you haven't been able to develop a vaccine is that this novel virus was engineered by the Dracs to perpetually mutate… never to be eradicated."

Echo had everyone's attention. "We Arrans have a vaccine that is being distributed right now to your CDC, NHI, and to thousands of distribution centers for immediate use by your physicians and scientists… once approval protocol is completed."

Hands went up and Echo simply ignored them.

"As soon as your medical leadership gives their approval and the proper international contacts have been established, the billions of vaccines that we have will be distributed worldwide."

As Pulse stepped away from his location, another image began to materialize. Within three seconds, a small, gray and non-human extraterrestrial image made a stunning entrance.

Echo announced another addition to the developing, alien stage production, "This is Aeon, of the *Grey* alien species, and a friend to the Arrans. As you can see, Aeon has eyes, but no other facial features. Not all species evolve with the same senses or the need for the same senses as you and I. Aeon does not communicate through speech."

President Sullivan was aghast. Sara was not far behind, but wondered,

<Echo, this is remarkable. Maybe too much for this group to digest.>

<We will see, Sara. I have much more coming.>

"Aeon has just informed me that she has returned the Apollo 18 crew, which was launched in April of 1975… back to your NASA complex in Florida."

Everyone, including Sara, was in shock.

"The *Greys* were able to intercede before the Dracs captured them while Apollo 18 was in Moon orbit in 1975."

Commander RJ Baker, having been patched in to the entire program, sent a group text that had everyone in total disbelief, adding to the incredible presentation by Echo.

"It has been confirmed by NASA that the confused, but healthy, crew of Apollo 18 was finally back home and hadn't aged a year!"

President Sullivan thought, *"And, of course, Apollo 18 was a secret mission… one that never happened… or so everyone thought until now. Shit!"*

Echo maintained her *in charge* demeanor. "Next in line for incoming teleportation is Arrans team member, Vibe."

Wearing the same uniform as Pulse, but with a black cape, Vibe was shorter in stature. Pulse looked like a linebacker… Vibe a swimmer.

"Hello, I am Vibe, and I am the cloaking expert. I have many other skills, but cloaking…"

Vibe motioned Sara over and whispered in her ear. Sara whispered back as Vibe finished his introductory statement.

"I have many other skills, but cloaking 'floats my boat,' as you say."

Echo lightly smiled and said to herself, *"That Pulse culture of humor just won't go away."*

"Madame Speaker and Mister President. You have a sergeant at arms of the House of Representatives outside."

"Yes, Mister Vibe," the speaker replied.

"Just Vibe. Could you have him come in here with his weapon?"

The Speaker looked at Cameron and the President nodded affirmative.

Moments later the sergeant at arms entered the chamber with his weapon.

Echo looked over to Vibe, who smiled at her, and then Echo spoke, "Sir, would you please fire your weapon at this person standing on the floor in front of me?"

POTUS rose and looked at Sara. Sara didn't hesitate. She nodded affirmative.

As the weapon was raised, Vibe asked crisply, "Wait!"

Everyone was on pins and needles.

Vibe touched his wrist device and said, "Now, please."

The sergeant at arms raised his weapon and fired once at Vibe.

The bullet struck Vibe and then fell to the ground.

"Again, please," Vibe could be heard.

This time several shots were fired directly at Vibe and all fell harmlessly to the floor.

Echo motioned for Vibe to depart.

Vibe grabbed the left lower corner of his black cape with his right hand, flung the cape around him and disappeared.

The silence in the chambers was deafening.

Echo continued defiantly, "This has been what you would call a 'visual aid.' It is frustrating to me that such theatrics are necessary, but we have problems to solve and we need you to believe that we have the capability to solve them."

Sara was so proud of her friend and mentor.

Then, Echo called for theatrics to be taken to a new level.

"Would everyone in the chamber please stand and hold hands."

Slowly they complied.

Once they were all standing and holding hands, Echo used her wrist device to levitate them about ten feet off the floor.

"You now have the three political parties' members from three previously closed partisan circles, represented in one single circle."

Allowing all of this remarkable action to sink in, Echo made a simple, yet profound statement, "That, my human friends, is what we refer to in our culture as UNITY!"

Echo snaps her wrist device, and all are slowly and calmly returned to their seats.

A stern Echo snapped, "This is not a warning. But I will tell you that evil aliens are coming, and you better put your petty bickering behind."

Glancing at Sara, "Listen to Sara Steele's ETRT, the President's Cosmic Storm committee, and the expertise being assembled. They are humanity's future."

In a much softer tone, Echo continued, "You cannot survive without our help. And Sara Steele is our chosen warrior princess. Tomorrow we fly into the magnetic wave with every intention of neutralizing the threat to your world."

Echo then gathered Pulse, Aeon, and Sara next to the podium, ignoring questions.

"Thank you and goodbye."

Echo looked down at her wrist telecom and commands, "Energize."

They had closed the small circle, and in a matter of seconds, they all had vanished.

40

WILL WORMHOLE WORK?

When they materialized, they were on the Moon, on Echo's Starship Destiny, including Vibe.

Echo had a disgusted look on her face, obviously not happy with the theatrics. Several of Echo's staff were talking and apparently giving her feedback on many issues, just while she was gone.

Sara could now see the enormous role and responsibility that her mentor had taken on.

Pulse muttered, "Echo, what a great strategy that was."

"It should not have been necessary," she replied harshly.

Echo knew that she had just opened an alien Pandora's Box and knew there was no going back.

"I am disappointed in their leadership. The President is a strong leader and a combat veteran. I don't understand why he can't get his people to join in."

"Well," Sara said, "they are not 'his' people."

Echo responded annoyingly, "I am now beginning to see this leadership culture as one that forever waits until tomorrow."

Pulse quickly responded, tongue-in-cheek, "And tomorrow is always the busiest day of the week."

Sara winked at Pulse's humor.

<Thanks Aeon, for returning the Apollo 18 crew.>

Aeon nodded to Echo with, <I am happy to have helped.>

Echo explained, via Aeon's telepathy, how the *Greys* interceded to spare the crew from being taken by the Dracs. Another example of this selfless and benevolent alien species.

Vibe chimed in, "The Cruiser Ghost is ready. Just need to set coordinates and we can be off."

"Ghost, Vibe? Cool name."

"Well, Sara, it is a ship for multi-tasking if ever there was one. It can pierce both a magnetic wave and remain undetected for even warp speed flights."

Sara asked respectfully, "The name comes from…?"

"The word ghost describes how this ship creates white holes to allow energy and light to exist in an otherwise black hole."

Sara thought how incredibly little she knew about the Arrans' technology.

A patience-challenged Echo ordered, "Preliminary info is now available on your devices. This is a timed event where logistics are critical."

Pulse nodded in agreement.

Echo offered Sara some basic details on wormhole theory, "We will build a temporary bridge and collapse the three-dimensional matrix around us as we approach the wave. So, the aperture at entry will remain open only long enough for us to get through."

Sara was truly absorbed in Echo's explanation and the excitement was obvious to everyone.

"Then," Echo continued stoically, "the bridge will collapse behind us as we pull through the wave."

Vibe added, "The accelerant that pierces the wave is made from exotic matter that we use for a variety of purposes, and it is available in raw form here on the Moon."

"I assume that any matter this exotic would have tons of applications," Sara uttered.

"Tons?" asked Echo.

"Sorry. Figure of speech," Sara replied.

Pulse added another wormhole fact. "The key issue with a wormhole is you can only go forward and can't go back in time."

Sara was getting more of her alien education.

"And," Pulse shrugged, "we need to use a relatively small craft to penetrate the wave and achieve the necessary warp speed."

"Why is smaller… better?"

Pulse explained, "Warp speed involves the speed of light and quantum physics. Matter is actually a deterrent to light speed… or in achieving warp speed. Think of it from Einstein's theory of relativity or Stephen Hawking's writings on the nature of space and time."

"Sorry, Pulse, but that isn't my strength."

"Fine. Hypothetically, think of the speed of light being energy, and not matter. Matter slows the light speed variable. In other words, the smaller the matter... the faster the speed!"

"I got it. I understand. In reverse, the larger... the slower."

"Exactly."

"Every day is a lesson of huge implications," Sara thought respectfully.

"So, coming back, in keeping with the smaller is better concept, we need to enter the exact same point as the one we went through getting through the wave at the exact same speed as the wave is moving toward Earth."

"That sounds complicated, Vibe" Sara responded.

"It is," advised Vibe.

"What happens if we don't execute the return precisely?"

"Well, Sara," Pulse responded, "it is a space-time element of quantum mechanics."

"Short answer, Pulse?"

Echo offers to answer Sara's question, **"If we don't execute the wave penetration precisely, we will no longer exist!"**

41

EYE IN THE SKY

The wave mission team climbed aboard the Ghost, and Vibe explained the protocol and seating requirements to Sara. She realized fully that this flight was one that required precision and expertise and became as serious as she could be as she listened.

All were strapped in… a pre-flight checklist was followed… and the Cruiser Ghost took off on its truly significant mission.

Echo looked at the preliminary specs and interception coordinates and advised Vibe, "Now that you have the same info that I have, what are your concerns, if any?"

Vibe's quickly announced his critical concerns, "I can see that the deceleration from warp speed to wormhole creation speed is critical. Inasmuch as we will be reaching the wave in fifty-seven minutes, I will finalize my preliminary calculations with only minutes to spare."

Pulse added confidently, "I will validate the shimmer formula for the accelerant now, so that is one variable that will be complete."

Echo glanced at Sara and said, "I will work with Sara on getting our telescope *Seraphim* properly assembled and ready for launch."

Sara murmured rather softly, "This is the part that I don't understand."

Pulse smiled and explained, "This machine is the most powerful and effective telescope in the universe, as far as we know. It is powered by a microreactor that can literally reach the limits of this galaxy."

"With this telescope," Echo advised, "we should be able to pinpoint the enormous heat source origin of the catastrophic power surge. Once we have the origin, we can calculate options to either destroy the device or stop its transmission."

"This is huge, Sara," offered Vibe. "If we can destroy it, the threat to Earth should be eliminated… or at least minimized."

Vibe paused, "But if we can only stop its transmission, the wave impact on Earth will still be substantial."

"I don't understand, Vibe."

"If we destroy the machine at origin, the waves in play will simply slowly go away at the source. Like waves on a pond when you throw a stone into it."

Sara understood and nodded.

"But if we can only stop transmission, that forward wave will not be deterred from hitting its target, your planet Earth."

"Then what, Echo?"

"Then, Sara, we need to mitigate the impact. That is Plan B. Plan A is to destroy the machine."

"Do we have a Plan B now?"

Pulse jumped in, "No, Sara, but that will be my job to figure it out. The data collected by Seraphim will be vital."

Sara had another question as she was trying to process all of the new info and strategies.

"You mentioned a 'shimmer.' What is that?"

Pulse was thinking as Echo was getting interested in just how her ops guy was going to answer Sara's question.

"Pulse has a magical way of describing and explaining things," Echo thought.

"Sara, are you familiar with the Superman comics and movies?"

"Of course. There was Superman, Lois Lane, Batman, Thor…"

"Well," Pulse responded, "You are actually mixing two competing comic adventures…Thor is in a different series."

"Whatever," was Sara's response.

Echo quipped, "Get to your point, please, Pulse. We are dealing with a big problem here."

"Sure, well, Superman was from the planet Krypton. And he had powers on Earth, but his enemies found that the Kryptonite from his planet actually diminished his superpowers on Earth and nearly killed him."

"And, Pulse?"

"And, Sara," Pulse advised, with a grin regarding his knowledge of comic books, "Shimmer is the substance that the Dracs left on the Moon after occupying it for millions of years."

"So," Sara added crisply, "shimmer is to the Dracs, what Kryptonite was to Superman."

"Bingo!"

"And you have a ton of it at your base camp?"

"Bingo number two!"

Echo thought, *"It's like I have teenagers on board."*

✦ ✦ ✦

With the wave now being felt by the Ghost, the small crew was seriously gathering their data and their wits. Even the experienced Arrans realized that any number of things could go wrong.

Pulse set the Ghost's autopilot and accelerator's auto-deployer for wormhole creation and the timing of the wave entrance began.

"Please buckle up," Echo ordered.

Moments later, a slight impact was felt as the ship seemed to orient itself within the confines of the collapsing bridge, just as Echo had explained.

Sara's ears popped and she noticed that the ship switched to backup power. She gazed over to Pulse who gave her a *thumbs up,* indicating that all was normal.

A mere few seconds later the Ghost had navigated through the wave to the relative calm on the other side of the advancing magnetic surge.

"Sara, let's get this telescope launched. Just give Vibe a hand with the final orientation in the launch bay."

"Got it, Echo."

Together, Sara taking her instructions directly from Echo, the pair of celestial device-builders put the Ikea-like pieces together and oriented the telescope into the launch bay.

"Are you ready?" asked Vibe. "We are all set here."

Three, two, one... the very sophisticated telescope, Seraphim, is launched.

The next thirty minutes were critical, as the crew of the Ghost were checking and re-checking their deployment data and calculations for telescope function.

Echo called for a report-out regarding key readings. Pulse summarized from a data screen that gave a three-dimensional view and predictive correlations.

"We are all good to go with our readings. Now, we just let Seraphim do its thing."

Vibe responded immediately, "I now have all the tracking and communication links set up with Seraphim; and with the telescope deployed accurately, we can monitor its progress from base camp."

"And our return, Vibe?"

"Echo, I have the general coordinates and wave speed calculated, and I'm just waiting to get the final fix on our entry point... just need a few minutes to verify."

Sara knew that the return would become the synchronization of the Ghost's speed and location, as Echo clearly explained.

"Buckle up, everyone," Vibe said. "We are less than a minute from re-insertion."

After a short pause, Vibe was back with his countdown. "Five, four, three, two, one... we are in."

All was eerily quiet...

Then everything went dark...

"Vibe, why are we suspended?"

"Don't know, Echo. Give me a moment."

There was some panic with the Arrans, as Sara could easily see. And her focus on every inanimate object in the ship was getting fuzzy.

"Echo, we have a problem."

"What, Vibe?"

"We have a very big problem!"

42

AGAIN, AND AGAIN, AND AGAIN, AND... AGAIN

Vibe began his countdown to reenter the wave, "Five, four, three, two, one... we are in."

All was eerily quiet and then everything within the ship went dark...

"Vibe, why are we suspended?"

"Don't know, Echo. Give me a moment."

Sara's focus on every inanimate object in the ship was getting fuzzy.

"Echo, we have a problem."

"What, Vibe?"

"We have a very big problem!"

Vibe began his countdown to reenter the wave, "Five, four, three, two, one... we are in."

All was quiet and the ship went dark.

"Vibe, why are we suspended?"

"Don't know, Echo. Give me a moment."

Sara felt her body was normal, but her Arrans friends were almost in a quasi-suspended, or nearly a two-dimensional version of themselves.

"Echo, we have a problem."

"What, Vibe?"

"We have a very big problem!"

Sara was beginning to sense some sort of déjà vu. While her visual focus was getting fuzzy, she knew she was feeling this sensation repeating itself.

"Echo, we have a problem."

"What, Vibe?"

"We have a very big problem!"

Sara knew she had to try something. Before Vibe could begin his countdown for the umpteenth time, she grabbed the partially full-size Vibe and the partially holographic Vibe and pushed him down to the control console… thinking to change the repeating algorithm.

A once fully distracted Sara was now completely focused and thinking.

"Vibe, we are in a time loop, reliving your entry into the wave. Do you understand me?"

Vibe was just beginning to return to his three-dimensional form.

"Yes. Yes, I do."

"And" looking over at a fuzzy form of Pulse, "each time loop is getting exponentially shorter."

"That is bad," a very worried Vibe admitted.

Echo and Pulse were re-emerging in their complete, non-fuzzy forms.

"Vibe… Sara. What is going on?"

"Echo, we are in a time loop," Vibe explained, "stuck in a steady-state unable to advance in time. Our time is zero. No movement. No seconds are ticking off. We are ghosts on the Ghost."

Pulse, regaining his composure, suggested the next steps, "Can you analyze the last moments before we went black, Vibe? Any data or time stamp to refer to?"

"I'm thinking…"

"It was essential to move at same forward velocity as the wave once we entered until our boost out," Vibe explained.

Vibe continued anxiously, "And it was also essential to replicate the same physical footprint of orientation, torsional rigidity, temperature, and balance. I verified all of those factors before I began my countdown and had zero doubt that it was miscalculated."

Echo, a much calmer Echo, simply asked, "All right, think… what is your diagnosis?"

"Echo, we can't physically survive this time loop for very long," Pulse snapped. "We are no longer repeating, and the ship is taking a beating."

"I know, Pulse," Vibe offered worriedly. "I'm trying to re-boot my last readings to see if something jumps out." Vibe was concerned and Sara was frantic.

"Pulse, check the ship's current physical condition."

"Will do, Echo."

Turning toward Vibe with her hand raised, Sara quickly offered, "I have a thought."

Vibe glanced back at Sara and asked, "What's your thought?"

"A virus… a computer virus. A hack!"

Echo raised her head and asked, "Vibe, is that a possibility?"

"Yes. Yes, it is. We didn't shimmer the Ghost going back because we had the coordinates."

Vibe was checking uploaded diagnostics.

"But, if a virus was in play, it would change all the entry specs and we would be extremely vulnerable. Give me a minute."

Pulse reported back, "Echo, we are beginning to feel an extreme pressure on our hull and our cabin is beginning to depressurize."

"We shouldn't be feeling this in space with an otherwise secure craft."

"No, Echo, you are correct. This virus has been weaponized."

"What is the timing, Pulse?"

"I would think we are less than twenty minutes from implosion!"

43

WAVE... GOODBYE!

Vibe pulled up a virtual diagnostic screen and he and Pulse looked at the pre-time loop and current readings for temperature, pressure, speed, and orientation.

"Pulse, I think the virus simply put a shadow on our telemetry from the actual readings to the hacked readings."

"And?" Pulse growled.

"And" Vibe was concentrating on the readings. "And what caused it… I'm not sure?"

"So, what do we do, Vibe?"

Sara added curiously, "Vibe, is it a coding thing?"

"Yes."

"Do you have a solution set in mind, Vibe?"

Vibe was busy calculating when he responded, "Actually, Sara, the fix lies in one of three possibilities that I see here, and I only have time to try one before we crash."

"Echo…"

"Yes, Sara."

"Using quantum communication real time, can you send the diagnostic map that Vibe is displaying to Connor?"

"I think we can. Pulse?"

Sara replied sharply, "Please do that, Pulse. Tell him we are in distress and only have fifteen minutes to determine which of the three fixes will work. Vibe, prepare transmissible forms of the three solutions."

"Doing it now, Sara."

"Vibe, have a 'best shot' ready if Connor is unreachable."

"All right, Sara." Vibe softly replies.

Moments later, Echo advised, "We now have Connor… and he is scanning."

Several precious minutes go by and Sara has awful, foreboding feelings that take her back to the cabin attack that killed Paul and nearly killed her.

"The same damn evil aliens," she thought angrily.

Pulse was looking at his countdown watch and saw that the Ghost was in the last four minutes before total decompression occurred.

About thirty seconds later, Echo firmly announced, "Option three, Vibe. Go with option three."

Vibe immediately uploaded this third option fix, pressed "run," and sat back.

"This should only take a couple of seconds."

Pulse, Echo, and Sara were holding hands. Sara had a distinct "family moment."

Then Vibe excitedly announced, "We're in. It worked. Sit down, strap in, and as soon as you can, Pulse, gets us the hell out of here."

Twenty seconds later, the Ghost shot forward in a rapid acceleration.

A boom, almost like a sonic boom, shook the Ghost violently as the frazzled crew could see that they were out of the wormhole prison that the virus had created.

"We are finally on our way home," a relieved Echo proclaimed. "Good job, everyone."

Echo glanced at Sara and smiled. "Sara Steele, your actions and decisions have saved us from certain death. You have earned every accolade that the Arrans race can bestow on a human... thank you!"

Sara was experiencing the highest of highs and responded, "I appreciate your kind words, but this was really a team effort, both from here in deep space and with the technology that enabled Connor to respond quickly and accurately."

Echo replied graciously, "We will meet with Connor personally and thank him. What a talented team member. I can see his value going forward."

A grinning Pulse added, "Yeah, I always liked that guy."

"As we head home," Echo exclaimed, "I think we need a new strategy going forward, given the reality of the physical issues facing Earth, the capability of the enemy, and the lack of high-level, global leadership."

Sara asked, "What is your strategy, Echo?"

"We need to consolidate all the resources that we can muster, into a fully focused joint effort."

Sara was concentrating on Echo's demeanor and candor.

"I am not sure, Sara, if humanity is ready to own their share of what will be needed... but we must move forward quickly."

Echo announced, "It's time to move our actions to the next level."
Pulse had already "read" Echo and was smiling.
"What would that be?" Sara inquired.

As Pulse winked at Sara, Echo answered, **"We need to quickly create a unified Galactic Force, with the mission of protecting the Galactic Civilization!**

44
MOON SHADOW

As the ship returned to the Arrans Moon base, Echo waited for some alone time with Pulse and Vibe.

"Sara, will you please excuse us?"

"For sure, Echo. It's time for this ET-for-a-day to 'phone home'. Don't want family and teammates to worry."

"Thanks, Sara. And thanks again for your help. ET-for-the-day saved the day."

"You are quite welcome, Echo. After all that the Arrans are doing for mankind, it isn't much."

With that comment, Sara gave Pulse a hug, excused herself, and headed to the Arrans' version of a mess hall to get something to eat.

Echo was visibly pissed. "Why didn't either of you see or sense that virus or have a contingency plan for that mess that could have gotten us all killed?"

Pulse replied distractedly, "Vibe, I'll take this one. Echo, I am sorry for our lack of focus and I have no excuse. I was in charge and failed to have an emergency plan for what we encountered."

"Pulse... what was the real reason?"

Pausing for a moment, Pulse said, "I was preoccupied with Sara and making sure she was comfortable with what we were doing and confident in our approach."

"If I said you were preoccupied with Sara from a physical sense, would you disagree?"

"No, Echo, I would not."

Vibe smiled politely as the implication was sent and received.

"When Sara returns, we will assess the mission, objective, and results from an operational perspective. Notify Engineering that they need to assess the damage to our ship."

A contrite Pulse responded, "Yes, Echo, I will."

Echo glanced over to Vibe with a request, "With the penetration data that we now have, we need to estimate the wave's potential damage upon impact with Earth."

"That will be done within the hour."

"Fine. Pulse, our next steps involve how to destroy the source of the power surge... once we find it."

"Yes, Echo, we must destroy the origin of the power surge, but that can't be done until we locate the source and evaluate its resiliency."

"Understood. Pulse, I am going to assume for now that we will need a powerful electro-magnetic pulse to disable or destroy the source."

"Yes, Echo. I will run EMP calculations immediately."

"And stay focused, Pulse?"

"Of course, Echo."

"Mostly," Pulse thought to himself... embarrassed but happy.

As Pulse regained his bearings, Sara returned.

"Sara, it is customary for us to complete a detailed report for every interstellar encounter we have... mission, objective, and results. I would like you, Pulse, and Vibe to complete that report now, while all is fresh in your minds."

"Of course, Echo," Sara added smartly. "I am used to paperwork demands from both my dad and grandad."

"They were well-organized men," Echo nodded.

✦ ✦ ✦

"Sara, I would like you to arrange a meeting with the ETRT for tomorrow. I know that is short notice, but time is critical now."

"It is, and I can. I will set it up as soon as we are done here."

"That is good."

"Do you have an agenda for the ETRT meeting, Echo?"

"Yes, I will telepathically describe my ideas and send a hard copy to your E-watch. You are welcome to add anything that I may have left out."

Sara thought to herself, *"Nada, nothing, zip, zero."*

Echo added, "I will need to meet with your team soon, as all of their skills and resources will be needed... and needed now."

Echo smiled and advised, "And I want to take a gift to Connor, to show our gratitude for his critical help."

<Sara, this is a first for Echo.>

<Really. How nice, Pulse.>

<You two know I can hear you, right?>

The three shared a laugh... a necessary laugh following a near-death experience.

Glancing at Sara with steely eyes and a stern look Echo informed Sara that Sara would be making a trip to the Arrans' home in Trappist One very soon. Turning to slowly walk away, Echo looked over her shoulder and said, "Pulse will explain."

Sara waved goodbye to Echo, and she and Pulse made their way to the aero-space hanger. As Pulse loaded some equipment into the Galactic Falcon, Sara was now somewhat worried and confused about the *Trappist One* remark.

Pulse looked over to Sara and said, "I will have plenty of time to explain Echo's plan for you to go to Trappist One. It's gonna be so cool."

Sara inquired, "Isn't Trappist One your 'primary residence,' as we say on Earth?"

"Yes, Sara, it is now our primary home base and a very special place. This system holds our version of mankind... the home life, recreation, lifestyle... and our primary personnel and military training planet."

"Excuse me... did you say a military training planet?"

"Yep. You will see it all!"

They got the Galactic Falcon airborne and Sara, once again, marveled at the view of the far side of the moon and enjoyed the greenish moon shadow.

As they travel back to Earth on Pulse's star runner, they have another opportunity to get to know each other better. Sara is always relaxed in his presence and Pulse can feel it.

Pulse, recalling Echo's curiosity about his feelings for Sara, kept his focus, at least for now, on the trip to Earth with his friend.

Pulse mentioned his travel back in time to the Apollo 17 incident in 1972 when he met and conversed with Command Module Pilot Robert Kelly. He also told Sara that he was supposed to clear Commander Kelly's memory, but decided not to.

"What you did... or didn't do... was good. And my grandad met and talked with Commander Kelly and that was another 'brick in the wall,' so to speak."

Pulse could have told Sara that he knew all about that fateful meeting, inasmuch as Pulse was coming from the future, but decided not to say anything at all.

"So, Pulse, what's up with my trip to Trappist One? I'm sure Echo isn't sending me on a vacation."

"Nope. On Trappist One, some forty light years away, you will undergo some serious battlefield training and likely get a cranial implant to optimize your capabilities."

"Say what?"

"You will go from tattooed crime fighter and alien chaser to a certified, badass Warrior Princess."

45

GALACTIC FORCE

Two days later, Sara called the ETRT for a meeting to give her team an idea of what Echo would be focusing on. Commander RJ Baker was also in attendance.

All members of the ETRT could see that Sara was *sky high* and in a very good mood.

"I have exciting news. Echo has asked to meet with us and that meeting will take place soon… real soon."

That remark got the eager team's adrenaline going.

"Today, I will cover several key issues and have some vital updates for you prior to that meeting with the Arrans' commander, Echo."

An anxious Connor asked, "The wave… what about that menacing magnetic wave?"

"Okay, fair enough. Let me go directly to the status of the destructive power surge headed toward Earth. I was part of the crew that was on an Arrans' ship that literally tore a hole in the wave in order to seek out its source."

"Really cool," thought Justin, as a few *yippees* could be heard.

"Yep. It was amazing. We launched a satellite with a telescope that will, hopefully, find the source of the surge so it can be destroyed. Nothing more for you right now."

RJ asked excitedly, "What is the ETA for the wave?"

"One hundred and twenty days," Sara responded firmly.

"And" Sara added confidently, "the Arrans team is already evaluating countermeasures to destroy the source of the incredible power surge."

"I'm getting ahead of myself," Sara continued, "but there will be breakout groups for deeper dives on a 'bunch of stuff' that I will outline soon."

Michaela thought, *"Well, 'bunch of stuff' is clearly not our normal Sara… She appears to be processing a 'bunch of stuff' herself!"*

Sara added crisply, "The ETRT will no longer be the unique driver of all things cosmic. We will be building a much bigger and much better galactic force to deal with the many issues and priorities that we are facing."

An inquisitive Tiffany asked, "So what will this 'galactic force' that you are referring to be called?"

Sara smiled and replied, "*The Galactic Force.*"

Smiles and some notable laughter ensued. Even RJ was amused by the simple designation for such an extremely complex undertaking.

Getting everyone's attention, Sara put up a slide of project 'current thinking.'

"We will need to integrate the ETRT into this Galactic Force and divide it into corresponding Galactic Force Divisions. We will work backwards from end game expectations for the various divisions and staff and equip accordingly. Does that make sense?"

"Yes, of course," Michaela replied. "Give us your first pass at the divisions."

With that, Sara projected on the screen the various needs that would require serious project development with the assistance of the Arrans.

1. *Echo's 8 technology capsules to solve serious problems on Earth.*
2. *Defense against the magnetic wave and contingency planning.*
3. *Research to address possible evil aliens' attacks, and to identify and root out secret alien invaders.*
4. *Data communication and daily briefs to global leadership.*
5. *Project Zeus definition, planning and execution.*
6. *Pulse's 8 highly confidential advanced technology capsules.*

At that moment, every hand was raised… no surprise to Sara.

"What can I say? It's a 'bunch of stuff.' Let me give you an overview.

"Number one is already familiar to you guys. With the exception of Tiffany, the entire ETRT is aware of these."

Tiffany noted, smiling, "Michaela has brought me up to speed with these."

RJ added, "My dad and I are on the Presidential committee that is working on them."

"Number two is our first priority right now and is being appropriately handled."

Pausing a moment, Sara continued, "I apologize for not being a better source of all things 'evil alien,' but believe me when I say that my learning curve isn't that far ahead of yours. Echo will be here soon and you will get all you need in info from her regarding number three."

"How soon is soon?"

"Connor, we will see her when she has a break in her duties at their Moon base. I would think in a day or two."

"And may I add... Connor was a real superhero in dealing with a near catastrophe in space on our wave encounter. Echo was totally impressed and will certainly bring it up during her visit."

Continuing, Sara felt an overwhelming *plate is full* with the ETRT, "Number four is kind of obvious and number five, Project Zeus, is currently in the exploratory stage, at best. Since it will involve building several spaceships, we will need to know what we are up against before we can design and build ships to confront those needs. Does that make sense?"

No pushback came from the team.

RJ then jumped in puzzled with one of the issues, "I was just getting up-to-speed with Echo's eight capsules... and now you have eight more?"

"Those eight capsules that Echo gave the world are for short-term development and will, hopefully, address the serious issues that are facing the planet right now."

"There are more, Sara?"

"Oh yes, RJ. Now you get to see the really good stuff."

Michaela took her cue and loaded the screen with the eight high-tech capsules that Pulse had given Sara in Dubai.

Michaela advised, "The ETRT has possession of the eight additional capsules that no government agency has seen and are our sole responsibility to implement."

RJ was impressed, as Michaela continued her explanation, "In fact, Echo has placed the entire implementation of these high-tech capsules in Sara's hands only. She and the ETRT are the gatekeepers for what you are about to see."

RJ asked, "What is the purpose of these capsules, and what makes them more sensitive or vital than the ones we have previously discussed?"

Sara responded crisply and confidently, **"The ability to implement these tools will determine whether or not humanity will survive mass extinction!"**

46

FUTURE PERFECT

Sara looked over to the smiling Michaela and with her laser pointer, Sara began her presentation one more time concerning the eight Pulse capsules, but this time with accountability and action plans for her team.

Michaela inquired, "You still going with the team leaders that we talked about last night?"

"Yep." Sara then began another pass at the awesome eight capsules, "In addition to all that we have on our plates, there isn't really anything more important or more critical than these eight capsules given to us by Pulse. I want to make sure we are all on the same page and we have true accountability and role determination for these vital issues."

Sara added forcefully, "Elonis will consolidate all project input data and daily production reports for real-time display.

"Okay, gang, listed below each capsule is the team leader and team. If anyone has questions, deletions, or additions, please contact Michaela or me..."

Capsule 1 will provide the entire plans and list of materials needed for terraforming Mars, a technique that we have used for thousands of years. Earth's technology will be able to use massive reflectors and mirrored devices to bring heat and light to Mars over a three-to-five-year period, rather than tens of thousands of years.

Michaela – RJ, Summar, and Mike Stevenson

Capsule 2 will give you a blueprint for taking the Artificial Intelligence that will be in the ongoing-development stage from Echo's Capsule 6 to the very essence of General Artificial Intelligence or Super AI where androids will perform any of mankind's needs in a socially responsible manner.

Tiffany – Jeremiah, Justin, and Rudy

Capsule 3 will enable you to understand and positively adjust significant weather patterns around the world. It will also enable you to control space weather and geo-magnetic energy, which will become a source of opportunity for climate management, or for dangerous consequences, if managed poorly.

Michaela – Elonis, Joyce, and Mark

Capsule 4 will teach you how to levitate and use various anti-gravity or negative gravity methods to your advantage, especially when colonizing other planets, by developing the upward forces necessary to cancel out the weight of the object so the object does not fall or rise, but can be steered.

Tiffany – Jacqui, Justin, and Robert

Capsule 5 will enable you to travel back and forth through time, using a four-dimensional fabric called space-time. Forward time travel is relatively easy, because it is based on speed. Backward time travel is risky, because it alters disease, catastrophes, and mortality. Reverse time travel was responsible for many of the major worldwide plagues and epidemics.

Connor – RJ, Summar, and Rudy

Capsule 6 will address quantum teleportation, which is our proven process for transmitting, atoms or molecular combinations, in their exact state, from one location to another using state-of-the-art communication and sharing quantum entanglement between the sending and receiving location.

Connor – Jeremiah, Justin, and Mark

Capsule 7 will enable you to perform superluminal spacecraft propulsion, also known here on Earth as warp speed, traveling at speeds greater than the speed of light by many orders of magnitude. Today, Arrans can travel from Earth to the Andromeda Galaxy in twenty minutes.

RJ Baker – Connor, Jacqui, and Mike

Capsule 8 will give you a blueprint for how you can defend your planet, if or when the time came to do so, with much of the technology that was just presented, a strong mastering of Full Artificial General Intelligence, accelerated evolving technologies and the use of antimatter microreactors.

RJ Baker – Sara, Matt, and Scott Woods

Sara added some clarification for a dazed group of overachievers, "As you know, these eight capsules are currently in Utah, and we will begin our work on these as soon as possible. Elonis and Michaela will advise the team once schedules are developed."

Sara glanced down on her E-Watch as a text message came in. She paused and the team awaited Sara's next words.

"We will need quick first passes on these eight assignments ASAP. Each team leader will need a brief report-out ready for ETRT review by tomorrow morning.

Michaela asks sternly, "Why now, Sara? Why so soon?"

"Echo and Pulse will be here tomorrow for their review."

47

2050 WORLDVIEW

Echo and Pulse arrived for the meeting with the ETRT as that team was restructuring into the Galactic Force with defined divisions.

The two aliens teleported without their military dress. Instead, they were wearing pants and collarless shirts with their identifiable glyph, matching their team and group colors. It was a refreshing change of pace... comfortable and relaxed.

Sara thought to herself, *"Casual Friday, I guess!"*

Sara also noticed a long scar on Echo's neck... battle memento?

Pulse carried a gold case, slightly shorter than a baseball bat, and obviously not a prop for the meeting.

"Good morning, ETRT," Echo began. "Thank you for all that you have done and for having our meeting on such short notice."

Sara nodded appreciatively, "We are delighted to have you both here today."

"First," offered Echo, "Pulse has a presentation to make."

Walking over next to Echo, Pulse proudly asked, "Connor, would you please step forward and join us here?"

A surprised Connor obliged.

"On behalf of the Arrans leadership team, along with Sara Steele of your ETRT, I am happy to present you with this battle sabre and hilt, a token of our thanks for saving us from that magnetic wave, using your badass skills."

"Badass skills,' Echo thought. *"Well, what do you expect?"*

A very surprised and smiling Connor walked over to Pulse, shook the alien's hand, and accepted the sabre and pulled it from its hilt for everyone to see.

"Thank you, Pulse and Echo. Thank you very much."

The normally fun-loving Connor was truly humbled by the aliens' show of gratitude.

As the ETRT members clapped and cheered respectfully, Echo moved to the lectern in the center of the room.

Echo then switched gears and sternly began, "I will now set the stage for life on Earth just twenty-five to thirty years out. It is scary."

"Back to the damn reality," Sara thought grimly.

No one was taking notes or preparing to take notes. All listened to Echo.

"All sea life will be gone from your oceans, and your oceans cover about seventy-two per cent of the Earth's surface. As a food source and for ecological balance, this will be devastating."

"This is gonna suck," thought a totally pissed-off Michaela.

"Subsidence will have destroyed nearly twenty-five per cent of the U.S. coastline and economies will crumble.

"Thawing permafrost will release extreme amounts of greenhouse gases into the atmosphere. Methane gas will exacerbate the global warming.

"Mutating viruses pose a danger. Without new medications, antibiotic-resistant germs, super bugs, will kill five hundred to six hundred million people a year worldwide by 2050."

"I had a hunch about this... and I was correct," thought Tiffany with an 'aha moment.'

"Alien engineered viruses are timed for climate change acceleration and targeting sick or malnourished. Needed food sources will disappear and hunger will be catastrophic.

"Evil alien species are likely planning either an attack on Earth or to invade and take control of Earth... we don't know yet."

RJ was thinking, *"That is one of the reasons I joined the Space Force."*

"Your Moon... your *artificial moon*... will become a strategic launch pad for our enemies. We will need to keep control of the Moon."

Hands went up in frenzied unison.

"I will address the Moon-thing in a bit," Echo ordered.

"I have asked Pulse to project all of this data, with supporting details and evidence, on your conference room screen and to all of your mobile devices."

All the data from Echo's description was shown.

"In addition to those issues, this team is trying to facilitate the eight capsules that you discussed yesterday, and we are facing a major attack from a destructive magnetic wave."

Michaela asked, "Echo, with this deep and dire list of critical issues, where do we start?"

Echo thought for a moment and walked over to address the team in the center of where they were sitting. "I believe we need some inspiration... we all need some inspiration."

Sara was eagerly awaiting Echo's idea as Sara felt a change in Echo's demeanor and perspective.

"Let's go visit that artificial Moon!"

48

PALE BLUE DOT

As the ETRT experienced emotions from ohmigod good to WTF not-so-good, Pulse left to get the Star Runner Falcon ready for its trip to the Moon, as Echo described Earth's artificial lunar body.

"This will surprise you, of course, but it is true. About two million years ago, a benevolent alien species, known as the Reticulans, or as we call the *Greys*, in a far-reaching strategy to create and preserve a wonderful world, literally brought an artificial satellite—your Moon—from a galaxy far, far away."

"Man," Sara thought. *"We should be in a dark planetarium right now."*

"Once the Moon was in place, in exact relation to your Sun, galactic matter, albeit large quantities, was gravitationally created, as were the other planets in your solar system."

RJ mentioned quietly to Michaela, "The Moon is in the wrong orbit for its size, and it is thought by renowned physicists that the moon is older than the Earth!"

Gazing at RJ, a smiling Echo added, "Your Moon is in the wrong orbit for its size, and the Moon is almost a billion years older than Earth!"

She continued, "The Moon is a hollow planet, whereby internal regions of the moon are much less dense than the outer part of the 'shell,' as we Arrans call it.

"When meteors strike the moon, it rings like a bell and reverberates for hours, and all craters, regardless of width, all have the same depth."

Even RJ was enthralled by Echo's revelation.

"Moon rocks contain brass, mica, titanium, uranium 236, Neptunium 237, and an undefined metallic crystal that has not been traced to any object anywhere in our universe."

RJ and Michaela had their ears peeled and were hanging on Echo's next remarks.

"In fact, there are trace elements of a unique metallic crystal that we believe is germane to Earth and could be a key threat to humanity from evil aliens wanting or needing this material."

Looking over at RJ, Echo added, "And, Moon dust composition does not resemble anything in the solar system."

RJ smiled, as Echo continued her presentation, "When we placed our Moon camp on the far side hundreds of years ago, huge pyramids, massive girders, and various machinery were in place."

Now, the ETRT members were taking notes.

"There was a black structure on the surface two hundred and fifty miles long, fifty miles wide with spire-like structures thousands of feet high. And underground plumbing existed along with enormous excavating equipment."

"What is your theory, Echo?"

"Well, Sara, this is important. Let me reiterate the facts as we know them."

Sara smiled, somewhat embarrassed, having heard this before.

"It was likely a hollow moon put in place by the highly-advanced, extraterrestrial race, the *Greys*, steered from some distant region of the galaxy into a circular orbit around a yet-to-be-placed Earth. That would explain the extraordinary mystery of rock and Moon-dust variations. We believe that intelligent life has existed within the Moon for millions of years. Our friend Aeon will neither confirm nor deny."

Echo paused before making a subtle comment that was as revealing as it was mysterious, "Spiritual intentions were likely in place, which I won't get into at this time."

Echo concluded with a truly heart-stopping comment, "When time permits, we will expose the artificial satellite for what it is to all of you. You will find it fascinating."

An eager Pulse held up his hand and got Echo's attention.

<The Falcon is ready.>

The ETRT moved outdoors and, once they were far enough away from all buildings, Pulse uncloaked the Falcon, to everyone's astonishment.

"Now I know what 'cool' really is," Connor murmured with a huge grin.

Sara was reveling in her new-found role in this amazing galactic venture.

Echo took the entire Galactic Force team on Pulse's star runner to the far side of the moon. They circled, flew low to show the base camp, and then landed.

"It is still breathtaking for me," Echo said softly, "every time I do this."

Before exiting the Falcon, Echo looked at her guests and began to recite something that was very familiar to Sara,

Look at that small dot. That's Earth. That's your home. That's all of you right now. On it everyone you love, you know, everyone you ever heard of, every human being who ever was, lived out their lives. The aggregate of our joy and suffering, thousands of confident religions, ideologies and economic doctrines, every hunter and forager, every hero and coward, every creator and destroyer of civilization, every king and peasant, every young couple in love, every mother and father, hopeful child, inventor and explorer, every teacher of morals, every corrupt politician, every "superstar," every "supreme leader," every saint and sinner in the history of our species live there – on a mote of dust suspended in a sunbeam.

The Earth is a very small stage in a vast cosmic arena. Think of the rivers of blood spilled by all those generals and emperors so that, in glory and triumph, they could become their momentary masters of a fraction of a dot. Think of the endless cruelties visited by the inhabitants of one corner of this pixel on the scarcely distinguishable inhabitants of some other corner, how frequent their misunderstandings, how eager they are to kill one another, how fervent their hatreds.

Our posturing, our imagined self-importance, the delusion that we have some privileged position in the Universe, are challenged by this point of pale light. Our planet is a lonely speck in the great enveloping cosmic dark. In our obscurity, in all this vastness, there is no hint that help will come from elsewhere to save us from ourselves.

The Earth is the only world known right now to harbor life. There is nowhere else, at least in the near future, to which our species could migrate. Visit, yes. Settle, not yet. Like it or not, for the moment the Earth is where we make our stand.

It has been said that astronomy is a humbling and character-building experience. There is perhaps no better demonstration of the folly of human conceits than this distant image of our tiny world. To me, it underscores our responsibility to deal, more kindly with one another, and to preserve and cherish the pale blue dot, the only home we have ever known.

Gazing at Sara, Echo uttered, "Yes, Sara, that is verbatim, the essay *Pale Blue Dot*, spoken by Carl Sagan in 1994."

Leaning over to Pulse, Sara murmured, "Pulse, Echo spoke that moving essay word-for-word, as if she had it memorized."

"Sara, Echo has what you call a 'photographic memory.' She remembers everything she has ever heard or seen."

"That is even more evidence of what an incredible leader she is, Pulse."

"And, Sara, it gives her another huge strategic edge."

"What's that, Pulse?"

"This is one more reason why her enemies fear her so much!"

49
ORIGINS OF ALIEN LIFE

"**E**cho, that was beautiful," Tiffany said with a tear in her eye. "And you spoke with such passion and resolve... thank you."

"You are quite welcome, Tiffany. That passage has moved me unlike any other I have ever seen or heard."

Echo went on, "So, here is the plan. Pulse and Sara will be leaving us now, as they have a much different agenda to pursue."

<Agenda, Echo?>

<Patience, Sara. Pulse will explain.>

Pulse took Sara's hand, and they exited the Falcon, waving to the ETRT.

"See y'all soon," Sara muttered.

"Not really." Pulse thinks to himself.

Laser steps forward to get his instructions from Echo.

"Laser, please take our guests on a quick tour of our basecamp with the shuttle parked outside. This is what humans call just a 'pit stop', as we need to return to Earth soon."

"Will do, Echo. Would everyone please follow me into the shuttle?"

Laser's brief tour of the Arrans' basecamp lasted about forty-five minutes, and then he escorted them to his star runner, which was ready to go with Echo on board.

As the ETRT boarded Laser's star runner for the trip back to Earth, Michaela asked Laser if his spacecraft had a name, since Pulse had his *Falcon* and Vibe had his *Mirage*.

"Why yes, Michaela, my star runner is named *Slipstream.*"

RJ beamed and thought to himself, given the fact that warp speed theoretically maxes out at nine, *"That makes perfect sense... quantum slipstream."*

✦ ✦ ✦

Back on Earth, Echo began to explain the origins of alien life for several species now part of the Earth's survival puzzle.

"I hope you enjoyed your brief visit to our base camp. We will have opportunities, I'm sure, to do a deeper dive in the future."

Michaela thought, "*Echo really is getting immersed in our lingo and slang. Cool.*"

"You are a wonderful collection of the best minds and work ethics of any group of humans that we have ever encountered."

The ETRT knew a compliment when one was given.

"So, you will appreciate my next comments."

Michaela thought kindly, "*I always do.*"

"It's foolish to think that Earth was the only place in the observable universe with life… Among the hundred billion galaxies, each containing a hundred billion stars orbited by a hundred billion planets."

RJ knew that something good was coming, at least from a knowledge perspective.

"If you just consider your Milky Way, the implications are staggering. Four hundred billion stars make up the Milky Way, and roughly two percent are G-type stars, which describe the sun and our solar system. So, eight billion are capable of having Earth-type planets."

Echo paused before continuing, "There are many alien cultures in the universe and must be recognized for what and who they are."

Tension filled the ETRT's meeting room as Echo began a game-changing revelation, "I would like to explain the origins of the Dracs, the Denon, and the *Greys* in more detail than was explained in D.C. For some this might be redundant, but I will just say it is repetitive for a reason… a life and death reason.

"The malevolent alien species that we are now encountering regularly are the Denon. They have evolved from human souls that have endured extensive torture in Hell by Alastair and similarly driven alien cultures from the constellation of Scorpius.

"In their evolution, they have become corrupted, extremely evil, and very powerful. They are what we call an entangled culture. Their current leader's name is Derk, but he now uses the name Scorpio, and his lieutenant goes by the name Singe."

Michaela and Tiffany were taking notes, and RJ was on the edge of his seat.

"They require a human vessel to walk and function on Earth and have the ability to roam in smoke form and can morph into recognizable human forms.

Death and destruction are always in their path. Earthly terrorist groups would be ideal hosts for their mission on Earth.

"The humanoid beings with reptilian features that are currently our biggest concern are the Dracs. The males are driven by massive ego and their own desires and have shapeshifting ability. The females have a chameleon ability and are more reserved, less warlike, and much more controlled than the males.

"The Dracs originated in the Alpha Draconis star system, which is only two hundred fifteen light years away, and was formerly the Polestar."

Pausing a moment, Echo continued, "The Dracs culture has two main castes; one is a dangerous warrior caste, at least eight feet tall, up to one thousand pounds, and are super-psychic, fast and cunning. Their leader is known as Vipor.

"The second caste is the highly advanced and intelligent race that has hundreds, if not thousands, of biological offspring here on Earth. They are indistinguishable from humans. Serp is their current leader."

"Echo, what is the likely alien purpose and strategy?"

"Michaela, we are connecting the dots, as you say. Pulse believes that a major supernova struck Earth in the very distant past, and left residue here that would be a huge mineral find for the Dracs."

"What kind of residue, Echo?'

"Well, RJ, if Pulse is right, and I would believe that he is, gold, silver, platinum, palladium, and titanium are all worth the hunt. But... there's more."

With her tone getting a bit creepy, Echo hit a nerve.

"The most coveted 'residue' left by that supernova was likely *Plutonium 239* and *Uranium 235.*"

"*Holy shit,*" thought a most serious RJ. "*Those are the common isotopes used in the manufacture of nuclear weapons!*"

Echo let that comment sink in before continuing.

"The cabin attack years ago was by design, as Serp surmised that Sara's team was getting close via the Pete Stevenson data. Vipor ordered the attack, against the wishes of Serp, according to intel from Aeon and the *Greys.*"

RJ was impressed with the knowledge and intel of Echo and the Arrans and was jotting down what-if scenarios on his notepad.

Echo advised, "More recently, the destructive magnetic wave was the 'first shot over the bow,' as they say in the military. It was meant to assess the defense readiness of planet Earth, along with worldwide allied strength, if it were in play."

Pausing, "Other general cosmic threats are credible, as we have no intel as to the joint capability and coupled alliance between the Dracs and the Denon."

With an impatient sigh, Echo concluded, "That is the baseline, evil alien info and as much intel as we now have. If you want to compose some more specific questions or need some help from any of us with the capsule issues, please contact us."

Tiffany inquired, "Can we contact you and your team directly, Echo?"

"If you do not have a direct link to us and the Arrans' database, let me know and I will take care of it."

Echo looked over to Michaela before pausing for one last comment. "Finally, Sara must go to our celestial planetary system in Trappist One for basic and advanced mental consciousness and physical battle training to be prepared for whatever aggressive confrontations are coming."

Echo became more serious. "It will be a life-changing experience for Sara. No human has ever gone through this Arrans' training."

Michaela glanced over to Echo and asked, "When?"

"Sara and Pulse are preparing to leave our Moon base camp right now for a trip that will take about three days at our fastest hyperspace speed to cover the forty-light-year distance.

Our Trappist One system, seven temperate, terrestrial planets in the constellation, Aquarius, is nearly twice as old as your solar system."

RJ and Michaela gazed at each other, realizing the enormity of Echo's words and Sara's pending trip to *another world*.

"Sara will be gone for two weeks and was not able to tell anyone of her trip, as time and family security is of the essence."

Looking directly at Michaela, who had a very serious look on her face, "I will be informing her parents today."

Michaela was relieved that Mike and Christine would be in the loop.

"Echo, when Sara returns, will we see any difference? Will she still be 'our' Sara?"

Echo answered Michaela with her usual open and honest perspective.

"Sara will become an extremely formidable opponent for the advancing aliens headed for Earth... a true Warrior."

50

TRIP TO TRAPPIST ONE

As they loaded a much larger spacecraft, Pulse described Trappist One to Sara, as Sara tried to process what was about to happen with both her journey and this incredible destination of Pulse's home planet.

"There are seven planets that make up the Trappist One system, and they are in much tighter orbits. You will be able to see celestial bodies with the naked eye that will be etched in your mind forever."

"I can't wait to see them, Pulse. I am so excited."

"One of the amazing differences between Earth and Trappist One is that the tighter orbits allow for viewing all of them at the same time from any one of them. I am unaware of any place in the universe where this is the case."

"Cool."

"And, Sara, the night sky is always beautiful and is nearly always in a dusk-like aura, making our home a most romantic place to be… a destination vacation, for sure."

Sara smiled as Pulse winked.

"Storms are rare on the Trappist System, and I will explain the differences in the seven planets as we get closer."

Pulse paused as additional supplies were being brought on board. Pulse signed a pad he was presented and thanked the two material handlers for their service.

"Our reddish dwarf star is smaller and not as warm as your Sun, so temperatures are cooler… in fact, cold at night. The days are temperate and most of our species do their socializing during the day."

Sara noted the larger-size ship than she had seen before and inquired, "Why such a large ship?"

"We are taking a larger spacecraft… this one is a two-level craft, about ninety-five feet long, to also bring back additional warriors, weapons, and equipment that Echo requested."

Sara was in awe… again.

"You will see some amazing 'reverse engineering' being done on this ship with highly technical AIs, building futuristic weapons from future intel that we don't have right now!"

"Holy crap, I'm trying to wrap my head around the endless list of 'ohmigod,' and it is mind-blowing."

"This is the same ship that I captained on that journey in 1972 when I met with Command Module Pilot, Robert Kelley. That was really our first step into the assimilation with your grandfather, Pete Stevenson."

"Whoa. That's nuts."

"I'll tell you what's nuts. Walk over to that triangular command desk."

Sara walked over to a very large desk, with a plethora of wrap-around screens, and gazed at how much more complex this cockpit and command center was compared to the Falcon.

"Now, move to your right and sit in that navigation chair to the right of the captain's command chair."

Sara glanced at the big chair, noting that there was one on each side of the captain's chair.

"This one?" Sara pointed to the chair on the right.

"Yep. Now, Sara, take a seat."

She was kind of puzzled, but did what Pulse had asked her to do.

Pulse walked over and sat in the captain's chair and looked over to Sara on his right side.

"You are now sitting in the exact same seat your Grandad Pete sat in when we took him on his memorable, galactic, space journey!"

51

JOURNEY OR DESTINATION

Sara was overwhelmed with emotion and sentiment. Capturing that moment was one that brought tears to her eyes, and she couldn't wait to tell her parents about the remarkable coincidence that she now shared with her deceased grandad… now a current highly advanced hologram.

Pulse got up, walked over to the aerobridge that was receding, and did a quick walk around to make sure that all was secure and ready for departure.

"Are you ready, Miss Steele?"

"Absolutely, Captain Pulse. Let's go!"

Now secured in their seats, Pulse began the simple execution of the spacecraft's launch. The ship lifted, hovered for a few seconds, and then speedily took off in a forty-five-degree angle. Sara had no duties… just an enchanted passenger on a very large spacecraft.

"Give me a few minutes," Pulse advised excitedly, "and then we can get caught up on those devilish details."

Sara smiled, once again, at his humor and knowledge of innuendo and quirky references.

"We have a flight 'check list' just like any human pilots do. All is good."

"This trip will take about three days at a modified warp drive… what we call a *slipstream*. Our travel time is calculated from point A to point B based on several factors and the size of the vessel traveling. Are you familiar with light speed?"

"Yes, Pulse, light travels at 186,000 miles per second."

"We use a superluminal propulsion system, equipped with a futuristic warp drive that travels by many orders of magnitude greater than the speed of light. Matter is the constraint. Think of light as energy and think of speed as energy and mass becoming interchangeable."

"So, Pulse, the bigger the mass of the spacecraft, the more difficult the warp speed becomes, and the smaller the mass of the spacecraft, the easier for max warp speed?"

"Exactly. Great understanding of this complicated concept."

"So, it would be a quicker trip to Trappist One with a smaller spaceship, right?"

"That is correct. But we need this vessel for the reasons I mentioned earlier, Sara."

"Got it. Thanks for the explanation."

"There is another part of this hyperspace travel that is awesome."

"All ears, big guy."

Pulse smiled. He so loved having Sara on board… now, he just needed to stay focused on the mission at hand.

"At our typical warp drive, travel to Trappist One would take about seventeen days, which is super-quick, given that we are going forty light years in distance."

"But you said the trip would take about three days?"

"That's right. We will be using a narrowly focused, quantum-directed field that bends the space-time vectors to create a subspace tunnel which will project ahead of this ship. Once we enter that tunnel, the incredible forces inside will propel us at unheard of speeds."

Pulse waited for this info to sink in with his terrestrial guest.

"To maintain the slipstream, we must deflect all forces acting upon this ship in order to literally stay in the geometric center of the subspace tunnel."

"Ohmigod," Sara thought. *"I can't even begin to appreciate what the hell is happening!"*

"Piece of cake, Sara… I call this speed… lunatic-quick."

Pulse winked at Sara. "Now, let's talk about your intensive training, both physical and virtual."

"Did you say virtual?"

"Yes, you will have a specific physical transformation, based on this schematic drawing that I just uploaded."

Sara looked curiously at a composite drawing that appeared on the nearest screen.

"That transformation will include a chip in your brain that optimizes integration of mirror neurons."

Sara was as passive as she could get, trying to absorb this *out-of-the-box* surgery.

"Then, you will begin training in a virtual reality world that will test your mental capability to react and respond to physical demands being placed on your new body… piece of cake."

"You're eating way too much cake, Captain."

"Yes and no, Sara. You are my cake!"

Sara surmised that Pulse was thinking sexually, and he was. Pulse was hoping that Sara picked up on the innuendo, and she had.

✦ ✦ ✦

Pulse put his massive spacecraft on autopilot and said to Sara, "It will be a few hours before I set up the slipstream tunnel. Let's get some food and drinks, okay?"

"Absolutely. What cha got?"

Sara and Pulse moved from the cockpit to the galley, where Pulse opened a series of white drawers holding a wide variety of processed foods.

"Kind of yucky, Pulse. They look like army K-rations."

"What do you know about K-rations?"

"Grandad Pete would always take them on our camping and water-skiing trips. He thought they were delicious, and we just went along with that. They sucked!"

"Well, Sara, for my special guest, I have the PIM."

"Okay, I'll bite." Pulse laughed when she said she would *bite*.

"What the hell is a PIM?"

"The *Pulse Individual Meal!*"

Pulse pulled out several white envelopes with coded letters on them.

"Even Echo doesn't know about these."

<Yes, I do!>

"What's your pleasure? I have steak, seafood, and Italian."

"Seafood, please."

Pulse opened his interesting meal packages. "Cosmic Cosmo?"

"Most definitely."

Pulse began preparing their drinks, while the dinners began to expand as they sat on dinner plates. Within five minutes, Pulse had their seafood dinners prepared, and they clanked Cosmo glasses in toasts.

"Here's to Sara Steele, Warrior Princess-in-waiting."

Chuckling, Sara offered, "Here's to Pulse, likely the best combination chef and bartender on Trappist One!"

After dinner, Pulse excused himself to head back to the Command Center to prepare the slipstream vectors.

Sara excused herself and headed to her sleeping quarters, finally succumbing to the events of a busy day.

✦ ✦ ✦

Sara was told to use the captain's stateroom for sleeping, so she assumed that she and Pulse would be sleeping together. As she unpacked her small bag of night clothes and bathroom essentials, she noticed an envelope that she did not pack.

Opening the envelope, she fell back, sitting on the bed. It was the Valentine's Day card from Doctor Matthew Palmer that she received following her rehab from his surgery saving her from life-threatening wounds from the cabin attack.

The card read, *I hope you feel loved and appreciated on Valentine's Day. Because you are!*

"This card was in my bedroom," she thought, as she gazed up from the opened card.

"Who the hell put it here?"

52
CONFLICTED

Pulse finished his navigational duties and headed to the stateroom and their bed. Sara was already in bed, so Pulse quietly got undressed and slipped into bed and gave Sara a warm embrace. He didn't have much time to test their sexual chemistry, as his navigation duties were close to full-time, but he was most definitely… ready to try.

As he placed one arm around her head and the other arm around her lower back, Sara tensed up a bit and said to Pulse, "Not tonight… we can talk in the morning."

Pulse knew that something wasn't right, given the enjoyable dinner and conversation, but he had too much respect for Sara to argue or ask questions. Plus, he needed to get back to his navigation.

The next morning was a bit awkward.

"Sorry I wasn't more attentive last night, Pulse. I was preoccupied and I have some things to sort out."

"No problem, Sara. I made some coffee, and you are just the push of a button away from a magnificent breakfast."

They both got a laugh from that remark.

"What cha doin' now?"

"Well, without a navigator, I really need to be here on the nav console most of the time, both day and night."

"Without sleeping, Pulse?"

"Well, I can catch some z's from time to time, but this subspace, tunnel equilibrium needs constant attention. Once we are back to, say, a warp four tomorrow, I can pretty much switch to auto-pilot."

Much of Sara's day was spent helping Pulse with any non-technical needs that he had. After lunch, Sara got some more details regarding the Arrans' training info from Pulse, and she was starting to get excited about the Trappist One adventure.

That afternoon, Pulse gave Sara the guided tour around this massive space-ship, and the one thing that stood out was that it was being manned by a crew of one! They returned to the command center and took their respective seats.

Then, out of the blue, Sara asked, "Pulse, have you ever been in love, or married, or in a long-term relationship?"

Pulse leaned back in his chair, turned to Sara, and softly said, "Yes."

"Do you want to talk about it, Pulse? I'm okay if you don't."

Pulse looked at Sara, paused, and suggested that he would get them a couple drinks. He got up and walked into the galley to pour a couple drinks. Sara knew that she was about to open a can of worms and was already planning to *walk-it-back,* when Pulse returned.

"I'm sorry, Pulse. I certainly don't want to pry into your personal affairs."

"Sara, I like you. I really, really like you. So, unless we are up front and honest with each other, our relationship doesn't stand a chance."

"Crap," Sara thought hesitantly. *"I can't even mention Matt's card."*

"I want you to try something, okay?"

"Sure. What cha got there?"

"This is labelled PNB, for your info, and you can get some from the galley whenever you want."

Sipping the drink, Sara was impressed. "Wow, that's some hot stuff. Bourbon, right?"

"Yes. It's PNB, which stands for Pulse's Non-alcoholic Bourbon."

"Seriously?"

"Seriously. It's my own brew. It tastes like Bourbon, but you can drink a gallon without getting a buzz!"

"You are full of surprises, captain." Tasting the concoction, Sara replied, "This is some really good Bourbon."

Toasting themselves, Sara used this opportunity to level the playing field before Pulse had even considered getting into any disclosure of his personal relationship.

"Pulse, you know about Doctor Matthew Palmer and me, right?'

"Yes, of course. Matt is a fine man and someone who I respect and admire. And you two are good friends, right?"

"Yes. So far, he has been the 'guy' in my life, following the death of my husband, Paul, in the cabin attack. When times get tough, he often slips into my mind, and in a good way."

"Sara, I hope he is always a strong force in your life."

"Well, he has been in and out of my mind since we left your Moon base, and I'm sorry."

"There is no need to apologize. I just want to be another 'great guy' in your life."

Sara moved over to a smiling Pulse and gave him a long hug and a kiss on his lips.

"There was a woman in my life, a long time ago."

"You don't need to go there, Pulse."

"Sara, I want to. Let me fill our drinks… I'll be right back."

Feeling a lot more relaxed, Sara was now going to hear what every woman wants to hear about… the competition.

Returning with fully loaded glasses of PNB, Pulse sat back down and began, "I met Ceria while we were both in training, similar to what you will be doing soon. We dated for many months and we were lovers and friends. We had a home on Trappist One that we shared with another couple, but our mission back then was stopping aggression from warring alien species."

Sara thought instantly, *"I probably shouldn't have brought this up."*

"During a hostile takeover of an extrasolar planet orbiting within the habitable zone of the sun-like star you call Kepler twenty-two in the constellation of Cygnus, we were in a sub-orbital fire-fight with our perpetual enemies, the Dracs."

"Oh shit," Sara thought worriedly. *"He is reliving a vivid memory!"*

"Ceria had been grounded that day and was not supposed to be on the fighter that I was piloting. Once we were in fight formation, she showed up to man one of the guns on my ship, having snuck aboard as we fueled our fighters from the interstellar carrier."

"Damn it… what's coming?" Sara sensed.

"During combat, we were hit and had to abandon ship. Ceria and I had our deep-space jumpsuits on and deployed from a burning ship in a daring space jump to the surface of the planet."

"I'm trying to visualize that jump, Pulse. It had to be frightening."

"Yes, but we trained for those scenarios, and all was well as we headed to the surface at about two hundred miles an hour. The problem was a saturated debris field. I managed to crisscross my way through that field, but Ceria was killed before she reached the ground."

"I'm so sorry, Pulse… so sorry."

"Thank you, but that is why, my lovely Sara Steele, I have adopted my human-type sense of humor. It helps me get through the tough days."

"Pulse?"

"Yes, Sara."

"Why was Ceria grounded and not allowed to fight?"

Pausing, Pulse gathered himself emotionally and replied, **"The planet under attack that we were helping to defend was her homeland!"**

53

COMMITTED

The next 36 hours were kind of tense and with a few awkward moments. Pulse and Sara both realized that the venting helped, but it didn't make their daily contact any easier.

The nighttime romancing was off the table as Pulse had to concentrate on staying within the subspace tunnel's navigational parameters. He had to focus on their flight vectors to keep them safe and alive.

The morning of their expected arrival on Trappist One, Sara got up, and not seeing Pulse, walked into the head for a quick shower. As she was toweling off, Pulse walked in on her nearly naked body, covered slightly by an over-sized robe.

"Good morning, Sunshine."

"Good morning, Captain."

"You smell good."

"Thank you, Pulse. Don't you need to be back at the controls?"

"No. Not anymore. We have now been out of the slipstream for about two hours and back to flying only at warp four. It's like your car going from two hundred miles an hour down to fifty-five."

Car-nut Sara could relate to his example.

She moved close to Pulse and gave him a wet, sloppy kiss. Pulse sensed that her mood had swung.

Pulse put his hands and arms through her robe and softly placed his big hands on her naked back and buttocks and lifted her slightly to his height and kissed her, while pulling her tightly to his body. The warmth of the shower was now being replaced by the warmth of her sexual arousal.

Tossing off her robe, Pulse set her gently on her bed and removed his shirt. As he bent over her, Sara put both of her hands around his neck and pulled his body onto hers.

"Do you like sex in the morning, Captain?"

"Yes, dear Sara. I think most guys do."

As Pulse slowly placed his body over Sara, she reached below his waist to unhook his belt. She could feel his arousal in his crotch and was stunned at the size of his *missile*.

In tandem, they did a mutual once-over. His eyes traveled down her body and hers down his. Sara was looking at a god-like figure, nearly seven feet of sheer sculpted leanness with big broad shoulders.

Sara drew her attention to every finely honed muscle, his beautiful, smiling face, and those sparkling blue eyes. She was warm, wet, and ready to take on anything this man had in his wonderful mind. ·

As Pulse slowly caressed Sara's breasts and backside, she opened herself completely as they kissed warmly and passionately.

Then, as if their timing was becoming a real-life obstacle, a flashing red light filled the stateroom, as well as throughout the ship.

"Echo?" Sara immediately asked.

"No. Not Echo. We have some sort of emergency. Let me go check."

As Pulse stood up, gained his composure, slowly straightened up and allowed himself to get back to *normal* physically, he said, "Stay here. I'll be back shortly."

After about five minutes, Sara put her robe back on and walked out to see what the emergency was. Pulse was busy on a pair of monitors and looking at a stream of data on a large viewing screen, sans shirt.

"What's up, Pulse? Problem?"

"Yes. Maybe a small problem."

"We have just received a 'Mayday' from a ship in distress outside our travel coordinates."

"What are you going to do?"

Checking his last data set, Pulse simply said, "I plan to ignore it and stay on course as planned. We are only about fifteen hours from home."

"Pulse. It's someone in distress… you can't ignore it. We may be their only hope!"

"Their location is outside our course plan to Trappist One, and it will cause us to lose precious travel time."

"Pulse, do you know anything about the vessel in distress?"

"Apparently, it is a Norwegian Medical Research vessel that will require us to change our course, and we don't even know if anyone on board is alive."

"Pulse, please. I insist we go check it out."

With a deep sigh, Pulse acquiesced. "Okay, Sara."

Pulse has a bad feeling about this!

54

MAYDAY MADNESS

P ulse slowed the spacecraft down to get his bearings on both his ship and the target ship. He also dug feverishly into the flight log on his data screen for identification, origin, and documented destination.

"This is apparently a bio-medical vessel that is not currently logged into any records or travel itineraries. That alone is a bad sign, Sara."

"Maybe we shouldn't go check it out, Pulse."

"We are here with a mid-course correction now needed, so I will look at the ship and get back as soon as I determine the status and need."

Pulse moved quickly from the ship's command center, took a jet pack with emergency supplies, and headed to the airlock.

"Sara, as soon as I am out, press this red button. The ship will stay locked for now, so don't worry. Upon my return, I should be able to open the airlock, but if I can't for any reason, press this green button."

Sara took one of Pulse's gloved hands and said, "Please be careful."

Pulse turned toward the airlock and murmured, "I will."

As Pulse employed his jet pack and exited the airlock, Sara thought about the space disaster that took Ceria's life.

"What the hell did I just ask him to do?"

Now Sara was worried, as Pulse was alone, headed to the idle Norwegian Medical Research vessel, and no human contact was made with the distressed vessel since the mayday was received.

Sara cannot see that Pulse had gotten inside the stricken ship. The silence was frightening.

Once inside, the ship was dark, until Pulse pulled his small flashlight from his sleeve. It was a ship of death. The crew was floating dead, and an occasional spark could be seen from odd places within the ship.

A closer look inside the craft revealed that it was being eaten away by what appeared to be thousands of metal-eating organisms. This was not a situation that this well-travelled space warrior had ever encountered.

As Pulse was taking a video, one of the organisms attempted to attach itself to his helmet, but the helmet material was not penetrable.

"This is a disaster in many ways," Pulse thought guardedly.

He set an explosive charge and exited the spacecraft quickly and returned to his ship. As he approached, Sara dutifully opened the airlock and Pulse entered quickly.

Once back on board, Pulse got his ship back to its warp-four cruising speed, and the Norwegian vessel exploded in a vivid dark sky. The shock waves from the blast could be felt on the Arrans' speeding spaceship.

Once they were out of danger's way, Sara asked, "What did you find?"

"A metal-eating organism that I have never seen before."

"You are upset? Sorry I made you go."

"No, I'm glad you made me go."

"Why?"

"I will need to give this info back to Echo. Hold on while I contact her."

    <Stopped for a vessel in distress.>

    <No, Pulse, you shouldn't have.>

    <Sara insisted.>

    <You did not follow protocol. We will talk when you return.>

    <Yes, of course. But I have both bad and good news.>

Pulse then explained to Echo what happened and finished his telepathic call.

"Again, Pulse, why are you glad I made you go?"

"This metal-eating organism is an entirely different weapon... purely tech-terror."

"And?"

"And, I don't think we have a way to stop its spread!"

55

EDGE OF AQUARIUS

With that amazing side trip and startling bad info under review, Pulse and Sara continued on to the Arrans' protoplanetary home. Located 40 light-years from Earth in the constellation Aquarius, Trappist One was an ultra-cool, red dwarf star slightly larger than the planet Jupiter, but having eighty-five times Jupiter's mass, according to Sara's research.

"Pulse, I see our hyper-warp speed four has us getting close to your home. An ETA yet?"

"Yes, with our combination of slipstream and warp, our total trip time was supposed to be three days. We lost about one-half of our last travel day with our side trip."

"Sorry."

"We are now going to slow to warp speed one point five for the next two hours, and then I will put the autopilot on for the approach and landing."

"I see you have been running calculations on the organisms since our encounter. Any ideas?"

"No, Sara. This is entirely new to us and frighteningly real. I'm sure Echo has my limited data and has her analytic team on it."

"I know when you get serious like this, you are concerned."

"Yes. We travel throughout the solar system, and this is a new organism, I'm sure. It has the elements of a significantly destructive weapon."

Pulse paused and smiled at his lovely companion. "Let me get us a couple drinks, and I will give you a Trappist One overview, okay?"

"Sure, Pulse, that would be great. Cosmic Cosmos, I assume?"

"Yep. Unless you would prefer something else."

"Oh hell, no. Your creation is just what this lady needs."

Sara's smile gave Pulse a warm feeling. He was really enjoying this special time with Sara, and he had to keep the mood upbeat, given how the tone and tempo would soon be changing for his human friend entering her training phase.

The fact that he shared the deeply personal saga of himself and Ceria still wore on him, but he believed it best to clear the air with Sara before they could move on.

While she waited for Pulse to return, Sara's mind raced with both anticipation and apprehension of what lay ahead for her... and where her relationship with this strong alien man would go.

Returning with their drinks, Pulse toasted their adventure, "With this moment, may you always know that I am focused on your well-being and will always be there for you."

Sara had two thoughts; first was *"How sweet,"* and the other was *"What the hell is about to happen to me on his planet?"*

"Thank you, Pulse. You and your ET family have changed my life forever and given me hope for the future."

With that, Sara took Pulse by the hand and said, "Let's go back to bed."

Pulse adjusted his navigational settings to give them some time and with Sara in hand, they walked quickly to the stateroom. Walking into the room, Pulse brushed up against Sara, sending a rush of goosebumps through her slowly relaxing body.

The effect he had on her was disconcerting. Her physical and emotional needs were never wanting with other male relationships, but Pulse had the *complete man* down to an art form.

As they stopped to gaze at each other, Pulse simply said, "Look at you," as he placed his hands on her face and neck. As he began to caress her body, running one palm down to her hip, Sara quickly responded... "Allow me," as she disrobed inviting Pulse to do the same.

Slowly lying flat on the bed, Sara took Pulse by the hand and brought him next to her, squeezing his muscular frame and feeling his throbbing manhood.

Sara's already rapid heartbeat sped up, if that was possible, and her already heated body rose another ten degrees... if that was possible.

A confident and focused man, Pulse put his finger to her lips and whispered in her ear, "Hush, my beauty. Put yourself in my hands and we will come together..."

Sara's *Master of the Universe* became the *Master of Sara's Boudoir.*

Sara had never been kissed so thoroughly before in her life... not by Paul or Matt or by any lover. From her temple to her toes, the warm and wet tongue of her alien god was mesmerizing and left her wanting more... much more.

She moved her body restlessly against his, ran her hands through his thick hair, and pulled his body close to hers. Her breath caught as she felt his firmness against her stomach.

Instantly, Sara wrapped her legs around his hips and drew his manhood toward her feminine core. Making love with Pulse would be a wild ride, Sara thought warmly, with the combination of pleasure and pain driving her crazy.

Minutes later, with Pulse's voice husky from desire and Sara moaning softly, a simultaneous climax set a new sexual baseline for this most compatible sexual couple.

Following nearly an hour of lovemaking, and both lovers thoroughly satisfied, Sara thought to herself... *"This sexual journey was as good as or better than the final destination will be!"*

✦ ✦ ✦

Pulse let Sara take a peaceful nap and returned to the command center to start the last stage of their journey to Trappist One. Many things were going through his mind... all good. As he attended to the relevant readings and travel data, Sara joined him with a smile and brought him a warm cup of tea.

"Thank you, Sara. Tea is just what I need."

Wrapping her arms around Pulse's neck, she added, "That was incredible, Pulse. I have never felt more a woman and so relaxed. I needed that... I needed you."

Pulse gave Sara a tender kiss and simply replied, "I am the happiest guy in the Trappist One System, thanks to you."

"So," Pulse began a more serious tone, "Trappist One is a very stable system that is actually older than your solar system. It has been here for about seven point five billion years, where your own solar system was formed about four point five billion years ago."

Sara asked in a frank manner, "Would that likely explain why life can exist here?"

"Yes, partly. There are seven temperate terrestrial planets orbiting our star, of which four are in what is called by humans the habitable zone. They are referred to on Earth as Trappist d, e, f, and g."

"Are you on each?"

"Yes, Sara, we have colonies on each, and each has a unique purpose."

"How so?

"Life evolved on one planet, and through a process called panspermia, the transfer of life from one planet to another, all three now sustain life."

"How cool is that?'

"Ultra-cool, eh, Sara? Like our cool dwarf star, right?"

"Funny. Damn, Pulse, I love your sense of humor."

"Thanks. So, one planet, Trappist One e, is home to the major elements of our civilization. Much like on Earth, its main purpose is to expand our society and sustain our life. Planets e, f, and g, are similar in size to Earth."

Sara was fascinated and enjoying the tutorial.

"One planet is for mining and the extraction of key minerals, and one planet is used strictly for training and the development of weapons and defense systems. You will be there, mostly."

Pausing for a moment, Pulse continued, "Trappist One d is important for being the one with the most water, but only along a ring known as the terminator line. It is tidally locked, with one side permanently facing the star and the other side in total darkness. Life does not exist there… only a huge source of water for our inhabited planets."

"What is the climate and environment like?"

"Our star is not nearly as bright and hot as your Sun, so the temperatures are moderate, and the sky on each is almost constantly in what you would call dusk. Very beautiful."

Sara smiled, picturing a never-ending dusk imagery.

"Due to close orbits, you can usually see all the planets from any one vantage point."

Pulse continued to give Sara details on the Trappist One system for the duration of the afternoon.

"Pulse, I'm gonna go freshen up and maybe lay down for a couple of hours."

"That will work. I'll come get you when we are getting close to visuals. You must see the entry into our worlds."

✦ ✦ ✦

Sara was laying on the bed, with an abundance of conflicting thoughts running through her head. She was awake but in deep contemplative thought as Pulse entered the room and sat next to her on the bed.

Her last thought as Pulse approached was concerning, *"So who put that card from Matt in my bag?"*

"How ya doing?"

"I'm good, Pulse. Are we there yet?"

Laughing, Pulse replied, "I just set the autopilot to take us in, as I mentioned earlier. Come see the incredible views of our worlds from space."

Sara jumped up, grabbed a comb to quickly brush her hair, and they both headed to the cockpit and viewport in the command center.

Hand-in-hand, they moved like a couple that was totally comfortable in each other's presence. Sara stopped for a moment, turned to Pulse and gave him a long, loving kiss.

"You're the best, my dear friend, Pulse."

Squeezing her tightly, "Thank you, my angel, the pleasure is all mine."

Once arriving at the command center, and looking out the starboard side of the spacecraft, Sara was in awe of what she saw with just the naked eye.

There was the Trappist One system, complete with the ultra-cool red dwarf star and seven orbiting planets, all appearing to be Earth-like in size.

As she consumed the magnificence of their arrival perspective, Pulse was on his own version of *cloud nine*. No human had ever seen what his Sara was seeing now, and that meant so much to him.

Unfortunately, this celestial perspective brought back bad memories of himself and Ceria, who was literally *lost in space*.

After several minutes of taking in this celestial beauty, Sara had an amazing summation, **"My God, Pulse, it looks like a cosmic travel poster!"**

56

TRAPPIST TRYST

Pulse brought his ship in for a landing on Trappist One e, and in a remote area that appeared to be a military-type outpost. Dark, secretive, and void of much noticeable activity, Sara was surprised with the lack of any greeting force at all.

Pulling his ship into a large bay, Sara could see that they had entered a large aviation center, with many crafts that were similar to Pulse's ship in formation.

"This facility is a 'backdoor entrance' to our main spaceport, and under high-level security. You can leave the flight uniform on your chair for the return flight."

"Sure. Why the secrecy?"

"Just for added security and appropriate safeguards. Don't want questions… because questions require answers."

"Got it." Sara folded her flight uniform and left it in the cockpit and slipped her shoes back on.

Exiting the ship, several attendees took over securing the ship, and without any words being spoken, Pulse led Sara to a small hovercraft that was similar to the ones they had on the Moon.

Outside the hanger, a car-like vehicle with Pulse's glyph was parked in a spot that had other reserved vehicles.

"Please, have a seat in front as I secure our bags."

Sara got into the rather spartan vehicle. It was surreal.

Pulse got in and touched the screen and they were off.

"We don't have much time, but before I deliver you to your next stop, I want to show you a place that is very special to me."

"Fine." Sara smiled and thought, "*Whatever it is, it will be awesome, for sure.*"

"Breathing okay?"

"Yep. Heartrate probably a little elevated, though."

Sara again was feeling the bittersweet emotions of both the high of enjoying the moment and the trepidation of what was to come.

Slow at first, and then with the speed of a *bullet train*, they were quickly covering a most beautiful terrain, and Sara was filled with joy and amazed with the tranquility of this new land.

"Where are we headed, Pulse?"

"To my retreat. You know how your grandad had his mountain retreat?"

"Of course. It was so peaceful there."

"Well, I have my lake, and when you see what this lake holds, I'm sure it will make you happy."

Twenty minutes later, they had arrived at a spectacular lake with a mountainous backdrop that reminded Sara of South Lake Tahoe.

Getting out of the vehicle, Sara asked, "What is this lake called?"

"Tranquility Lake. Very apropos, don't you think?"

Sara laughed. "That name is literally what my first impression was when I saw it… tranquility."

Leaving the vehicle, Pulse walked over to the shoreline and removed the cover on a small boat. "Hop in."

Sara was having mini-flashbacks to her time with her dad and granddad in that cabin on the lake in the Sierra Nevada.

Climbing into the boat, Sara sighed and said, "This is spectacular… almost heaven-like. It takes my breath away."

Pulse took Sara out on the lake at dusk… it was always dusk, as he said. And all the planets were visible.

In about fifteen minutes in a small boat that didn't appear to have any power, yet was moving along the water just fine, Pulse announced that they had arrived.

"Pulse, this is beautiful. What is it you want to show me?"

"It's not here… but close."

"I don't understand."

"Sara, take off your clothes."

57

SEA OF LOVE

"What! Why?"

"Trust me, Sara. You don't want to get your clothes wet, do you?"

"Huh?"

"We're going swimming. That is what I want to show you."

"Okay. But you too?"

"Sure."

With that, both disrobed and left their clothes in a neat pile on the anchored boat.

Pulse thought to himself, seeing Sara naked, *"What a strong and beautiful woman."*

Sara thought to herself, seeing Pulse naked, *"He looks like a Greek God. Tall, muscular, long arms, a chiseled body, and such big hands!"*

Pulse took Sara in his arms. One arm was around her waist and the other hand was holding her head with a thumb and index finger covering her ears.

"We will be going deep, and I need to help you breathe. So, this kiss will last a while."

With that remark, Pulse grasped Sara tightly around the waist and kissed her gently... then firmly.

They fell into the water and descended to the bottom of the lake.

Being a PADI-rated scuba diver, Sara had no sense of pressurization problems as they made their descent. His hands on her ears seemed to mitigate the ear pressure completely.

They came to a stop on the bottom of the lake. Still in his arms, Pulse carried Sara through a waterfall-like curtain into a totally dry under-lake home, or retreat, or just plain getaway place.

Setting Sara down, Pulse said, "Welcome to what the men on your planet call their 'man cave.' Let me get you a robe..."

A totally disoriented Sara wraps her arms around her wet body as Pulse made a hasty move to another part of the "house." He returned with a soft robe and a warm towel.

"This is where I come when I need some peace and quiet or just need to think. Ever have those times?"

"You know I do. This is incredible. Everything is incredible."

"Are you warming?"

"Yes, Pulse, thank you. Your robe is… kind of big?"

"Oh, right. I'm not used to having company."

Sara thought, *"That's good. No girlfriend playpen here!"*

Pulse grabbed the other robe and put it on.

She is blown away by both his sensitivity and his skills. She wants to tell him that… but isn't quite ready yet.

"Sara, I have feelings for you that I have not felt before… never before. I have a desire to be with you and never let you out of my sight. It is selfish, as you have a fateful journey ahead of you that will challenge your strong faith and relentless hope."

Taking him by the hand, Sara offered, "I share your feelings, Pulse, and I have never felt happier or safer than when I'm with you."

They kissed and Pulse drew Sara closer.

"This is my place, not yours, Sara."

"And?"

"And I can change that." Pulse placed his right hand on Sara's temple and said, "Think of a different place that you can imagine. Your space… your getaway. Think."

Sara thinks intently and Pulse creates a *visual* based on Sara's thoughts and immediately the man cave becomes the kitchen in Sara's home, and the entire setting is transformed into Sara's home from Pulse's man cave.

She simply said, "Dear God!"

Enjoying that visual image turned into a physical transformation, Sara smiled and closed her eyes again.

Pulse smiled as he picked up a remarkable new setting transformation, given Sara's thinking.

Now, they were in Sara's bedroom, with soft candles flickering and the sound of the sea on a recording in the background.

Following this surreal scene, Sara's mind aligned once again with Pulse. They fell onto the bed, embraced, and feelings of intimacy reverberated intensely.

"Do you want me, Sara?"

"Yes, Pulse, I do."

"You are my beautiful warrior woman," Pulse murmured as he placed his strong arms through the opening of her robe and found her hips and gently moved his hands upward until they rested under her breasts.

"I feel so safe, so secure, and so loved when we are close like this, Pulse."

As Pulse kissed Sara's neck and cheeks and then finding her soft lips, he could sense her sensual movements and became aroused as she parted his legs with her bare foot. Rolling on top of him, Sara began running little kisses and nips on his shoulders and chest and moving those kisses gently down his stomach.

Then, lifting her body so she could peer into his dark and mysterious eyes, her legs moved around his waist. With a subtle but firm motion, Pulse slid into Sara, pulling her body tightly against his as he moved in and out with passion and warmth.

Once again, they enjoyed and pleased each other for nearly an hour, now understanding what was required both physically and emotionally to satisfy their partner's desires.

The two lovers were now getting to know each other better and able to meet each other's sexual needs. Both liked to have some control when having intercourse… when it's his call, it's him on top. When it's *lady's choice*, she is the *cowgirl in charge*.

Pulse thought… *"I have never been happier."*

Sara thought… *"This sex is what I would certainly call, out of this world."*

✦ ✦ ✦

After making love and talking for hours, Pulse realized that he must bid farewell to Sara soon and get her back on track for the training that is the only reason for her to be on Trappist One. To say they have become comfortable as friends and lovers would be an understatement.

With the *man cave* restored, Pulse took Sara on a brief tour of his actual home under the lake.

"You have movie posters from American movies and photos of our space program in every corner of your home."

"You know I'm a big fan… never bigger than right now."

"Ohmigod, there is a photo of you, Echo, Laser, and my grandad! Thank you."

Sara gives her alien host a big kiss and gets back on point.

"So, what's in store for me now, Pulse?"

"Fair question. First, they will do a neurological scan to see what, if any, implants can be used to increase your consciousness and self-realization. They will describe the nature of mirror neurons, which are key in the implants."

"Yes, Echo briefly explained that to me."

"Not everyone is a candidate, Sara, so you must not be disappointed if there are no implants. I would think from your behavior and life experiences that you will be a perfect subject."

"Thanks."

"Then you will go from the lab to the training compound. Your regiment will be determined based on a psychological and physiological profile that they will conduct."

Pulse described Sara's training and the introduction and use of new equipment and technology, which will be far advanced from anything she had seen on Earth.

Sara was beginning to get excited about the prospects, given the latest techniques shown to her by Pulse.

"There will be what you humans would call a 'badge of courage' awarded to those who complete the training in its entirety. And very few Arrans candidates actually complete the entire program."

"You did?"

"Yes. Echo holds the record for highest point total, an award that she is very proud of but never mentions. Such respect for our wonderful leader."

"The suspense is killing me, Pulse. Finish? Award?"

"Echo is very fond of the French people and their language."

"I know. And I know you have a small outpost in France."

"*Oui.*"

"Why is that important here?"

"Echo has very high value for what you will try to attain in this rather select training."

"What is that?"

"It is referred to as the *Croix de Guerre.*"

"What does that stand for?"

"Cross of war!"

58

BEAUTIFUL BONES

Pulse and Sara returned to the area where they landed and Pulse took them in his vehicle to the Arrans' military headquarters, about an hour away.

Sara was now beginning to see the vast outpost as more of a highly sophisticated city… and a modern one at that.

They stopped for a quick meal before Pulse escorted Sara to the medical lab, which would be her first stop.

"Goodbye for now, Sara. I'll leave you in good hands and will be back to pick you up in six days."

Sara and Pulse embraced and gave each other a longer than usual parting kiss.

"Hi, I'm the Chief Medical Officer here. My name is a long one. Pulse suggested that you just call me *Bones*. He said it would make sense to you.'"

"He's a fan… and it does."

Sara was already feeling at ease with Bones and his stark-white lab coat. She knew she was, in fact, in good hands with the smiling alien doctor.

"We will be doing three separate procedures with you, Miss Steele."

"Please call me Sara."

"Yes, Sara. First, we know you have some added bone, muscle, and tissue enhancements, and we will take some X-rays and assess your strength and general health in a very quick and simple procedure."

"I assumed as much," Sara added confidently.

"In fact, if you are ready, we can do that now."

"Sure. Go ahead."

Bones led Sara to a small room that held medical equipment that was foreign to her. She had expected MRI-type machines, but these were handheld that appeared to be very basic… almost primitive.

"Please slip this gown on. You can use the Relaxation Room on your right."

Sara went in, and proceeded to change in to what seemed like scrubs.

Upon exiting, Bones had Sara walk slowly through two vertical machines, stopping for a moment inside each one, and afterwards, Bones took a blood sample from Sara's finger.

Bones was met by another staff member in a white lab coat who smiled at Sara but did not speak.

They all moved to a room with a large table and Sara was asked to lay on her back on the table. Over the table was a set of photos or X-rays or whatever, beginning to materialize above her.

Bones surveyed the medical data and almost immediately noted, "I can see why you have, as you say, superhuman strength. Your human medical team did an outstanding job of muscle, bone, and tissue enhancement."

"Thank you," Sara replied and thought of Matt, "*I owe that man my life.*"

"This is very good," Bones advised confidently. "We will further enhance your bone and muscle materials with much stronger elements, once your blood work and analysis results are in. If you are a compatible patient, we can begin the work today."

"Today? Now?"

"Why, yes. Is that not acceptable?"

"Bones, I'm having a hard time processing all this newness and your pace. Sorry."

"No need to apologize. Would you like to talk to Echo in a virtual state?"

"You can do this? Here?"

"Yes, of course. She can be anywhere anytime. Her virtual 'self' is simply a program."

"Oh my God."

"You can talk to her knowledge, not her person."

"I'm good, Bones. Carry on."

"Echo said you are special. She was right. You are."

That was all Sara needed to hear. She was totally on board.

A giddy Bones advised, "Okeydokey."

Sara had to laugh and think. "*More Pulse!*"

"We have made the incredibly complex… awesomely simple," Bone boasted. "By that I mean, we will conduct the surgery right now, and have you all healed and ready to leave by this time tomorrow."

"Excuse me," a shocked Sara quickly countered. "Explain. Please."

"But of course. We will put you into a coma-like state. This process will take about three minutes. My team will then perform the surgery on your arms, legs, and hips to enhance your body parts, as I noted."

Sara was getting a good dose of the future of medicine.

Bones continued emphatically. "I would estimate the surgery to take three hours and seventeen minutes, give or take a few seconds. We will evaluate the surgery results, and when all is deemed verified as designed, we will put you into our *extrapolator*. Did not Pulse explain the extrapolator?"

"No. Hell no."

"Sorry, Sara. The extrapolator is a time machine… one of many varieties that we have. It will take your body into the future about five and one-half months, so you can 'heal.' You will then return to this time frame fully healed and will have been gone but a few minutes."

"Holy cow." Sara was astonished and thought, *"This should be an episode on the Ancient Aliens series!"*

"On the next day, a therapy team will meet with you and evaluate your capabilities and your readiness for the second stage."

"Second stage?"

"Yes. Mirror neurons for learning new skills will be part of your cranial implants. This is what you would call a 'slam dunk' in sports vernacular, I believe."

Sara was speechless.

"You could learn a fighting skill or an operational skill or a new language skill is micro-seconds with these implants. Sara, I went from burning toast to a Chef de Cuisine in an instant!"

"So, Bones, I could learn Kung Fu or Tae Kwon Do or the French language in a few seconds?"

"Oh, not in seconds… Faster."

59

MIND OVER MATTER

The Bones' surgical team gathered and prepped Sara for this minimal-time, major-event surgery. She thought of a trip to the dentist or a visit to her OB/GYN doctor, but it was much different. It was an absolutely peaceful feeling.

To Sara, the actual surgery was a non-event... it was like it didn't even happen. One minute she was going to have surgery and the next minute... it was over... or so it seemed.

Whether Sara was gone for mere minutes, hours, days, or months, she couldn't tell. And, in a nice surprise, only lovely thoughts filled her mind while she was *out*.

Back from her trip through time, and with the first part of the transformation from the neural implants complete, Sara was escorted by Bones to the neurology center, where the implant work would be done.

Again, the entire prep, implant surgery and recovery took less than an hour.

After that, Bones took Sara to lunch with two of his associates, who were there to conduct a cursory analysis and patient evaluation in real-time.

This pace of fast to slow to fast, etcetera was a little disorienting to her.

Following lunch and a *thumbs up* from Bones' two colleagues, Sara was led to the training compound.

Expecting a vast, military-type training facility, Sara instead was taken to a small room with several chairs resembling her dentist office.

Bones was still her liaison and spoke, "I'll be turning you over to Link, who will explain what will happen on days three, four and five. Farewell. I have enjoyed working with you, Sara."

"It was my pleasure, Bones. My human hero is a Doctor Palmer. My Arrans' hero is Bones."

Bones smiled as he departed.

✦ ✦ ✦

Day three began with her introduction to Link, who announced, "I have reviewed your paperwork and the results of the physical transformation up until now. You are a remarkable human and I am excited to be working with you."

"Thank you, Link. What's the plan?"

"Please lay on this table while I get what you would call an EKG-like machine hooked up."

As Link attached several monitoring leads to Sara's neck and head, he said, "You do remind me of a younger Echo. You are 'to the point.' You and she seem to be similarly wired."

"Why, thanks. Echo is at the top of the mountain, for sure."

"Sara, do you have any aches or pains, either in body or mind?"

Hesitating, Sara responded. "No pain. Even with the cranial surgery and neurological impact, I feel fine. Not even a headache. You mentioned the mind?"

"Yes. I need to be sure that your mind is uncluttered and free. The energy that I am monitoring through the attached leads will answer that for me. As of now, I would say you are very ready for the next step."

"As ready as I will ever be," she figured.

"Sara, you have had a physical docking device implanted in the back of your neck."

"Yes, Bones explained the process and that it would not be visible on my neck."

"That's right. It is not. But what it will allow us to do is upload any number of programs into your brain… into your mind. You will be able to literally do anything you want to do or are faced with doing."

"Link, I feel like I am in a science fiction movie." Sara also thought, *"I don't remember any episodes of this stuff on the Sci-Fi Channel."*

"Sara, this is now science fact, and in a moment, you will see what I mean."

"So, if I get into a situation where I need to fly a starship, I get the training uploaded and go?"

"Not yet… But yes, provided you get through this intense training cycle."

"I'm ready, Link."

"I will place this headset on you and when it is engaged, you will be in a virtual reality environment that will appear to be one hundred per cent real. But it exists only in your mind."

"Whoa!"

"You will move from one training segment to another and stay there until you either master the skill or cannot advance any further. You will get three attempts to master each of the eight tasks."

Sara thought about Echo and… *"Another number eight. Capsules, training…"*

"Some of the training will involve hand-to-hand combat, some console battles like a human video game, and some will simply be physical challenges."

"Physical challenges?"

"Yes. You will actually be doing what you will be feeling… physical training in a programmed simulator. If you strike… you will feel that you struck. If you are struck, you will physically feel that strike."

"Wow."

"I am monitoring your 'vitals' and will be here to disengage if the need arises, and if your health and well-being are being compromised."

"Holy crap… this is freaking serious!"

"Sara, only your mind can tell your body if you can achieve those tasks."

"Mind over matter."

"That is correct, Sara. Very much so. Shall we begin?"

"Yes, please."

"Please relax and clear your mind. Focus on a good thought or a wonderful place or a friendly person."

"Or I'll combine those all into one image, Link."

"Never thought of that. Ready?"

Pausing a moment, Sara replied. "Ready."

✦ ✦ ✦

Sara was experiencing uploading on a major scale, but it felt so natural that even when the VR was fully engaged, Sara felt like she was on *terra firma* in the middle of an actual training complex.

This intense training process would require three grueling days, and Sara knew her physicality would be tested.

The first challenge was hand-to-hand combat. Sara was engaged in hand-to-hand combat with a single opponent, then several opponents. From that venue, she had sword fights with as many as six opposing warriors.

Following a momentary training upload, Sara fired several weapons that she had never seen before at a variety of objects and people, requiring both direct and peripheral vision.

For one venue, she dove thousands of feet into the sea, and engaged in both hand-to-hand and weaponized battles with aliens of a variety of body types and sizes… some were even reptilian in appearance.

For one challenge, she was required to run thousands of miles in mere seconds and reach a vertical leap of nearly three hundred feet. That particular event was quite odd. Sara actually could feel herself far exceeding the leap parameters... almost flying!

In her last challenge, she was suspended for several seconds as another major uploading session was underway.

When that program was successfully installed, Sara took an alien warship and engaged in a fierce space battle against four malevolent attackers.

One battle setting was as if she was in a *house of mirrors* in a carnival. The attackers relentlessly came at her from all sides, and she had to rely on both newly acquired skills and never imagined instincts.

When the VR training was over, Sara was extremely tired and physically drained and had no idea if she had been *fighting* for minutes, hours, or days.

On the final day of training, Link welcomed her back to the reality of the training center and his only comment was. "Congratulations, Miss Steele. That was an awesome performance."

"Thanks, Link. I feel pretty drained... but proud of the way I handled those events."

Sara Steele had set records in five of the eight advanced virtual reality categories, besting Echo, who had held those lofty records. That info was not divulged to Sara.

Sara had but one thought... *"How I wish my family was here to see this... especially grandad Pete."*

On the very next day, an awards ceremony was planned, as was the case with any Arrans' training participants.

With Pulse joining Sara in attendance, Sara was aware that she had reached a very high goal. She was still a little tired, but otherwise ecstatic.

When requested, Sara gave Pulse a gentle kiss and walked up to the small stage in a rather austere room, lacking any indication of fame or glory.

Once the few attendees were situated, the speaker for the ceremony announced, "We will now have the *Croix de Guerre* presentation."

Even though it was a small but energetic group of Arrans gathered, they all seemed happy for Sara and were smiling at the thought of a human being honored.

"Will the Program Master please step forward to present Sara Steele with her award."

With that comment, Pulse stood up and proceeded to meet Sara on the small stage.

This was a nice surprise, or what?

"Pulse...you?"

"Yes, this program was my creation, and I couldn't be happier to present this cross to you."

Pulse gently placed the medallion around Sara's neck. He kissed her on the cheek. She smiled.

Sara wanted to hear more about Pulse and this Master's Program... but that could wait.

Sara was awarded the Cross of War.

60

SEA OF REVELATION

Following the ceremony, Sara and Pulse returned to Tranquility Lake using Pulse's boat to again revisit his man cave.

Securing the boat, Pulse asked to see her newly awarded cross. With a big beaming smile, Sara showed Pulse her cross.

"Now, you and Echo have something else in common. First was the Battle Saber, Destiny, which is in your possession, and now the Cross of War. Congratulations!"

Sara paused and respectfully asked, "Pulse, do you have one?"

"I have what you would call an 'honorary' cross."

"What does that mean?"

"As you know from the awards ceremony, I was one of the creators of the warrior program that you just completed, so they honored me at the launch of the Master's Program."

Sara nodded, "Not surprised." She thought to herself, "*and humble, too.*"

"Since I needed to perform all the requisite tasks within the program, naturally I completed them."

"That's impressive," Sara winked.

Sara handed Pulse her chain and cross, quickly disrobed, and dove into the lake, snapping, "Beat cha!"

Pulse smiled broadly and quipped, "Aha, a race!"

Under full control, Sara knew exactly where the man cave was located and had a head start from Pulse. Being a certified scuba diver, she knew how to navigate deep water, but *freestyle* dives were never her *thing*, until now.

Roughly halfway to her target, she saw a sleek silver image of her friend, Pulse, gaining an advantage. He pulled up... embraced Sara, and they together spiraled down to the lake bottom.

Moments later, they were once again in a dry and comfortable place, both smiling brightly.

"My God, Pulse, that was exhilarating. What an unbelievable rush!"

"Sara, you were spectacular. No fear… no hesitation… just go!"

"Pulse, it was so natural, as if I had done it a thousand times. I have control of my mind and body unlike I ever dreamed I would. I can't thank you and Echo enough."

"There will come a time when you will need that speed, strength and new skill set… you will be challenged."

"I will be ready, Pulse."

"Sara, we haven't got much time. We need to start our journey back to Earth. What's your pleasure right now?"

"I want to try something, Pulse."

"Sure." Pulse was getting excited and partially aroused, given the performance of Sara, his girlfriend and athletic equal.

He was thinking about having more of that great man-cave sex and asked, "What is it that you want to try?"

Sensing his thoughts, "No, Pulse, not that… at least not right now."

Pulse relaxed and shifted gears to her current thinking.

"I want to use my skills, as you did, to create an occurrence from my memory."

"You have something in mind, don't you?"

"Yes. Yes, I do."

"Very well. Clear your mind and focus."

Sara looked inward to her mind and thoughts and did focus on a time and place. Pulse could read the extreme concentration in his new prodigy.

Within seconds, Sara recreated a clear and unmistakable scene, and it was Grandad's cabin in the Sierra Nevada Mountains.

Pulse was very pleased that Sara had now successfully used one of her new skills, combining visualization, materialization, and event horizon re-creation.

"Wow!" Pulse couldn't believe his eyes.

Sara recreated the cabin in full detail, and Pulse was overwhelmed with the depth and detail of the transformation.

"You know, Sara, I was once in Pete Stevenson's cabin. I had such admiration for that man."

Sara smiled. Then she virtually went forward in the stark cabin recreation to the exact time that the ETRT discovered the hidden alien artifacts and computer data that began the journey from informed speculation of alien existence to irrefutable truth.

"This is a very difficult image for me, Pulse. The memories are the highest-highs and the lowest-lows."

Pulse gently took her hand in complete support. He thought to himself, "*No human has ever done what she has just done.*"

Then, in a time-travel twist that Pulse did not see coming, Sara again traveled forward to the exact day and time of the missile attack that killed Paul.

"Sara, what are you doing? What the hell are you doing?"

"I'm 'seeing' something that I need to project."

"Be careful, Sara. I'm not sure you can sustain this image. It is too damn real!"

"I am feeling an event that I did not see. I am able to mentally 'time travel' back to the attack."

"What are you seeing? Is your imaging clear?"

"Yes, I have an 'eye in the sky' and everything is in front of me."

"What do you see, Sara?"

"I can visualize the origin of the missile to a launch sequence from an unrecognizable spacecraft."

"Can you describe the craft?" Pulse was stunned.

"Yes." She paused. "It is a long ship, maybe several hundred feet long, silver, but with an odd shape."

"Take your time. Describe the ship."

Sara moved her arms and hands as if to create an image she could touch.

"It has two curved launch ports on either side of the cockpit and is shaped like a… like a scorpion with a long tail that has a curved mast or tail."

As she was still describing details of the ship, Pulse contacted Echo telepathically,

<I am in my cave at Tranquility Lake with Sara.>

<You are with Sara in your romantic hideaway and you are contacting me? Is Sara all right?>

<Oh yes, more than all right.>

Sara could see that Pulse was on a telepathic discussion, and that he was clearly in a serious demeanor.

<Riddles are not my thing, Pulse. Explain.>

<Sara has recreated her grandfather's cabin in the mountains, which I expected, given her new implants and training.>

<And there is more?>

<Yes. Sara has taken that new skill and traveled back in time to the day of the attack on the cabin that killed her husband and severely injured herself.>

<That is very promising.>

<There is more…much more.>

After a brief pause, Pulse continued,

<She back-traveled to the exact time and source of the attack and described the spacecraft that launched the missile.>

<Did you recognize her description?>

<Yes. It was a reptilian battle vessel from the constellation Scorpius.>

Echo paused for a moment and responded,

<It was an elite force of the Draconian species that attacked Sara in what was their first indication of warring intention.>

61

CULINARY CREATIVITY

Michaela hadn't heard from Sara since she departed for Trappist One, but she knew that Sara was in the best hands.

Meanwhile, Michaela's project to study Darwin's Theory of Evolution, courtesy of Tiffany's research, was well underway.

With direct help from Tiffany and RJ providing consultation with several key subject-matter experts, Michaela had gathered a plethora of scientific data and quantum physics research around the Darwinian Theory of Evolution.

The three researchers were set to meet in Tiffany's home and Michaela was excited as she knocked on Tiffany's door.

"Hi Michaela. Good to see you."

"Good morning, Tiffany, likewise."

"Come on in. Where is RJ?" Tiffany asked cheerfully.

"RJ said he was sorry, but he has military obligations at the JPL that require him to work remotely. He will be available to video chat whenever we are ready."

"That will be great," Tiffany replied calmly. "Can I get you a coffee, Michaela?"

"Sure, Tiffany. Thanks. Just black, please. I brought you some of my made-from-scratch croissants."

Michaela handed Tiffany a bag of goodies that was still warm.

"Wonderful. Thanks. I know you are an awesome cook. One hot cup of coffee coming up."

As both ladies walked from the foyer to the kitchen, Michaela was preoccupied, and Tiffany could sense it.

"What's up, lady genius?"

Michaela smiled and paused a while. "Oh, just a couple things on my mind right now. Usually I can focus pretty well, but I'm having a little trouble at the moment."

As she poured Michaela a cup of her strong Italian-blend coffee and set out a couple croissants, Tiffany inquired, "Wanna share anything?"

"Of course. Nothing major, though."

Tiffany motioned to Michaela to have a seat and Michaela explained her anxiety.

"First, I'm worried about Sara and that is not normal. If ever there was a person that could take care of herself, it's Sara Steele."

"I understand, Michaela, and you guys are close. But it's not like she can pick up a phone and call you from a place forty light-years away."

"Well, when you put it that way, I guess I'm being unrealistic."

Tiffany continued emphatically. "Plus, look who she is with. The Master of the freaking Universe... that's who!"

"No kidding."

"Okay, Miss Marx, what else?"

Taking a sip of her coffee, Michaela reluctantly began. "I can't get this guy, Commander RJ Baker, out of my mind. Have you met him?"

"Nope. But the grapevine has it that he is some sort of Adonis-type mortal. Am I close?"

"Damn straight. What a hunk... and smart, too. He has a PhD in Celestial Mechanics. How cool is that?"

Tiffany nodded.

"But sexy, Tiffany... so damn sexy."

"So, Aphrodite, what cha gonna do about it?"

"Clever choice of names, Tiffany, as those two were lovers in Greek Mythology."

"I have an idea, love-struck woman, which I'd be happy to describe. Let's head over to my office and talk."

✦ ✦ ✦

As they entered Tiffany's lab-like office, Michaela was again impressed with her colleague's high-tech and awesomely equipped office.

"What's your idea, Tiffany?"

Setting down their coffees and croissants, Tiffany offered her proposal, "Okay. What is the one thing about you that no one is aware of?"

"Excuse me?"

"Michaela, what is one thing of a personal nature that you don't really share with anyone?'

"Sorry, Tiffany, but I don't get it?"

"You are an incredible cook, baker, and generally speaking a master chef, at the very least, a sous-chef."

"That may be a stretch. But what does that have to do with me and RJ?"

"Seriously? No clue? Galaxy to Michaela."

Tiffany smiled and proceeded to explain her idea, "What has become a lost female art in our world?"

"Cooking?" Michaela asked inquisitively.

"Yes, of course. In the old days, women cooked while men hunted for food. Well, maybe that's a little too far back."

"Ya think?"

Both ladies laughed at the historical reference.

"Let's face it, Michaela, women just don't cook anymore. Unless it was handed down to you, it's a lost art and guys no longer expect their lady friends to be the 'housewife' types."

"I guess you're right about that."

"So, Miss Marx, have your Adonis-guy over for a meal he will never expect nor ever forget!"

62

DARK DARWINIAN DISCONNECT

As Michaela thought about Tiffany's suggestion, she focused on the job at hand. Unpacking her case to get to the Darwin file, she announced her intentions to Tiffany, "Let's get as much baseline scientific data as we can today, so I can work with Elonis on the number crunching."

Tiffany nodded in agreement.

Michaela continued to be on point, "By my observation, and discussion with you and RJ, we might be ready for some serious analysis soon."

"Okay, Michaela. Want me to dial up Adonis?"

"Please. Serious mode now, all right?"

"Yep."

Tiffany set up the video chat with Commander Baker and within a few minutes, all three were engaged in the meeting and ready to roll.

"Hi RJ," a smiling Michaela said.

"Hi Michaela. Hi Tiffany. It's good to meet with you. How're you guys doing?"

Tiffany responded quickly, "Hello RJ. Nice to meet you. We're fine. Just talking technical stuff, of course," as Tiffany winked at Michaela with that remark.

"What's your agenda this morning, Michaela?" RJ asked directly.

"First, is this still a good time to meet?"

"Yes, it is. I had this meeting in my planner and the project guys know that I am involved in some ETRT stuff."

"Great," Michaela was ready to begin.

Tiffany offered her thoughts, "I'll capture all of our notes and place it in either a Gantt Chart-type timeline or event line, given we will be going back millions of years."

"That'll work," Michaela responded.

RJ inquired, "We are talking only about AMH, correct?"

"Yes," Michaela responded. "Only anatomically modern humans are being researched. We are looking to support human evolutionary theory via the evolutionary tree of life inferred or speculative evidence to confirm."

"Yes," answered Tiffany. "My research has a disconnect regarding that physical evidence piece."

Michaela chimed in, "Creation versus evolution and competition for survival of the fittest has been discussed zillions of times and no clear conclusion can be drawn. That's why I believe Tiffany's project is so vital."

"What are the key facts accepted today?"

"Well, RJ," Tiffany advised, "we know that our DNA does not match Neanderthals, and there is a two-hundred-thousand-year mystery whereby we have no DNA that would reflect any evolution whatsoever."

"Can you explain that mystery, Tiffany?"

"Yes… well, sort of Michaela. If we have been evolving for billions of years, why would our skull size, and more importantly, our brain size, increase noticeably over a span of only the last two hundred thousand years? That is a relatively small timeframe in evolution."

Michaela raised her eyebrows as Tiffany added a remarkable fact, "And no human skulls have yet been found that show any sort of this particular evolutionary process."

An excited RJ jumped in, "I did some reading about human chromosome two and the gene TBR1, which is responsible for an enlarged human brain. Let me get the actual data to you to download and integrate."

"Great," Tiffany replied enthusiastically.

Michaela was getting excited as her research was now in play. "I have been studying mirror neurons found in this 'newer' neocortex that are unique to the human brain. A so-called 'rosehip' neuron that controls info flow and expands consciousness is again what appears to be a non-evolutionary phenomenon."

"Whoa," snapped RJ. "That is kind of chilling."

For the next hour or so, they continued to report their findings on various aspects of DNA, gene research, chromosome understanding, rapid human brain development, and several apparent misassumptions of the Darwin Theory of Evolution.

Michaela, with an impatient sigh, added, "Okay, guys, we have been at it for over two hours, and I think I will have enough data to start crunching with Elonis."

RJ blurted, "From what I've heard about your metahuman Elonis, even my military resources can't help much."

"Nope," Michaela replied. "We're pretty much at the top of the problem-solving pyramid with Elonis. I'll let you know if I need anything, though."

"I'm gonna excuse myself and head to the kitchen." Winking at Michaela, Tiffany added, "You two can finish up here."

RJ nodded. "Fine. Thanks in advance for your continuing help."

Michaela realized that Tiffany gave her an opportunity.

"So, RJ, we really appreciate your expertise here."

"Glad I'll be able to help."

Pausing, RJ was about to say goodbye when Michaela blurted out, "Hey, I have an idea."

"What's that, Michaela?"

"How would you like to come over to my place for dinner this Saturday night?"

"I'd love to!"

"Great. Say, eight o'clock?"

"Eight is fine. I'll bring Chinese or Thai food."

"Oh no, that won't be necessary, RJ. I'll cook,"

"Really! Uh, okay."

63

DINNER AT EIGHT

RJ arrived at Michaela's high-rise condo sharply at eight o'clock and was greeted by a smiling and brightly attired Michaela Marx.

"Hi, Michaela. Cool building."

"Thanks, RJ. Come on in."

The tall, statuesque Michaela wore a conservative slip dress in shades of green, the lightest of which perfectly matched her hazel eyes. She wore large hoop earrings of tiny diamonds to match her sparkling silver platform shoes that placed her eye-to-eye in height with her dinner guest.

As a smiling RJ stepped inside, he handed Michaela a bottle of wine from his neoprene wine sleeve. "Assuming we are still having sea bass tonight, this is one of my favorite Cabs."

"Thank you. Yes, we are having one of my favorite dishes, Drum, a white sea-bass which is not technically a bass. It is white-fleshed and meaty and low in fat."

"Too much detail, dummy," Michaela thought to herself.

"Healthy and delicious, I'm sure."

"Yes, RJ, it is a healthy choice and mild-tasting, which makes it the perfect flavor carrier."

"Wow, Michaela, I never thought of this super-smart astrophysicist as being a gourmet cook. How'd that happen?"

"Well," a much more relaxed Michaela said, "I use my cooking time to think and plan. Everyone has their technique… that is mine. What's yours?"

"I'm into space exploration and do my thinking in all of those opportunities that give me solitude."

Michaela knew exactly what RJ meant by that. "Yes, there is a big difference between loneliness and solitude."

"Exactly." A very relaxed RJ offered, "My contribution to dinner tonight is this 2017 Hess Collection Small Block Reserve Series Cabernet."

"Yes, we will definitely open that wine. Come on into the kitchen where I have some snacks. I'll get my wine opener."

Her not-so-subtle Paris perfume Fracas left a trail of intoxicating scent as she floated ahead of him into the kitchen.

RJ was dressed in his signature military casual dress. He favored black and had black jeans, a white, crewneck shirt, and a light aviator jacket that was black and trimmed in silver. A silver Space Force cross necklace with two similarly matching bracelets screamed successful military man. At over six feet tall, and with GQ looks, Commander RJ Baker was certainly a gentleman that garnered *second looks.*

"Let me take your jacket and show you around my place. Would you like something to drink?"

"Just some water with a little lemon for now would be great. Thanks."

As Michaela poured the commander a cool glass of water, he inquired, "You are on the top level of this building, floor forty-four. You don't mind the height?"

"Oh gosh, no. I really like being this high. I can see everything. And, our pool is on the roof, which is close for me. I like to do night swims."

As Michaela walked through her condo, RJ was marveling at her memorabilia and photographs. Many were recognizable to him.

"On the left is my bedroom, which has a great view as well, and on my right is my somewhat cramped office… lots going on these days."

"Your view is breathtakingly beautiful. Your condo is very impressive and very comfortable."

RJ thought, "*Would like to spend some more time in that bedroom with this foxy young woman.*"

"Thank you. Let's head back to the kitchen, as I have some work to do there."

✦ ✦ ✦

As they walked toward the kitchen, Michaela got a text from Tiffany. "Excuse me, RJ, I have a text from a colleague that I probably should take."

"No problem. I'll just enjoy the sunset from your balcony."

> "Hey, girl, what's up?"
> "Just getting dinner ready."
> "Is the incredible hunk there?"
> "Yes."
> "Did you show him your bedroom?"

"Yes. I mean, no. Gotta go."

"For sure. Enjoy the evening"

"Will do."

As they finished their brief texting, Michaela was back in the kitchen and RJ joined her. "So, Miss Master Chef, what can I do to help?"

"Here's the opener. Get our Cab ready, okay?"

"Got it. What's the plan?"

"I like pan seared. It's a quick cooking method and it produces a flavorful, crisp exterior, which acts as a little barrier allowing the fish to remain tender on the inside as it cooks. I always prefer a large cast iron skillet which does well to transmit the heat evenly."

Michaela had the skillet on the stove top as RJ poured wine into the two glasses on the counter.

"Before searing in olive oil, I first give the sea bass here a quick coating of Mediterranean spices, ground coriander, cumin, and sweet Aleppo pepper."

"What do you serve with this scrumptious sea bass?"

"My serving is both a part-Italian and part-Greek addition... a bright garlic and bell pepper medley. Not just a pretty embellishment, trust me. The sweet peppers, combined with the salty Kalamata olives, are the tastiest complement to this wonderful sea bass recipe."

RJ moved closer to Michaela and murmured, "Miss Marx, you are amazing."

With that remark, RJ gave Michaela a quick kiss on the cheek.

Michaela smiled, "Okay, dinner is served, Commander."

They sat down to a most enjoyable and unforgettable dinner. As they were finishing, Michaela put on her serious face. "Ya know, RJ, we have a ton of data on that Tiffany expose concerning Darwin's Theory."

"Yes. The first glance was remarkable... and quite scary."

"I will be working with our metahuman Elonis next week and hope to have a conclusion of sorts by the following week."

"That would be a super-quick turnaround, Michaela. I'll send you my thoughts next week."

"That would be great."

"Meanwhile, I have something to ask you."

Michaela was getting excited and nervous. She knew that he enjoyed the dinner... because it was an awesome dinner. So far, all had worked out well.

But she had a laser thought. *"What does he have in mind? How do I look? Does he find me attractive? Sex?"*

"I'm listening," she said wistfully.

"You're okay with heights, right?"

"Well, yes… I guess. What do you have in mind?"

"Have you ever skydived?"

"A few times."

"Well, I'd really like to re-pay you for this lovely dinner."

"RJ, that isn't necessary."

She then thought excitedly, *"Yes, it is!"*

"Okay. But the ball is in my court."

Pausing a moment, RJ continued, "I have been into skydiving since my college days and I love it. I'd like to treat you to a dive you will never forget."

"But I have skydived a few times already."

"Michaela, nothing like this."

Coming back down to Earth after her intimacy expectations were shelved, "Like what?"

"Not a typical sky dive, Michaela."

"You have my curiosity aroused. What then?"

"A high-altitude space jump!"

64

GALACTIC VOYAGER

Three days later, Commander Baker was at a remote landing strip on the out-skirts of the military base in Roswell, New Mexico, waiting for Michaela to arrive. She would be flying in on Scott Woods' private jet piloted by the dear friend of the ETRT, Ken Darragh.

Right on schedule, Michaela's plane landed and taxied over to the small terminal and refueling stations.

RJ walked over to greet them.

Michaela exited the plane, flight bag in hand, walked down the portable stairs arranged by an airman, and gave RJ a big hug.

"It's great to see you. Good flight?"

"Oh yes. Captain Darragh is one of our favs."

"Thank you for that incredible meal, Michaela. It was awesome."

"I'm glad you enjoyed it, RJ," she replied. "*I had much more in mind,*" she thought somewhat disappointedly.

Moments later, Captain Darragh exited the plane and introduced himself to Commander Baker, "Hello Commander Ken Darragh. Nice to meet you."

"The honor is all mine. I've heard about your courage and accomplishments in getting the ETRT and its mission to where it is today."

"Why, thank you, Commander. You've got quite a reputation yourself."

"Well, some people call me a bit of an overachiever, I guess, Captain. Where's the Galactic Voyager?"

"She'll be in around fifteen hundred hours tonight, leaving from the hanger in Fremont. You guys will be all set for departure first thing in the morning. Well, gotta go and take care of my plane. Good to meet you and all my best tomorrow."

"Thanks. And really appreciate you bringing Michaela out."

"She's a special someone, Commander."

Exchanging smiles, the two left Captain Darragh and headed over to the barracks and mess hall.

"You okay bunking here tonight?"

"Oh yeah. This is perfect. Not many people and not many questions."

"Good point, Michaela."

They walked over to the dimly lit mess hall, where nearly everyone on the base had already eaten. Fixing themselves plates, RJ was anxious to get the next day's agenda out for Michaela to understand.

Sitting down, RJ began, "We will be doing a wingsuit, HALO tandem, free-all jump from about thirty thousand feet."

"HALO. What's HALO?"

"HALO stands for High Altitude, Low Opening, and it describes our tandem dive."

"Okay. Thanks. There is much more, I'm sure."

"Michaela, normal skydiving altitudes are around ten to twelve thousand feet. You said you are fine with free falls."

"Yes, it seems pretty natural to get your bearings and orientation."

"Well, Michaela, the wingsuit simply gives you more control. I'll have time to explain everything involved in the jump and both of our suits tomorrow."

"I trust you, RJ, and I'm a quick learner."

"The Galactic Voyager's mother ship will get us to altitude; and according to your friend Scott's crew, we will jump from the rear of the craft. I'll go over everything tomorrow so it's fresh in your mind."

"That makes sense, RJ." Michaela thought, "*This guy is smart, curious, serious, and fun. Hot damn.*"

"Michaela, you said you've done several dives, but none lately. Did you not like the sport?"

"Oh no. That wasn't it at all. I actually did like sky diving a lot. It was flat-out exhilarating."

Pausing, "Sara and I have also scuba dove before… deep dives, night dives, drift dives, and even cave dives. She and I are both certified. But nothing compares to my skydiving. Nothing!"

"So, why did you stop?"

With a slight grimace, Michaela scowled a bit with her answer, "I was dating a guy that had a passion for the sport. He had like seven hundred sky-dives, I think."

"That's a lot. May I ask what happened?" RJ asked with a smile.

Michaela thought about her answer a moment before she said, "I guess he was just into diving more than he was... into me."

At this point, guy and girl sexual thoughts collided...

RJ knew that there were times to be silent... this was one of those times.

"So, RJ, we are jumping from a spaceship at thirty thousand feet, which is pretty darn high. Gosh, that's the height of Mount Everest!"

"It is Michaela. It's literally at the limit for commercially allowed diving... that ceiling is twenty-eight thousand feet. The FAA requires both the pilots and the plane to be certified, which we will not be."

"So, that's why we are here in Roswell, away from regulations?"

"Yep, Michaela. You okay with that?"

"Sure. I hang around with a bunch of renegades, as you know."

"Or so I've heard."

"And, RJ, you have done a ton of these, right?"

Smiling, RJ uttered, "Not seven hundred, but over one hundred high-altitude space jumps."

"So, high-altitude jumps have unique requirements?"

"Oh, yes. Oxygen is required and a special breathing mask and headgear is required."

"How high have you jumped?"

Pausing a few seconds, RJ winked at Michaela and responded, "I have jumped from one hundred and fifty-eight thousand feet."

Michaela was doing some mental calculations...

"Holy crap. That's thirty miles!"

65

LEAP OF FAITH

The next morning Michaela and RJ walked from the barracks to the mess hall as RJ received a text message from the Galactic Voyager regarding the plane's ETA.

"It looks like they are only about an hour out, so we will have plenty of time to grab some breakfast and head over to the terminal."

"That's great, RJ. I didn't realize you knew Scott Woods and was up to speed with his Voyager craft. The guy's got money, brains, and ambition, for sure."

"Yes, Michaela, and to fund and oversee the ETRT's vast resource challenges, you couldn't be in better hands."

"RJ, did you hear about what happened to his wife, Amanda?"

"Yes, I did. What a hellish ordeal. But again, your team literally came to the rescue."

"Yeah, not a habit we want to get into…"

As they finished their simple meal, they left the mess hall and walked a couple hundred yards to the terminal and flight training school.

Once inside, and with no one else in the buildings, RJ led Michaela over to the rack with the special diving suits.

A curious Michaela, recalling last night's comment, asked RJ about his space jump from thirty miles high, "Well, it required several key variables that needed to go perfectly well. I had to don a pressurized space suit and take a helium-filled balloon on a vertical ride that took nearly three hours."

Michaela was already impressed with this daredevil of a space diver.

"When I reached my target altitude, a small explosive charge fired and cut me loose for my rapid plunge toward Earth."

"Oh my God," Michaela uttered in total surprise.

"I was in freefall for about six minutes, reaching speeds in excess of eight hundred miles per hour, and I was going so fast that my body broke the sound barrier, creating a boom that the guys on the ground heard."

"You gotta be nuts!"

"Michaela, I am a curious guy that is always pushing the limits… and I like speed."

"So, then your chute opened?"

"Yes, my main parachute opened at seventeen thousand feet. I landed in a field about six miles from where we are right now."

"I Googled high-altitude jumps, and yours isn't even listed, much less reported as a record jump."

"Well, I'm glad you took the time to look into space diving, but my entire jump was done without any knowledge or approval of the government or military. I applied for the jump and it was denied."

"Why?"

"They told me it was too dangerous. The balloon was provided by a division of *Stargate LTD*."

"That figures, RJ."

"Yep, Scott's rather cool equipment, again. He is building some wild flying machines in his Fremont, California, facility."

✦ ✦ ✦

Out of the window, Michaela and RJ could see that the Galactic Voyager had landed and was taxiing over to the main terminal.

"It will take them thirty to forty minutes to get the plane refueled and ready for us. Let me show you the equipment, and we'll go over the flight plan and jump plan."

Michaela was a lot less nervous, given what her flyboy had just described as a heart-stopping space leap.

"It will take the plane about forty-five minutes to get to altitude and circle a bit to get us into a reasonable, Roswell drop zone."

Michaela is thinking… *"Roswell. How fitting."*

"We will suit up as soon as we are about ten to fifteen minutes from drop. The white suit and helmet are yours, and you will have this camera that attaches to your arm."

RJ pulled out a Go-REAL, state-of-the-art sport camera.

"A helmet-mounted camera will also be engaged. I'll be in the black suit hooked in tandem to yours, and I will be attached to the chute, which I have already packed myself."

Again, Michaela was reassured.

"It may look complicated, Michaela, but I have done these so many times that the dive prep is kind of dull… but the dive itself is unlike anything you could imagine.

✦ ✦ ✦

The pilot of the Voyager walked into the terminal hanger and introduced himself, "Hi, I'm Captain Voss and I'll be taking you up today."

"Hi, Captain Voss. I'm Commander RJ Baker and this is Michaela Marx."

They all shook hands and Captain Voss immediately asked RJ about flight clearance.

"Yes. I am logging this flight as a test of a tandem evacuation chute for emergency-only deployment. Paperwork is already filed."

With that, the three left the hanger and got on board the Voyager. Moments later it was taking off and Michaela was getting a bit anxious.

Sensing her apprehension, RJ explained the rather simple space-dive program, "We will deploy via the belly of the aircraft using the ramp that will be opened by forty-five degrees. My release belt will hold us until we get the green light that our speed has been dialed back to a safe exit speed."

Michaela listened and nodded approval as they donned their spacesuits.

"We will enjoy about a two-minute free fall that will reach speeds around two hundred miles per hour that you will sense, but will not upset our orientation or forward direction."

"RJ, I am so ready for this," a confident Michaela announced.

About fifteen minutes later, Captain Voss came on the intercom and said, "Okay, get yourselves suited, strapped, and ready. We will be at our drop zone in less than ten minutes."

The two divers stood up and walked over to the top of the ramp. Moments later, the ramp began to open and a yellow light appeared.

The ramp stopped at a 45-degree angle and the green light appeared.

Disconnecting his safety harness, the two jumpers were gone and in freefall.

Michaela was seeing a sight unlike any other. The Earth from that altitude was breathtaking. RJ guided the pair securely through their two-minute freefall and then deployed the massive parachute as they began their quiet and steady descent to the ground.

From unbelievably fast to serene and calm… the last part of the descent was magical.

Michaela felt an overwhelming state of harmony and peace.

"This is the best day of my life!"

66

SEX, DIVES, AND VIDEOTAPE

With yesterday's incredible skydive vividly etched into their minds, RJ invited Michaela over to his place to have dinner, view the video of the dive, and enjoy another wonderful evening together.

Michaela arrived at RJ's house in a V-neck, sleeveless, ribbon-belt, floral-print evening dress with black open-toe stiletto heels. A very tall, beautiful woman was standing before RJ… statuesque as a runway model, if ever he saw one.

"Oh my, Michaela, you look absolutely stunning."

As RJ gave Michaela a kiss, she replied, "Thank you. And thanks for having me over."

RJ took her hand and they walked from the foyer into the living room. A contemporary home, it had the looks of a man's house, but not excessively masculine.

"I love your dress and must say that my home looks much better with you in it."

That remark surprised Michaela, "Thank you, RJ, for both compliments."

Michaela thought longingly, *"I like being in his home… but I'd like much more!"*

"Can I fix you a drink?"

"Sure, that would be great. And I'd love a tour of your gorgeous home."

"Of course, Michaela. I know you like a good cab and I have one here for you to try."

Michaela followed RJ into the kitchen where a bottle of Chappellet 2020 Hideaway Vineyard Estates Cabernet Sauvignon was chilled. RJ poured a taste for Michaela and waited.

"RJ, this is divine. I love it."

RJ finished pouring Michaela's glass, poured one for himself, and smiled. "Tour time."

They moved slowly through the house as RJ showed Michaela the dining room, his office, a fitness room that was well equipped, a media room with viewing equipment and seating for movies, and the master bedroom.

Every room in the house was light, bright, and decorated with assorted military and space mementos. Each room lighting system was voice-activated.

Michaela, looking at his bedroom and that enormous bed, thought to herself, *"I'd really like to 'mess up' his neatly made bed."*

From the tour, they moved back to the kitchen where he had a wonderful seafood dinner planned.

"I know you love seafood, Michaela, so I have prepared something that I hope you'll find a little different and enjoyable."

He led Michaela over to the stove top and she could already smell the wonderful aroma of his dinner selection.

"Okay, chef-of-the-night, what cha got?"

"This is one of my favorites. It's a Furikake Salmon Bowl. Seared salmon seasoned with Furikake, served with sesame cabbage, avocado, shiitakes, and rice. Let's fill our bowls here and sit down in the dining room. I'll bring the wine bottle."

Following a very enjoyable dinner, the pair compared cooking notes, as they were both no slouches in the kitchen. They took their bowls back to the kitchen, refilled their wine glasses, and headed to the viewing room to watch the space-dive video.

Glancing at his beautiful house guest, RJ set up the video and thought to himself, *"This is going to be a great night... I hope!"*

As they watched the video, RJ had the space jump timed to a celestial music track... what a special effect.

"Wow, this guy thinks of everything," Michaela thought as she listened to the track.

As the video ended, RJ put his arm around Michaela, and she responded by turning into him and running her hand through his hair. They kissed firmly and passionately for a couple minutes.

RJ stood, picked his lady up, and carried her to the bedroom. He placed her on the bed, removed her shoes, and removed his shirt and shoes. She knew he was going to kiss her, but when his hands surrounded her face with a gentle kiss, his dark, silky hair fell forward, and her temperature sizzled like melting butter.

He placed his hands upon Michaela's hips, and the gentle kiss became wet and passionate. Stopping for a moment and turning to his nightstand, RJ touched a remote key that began the soft, flowing music of gentle rain and utter relaxation.

Returning to kiss Michaela, and with his hand slipping fingers through her hair, he said, "I have been starved for you since we met... but especially since that body-on-body sensual feeling of yesterday."

Michaela was getting aroused, and... she could see her man was as well. He slowly descended onto her body like a gorgeous cloud, bracing himself with one hand so as not to place too much weight on her lovely frame.

They embraced, and then rolled over to where she was on top of him. Michaela let RJ move her dress straps away from her shoulders with his fingers, exposing her bra.

They kissed again and Michaela slipped out of her dress and bra, leaving her with only the tiniest bikini briefs. RJ had already stripped down to his black, silky boxers and the *rain*, as if sensing a sexual drought, which set the magnetic mood immediately.

As she settled over him, her warm body and trembling legs were feeling his big, strong hands on her thighs, positioning his boxers in contact with her bikini briefs. She removed both items and used her hand to guide his throbbing manhood into place.

Her mind, body, and soul opened wide, to soak in his manliness. Moments later, he was in... and they were both on fire, she writhing in pleasure and he with his arms around a goddess and a soul mate... an orgasmic leap of faith and love.

Michaela, clenching the last moments of her sex against his... thought ecstasy.

Several minutes following a complete physical relaxation and with RJ's warm body pressed against hers, Michaela thought longer term, *"Hot sex after a wild space jump... this is a routine a girl could get used to!"*

67

ALIEN INTERVENTION

Two days later, Michaela, Tiffany, and RJ met at the main conference room of the ETRT to discuss and present their findings on the DNA-focused Darwinian Theory of Evolution.

Michaela and RJ came together and were obviously sharing a funny story or some enjoyable humor.

Elonis joined them with soft drinks and a few snacks. Tiffany was anxious to get the scoop on Michaela's space jump.

"Well, space cowgirl, how did your space jump go?"

"Space cowgirl... how apropos," Michaela thought as RJ winked.

RJ was intrigued as to how Michaela would reply.

"It was the most exhilarating and unbelievable experience ever. You can't describe it... you'd need to be there... to do it."

"Michaela did terrific," RJ chimed in firmly. "This lady is fearless and so determined. It was a great experience for me as well."

Elonis added an additional perspective. "We were tracing her vitals the whole time. They were very good."

Switching back to the meeting at hand, Elonis was her usual serious self. "Now, the subject matter info is ready to discuss."

With the fun stuff behind, it was on to the meeting agenda.

Elonis teed up the presentation on the large conference-room screen, and she had all of the portable devices programmed to pick up each slide and create a consistent file.

Michaela was still thinking about her wonderful adventure two days ago... and most recently, last night, as Tiffany muttered, "Okay, space lady, anytime now..."

"Yes. Of course. First, I want to thank Elonis for the amazing job of crunching tons of numbers to get to where we are today."

"It was very satisfying, Michaela. It is what I do."

"Nonetheless, you are an invaluable asset that we often take for granted."

RJ glanced over to Michaela and smiled. He was also thinking about how much he enjoyed their last two days.

A now focused Michaela began, "Our mission was to consider only the anatomically modern humans, or AMH, and within the evolutionary tree of life, is there inferred or speculative evidence to support human evolution. This was the original premise that Tiffany gave us."

All nodded and Michaela continued, "If you look at the first two graphs, you will see that the standard model of our origin millions of years ago is broken."

Elonis had the graphs displayed.

"Our DNA does not match Neanderthals at all, and it appears that the current human species interbred with Neanderthals."

"So," Tiffany conjectured with a smile and nod, "we simply shared Earth with Neanderthals… not evolved from them."

RJ then offered his research on skeletal remains.

"If you look at slide number three, there is a noticeable absence in human skulls found up to a period about two hundred thousand years ago."

With a laser pointer, RJ focused on a particular time frame. "And those 'newer skulls' were longer and the brains within those skulls were larger."

Michaela added excitedly, "Yes, it is as if modern humans appeared suddenly, two hundred thousand years ago with the capabilities and cranial capacity that we have today. How, I might ask?"

This startling revelation was as thought-provoking as any info could have been. Michaela then gave credit to her super metahuman friend, "Elonis uncovered a remarkable fact that appears on the next slide, and I'll let Elonis explain."

"Thank you, Michaela. There is now quite a mystery regarding human chromosome number two. One gene alone is eight per cent of human DNA in each cell. It is called gene TBR1, and it is responsible for the enlarged human brain, again, only traceable back two hundred thousand years."

RJ offered a foundation perspective, "Let's refer to that two hundred thousand year period as the 'new' period going forward."

There was no pushback.

Michaela interjected, "Gene TBR 1 determines our capacity for emotion, sympathy, empathy, compassion, and likely the self-regulation of our biology 'on demand.' Also, mirror neurons found in the 'new' neocortex are completely unique to the human brain."

Elonis nodded and eagerly added, "And the so-called 'rosehip' neuron is unique to this 'new' brain."

Michaela again explained, "The 'rosehip' neuron is remarkable. It regulates and controls the flow of info to the specific portion of the brain to facilitate and expand consciousness, and it is only found in the human brain."

"Excuse me," RJ advised, "but I have a text message to take that is important. Just give me five minutes."

With that, Elonis began to refresh everyone's drinks.

✦ ✦ ✦

"Commander, we have the DNA test results
back that you requested."
"The one from the astronaut?"
"Yes. The incident involving the astronaut and the spacewalk."
"What did you find?"
"The DNA taken after the spacewalk incident
does not match the astronaut's baseline DNA."
"What conclusion can be drawn?"
"We can't explain our results.
The DNA seemed to have been altered."
"And you are 100% certain of your findings?"
"Yes."
"Thank you."

✦ ✦ ✦

Returning to the meeting, a somewhat preoccupied RJ asked, "Sorry everyone, where were we?"

Michaela glanced at her Adonis-in-motion and continued her presentation, "The next series of slides are timelines and scientific analyses of the human chromosome two and arguably cannot be interpreted by any other explanation than the following…"

Michaela paused to get everyone's attention.

"This 'new' chromosome is an indicator of an ancient DNA fusion of two unique ancestral and alien chromosomes that are not seen in nature… therefore, not natural."

An excited Tiffany inquired, "Are you suggesting that these chromosome mutations strongly indicate intentions and imply purpose?"

"Yes, Tiffany. Yes, I do."

"The data complies," snapped Elonis.

"You can infer from that one slide," RJ added, "that the altered DNA had resulted in a fifty percent growth in the human brain that wasn't explainable in the theory of evolution."

With an audible sigh, Michaela advised rather calmly, "We obviously have an ancient DNA fusion. The timing, precision, and specific genes being modified suggests something occurred beyond evolution from two hundred thousand years ago."

Following a short pause, Michaela concluded her presentation with icing on the *evolution cake.*

"For seventy-five million years, there was no physical indication of any evolutionary change in chromosomes… then, two hundred thousand years ago, massive, random-like changes to our 'new' brain and 'new' capabilities."

"There is a fascinating quote from British astrophysicist, Sir Fred Hoyle."

"What is that quote, Tiffany?"

"The odds of today's human DNA forming randomly are the equivalent of a tornado sweeping through a junkyard… and assembling a Boeing 747 from the scattered debris."

Michaela quickly interjected, "My God, do you know what this all means?"

After a short pause… RJ replied confidently, **"The only conclusion that you can draw is *Alien Intervention!*"**

68

WEAPON OF MASS DESTRUCTION

Sara had not yet returned from her Trappist One training, but Echo and Pulse had gathered enough info on the approaching magnetic wave to call for a meeting with President Sullivan. It was now less than ninety days until Earth impact.

POTUS arranged for a meeting with Michaela, Commander Baker and the Arrans' contingent at St. John's Episcopal Church, one block from the White House and often called the Church of the Presidents.

Arriving at the church at nine o'clock PM, with minimal security, President Sullivan dismissed all but three of his security team. He knew what was about to happen, and he wanted to maintain as much secrecy as possible.

"So, you and Commander Baker participated in a taxpayer funded test of HALO space suits, eh?"

"Yes, Mr. President," Michaela laughed, knowing POTUS knew everything.

"I would have enjoyed that dive when I was younger."

"Tell ya what," RJ offered seriously. "Let's you and I do a space dive sometime soon, okay?"

"I would really love that. As soon as we get some idea about this incoming destructive magnetic wave, maybe we can figure something out."

"Michaela, have you heard from Sara?"

"No. You know where she is, right?"

"Yes and no," the President replied with a frown. "I know what I was told... just find it hard to believe."

"Well, Pulse and she should be back on Earth next week," Michaela advised, smiling.

"Our reality here seems so dull and boring compared to what is out in our universe," the President uttered.

With that comment the *what is out in our universe* point became apparent.

With little fanfare, a soft haze appeared in the middle of the church's vestibule. From a fuzzy image to two people in mere seconds, Echo and Vibe appeared.

"Hello, all," Echo said, managing a brief smile. "Vibe and I are pleased that we could meet you here today."

"Hello, Echo. We are happy to have you here," the President said.

"Michaela, Sara sends her best," Echo offered, glancing at Sara's BFF.

"She is good?"

"Yes, Michaela. Sara is exceeding our expectations… their expectations. From what I am told, she has earned the *Croix de Guerre*, or Cross of War."

Pausing, Echo spoke forcefully, "She is now *Sara Steele, Arrans Battle Warrior.*"

Silent for only a moment as Echo wasted little time in updating the group, "We have info regarding the magnetic wave."

"Yes, Echo, that's why we are here," the President replied.

"As you may know, we were able to penetrate the wave by creating a wormhole and launched an exploratory satellite with a strong telescope designed to determine the origin of the wave."

"Were you successful?"

"Not yet, Mister President," Echo advised. "We hope to have the origin located soon… maybe within days. Having gone through the wave, we do have our first evidence for potential damage from that magnetic wave."

Vibe interjected, "We have a ninety-nine-point-five probability of discovering the origin of the power surge within the next thirty-six hours."

"Thank you, Vibe," Echo responded.

"Do you have any ideas, Echo?"

"Well, Commander Baker, our recon team that crunches data thinks the machine that launched the power surge did so from the near-Earth asteroid known as Apophis. That would make sense as the asteroid would be passing through a gravitational keyhole that would accelerate the wave."

RJ chimed in, "But that asteroid is only about four hundred meters wide. That's relatively small to be launching that type of firepower."

"That is correct, Commander, and you are most knowledgeable." Echo was pleased at RJ's knowledge and input.

"This could be good news," Echo continued. "We believe the surge is the work of an elite faction of the Draconian species, an evil alien race that has apparently set its sights on Earth. We will get into that issue later."

"What's the good news, Echo?"

"The good news, Michaela, is that this would not be anything close to their worst weapon. I believe, and many of my team believes, that this power surge, although still a possible catastrophic event, is meant to determine the level of Earth's defensive technology."

"Whoa, does that make sense?" responded the President. "Do you have a theory regarding their strategy, Echo?"

"Yes, Mister President. We believe that the Dracs have no desire to destroy Earth and likely need Earth's minerals, resources, land mass, people for labor… we just don't know any of this with any degree of certainty just yet."

POTUS was getting a lesson in the new normal and was worried.

"Echo, do you have a plan yet?"

Vibe smiled and thought to himself. *"Echo always has a plan."*

"Yes, Mister President. We first must destroy the machine at the source of the surge. Once we have its location determined, we can arrange for its destruction."

"Will that be a problem, Echo?"

"No, sir. We must then create a countermeasure for the approaching wave."

The President asked hesitantly, "Won't the destruction of the machine at the source take care of the wave?"

Sensing RJ's interest, Echo glanced over to him and said, "Commander?"

"Mister President, the machine will no longer send out any destructive power surges, but the magnetic wave in route to Earth will not be affected. It will continue until it hits our planet or is destroyed in route… or destroyed hitting Earth."

"For the love of God!" President Sullivan was visibly upset.

Echo quickly added, "We don't know yet if it is an enhanced radiation weapon, a fission wave, or simply a strong magnetic weapon that would render the entire planet's infrastructure inoperative."

RJ responded with specifics, "Mister President, that would be a disaster. All of the electric grids, communication, computers, power sources, lighting, and all things energy related could be destroyed."

Sensing the President's concern, Echo advised calmly, "We believe we have a countermeasure established that involves an EMP, or electro-magnetic pulse, that can be greater than the oncoming wave, and be used defensively. That is what we are working on at this time."

RJ added encouragingly, "That would be a logical countermeasure."

The President, still nervous, asked curiously, "And if that doesn't work, Echo?"

Michaela scowled and spoke, **"Possibly the end of humanity as we know it!"**

69

ORGANIZED CHAOS

Michaela's words brought a collective silence to the group.

As Echo surveyed the quiet of the church and was reading the body language of those around her, she said to the President, "Could I have some one-on-one time with you?"

"Of course."

POTUS bid farewell to Michaela and RJ, and Vibe zapped himself elsewhere. President Sullivan and Echo moved to a small antechamber, so they could talk in private.

The President began with a question, "In Dubai, you announced to the world that you were leaving Earth for a while to address issues regarding other civilizations in our solar system or possibly in our known universe."

"That is correct. That was our intention."

"So, Echo, in addition to this magnetic wave, what changed your plans?"

"I'm going to address that issue now. Our priorities have changed regarding Earth and its current potential extinction."

"Extinction? What the…"

"Yes, Mister President, and that is no exaggeration."

Echo began with a startling statement that she would use to explain her thoughts on the issues at hand and what is at the essence of the world's problems, "If someone or something were to introduce a little anarchy, upset the established order… everything becomes chaos! That is at the core of what you are facing today."

The President, respectful as always, was listening.

"Before I get into some important details, I still want to meet your Vice President, Samantha Worthington."

"Echo, I did make arrangements for her to head over from her office whenever you are ready."

"Thank you."

"Echo, what would be the nature of your meeting with her?"

"Just a hunch and to follow up some concern that Sara mentioned to me regarding astronaut Worthington's space accident."

"Fine. That's good enough reason for me. Truth is… I'm not sure if I can even trust her."

Echo could see the seriousness in the President's comment.

"Let's begin with the terrorist attack on the North and South Poles a couple years ago. Those explosions not only destroyed irreplaceable and critically needed land masses, but it accelerated the effects of climate change resulting in advancing global warming by decades."

"Yes, and the human toll and economic toll from global sea level rise has been enormous."

"The cabin attack in the Sierra Nevada Mountains that severely injured Sara and killed her husband was a terrorist attack."

"Yes, Echo, and we still don't know who was responsible."

"I can now shed some light on the perpetrators of the attack."

"You know?"

"Yes, and all of what I will tell you ties many loose ends together."

The President was beginning to grasp where Echo was going with her montage of evil.

"There have been several nuclear missile interruptions or absolute shutdowns within many countries that have nuclear capability. I will go into the source of those interventions."

Cameron sat back with arms folded.

"Now, you still have the Covid-19 pandemic, which continues to wreak havoc on this planet. This was an engineered, biological weapon that is still mutating to this day. It was designed in such a way that no current human technology could cure it… and that has been the case."

"But…"

"Please, Mister President, I will recap all of this very soon." POTUS nodded.

"There has been no vaccine found yet, and never would have been without our intervention. It took our leap into the future to secure the vaccine, which I stated at an earlier meeting, and has been in distribution protocol ever since."

"And we thank you."

"And, finally, this destructive magnetic wave headed to Earth. This has become our number-one priority, of course."

"I do believe you have connected most of the dots, Echo."

"Yes. Yes, I have. There are three alien species now on Earth, and their agendas are quite different. The *Greys* are friends of ours and have been on your planet for many thousands of years."

"Yes, Echo, you introduced Aeon, leader of the *Greys* to us at our meeting with Congress."

"Yes. Among other things, they powered down the nukes to avoid wars over the years and are responsible for most of your abductions. They also, as you know, returned your Apollo Eighteen crew before that crew was abducted by an evil alien species."

"And that is leading to what we would likely refer to as the dark side?"

"For sure, Mister President."

"There are two evil alien cultures that have now targeted Earth for various reasons, and that was not evident during the Dubai encounter."

"Two?"

"Yes, Sir, there are two alien species that we have encountered many times, and as of now, they are making their presence known on this planet."

Pausing, Echo continued with a very serious tone of voice. "One species we call the Dracs, from the Alpha-Draconis star system. They are a very dangerous reptilian caste that can live on the surface or subterranean. They attacked the Stevenson cabin and tried to abduct the Apollo Eighteen crew."

The president reacted expressively, "Dear God!"

"The Dracs are responsible for the power surge wave headed toward Earth."

The President took a deep sigh.

"The second species we call the Denon, likely now found in the Constellation of Scorpius, some twenty-two light years away. I believe they are led by their leader who has now taken the name Scorpio; and who, with his group of terrorists, were likely responsible for the attack on the polar regions."

"And that is why you wanted them sequestered in Colorado."

"Yes. We need to keep our eyes on them. They are extremely violent and are what we call an entangled culture, absorbing many similar, but smaller, species as they move through the galaxy."

"Echo, this is the mass extinction possibility that you were referring to?"

"It is one of two mass extinction possibilities facing your Earth!"

70

ΛLTERED DNΛ

With that sobering thought, President Sullivan knew that Echo was about to share more devastating information.

"I am sorry to burden you with such dire thoughts, but we need to work together if we are to save the planet."

"My gosh… save the planet. I always thought our demise would be due to man-made calamities."

"Well, that gets me to the second mass-extinction possibility."

Waiting to get Cameron's full attention, Echo continued, "Your planet is dying. There are many contributors to this dilemma, and that is why we brought the *Eight Capsules*. We must find a way for world leaders to understand the technology behind them and implement the solutions.

"You and I will spend some time discussing a number of critical success factors and build a consensus for implementable solutions. But for now, I see a number of socio-political needs to be addressed."

"Please, Echo, go ahead."

"You need baselines for governments, countries, and leading nations to focus on world order. It is the only way you can measure progress being made.

"You must remove the myths and replace them with new, pure facts. Let your scientists and technology leaders dictate policy and procedures.

"You must consider a groundbreaking, global management doctrine, a current Earth's Magna Carta.

"Before any democratic fabric can be developed, you must consider a socialist state."

That one baffled the President, who grimaced, but still listened patiently, and thought, *"That isn't gonna happen."*

"Political and economic conspiracies must be identified and flushed out, and your secret space program needs to be revealed."

"Hell, I may not know as much about our secret space program as she does," thought an overwhelmed President Sullivan.

"Suppressed technology issues have become critical and are slowing growth constantly. We have intel that indicates that Scorpio and the Denon here on Earth have played an integral part in suppressing technology. Assets, liabilities and socio-political alliances must be established… both foreign and domestic."

POTUS was trying to take mental notes, but Echo's rapid-fire *issues list* was intimidating.

"Reading your thoughts, Mr. President, I will follow up with these critical needs and provide them to your admin staff."

"Thank you. Please continue."

"Your American military will be pressed into service to build advanced offensive and defensive spaceships and must allow the Arrans to become the joint developer of same."

The President groaned as Echo completed her to-do list.

"An impenetrable compound or fortress for the ETRT and their activities must be prioritized. They know it but will obviously need your help in the implementation."

As Echo indicated she was finished, and that the President could call on her at any time, Cameron texted his VP to come to the church.

Echo added sharply, "I think we should consider having a meeting of the World Council as soon as we deal with the magnetic wave and have some strategic planning underway."

"I agree, Echo. I will look to see how quickly we can convene that group. Meanwhile, we can develop an agenda."

At that time, Vice President Worthington entered the room.

"Hello, Samantha."

"Mister President."

"You haven't met Echo yet, the Commander of the Arrans."

"No, Sir, I haven't had the pleasure."

As they shook hands, Echo forced a smile and simply said, "Nice to meet you."

What followed was some small talk and non-confidential dialogue among the three people. Then, as Vice President Worthington was excusing herself to exit the church, Echo added a surprising comment, "Vice President Worthington, we will be having a fully staffed ETRT meeting in a couple of days, with a returning Sara and my leadership team. We would love to have you attend."

Turning to look directly at Echo, VP Worthington responded, "I'd be delighted and will make arrangements ASAP. Thank you."

As the VP exited, a confused POTUS asked, "That was a strange invitation. Why would you want her there, given what we all believe is a woman with her own agenda?"

Echo answered. "Just a hunch."

"Well, Echo, your hunches are pretty sound."

"Thank you, Mister President."

"And you needed to make physical contact, Echo, and you did, right?"

"Yes. That is correct."

"And do you have a conclusion?"

"It is as Sara surmised."

"What's that, Echo?"

Your Vice President is no longer human!"

71

TAKE ME ON

Two days later, Sara had returned from Trappist One, having been gone for nearly two weeks. She returned to a hastily called ETRT meeting that Echo insisted on having. Scott was brought in as well, given his huge stake in future developments.

As a much more serious Sara entered the ETRT conference room, she was greeted by a standing ovation. Sara hadn't talked to anyone since her return the previous night, which was thought to be odd by many of her teammates, especially Michaela.

"Hello everyone. It's nice to see you and it is great to be back. I see we have a full team here, including RJ and even Scott Woods. Hi Scott."

Scott quickly walked over to Sara, gave her a warm hug and said, "Hi Sara. Welcome back."

Echo, Pulse, Laser, and Spirit appeared, beamed into the meeting from their Moon base.

"Hello, ETRT," Echo said loudly. "Thanks for meeting with us and it is with great pride and pleasure that we welcome back, Warrior Princess, Sara Steele."

Echo had the entire ETRT assembled, and Sara could see that most of Echo's elite leadership team was present, which was unusual.

Echo interjected notably, "I was told by President Sullivan that Vice President Worthington was invited... but cancelled."

Pausing for a few seconds, Echo then inquired, "Sara, while we get our program pulled together, could you describe the Cross of War that you earned and the training that you went through?"

"Of course, Echo" Sara replied eagerly.

At that very same moment, Vibe appeared in the room, holding a small device that resembled a key fob. "Hello everyone."

"Hi Vibe," was the immediate response from several team members.

As the Arrans team huddled, Sara pulled out her Cross and began to provide details on her training, deciding to exclude the physical implant part of the process. She described the video game-like training and her medical friend, Bones.

Michaela thought reflectively, "*Sara is much more serious... much more focused. Changed.*"

Sara demonstrated how she could mentally create holograms for people or objects, and did so with several images of Trappist One, getting an *ooh* and *aah* from several people.

Scott looked directly into Sara's eyes and recognized a much different Sara... a calm, focused, and somewhat detached Sara.

Sara had a momentary pause in her talk as her mind apparently went from her talking points to a totally distracted mental red-flag. Her head jerked up as if a sound or light or thought had interrupted her dialogue.

At that exact same time, Echo excused herself and took her team into an adjoining meeting room.

As Echo was leaving, Sara also excused herself from her ETRT team and briskly walked over to Echo and they looked into each other's eyes.

Echo stopped. Sara leaned over to her and both had the same chilling thought... and not unexpected.

<Sara, do you sense it too?>

<Yes, Echo. I will alert everyone.>

Sara and Echo shared the same thought.

"We are in imminent danger."

72

DOME SWEET DOME

Echo knew that there was a pending danger, as she had expected it ever since she mentioned to VP Worthington that a fully manned ETRT would be meeting on this day in this place.

She wasn't sure if Sara would pick up the same subconscious warning, but she did. Echo thought confidently, *What they said is true. Sara Steele has gained special skills... how many and which skills is still to be seen.*

Echo's hunch was to bait the VP into showing her hand. If nothing happened... fine. She would have been wrong this time.

"All diagnostics in place, Vibe?"

"Yes, Echo."

"And the dome?"

"Yes, Echo, the dome has been installed and the shield is now functional."

"Very well. Good work."

Echo paused a moment. "We are about to be attacked by Dracs, as I had surmised, and our countermeasure will deter the attack, but..."

Pulse asked, "But what, Echo?"

"Pulse, this will indicate that our war is now official. They are on notice."

"As are we," Spirit announced defiantly.

Echo and her team moved quickly back into the main conference room where Sara had gathered the ETRT.

Echo looked directly at Sara and spoke, "Sara, please make the announcement."

Without hesitation, Sara simply said, "We are about to be attacked by the evil alien race, the Dracs."

Sara glanced back at Echo, nodded and continued, "A shield has been installed by the Arrans that will protect us from this attack. It is likely we will feel only a momentary shudder, right Vibe?"

"That is correct, Sara."

Complete silence and nervous anticipation described the air in that room. About ten seconds later, the aerial attack was felt, but only for a moment.

Echo spoke calmly, "The attack on our location by the Draconian forces was neutralized. We are safe."

With frazzled psyches and unbridled fear and concern dominating everyone's discussions, Pulse looked over to Echo and spoke, "From this bad event will come some good."

"How so, Pulse?"

"They have awakened a sleeping giant!"

73

FULLY FUNCTIONAL FORTRESS

Sara took on a greater leadership role following the attack. As she reassured everyone that they were safe and the attack was thwarted, she asked Echo for some specific explanation.

Echo provided Sara with some details, "It appears that the Draconians used a highly sophisticated drone to launch an armed missile at your building. It is an undetectable mode of aggression that we have seen before."

Sara had an *aha moment*, thinking back to the cabin attack that got her husband, Paul, killed.

Echo announced to the ETRT, "We are heading back to our base to continue our work to mitigate the magnetic wave. Sara is in charge and we will follow her advice."

Sara did not bat an eye. She now knew her role explicitly.

High fives and handshakes amongst the attendees were a sign that all was going to be okay. As Echo assessed the moment, she walked the few short steps to Sara and implied in a whisper in Sara's ear, "You are special Sara... very special. What you accomplished at Trappist One was, as you say, 'off the charts.' You exceeded all expectations."

"Thank you, Echo. I have you to thank and I am so appreciative."

Again whispering, "Sara, whatever your mind believes... truly believes... your body and spirit will make it happen. Trust yourself and what you are now capable of doing."

Echo gave Sara a long and warm hug.

"Goodbye, for now Sara. Let us know when we need to reload our social matrix. I will keep you posted on the wave progress."

Sara smiled and the Arrans team was gone.

She knew that Echo's mention of a *social matrix* was to focus on how to integrate the platforms of humanity and aliens to educate and communicate to the global masses… and all those deniers and obstacles.

Sara sent a text message to POTUS.

> "ETRT was attacked by Dracs. Everyone okay.
> VP was absent. You need to find her and arrest her."

Moments later, POTUS responded.

> "Got it. Glad all okay.
> Working to locate VP. Take care."

"Can I have everyone's attention?" Sara said firmly addressing the ETRT, "We need to move quickly to the final phase of completion of the Utah compound, I will get with Scott shortly and we will discuss our next steps. I want everyone moved to the compound as quickly as possible with a seamless transition."

"Yes, ma'am," Scott replied respectfully.

That comment did get a brief smile from Sara.

"What about the wave, Sara?"

"RJ, Echo has indicated that we will have a preliminary plan soon. I will let you know tomorrow what she has determined to be our best shot. It would appear that an electro-magnetic pulse will be required, and they can provide that technology."

Hearing no pushback, Sara continued, "I also want to consolidate all of our R&D activity in California, our current Texas supply chain, and Utah complex into one division within the Utah compound. Connor, would you and Justin take on the logistics?"

"Yep. Will do, boss." Connor replied.

"Michaela?"

"Yes, Sara."

"Echo has asked us to do our best at the interrogation of Scorpio and the terrorist group currently being held in the maximum-security prison in Florence, Colorado."

"And you want me to do that?"

"Yes. Maybe RJ can go as well."

"Fine. RJ?"

"I'll check my schedule and see."

"Thanks. Michaela. Echo needs to get as much detail as possible and we can't use the authorities."

"Understand."

Sara received a text message from her dad, Mike.

"Excuse me. I have a text from my dad.

"Hi Honey, you okay?"

"Yeah, Dad. Fine. Sorry I didn't call. Been busy."

"Of course. Echo has kept us informed of your adventures."

"Yes, I had faith that she would."

"Can Mom and I talk to you now?"

"No. We just had an attack by the Dracs."

"Ohmigod. You okay?"

"Yes. All good. Will call later."

"That would be great."

"Bye."

"Bye, Sara."

Sara motioned for Michaela. "Got a couple personal admin things to do. Can you help?"

"Of course, Sara. What do you need?"

"I want to get Mike and Christine moved from Ohio to our compound."

"Your parents?"

"Yes. Mike and Christine. Can you help with that?"

"Sure. What else?"

"I haven't talked to Doctor Palmer for quite a while."

"Sara, you mean Matt, as in boyfriend Matt?"

"Yes. It has been a while since we talked. Could you discuss with him the need we have to consolidate our resources into the Utah compound?"

"Seriously? You want me to talk with your boyfriend when you haven't even let him know that you are back? And you are alive and well?"

"When put that way... you are right. I will call Doctor Palmer after I call Mike and Christine."

"*Oh boy,*" Michaela thought. "*This is a different Sara. This adjustment is gonna take some time to get used to.*"

"Sara, we should have Pete there as well. You want us to take care of that?"

"No Michaela. I will handle the hologram Pete. Pete and I need to talk."
"About what, Sara?"

"The accuracy of our individual and collaborative future visions."

74
CALLS OF THE WILD

An extremely focused Sara headed back to her office with Tiffany hotly in stride.

"Sara, ya got a minute? We need to talk."

Turning to Tiffany, Sara took Tiffany's hand and impatiently muttered, "What's on your mind?"

"It has to do with…"

"With the Darwinian Evolution Theory."

"Well, yes, Sara. We had a game-changing experience."

Sara put her other hand on Tiffany's forehead. "I am sensing your excitement and I am feeling your thoughts."

Within a few seconds, Sara withdrew her hand from Tiffany's forehead.

"I now know all of the results from your study. Remarkable work. Thank you. Now, I need to make a few calls."

Sara turned, walked away, and entered her office. She looked over to the speechless Tiffany and closed her office door.

"Egad," thought Tiffany.

✦ ✦ ✦

Sara took a deep breath, noticing that her blood pressure was a little high and realizing that her new skills were coming with a downside. She sent a text message to Michaela.

> "Got a minute? Need to talk."
> "Sure. Be there in a few."

As Michaela arrived, Sara got a couple of cold soft drinks.

"Thanks for coming right up. I need a sounding board."

"I bet you do," responded Michaela.

"Sara, you just covered a life-changing transformation of yourself with your dearest friends in a matter of minutes. What gives?"

As Sara began to pour their drinks, Michaela interrupted her, "Whoa, ya got anything stronger?"

Sara forced a laugh, paused and said, "Understand. You got it."

With that, Sara got a bottle of wine from her office wine rack.

"Stronger?" Michaela was looking for a little more relaxation.

"Okay. Fine. I have a smooth, sherry oak Scotch here. It's a Macallan, eighteen-year-old, single malt Scotch Whisky that is one of my favorites."

"Neat," Michaela said.

"Okay, straight, coming up." Sara was getting relaxed before even having a sip of her Scotch. The mere presence of her bestie, Michaela, calmed the hyper Sara.

Finding the Scotch and setting up their drinks, Sara realized that her stream of consciousness was oscillating between the pre-Trappist and post-Trappist events.

Sara poured the two drinks and they touched glasses and toasted, "To us."

"To friends," Michaela responded.

"Always and forever," replied a now more relaxed Sara.

They spent the next thirty minutes discussing Sara's adventure and the incredible task at hand for the ETRT and everyone involved. Michaela was the perfect sounding board for Sara, and she felt nearly *normal* again.

They hugged as Michaela uttered, "Got to go. Will leave in the morning for Colorado. I'm glad we had a chance to talk."

"Me too, Michaela. Sorry to make you take this trip, but Echo respects you and she knows you will find a way to get some info out..."

Sara smiled. "Have a safe trip."

"Will do. Now you go make those calls, okay?"

"Yes. Right now."

✦ ✦ ✦

As Michaela left, Sara refilled her drink glass and dialed her dad.

"Hi, it's me. Sorry about earlier."

"Sara, it is so good to hear your voice. Mom's coming."

"Great, Dad. How are you guys doing?"

"We are fine. Just a little nervous about you, naturally. Echo gave us almost daily briefings. Here's Mom."

"Hi Sara. Oh gosh, it's good to finally talk to you. You okay?"

"Mom, I'm great. That experience was 'stellar'… 'Out of this world'…"

All three laughed. Sara went on to describe her time on Trappist One and teed up her request that Mike and Christine pack up and head to the Utah compound. Mike was on board, but Sara could tell that her mom would need some coaxing.

Sara feigned an incoming call so she could end the conversation. She noticed the obvious… she had even less patience than before.

Sara then moved to an even more awkward call with Doctor Matthew Palmer, Sara's chief reconstruction surgeon from the cabin attack days, and her current boyfriend and lover.

"Hello, Matt. Sorry I've been out of reach for a while, and sorry you've had to get your news about me secondhand."

"Hi Sara. Thanks for calling. I have been disappointed that you couldn't have found some way to inform me of your travels."

Sara thought, *"It's white-lie time."*

"Matt, communication from that far in space was impossible." Continuing, "And, we are now coming to terms with the fact that an evil alien race has targeted Earth, and we just lived through a thwarted effort to attack the ETRT."

"My God, Sara. That's awful. Is everyone okay?"

"Yes. Echo and the Arrans had a strong suspicion that this attack was coming and installed a dome to protect us. But this is why I haven't been able to communicate directly with you and my parents."

Sara waited for a response from Matt, which did not come. "So, until we can get everyone relocated to the Utah compound, I need you guys to be out of sight and out of their minds… that is the evil Draconian alien race."

Sara concluded the uncomfortable call with a promise to make a trip to Matt's Utah lab very soon to see him. Little did Matt know that Sara's main reason for making such a trip was to reach out to her grandfather Pete's hologram.

And little did Matt know of Sara's tryst with the alien Pulse. Oh my!

✦ ✦ ✦

To add another stressful call to the day's mix, Sara got a call from RJ who seemed stressed himself.

"Hi Sara. Glad to have you back."

"Thanks, RJ. It's great to be back. What's up?"

"I didn't get a chance to tell you earlier, with attacks from aliens becoming our priority, but we just got the final results back from VP Worthington's DNA analysis."

"Not good news, I bet."

"No, not at all."

RJ paused. He was unusually serious and seemed quite concerned.

"Is Michaela there? I want to run something by her before I close the report."

"What's that?"

"I need her opinion regarding epigenetic change in DNA stemming from extended time in space coupled with the VP's accident in space."

"Yikes. You will need to talk with her, for sure. She is not here right now. She just left to pack for that Colorado trip. If you miss her tonight, she will be reachable tomorrow."

"Colorado trip? Refresh my memory, Sara."

"To the Colorado prison trying to get some info from Scorpio. I couldn't face the low-life that killed our close friend, Kathy."

"Oh, that's right. I heard you guys talking about that earlier. Okay. I'll catch her later… it can wait."

"Can you share your preliminary DNA results with me?"

"Of course. We have confirmed that VP Worthington's DNA is not only different from her earlier DNA test…"

"I'm not surprised."

"And our DNA results have been one hundred per cent verified by two sources."

"All ears, RJ. What are we dealing with?"

"Sara, VP Worthington's DNA is not human DNA!"

75

NIGHTMARE
DESCENDING

Only 24 hours after the Dracs' attack, Michaela found herself at the Florence, Colorado, prison to interrogate Scorpio and, hopefully, get a sense of what part his terrorist group had been planning.

She sent a text message to RJ but hadn't heard back. She thought, *"He's a very busy guy… but I already miss him so much."*

Michaela looked at a notepad of questions to ask Scorpio and she was still editing this hastily drawn up checklist. She knew she wouldn't have access to her computer.

Armed with a bogus *deal* for some solid answers, Michaela reluctantly entered the prison. She knew that this info could be important, and she also knew that Sara couldn't do this task given the Kat murder implications.

Michaela thought, nervously, *"This is gonna be a crappy day."*

POTUS had made arrangements for Michaela to be shown into the prison via a back door, so as not to alert the press. This would be the kind of publicity that the ETRT and the joint efforts did not need.

"Good afternoon, Miss Marx," the prison security guard said crisply. "We were expecting you."

"Thank you. It's… well, okay."

Once through the security detector, they attached a visitor's badge to Michaela's blazer, took her cell phone and laptop, and walked her into a narrow corridor.

The atmosphere was cool and dimly lit and not one that Michaela could tolerate well. She had just arrived but couldn't wait to leave.

However, a surprise awaited her as VP Samantha Worthington was waiting to meet her there.

The security guard brought Michaela to the end of the corridor and announced, "The vice president has been waiting for you."

Michaela knew that she was not supposed to be there. She assumed nervously, *"wasn't there an arrest warrant out for the VP?"*

"Hello, Michaela. The President thought I should sit in on the interrogation."

Now, Michaela was going from nervous to frightened… She frantically thought, *"Why is she here and what does VP Worthington have in mind. I need to be alert!"*

As they were being led to the main area where all members of the New World Order were being housed, a frantic Sara tried to reach Michaela, who had to surrender her cell phone at security.

Sara could sense that Michaela was now in the company of the vice president, and Sara was concerned with Michaela's safety, given the facts from RJ and an overall bad feeling.

Once Michaela and Samantha Worthington were inside the massive cell block that housed Scorpio and about fifteen of his associates, an explosion shook the entire prison.

When the smoke cleared, the results were both shocking and unrealistic.

Michaela, Samantha, and the entire Scorpio gang had disappeared through a large, dark and dusty hole in the prison floor.

76

MIND WIDE SHUT

Michaela had been abducted in a bold and brazen escape by the terrorist gang. She was not conscious when she reached the escape destination where Scorpio, Vice President Worthington, and fifteen hideous reptilian aliens were now in a cold, dank, and dark, cave-like meeting room.

With heavy moisture on every wall, it appeared to be either a subterranean cave or an undersea alien hideout thousands of feet below the surface of a vast sea.

Within the dark and foreboding room, these were Draconian reptilian creatures, and they were sitting in a semi-circle with a naked, bound and dirtied Michaela sitting facing them, wearing a large, hideous gold mask, resembling a VR goggle, and then she was roughly cloaked in a red robe placed on her by a large, reptilian alien.

The air was hazy, and a heavy layer of incense was strong and pungent. It was cave-like in its aura of doom and death.

Suddenly poked with a large, metallic shock rod, Michaela slowly awoke, but in an induced trance. She was not cognizant of anything in the room and had been put into a state of partial sleepiness by her captors.

The alien Scorpio was discussing with VP Worthington their need to find and interrogate Sara Steele and getting her location from Michaela was vital.

The Scorpio's voice was the first spoken word that she heard.

"Michaela, relax. Can you hear me?"

With no response from his captive, Scorpio continued his questioning, "Michaela, think warm and comforting thoughts."

Sitting down next to Scorpio was VP Worthington, who seemed at ease with the bizarre environment. She was obviously part of whatever conspiracy was about to play out.

A dazed Michaela felt her mind and vision becoming cluttered with many of the wonderful memories that she had; and with the smell of incense, she became relaxed, almost in a dreamlike state.

As her brief shaking subsided in that cold, dank dungeon atmosphere, she began to relax and experience the trance-like mind-set in which her abductors had immersed her.

VP Worthington, in a soft and friendly voice, asks her captive, "Are you happy and joyful?"

A now relatively cognizant Michaela replied, "Yes."

"Can you see your family and home where you grew up?"

"Yes."

"Are you in a good place?"

"Yes."

"Would you like to have your friend, Sara Steele, be there with you?"

Pausing a moment, "Yes."

"Where is Sara?"

Silence from Michaela.

"Where is Sara located right now, Michaela?"

Michaela was still silent as her body began to tremble.

Scorpio, whose roots were in the constellation Scorpius and where he learned the *art* of prisoner submission, was now becoming impatient. He took the *passive* interrogation to the next level.

"We will bring Sara to you, Michaela. But you must tell us where she is."

Still no comment from an agitated, albeit semi-conscious Michaela.

With that, the reptilian creatures morphed into the human forms they had in the prison.

Samantha Worthington got up and walked behind the seated Michaela, so as not to be recognized by their captive.

She took the goggles from Michaela's face, and the incense was immediately removed.

Michaela was now awake, almost as if a switch was pulled, and was lucid, frightened, and aware that she was now a prisoner of an alien race. The room had the atmosphere of a dungeon.

Scorpio ordered defiantly, "We need to know where your friends are located and what their relationship is with the Arrans. If you cooperate, we won't hurt you. We just need information."

Michaela shot back, "My friends are on Pluto, and I don't know what an Arrans is, you ass."

"We will get the info we need from you, one way or the other. So, where are your friends?"

"Go to Hell!"

"Take her to the Tank!"

77

GARDEN OF EVIL

Michaela was taken forcefully by three humanoids down a long and winding passageway to a lower floor, even darker and danker than the other room. The pungent odor of a cave-like setting was now replaced by the smell of mold, mildew, and pungent water.

They removed Michaela's red robe and placed her dirty, naked, and trembling body in a large tank of water, bound her hands and feet, strapped a large breathing tube to her face, and then totally submersed her in the tank. Electric wires were placed on a headset on a now totally submerged Michaela, and all captors left her there… alone and scared!

Michaela had no idea that she was now in a Dracs' torture chamber with hideous devices meant to extract information from captives in whatever manner was necessary. Large, liquid-filled cylindrical tubes held bodies, some human and some non-human, and some alive and some in suspended states.

The backdrop from Michaela's tank was even more eerie. Scanning back to a wall hundreds of feet behind the tank, a virtual garden of triangular rocks was arranged in rows and columns that likely totaled several hundred thousand. The rocks looked like eggs ready to hatch!

Michaela was alone, in the dark, submerged in a tank of cold water, and then it began. A slow siren-like sound overtook her sense of hearing and was now her obvious sense of immediate peril. This severe noise flooding her ear drums was the torture that Scorpio had selected.

Minutes turned to hours before anyone came to her. When they did, the sound stopped, her head was lifted from the water tank, and she was asked, "Where are your friends?"

A shivering Michaela didn't respond.

"Where are your friends?" the voice snapped.

Michaela was still silent.

Just like that, she was back in the tank. Only now, the siren-like sound was noticeably louder, and Michaela knew that this terrible torture method would likely become fatal.

Along with the captors was VP Worthington, who asked the attendant, "What's the plan?"

The alien attendee responded, "This is noise that will continue to affect hearing and she won't be able to last more than a day. It is fatal torture, bursting ear drums, and causing aneurisms or rupture."

"So, she either tells us what we need to know, or she dies?"

The alien attendee looked at VP Worthington directly into her eyes, **"She dies either way!"**

78

DRACONIAN EMPIRE

President Sullivan sent out a Level-Five, terrorist alert immediately, as the scary details of Michaela's abduction and the VP's defection to an alien society were now known.

The ETRT met within the hour and was patched into the President's Situation Room. Echo was alone with POTUS and Pulse was with the ETRT.

Echo took the lead. "We now know that the enemy has made their first move. Whatever they have been hiding and why they were hiding it, is a moot point. This is Earth's wakeup call."

The President asked nervously, "Echo, do we know anything?"

"We know three critical things... First, the Draconian aliens used a black hole with well-coordinated time slips to get to their lair, wherever that is. And they certainly didn't try to hide it.

"The explosion itself was crude... theatrical. They didn't need a blast to escape."

"And number two, Echo?"

"They had help from the Denon species that are led by Scorpio, to make such a subterranean exit. I did believe that much of your terrorist problems were brought on by the Scorpio-driven groups, but now I can accurately say that Scorpio is a Denon."

Pausing a moment, the President asked, "Number three, Echo?"

"Michaela is in grave danger, Mr. President. We don't even know if she is alive... if she survived the explosion and, if alive, where on this planet she could be!"

Echo suggested a grueling recap, "To determine who took Michaela and why, and what we can do about it, we need to do a quick analysis of all of the cultures, their motives, and their immediate intentions. That way, we can get everyone's opinion as to a choice of action."

Everyone at the ETRT was listening, as Commander RJ Baker just walked into the conference room to observe the video call. He was not yet aware of Michaela's abduction.

Echo began her analysis, knowing that this would be a long and difficult explanation. "The malevolent alien species that you would see as the direct opposites to angels, are the Denon. They are an entangled culture that has evolved from human souls that have endured extensive torture in Hell by Alastair and similarly driven alien cultures. In this process, they have become corrupted, extremely evil, and very powerful."

A puzzled Connor asked, "They exist?"

"Oh yes. Very much so."

"They require a human vessel to walk and function on Earth. They can roam in smoke form until they morph into actual human beings, sometimes able to duplicate a specific person's body. Death and destruction are always in their path. Your Earthly terrorist groups would be ideal hosts for their mission on Earth."

"Scorpio!" Sara was again putting the puzzle pieces together.

"The humanoid beings with reptilian features are the Dracs. The males are driven by whims and their own pleasures and have shapeshifting ability. The females have a chameleon ability and are more reserved and controlled than the males.

"The Dracs originated in the Alpha Draconis star system which is only two hundred fifteen light years away, and was formerly the Polestar."

Sara enlightened the ETRT so they would have a point of reference.

"A Polestar is a bright star closely aligned to the axis of rotation of an astronomical object and is used for navigation since it stays in the same place. It holds still in the sky while the entire northern sky moves around it."

Echo continued, "The Dracs have two main castes; one is a dangerous warrior caste, eight to ten feet tall, six hundred to one thousand pounds, and are super-psychic and super-fast.

"The second caste is the highly advanced and intelligent race that has thousands of biological offspring here on Earth. They are indistinguishable from humans."

Echo waited for a moment as those in the ETRT were getting nervous, but doing their requisite notetaking.

"Also, there are likely sub-ocean clusters of pre-humanoid Dracs, a devolution that we can only speculate about at this time... just don't know."

Pulse added harshly, "This dangerous galactic species is a tall, reptilian, elite and highly advanced culture. We know they are flesh-eating and blood-drinking humanoids resembling the fictional *Creature from the Black Lagoon* from that 1954 movie."

"I assume Pulse is correct about the 'Creature' part," Echo noted. "We believe we can even better categorize them as the super-elite Draconians, stemming from the Devonian geological period.

"Even though the Denon are an entangled culture, their very 'being' can be traced to ancient mythology and what was written and studied at the time as the seven deadly sins. This species can be characterized by anger, rage, hostility, and death as a result of their social domination. They believe in reward as being total damnation, achieved by doing horrible atrocities.

"I believe what we are seeing is a collaboration of the two species, and I hope I am wrong… it's a hideous thought."

"What about the *Greys,* Echo?" asked President Sullivan.

"As we have mentioned many times, the *Grey* aliens are Reticulans and are, for the most part, a good species… a kind species. They are non-violent, meek, and not very strong. They are aptly portrayed in many American movies regarding extraterrestrials, I assume because many had been caught by the U.S. government."

POTUS flinched with that statement while Pulse nodded appreciatively.

"They befriended humanity and traded technology with the German Empire directly and with the U.S. government, indirectly. We look at them as fixers and a helpful species. They are the ones that messed with nuclear-armed missiles when confrontations were likely."

"Oh, the good guys, eh?"

"Yes, Connor… the good guys."

"For those of you who are unaware, they are short, gray-skinned, and small with large heads. Even being short, they have long limbs, no nose or ears, and large black eyes."

Pausing, Echo continued. "They do not speak but communicate telepathically. That is why humans were never comfortable in their presence. So, I believe we are seeing a Draconian Empire revealed in the abduction of Michaela."

"What!" Commander Baker jumped up. "What!" He was hearing this for the first time.

"RJ," Sara said softly, "I will update you in a few minutes. I'm sorry you are hearing this for the first time under all this alien noise."

Commander Baker slowly sat down, visibly shaken, and with clenched fists. Sara immediately inquired, "So, Echo, what is their 'end game'?"

"I don't know. Until we get our Michaela back, only probabilities and simulations can be established."

Sara and Pulse walked over to Commander Baker to debrief him on Michaela's abduction.

Connor and Justin were somewhat optimistic as Connor spoke to RJ, **"At least we have the undetectable tracking device, like how we found Amanda."**

79

HALT AND CATCH FIRE

"**S**ara, Echo and I are going to sign off. I want to talk to Echo in private. Please get me an update on Connor's tracking assumption as soon as you can."

"Will do, Cameron. I'll link my thoughts to Echo if we have anything right away."

"Ah… okay," replied a somewhat confused President Sullivan.

By that time, Justin and Connor were already in the computer lab running a diagnostic scan on Michaela's tracking device.

> Sara texted Connor, "Anything yet?"
> "No."
> "When?"
> "Need a few minutes."

Pulse and Sara spent the next ten minutes explaining to RJ what happened to Michaela at the prison. They had no idea what happened to VP Worthington, but presumed that she defected.

RJ hissed, "Michaela asked me to go with her, but I couldn't clear my schedule quickly enough."

Pulse gave RJ a totally unexpected hug, as they both realized the sense of urgency of the moment. Sara was pleasantly surprised by Pulse's show of support and affection for RJ and acknowledging and understanding the dire situation.

Justin looked over to Connor and was shaking his head. "Connor, it looks like our code may have been broken for the tracking device."

"What?"

Just a few seconds later… "Damn, the code has been broken," a devastated Justin glared.

"If that is true, Justin, we can't locate Michaela."

Justin pipes in, "*Halt and Catch Fire!*"

"What, Justin?"

"Just thinking about something my grandfather used to tell me."

"What the hell ya talking about?"

"Connor, this reminds me of my grandfather's account of early unreliable computers. Often, he would tell me, they would not respond or simply stop working and sometimes caught fire."

"Justin. You're making that up."

"Nope. *Halt and Catch Fire* was a 'thing.' Look it up."

At that moment, Sara, Pulse, and RJ entered the lab.

Sara quickly asked, "Well?"

Connor had the bad news to tell. "Sara, Michaela's tracking device has been disabled."

Sara snapped, "How could that be? You ran endless simulations before the Amanda incident and never had a potential problem."

A bewildered Connor scowled, "We have a malfunction that was never in our list of possibilities with this tracking device."

Pulse then stated the sad truth, **"Obviously, your list was one issue short!"**

80

ENERGY TRACING

Sara telepathically informed Echo of the disastrous conclusion raised by Connor and Justin, and that they would continue to work on the problem. She immediately alerted the President.

"Mister President, Michaela's tracking device was disabled. Apparently, we don't know where she is or even if she is still alive."

"My God!" The President was in shock. "I'll contact the prison security and see if anything turns up on their cameras during the minutes leading up to the explosion."

Echo got a frantic message from Vibe, "When we contacted Connor to help with the dilemma of our ship and the wave mission and our repeating cycle of time, it appears that a very high level of cyber hacking followed."

"Explain, Vibe."

"It looks like the Dracs were able to access Connor's entire database via their virus while we were with him for those few short seconds. Remember, there was a time-stop."

"So, Vibe, that would explain how they were able to disable Michaela's tracking device."

"Yes, Echo. Very clever and predetermined. Their plan was to capture Michaela, knowing we had no way to track her or to save her."

Vibe quickly added, "I have alerted Connor and Justin and they are rapidly at work de-bugging their systems, checking other trackers for function, and installing new firewalls."

A very concerned Echo was thinking of any scenario that could be employed to find and rescue Michaela. As she thought, President Sullivan contacted both her and Sara with feedback concerning VP Worthington's prison incident.

"Our cameras show that Scorpio and the VP had conversation moments before the 'hole' opened up. So, they were in this scheme together."

"Thank you, Mister President."

"You are welcome, Echo. Sorry I don't have any more info at this time. Does your team have any ideas?"

"No, sir," was Echo's response.

"Sara, does the ETRT have any optimistic info at all?"

"No, Cameron, we do not."

Pulse approached Echo excited and with a slight smile. "Echo, I have a plan."

"Go ahead, Pulse."

"This is about energy. We need to capture her energy field… her spirit."

Echo said, "All right… very well. I believe I know where you are going with your thoughts."

"Yes," replied Pulse with a sense of purpose and conviction.

"Echo, we need our energy expert, Vigor."

81

TOO LITTLE...
TOO LATE?

Sara was informed of a tentative plan as Echo summoned Vigor. Echo explained to Sara, while they waited for Vigor, that Vigor was Echo's energy guru and a brilliant tactician for all things regarding zero-point energy and vacuum energy in quantum field energy theory.

Vigor arrived in his usual frantic state. Calm and collected were not his trademarks.

"Vigor, you are reading our collective thoughts."

"Yes, Echo. I have a firm understanding of the situation involving the abducted human."

Sara asked respectfully, "Can you tell us what you have in mind?"

Vigor replied, "Steady and dynamic states as the origin of dark energy and dark matter put out spherical clouds of photons."

"Bottom line, Vigor?"

"Yes, Sara. This means that we may be able to locate Michaela from the smallest amount of her energy and trace her location in a kind of 'energy gravitation,' so to speak."

"That sounds complicated, Vigor."

"Not really, Sara. All I need is something personal of hers... something like clothing or a uniform or something that would encapsulate her energy essence."

Even Echo was struggling with this description.

RJ jumped up. "I have it! Her flight suit from our space dive."

"Yes," answered Vigor. "That would be perfect."

Pulse ran over to RJ and said, "Do you know where that suit is right now?"

"Yes, I do. At our Roswell base."

"Hold on, Commander," as Pulse took RJ in his grasp. In an instant... poof, they were gone... headed to the military base at Roswell.

Echo tried to explain in non-technical words what her guru, Vigor, was thinking, "If we can find enough energy in that suit, we might be able to trace her whereabouts.

"How?" Sara asked.

"Energy can neither be created nor destroyed. It is constant in the universe. If we can isolate enough of her energy, we have systems that can literally trace that energy to the current state… hence, her location."

Vigor excused himself as he needed to run simulations on the various amounts of energies that might be available in Michaela's jumpsuit.

Sara and her team kept busy trying not to dwell on Michaela's situation, but found that next to impossible.

In what seemed like hours, but was actually less than fifteen minutes, Pulse and RJ returned with suit in hand.

Pulse offered some light humor, "As Commander Baker was needed to fill out paperwork before we could go… we just went. Must have surprised the officer-in-charge.

"Yeah, I'll have some explaining to do," offered a more composed RJ.

A returning Vigor grabbed the suit and scanned it.

"This is great. I have more than enough random quantum fluctuations of the electromagnetic force field present in the vacuum of this suit. In other words, this 'empty' vacuum is actually a cauldron of energy."

"Can you tell us what that means, Vigor?"

"Yes, Sara. Yes, of course. We can find your friend."

Echo, Pulse and Vigor huddled and discussed next steps, then, Echo advised, "We have a plan. Pulse will follow this energy 'lead' to its source. Pulse will literally follow Michaela's energy signature to its current location."

"I want to go to," Sara added. "I have those skills."

"It is true, Sara, that you have those skills," Echo advised, "but only Pulse has the necessary experience to confront unknown obstacles if or when they occur."

Sara knew that Echo was right and nodded affirmatively.

✦ ✦ ✦

Armed with a battle helmet, saber, and wrist weapon, Pulse got his last-minute briefing from Vigor and was gone.

Sara could see that Echo wasn't her usual, confident self.

Sara whispered to Echo, "He'll be fine."

Echo smiled, noting a kind of *reverse mentoring*.

Several minutes later, Pulse connected telepathically with Echo, Vigor, and Sara. Pulse had found Michaela, barely alive, submerged in what was obviously a severe interrogation tank meant to torture its victims.

<Pulse, can you bring her back?>

<She appears to be in a coma, Echo, or under the influence of a drug.>

<Do you sense harmonic oscillations?>

<Yes, Vigor, I sense continuity as her energy surges.>

<Vigor, what do you think?>

<Due to the death, energy, soul transfer... Pulse needs to bring her back immediately.>

Sara asked Echo for an explanation of that statement.

<Later, Sara, not right now.>

✦ ✦ ✦

As Pulse disconnected his telepathy with the group, Echo and Sara, having linked their thoughts, were busy assembling a medical team from many geographical locations.

Echo had her medical version of Bones plus Laser, Vibe, Spirit, and Peace. Bones brought what Echo called a *regeneration bed.*

Sara countered moments later with Doctor Matthew Palmer and Jeremiah.

They all met in the Medical Center and Sara had the staff prepare for surgery or whatever was coming their way. The aliens and Sara could *feel* that Pulse was on his way. They assumed he had Michaela.

Echo noticed that Sara was praying; something she had never seen Sara do before.

Then, like a ghost landing amongst them, a kneeling Pulse appeared holding a dripping wet Michaela, draped in a heavy, soggy, filthy robe. Pulse placed her limp body on the table and a flurry of hands, waving and pointing, began the immediate assessment.

Echo stepped into the circle of medical professionals undertaking a rapid and focused analysis of Michaela's condition, and the flurry of activity nearly stopped as Echo touched Michaela's forehead.

Echo turned toward Sara and the team.

"Michaela is brain dead. It appears that her captors raised enough volume in that tank to burst her eardrums and caused an aneurism."

Sara broke out in tears, again seeing a loved one die at the hands of bad people.

Echo continued. "She will be placed on a ventilator and can't live without the ventilator while we decide what, if anything, we can do."

The mood was very grim. RJ was devastated and Pulse… visibly angry.

Echo met with Laser, Vibe, Vigor, Spirit, and Peace for a few minutes, obviously discussing something important.

As they concluded their talks, Vigor provided an idea to the humans in the room.

"We need to travel back in time… take a very short trip!"

82
MIRROR-VERSE

Echo completed her discussions with the Arrans' team and informed the humans of their plan, "We will use a technology that we haven't introduced to Sara and the ETRT yet. It's called a prismatic refractor, and it breaks matter and light down and converts those components into energy."

Pulse added specific info, "We will also use a *Mirror-verse*, or a means to look back into the recent past using energy only. We can't go too far back because the energy field will impact the soul and reincarnation."

Sara utters what everyone feels, "What? Reincarnation?"

Echo responds, "Spirit, can you offer some enlightenment?"

"You must look at the body as energy and not matter. We Arrans believe that when the body is gone, through death or signal transduction, the soul is free and answers to a more spiritual calling. We do believe in reincarnation."

Echo advises impatiently, "We must move quickly and suspend our discussion on this subject until later. Pulse, what is your thinking?"

"I will take Michaela's body through the Mirror-verse and we will travel back in time to where I found her in the tank... but just after her immersion. That should be safe since no one was with her at the time."

"Michaela's body will crystallize and fall to the floor as she and Pulse enter the mirror," Echo explains, "and Pulse will 'wear' both a protective membrane to protect his body from disintegrating and a 'shimmering' to protect him from Draconian bacteria."

"That sounds incredibly complicated," Sara mutters.

"Yes," RJ adds with noticeable nervousness, "How often have you done such a thing?"

"Never with a human," Vigor replied, "but we have designed it with a 'fail safe' feature that will return them at the instant that a failure is detected."

"So, Vigor, they could return before Pulse has reached a living Michaela?"

"Yes, Sara, that is a possibility."

Echo orders, "We must go now, as Michaela is literally on 'life-support' and death could be near."

Vigor opened the mirror portal and a swirling haze of bluish light transformed into a mirror-like object about ten feet high and six feet wide.

Pulse had already obtained the smallish prismatic refractor and prepared himself with the needed precautions, lifted the limp and lifeless body of Michaela, and together they moved through a swirling mirror of light and energy.

Michaela's body crystallized as soon as it entered the mirror and fell to the floor in glass-like pieces.

Echo reminds everyone, "Matter doesn't matter."

Pulse entered the mirror with the opened refractor, presumably trapping Michaela's energy. Then he closed the refractor and was gone.

✦ ✦ ✦

Pulse went back in time to just before the tank torture began and Michaela was alive, alert and still in good health. He surveyed the area and saw that they were alone. Michaela cannot see him. He also saw a disturbing sight that wasn't part of the virtual scan.

Pulse stopped time and *captured* the live version of Michaela and allowed the contained energy field from the refractor to encapsulate the inanimate Michaela, now lacking consciousness.

He checked her vitals and once again surveyed the area for any potential alien encounter.

Then, only minutes after he entered the mirror, Pulse returned with Michaela, now very much alive. He handed her to the medical team and nervously told Echo, "I must go back. I need a Level Four containment vessel."

Laser had the vessel teleported immediately. Pulse turned toward the mirror when Echo said, "Please be careful."

Sara thinks pragmatically, *"Echo never says please."*

Michaela was now on the table and was under the observation of the entire medical staff. They agreed that her vitals looked good; almost normal. She was apparently asleep and not in a coma.

<What are you going back for, Pulse?>

<I am going back to get a 'rock.'>

<That's why you needed the Level Four?>

<Yes, Echo. This is not good.>

<Be careful.>

<Yes, Echo.>

Meanwhile, Sara looked over to RJ, who was visibly relieved, and winked, "Okay, handsome prince. There's your *Sleeping Beauty.*"

With that warm thought, RJ walked over to Michaela, leaned over, and gave her a big kiss. Almost on cue, Michaela's eyes opened, and she turned to RJ and said softly, "Hey, what's going on? Where am I?"

A warm applause ensued as Michaela was reunited with RJ and her friends. Everyone was now anxiously awaiting Pulse's return.

Echo smiled, knowing Pulse was nearly back. A couple seconds later, Pulse emerged through the mirror. He had a *rock* in the containment vessel and explained that it was likely an egg in a vast Draconian hatchery.

"This is just one of what I saw of tens of thousands of eggs about to hatch!"

83

ARRANS RISE UP

Echo glanced from Pulse to Sara and uttered an alarming warning, "We are now on the verge of a major confrontation with either the Draconian separately or a joint military assault that includes the Denon as well."

As the people surrounding Michaela were cheerful and relieved, Sara knew it was time for a re-boot back to reality.

"Echo has a thought and I concur. Let's meet in the lab with her team and have them give us a weapons overview."

"Yes, Sara, we need to get our resources and thinking on the same page."

"Echo, I will try to get POTUS patched in as well."

"Good, Sara. Let's go."

Those not staying with Michaela walked to the lab where Laser and Vibe had begun to assemble the inventory. RJ, having said goodbye to Michaela, allowing the medical team to take over, joined the others in the lab.

"Duty calls," was his thinking.

Echo turned things over to her team. Sara had added the President to the audience. "Hello, Mister President."

"Hello, Echo, and congratulations to Pulse and to all of you for a truly magnificent victory. What you were able to accomplish is nothing short of science fiction... now alien fact."

"Appreciate your trust and continued support," Echo responded with a noticeable sigh.

Laser opened with his description of the prismatic refractor, looking at the one from the medical lab in front of him, "This device has the capability, as you witnessed, to convert matter and light forms into energy. We have various sizes of these refractors; and if you can imagine, we can almost transport groups of people or artificial light to areas without light... or heat."

"Almost?" Sara was curious.

Pulse replied, "We are working on the larger device that Laser mentioned. Laser show them the extrapolator.

"Sure. This technology is at the top of the hierarchy of advanced technology, and we have been refining it for hundreds of years."

RJ was extremely engaged.

"Like with any innovative technology, this one has a complex set of both hardware and software. It is our time-travel machine.'

Sara thought, *"Been there... seen that!"*

Laser set up the incredible visual aid in two stages. First, he showed on a display table, a large, pyramid-shaped machine that resembled a metronome, a device used in music to produce an audible click at regular intervals.

"This machine holds the software, and it can be programmed to start at present and end at some future date in time. We can usually select a future year, day, hour, and location."

Then, moving over to an empty space on the floor while holding a remote-control device, he signaled the *metronome* and instantly a whirling, elliptical-shaped doorway opened to a three-dimensional passage or portal that was apparently the entry point for the time traveler.

"Holy crap!" Sara was shocked, not having seen the device actually engaged.

Echo exclaimed, "This is the best of the best. We have been able to go nearly one hundred years into the future, so far, and that is primarily why we are so concerned now about the future of this planet. The future of Earth is annihilation if we don't intercede."

Laser continued, "We have one more special item to show you. It is our antimatter microreactor. If you think of this formula…

"Dark matter equivalence = axion motion = kinetic misalignment."

"You would concur that dark matter is a key to energy optimization. Dark matter is only part of the matter-energy equation. It also includes radiation and ordinary matter. We have developed an extraordinary process to harness the power of dark energy, which comprises nearly seventy percent of the total energy in the observable universe."

RJ, feeling so good about Michaela's return, was thinking, *"Here it comes… the ultimate power-source!"*

Laser went on, "The density of dark energy is also very low, which allows us to build enormous power from our highly developed antimatter microreactors. One the size of our wrist weapon could soon power the entire U.S. fleet of planes, ships, and satellites."

✦ ✦ ✦

As Doctor Palmer joined the group, everyone wanted to hear about Michaela's condition.

With Matt and Pulse in the same room with her, Sara is thinking, *"Kind of awkward!"*

"She is stable and in remarkably good health. Her vitals are all good, and she doesn't seem to be suffering any adverse effects."

"However," Doctor Palmer added, "something very odd occurred that we cannot explain."

RJ asked, "Odd like in 'okay' odd …or 'oh shit' odd?"

"Okay, odd, RJ. When Pulse returned with Michaela, she was naked, limp, and wet. After we performed our diagnosis, we covered her and left her alone to rest."

"Yes," RJ responded. "That's when I left."

"Well," Doctor Palmer muttered, "When we returned, she was awake and smiling and clutching something in her hand that she definitely did not have when we left her."

"And what was that… what is that?

"I ran it by the ETRT, and Tiffany claims it is a *dream catcher.*

"How she got it," Doctor Palmer added, "we haven't a clue!"

Sara went from puzzled to processing…

Pulse paused a moment and then asked, "Does she remember anything at all about her abduction?"

"Not really, Pulse. Her last clear recollection was at the prison when the floor opened up."

Sara nodded, "That is very good news."

Doctor Palmer glanced at Pulse and added, "What you did was truly amazing. We are all so impressed and so thankful."

"Thank you, Doctor Palmer, I am both happy and relieved."

With that, Echo brought the group back to reality, "We need to focus on a strategy. Sara, what are your thoughts?"

Sara thought for a moment before she responded, "Well, we now know much more than we did just a few short days ago. I think we need a short-term plan and a long-term plan."

"I agree, Sara," Echo advised. "What is your current thinking?"

"The facts are we have a destructive magnetic wave headed towards us. Echo, have you any detailed info yet?"

"Yes. Our analysis has confirmed that the origin of the power surge is on the asteroid Apophis, and our military is planning the destruction of that machine within the next thirty-six hours."

"That's good, Echo."

RJ chimed in, "Not necessarily, Sara."

"RJ is correct," Echo said. "RJ, explain."

"Of course. Even though the surge at the source will be destroyed, the waves in route to Earth are not affected... at least, not significantly"

"Damn it!" Sara shouts back. "Echo... Pulse... what's the plan?"

"Sara," Laser chimed in, "we are calculating what return electro-magnetic force will be required to neutralize the wave, and from where on Earth that countermeasure would be installed."

"So," Sara muttered, "we are on top of this."

"Yes, Sara," Laser advised, "we are."

Sara paused a few seconds before continuing, "Okay. The other short-term issue is the 'rocks' and Pulse has a sample."

Pulse responded, "I have already sent that specimen to our lab. I should have results back soon, and the scope and scale of that potential problem will be determined."

"Sara, you referred to a long-term strategy. What are you thinking?"

"Echo, we have been forced to respond... react... defend, so to speak."

"That is correct, Sara."

"Well, I strongly believe that we should go on the offense."

"Meaning?"

"Meaning, Echo, we should immediately pursue two courses of action... related, but uniquely different."

A smiling Pulse interjects, "I like taking the aggressor role. What are you considering, Warrior Princess?"

Sara snaps back quickly, "This Warrior Princess thinks we need to declare War!"

A calm and rather reticent Echo inquires, "I don't disagree. With what and how?"

"I think we should get Pete's vision of the future along with any simulations that the Arrans can put together, and literally visit the specifics of the 'future state' to see what we will be facing. It might be fuzzy, but better than no idea at all."

"I love it," offered Laser.

"And the second course of action, Sara?"

"Sure. It's now time to invest hard and heavy into Project Zeus... our own fleet of Galactic Starships."

Echo responded enthusiastically, "I completely agree, Sara."

As the entire group nodded their agreement with Sara's conclusion, Pulse leaned over to Echo and told her that Sara achieved something in her training that no other participant ever achieved, including Echo.

He whispered to Echo, not wanting Sara to pick up on their telepathy.

"I need to share something remarkable with you."

"What's that, Pulse?"

"Sara can fly."

"You mean she can leap?"

"No. Sara Steele can literally fly!"

84

FLYING MIND

Echo and Sara met to discuss the timing and logistics of such a proposed simulation.

"So, Pulse tells me you have acquired a skill that is unique to anyone that has gone through the warrior training?"

"Yes. I can visualize a destination, albeit one that is close to me, and I can fly to that location… it's like teleportation, but with actually feeling and seeing and making the journey."

"And you discovered this ability soon after the virtual training on Trappist One?"

"Yes. I showed Pulse my gift, assuming that was a common end-result of the training."

"I can assure you, Sara, it was not. I'm thrilled for you and puzzled as well. Congratulations."

"Thank you."

As Echo was trying to make some sense of this new skill of Sara's, she sent a thought to Pulse… she was most curious about Sara's *gift*.

<Would you get a sample of Sara's DNA from the Trappist training and find a way to check it against the DNA in Doctor Palmer's lab from Sara's earlier surgery?>

<Sure. What are you thinking?>

<I'm thinking there is more… much more to this than we can even imagine.>

<Good… bad… where are you leaning, Echo?>

<Just need to get an answer. A legitimate answer.>

With that thought, Echo turned to Sara and got back on track. "I think we should convene at the Utah lab where the hologram of your grandfather can be our launch point for the simulated future state."

"That will be fine," Sara noted. "Who else will be involved?"

"I want to assemble an advanced, technical team from both Doctor Palmer's AI lab and members of my leadership team. I also think that Commander Baker should be there, if it is possible."

"That can be arranged," Sara replied crisply. "Who will actually be involved in the forward simulation?"

"Sara, just you, the hologram Pete, and I will make this 'journey.' I still have much to do to prepare for this event."

"Echo, I would also like to assess the progress of building the compound. Scott should be there as well."

"That would be fine, Sara."

Noticing that they were alone, Echo changed to a different topic. "I am well aware of your feelings for Doctor Palmer, and I can clearly see that you and Pulse are growing closer."

"Yes, on both fronts. You have an opinion, I'm sure, and I would appreciate your feelings."

"Sara, you are now a complex person with extraordinary skills, and you will be challenged beyond anything you can imagine."

"I am beginning to see and understand what you see and understand, Echo."

"And I am sure you do."

"So, Echo, do you have some advice?"

"Sara, we are talking about 'boyfriend' issues, plain and simple. They can be distractions at any time. But in your case, given what will be asked of you, those issues could distract you enough to result in disastrous consequences."

"And your opinion Echo?"

"You need to make your choice so we can move on with our mission."

85

FUTURE STATE

The following day, assembled at the Utah lab were Sara, Michaela, and RJ from the ETRT; Scott Woods, Doctor Palmer, and Jeremiah from their lab; and Echo, Pulse, Laser, Vibe, and Vigor.

Pete had been programmed to narrow his view of the future to specific events that he warned Sara and Matt about during an earlier *aha moment* in Jeremiah's lab.

The Arrans team had created the extrapolator portal with an event horizon of one hundred years into the future.

The humans were absolutely mesmerized with the set-up of the Arrans' extrapolator and could see that their respective lives and work would soon become linked to this marvelous alien technology.

The journey begins…

Echo takes Sara and Pete's mind into a future state that is as actual as can be imagined. It is a highly advanced virtual reality that literally places the travelers into a world of unbelievable chaos and devastation.

The Arrans' Moon basecamp had been totally destroyed, and the Moon itself was partially destroyed. And, without the Moon, humanity could not survive on Earth.

Snippets of the multiverse fill Sara's mind, well beyond the 100-year-event horizon.

The Dracs are at the Alpha-Draconis star system, over 200 light years away.

The Denon are at the M-dwarf Star GJ 677C, F and E, 22 light-years away. Together, they have colonized Mars and they have a joint military venture on what Pete insists is an Earth-size exoplanet nearly 100 light-years away… a location that scares Echo, as it is *homeland* for the Arrans.

Sara shares her multiverse projections with Pete, who then gives his VR-indicated time and location coordinates to Echo for verification when they return. Echo logs that info.

Echo knows that if what Pete *saw* was accurate, those are the likely locations where the massive alien military bases' weapon-development centers were to be built.

In one after another Milky Way location, Sara sees death, destruction, fire, and annihilation. The future isn't just dark… it is gone!

Upon returning to current reality, Echo and Sara conclude that they both *saw* many of the same images and agreed that mankind and the Arrans culture must become much more aggressive.

"Sara, this has been a nightmare, even for me." Echo has been visibly affected by this surrealistic journey.

"Sara, this is the first time that I have been able to connect the cosmic dots… it is frightening."

Looking directly into Echo's eyes, Sara had never heard or seen her alien friend this upset and this de-energized. Always so full of determination and positivity, this time it all was sinking into Sara.

Sara knew that she had experienced far more multiverse chaos than Echo had seen, and she thought decidedly, *"I know what we need to focus on."*

"Echo, we need to accelerate a strategic plan that has us both defending Earth and attacking our enemies."

"I agree, Sara. First step?"

"We need to build warships… and as soon as possible!"

86

CLICK YOUR HEELS

Given the shocking glimpse of the future and realizing that her parents could be in danger, Sara planned to travel to Ohio to meet with Mike and Christine and bring them up to date on the current alien and magnetic wave situations.

Getting a grasp on recent events, Sara took a deep breath and phoned home, "Hi Dad, it's me. How're you and Mom doing?"

"Oh, hi Sara, thanks for the call. We are fine. Echo has been great keeping us updated on your travels and your training. We would have worried sick, if not for her. Are you coming out for a visit?"

"Yes, Dad, I am."

"Soon, Sara?"

"Yep, we need to talk, Dad. Is Mom there?"

"Yes, she is. Do you want me to get her?"

"No. Not yet."

"Are you okay, Sara? You sound like you are a little stressed or maybe you are just tired."

"I'm fine. Just busy, ya know."

"Where are you now? California or Utah?"

"At the Utah lab. Dad, are you okay with a visit now?"

"Of course. Get me your flight itinerary and I can pick you up at Cleveland Hopkins Airport."

"No, I mean are you okay with my visit right now?"

"Sure, Sara. I don't understand."

"You will, Dad. I'll be there real soon."

As they both hung up, Mike when into the kitchen to tell Christine what had happened with the call to Sara.

"And she said she would be right over, Mike?"

"That's what she said."

As Mike helped Christine with some kitchen chores, a swirling, hazy mist filled the breakfast nook. Within seconds, Sara appeared to a stunned and speechless Mike and Christine.

"Well," Christine muttered, "you certainly aren't Sara Stevenson anymore."

Mike smiled as Sara replied firmly, **"I'm not even Sara Steele anymore!"**

87

I KNOW A PLACE

"That was quite an entrance, honey. Give your mom a hug before you disappear into cosmic Disneyland."

A smiling Sara walked the few steps over to her parents and embraced them both.

"Damn, Sara, that was impressive. Ya gotta teach us that trick."

"Afraid I can't do that, Dad. But I can do something similar that you will certainly enjoy. Let's just take a moment and relax, okay? I've been on a roller coaster these last few days."

"Can I get you something, Dear? Or did you have a drink on the long trip over here?"

"Funny, Mom. Gosh, I'm glad you guys are good, and all is well."

Sara smiled and glanced over at her dad.

"Mom," Sara said grinning, "you are especially calm and cool… you on meds?"

"No, Dear. I just finally accepted the fact that our daughter is a superhero!"

An excited Mike chimed in, "We are so proud of you, Sara."

He gave Sara another hug as Sara added her concern, "With the lingering Covid-19 and all this alien stuff, a girl can worry about her parents being okay."

"A girl can," Mike offered, "but a Warrior Princess can't."

Christine added, "Let me get you something to drink. What's your preference?"

"Just some iced tea or lemonade would be fine. I'd like to bring you guys up to speed on current ETRT events, and then I have a little surprise."

Christine brought out a pitcher of lemonade with ice and some glasses as Sara began to bring her folks into the loop.

Sara decided to bypass the Michaela abduction for now, given Christine's depression following the abduction and murder of close friend Kathy. Sara would get with Mike later to cover that episode.

Christine poured the lemonade into three glasses, stirred the clanking ice cubes, and handed them out, and said with a grin, "Cheers to the space cadet and the old folks!"

Sara burst out laughing and thought, *"Mom was always the conservative and reserved one... now she is Miss Funny Pants. I love it!"*

"Okay, guys, I have three things on my agenda for today. First, I need to bring you up-to-speed on a shitty glimpse into the future."

Sara had a change of plans regarding this next issue, thinking, *"I need to sugarcoat this, or Mom will freak out."*

Echo and I, using a Arrans' device called an extrapolator, recently used a complicated galactic data set and images from a variety of sources, to teleport our minds into the future... the very distant future... a simulation, of sorts."

Sara winked at her dad, who now knew that the unsavory details would be for his ears only at a later time and place.

"What this telepathic trip into the future showed us was that an annihilation of Earth... an apocalypse causing an extinction-level event was in our future."

"Oh my," uttered Christine. "I don't want to hear the details, but... when, Sara?"

"Sorry to scare you, Mom, but not soon and never, if we take action now. The whole purpose of this simulation was twofold: to give notice to global leaders that we are facing a catastrophe, and to take immediate action in a human-alien alliance."

Mike jumped in, "And you are doing that, right?"

"Yes, Dad, we are. But the threat is real, and it is closer than ever."

Sara uttered, "Let's move on to something a little more pleasant, okay?"

Christine smiled and replied, "Of course, Dear, pretty please."

"Great. This is number two on today's agenda." Mike and Christine held hands as an excited Sara had a proposal.

"Remember back about twenty years ago when you guys flew to Portofino, Italy, to celebrate your wedding anniversary and renew your vows?"

"Of course, my good friend, Betty, was maid-of-honor and Dad's best friend, Kenny, was his best man." Christine added, "And you were the lovely young flower girl. How could we forget? Dad and I cherish the photos of that wonderful occasion and think about it often."

"Well, go change into some traveling clothes, because we are teleporting to Portofino, Italy, as soon as you can be ready!"

"You mean virtual, right Sara?"

"Nope, Dad. We are going to literally be on the very same streets as we were way back then."

Christine got a little faint and had to sit down. An eager Mike offered his suggestion, "I'll get our passports, my Italian Lira, and some Euros for the trip, Sara."

Sara smiled as Christine stood up and said, "Give me a moment to catch my breath and then we'll be off. Now I'm excited!"

Sara mentioned some admin facts to her parents as they prepared for the *trip*.

"The current temperature in Portofino is seventy-two degrees, with partly-cloudy skies and winds out of the east at ten miles an hour. Be sure to bring your boat shoes, as we will be taking a cruise around the bay and harbor."

Sara took a moment to upload the Italian language into her newly acquired software skill, using her wrist device and implant, and was anxious to try it out on the locals there.

About thirty minutes later, the three international travelers were ready. Mike had secured the house, not realizing that they will be in a perpendicular time-stop and would return to Ohio at about the same time as when they left.

"Ready, Dear. I have our old travel itinerary," Christine announced, "and even old photos to compare with the present."

Sara smiled… held hands with her parents… and in an instant, the three Ohioans were in Portofino, Italy, in the city referred to as the *Italian Riviera.*

As the three materialized on the picturesque harbor front, Christine uttered, "This is as beautiful as I remember… and so real!"

"Mom, it is real. We are real and this moment is real."

Christine and Mike both gave their amazing daughter a hug, as the gorgeous commune of *Portofino* exploded with the colorfully painted buildings that lined the shore.

Mike said, "I want to have lunch at *Trattoria Tripoli* in the *Piazza Martiri dell'Olivetta,* where the meatballs are 'delizioso,' and after that, go for a short fishing trip."

"Can do, Dad."

Christine chimed in, "I want to go to the *Abbey of San Fruttuoso,* where Mike and I exchanged vows."

Sara answered with an idea to run by her very excited Italian visitors.

"That abbey is located closer to Camogli than to Portofino. Let's make it our last stop before heading back home."

"Excellent idea," Mike confirmed.

The happy *tour group* spent the entire day and early evening doing all the things that Mike and Christine wanted to do, including souvenir shopping, which Sara said was okay. They even managed a short boat cruise.

After an exhausting day, they went to Christine's favorite eatery, *Ristorante Taverna del Marinaio*, for a scrumptious seafood dinner. Sara's parents were amazed at Sara's grasp of the foreign language, as was Sara amazed.

Following dinner, Sara took Mike and Christine to the Abbey, where they went inside and spent about thirty minutes reminiscing. As they left the church, about to head home, Christine looked into Sara's eyes and said to Sara what Mike was surely thinking, "You have made this the happiest day in our lives. Thank you for taking time to 'stop and smell the roses' with your very grateful parents."

"The pleasure has been all mine, mom."

With that, they embraced and zap... back to the present day in Northeast Ohio.

Upon arriving back at her parents' home, she noticed the time on the kitchen clock. It was nearly 11:00 pm Ohio time when they left, so given the seven-hour time difference, arriving in Portofino early in the morning, Italian time, was to be expected.

What wasn't expected was the clock in the kitchen did not read 11:00 pm... the clock actually read 5:00 pm that same day. Sara thought, *"We arrived back in this house... six hours before we left!"*

Sara thought of a limerick she saw in Pulse's man-cave at the bottom of Tranquility Lake:

> **There was a young lady so bright,**
> **who traveled much faster than light,**
> **She departed one day,**
> **in a most expeditious way,**
> **and arrived on the previous night.**

"Not only was that freaky," she thought curiously. *"I now have a photographic memory!"*

Glancing at her parents, who were basking in the glow of a most memorable trip, Christine cut into Sara's head-scratching with a question, "So, you had two issues for your dad and me... what's your issue number three, sweetie?"

Sara's demeanor took on a very serious tone.

"We need to move you guys to the Utah compound, before a destructive magnetic wave strikes Earth!"

88

PROJECT ZEUS

Sara left a tentative logistics plan with her parents so they could pack up the house and put together enough belongings for at least six months. Christine looked at this sojourn as an opportunity to spend time with her daughter, not realizing the time demands on Sara.

Back at the Utah lab, the remaining members of the ETRT that had been stationed in Palo Alto, Team-Arrans and Matt and Jeremiah started to put the feasibility plan together for the most ambitious project in American history.

The reduced R and D time, prototype development and build, and testing of battle-ready spaceships still put the whole project on a timeline that was ten times faster than the development of the atomic bomb.

As Sara was literally zapping in from Ohio, following her momentous visit with Mike and Christine, she was delighted with the *hair-on-fire* atmosphere she was seeing.

"Hi guys. What's our plan?"

"Hi Sara," an excited RJ responded. "How was your Ohio visit?"

"Oh, pretty normal… just catching up, you know."

Seeing both Scott and Matt, Sara waved, noticing that both men were engaged in a spirited conversation.

Echo came over to Sara and, with a gesture that was becoming as pleasant as it was unusual, hugged Sara and whispered in her ear, "What you did for your parents was wonderful. We tend to leave those we love on the outside too often."

"Thanks, Echo. It just was so 'right,' and looking back, it made me think of all the things we have missed because of this game-changing alien disruption."

Pulse then walked over to Sara, Scott, and Echo with an assessment. "Echo and I agree that we need both starships and warships."

Echo took the lead. "Let's scope this project out from the 'big picture' perspective."

"I agree," answered Scott excitedly. "Throw something up there so we can get some dialogue going."

Using a whiteboard in the lab, Echo wrote down their priorities:

1. *How many of each?*
2. *What are the design criteria?*
3. *Who would design?*
4. *What role would both the ETRT and the Arrans play?*
5. *Where will they be built?*
6. *Who will man and crew them?*
7. *What will be the major obstacles?*
8. *What will be their mission or destinations?*

Pulse looked at Sara and thought to himself, "*Eight more from Echo... how consistent... how mysterious.*"

Sara glanced at Pulse and was ready to move the meeting along.

"Okay, let's break out into groups and put some basic plans together."

A thoroughly engaged RJ advised, "Timing will be critical. It is obvious that we don't have traditional timelines to design, build, and test these crafts."

Scott, who had been busy taking notes and formulating a project management strategy, agreed as they broke out into work groups. He added a request, "Sara, can we count on your dad to get involved with some of his ops and project management expertise?"

"Absolutely. I have it on good authority that he will be here in three days."

Echo, Pulse, and Sara moved to a smaller room where they could talk in private. Sara was seen busily texting as they walked.

"I've got Mara Wallace, the President's chief aide running Cameron down right now in the White House. We need to get him involved right away."

"Good call, Sara," Echo responded. "Whatever we do will require a huge commitment from President Sullivan and his military arsenal."

Noticing Pulse making some notes, Sara asked, "What cha doing, Pulse?"

"I think we need at least three Galactic-class starships plus Echo's Destiny. I even have names for them."

"Okay," a half-hearted Sara inquired, "what are they?"

"Number one would be *Orion,* Pete Stevenson's secret nickname. Number two would be *Intrepid,* for being fearless and adventuresome, and number three would be *Prometheus*... no gain without pain."

With an impatient sigh, Echo added, "Pulse, focus. Please."

✦ ✦ ✦

President Sullivan and a small cadre of military leaders were now in place in the Situation Room, so a secure video call could begin.

Due to the large number of scattered off-site attendees, and a lack of a relevant agenda, Sara took the meeting lead, and laid out the view at 30,000 feet.

During the meeting, some preliminary answers were reached, and preliminary roles and responsibilities were presented and agreed upon.

Sara began a brief summary of conclusions and agreements.

"The design-versus-need criteria signaled a plan for three to five starships and a fleet of warships numbering at least fifty. I would name this 'bucket' our *Galactic Federation.*"

Over-the-top was the general consensus discernment of the assembled personnel.

"The ETRT role and Arrans' role will be combined, and would focus on software and AI, GAI, and various deception-oriented battle tools and disruptive technology."

The techies in the group were getting energized.

"The likely manufacturing sites would be in Alabama and South Carolina, where many joint manufacturing plants were already in place."

Scott lobbied for his interstellar voyager ships to continue to be made in California. They would.

"Manning would be on a need-by-need basis, but it was agreed that all starship leadership personnel would be made up of cross-cultural and cross-functional staff."

There seemed to be no dissent.

Sara was pumped up and continued. "Crews would literally be galactic and accept any and all volunteers."

Major obstacles, roadblocks, impediments, and literal showstoppers were discussed and tabled for the present time.

Mission scope and scale were determined to be any and all of the offensive and defensive needs that galactic intel presented. Initial targets, strategic special deployments, and future destination journeys were generally discussed and were also tabled.

At that time, President Sullivan called for a thirty-minute break. Echo took that time to meet with Sara and Pulse.

When the President returned, he was alone and noticeably pissed.

"Sorry for the meeting disconnect, but I am having my own personnel disconnect. I have gotten serious pushback from two of my trusted commanders, as well as one senior staffer."

Sara asked distractedly, "Pushback on what, Cameron?"

"There is a small contingent that, while understanding the gravity of the situation, do not believe that Sara's young team of overachievers and the friendly Arrans aliens need to be at the center of any military deployment."

"Mister President, what do you intend to do?"

"It's already being done, Echo. I am replacing those dissenters."

A somewhat scowling Pulse added, "So that early turmoil basically defines our Project Zeus resource base going forward."

"I have a better name to define our project, Pulse."

"What's that, Sara?"

Serious and cynically, she simply uttered, "Badassery."

89

CAMP DAVID II

Two days later, and following the tense session from the high-level video conference, it was time for the committee that the President assembled to give reports on the progress being made regarding Echo's initial eight capsules at the second Camp David meeting.

POTUS had invited Echo, Pulse, and Sara to be on-site for that meeting, and only two days after Sara's *Badassery* conclusion, the fully committed three-some arrived at Camp David and were welcomed by the President.

"It's good to have you here in this place where some of the most significant American alliance meetings were held. Let's hope today's will be memorable."

Echo thought sarcastically, "*It will be memorable, I'm sure!*"

"Hello, Mister President. Pulse and I are happy to be here and we are both optimistic that this will also be a significant meeting."

"Hi Sara. Are your parents safely located in the Utah compound?"

"Yes, Cameron. In fact, we just finished their orientation a couple hours ago."

"Good. The committee is seated and in place. Let's head into the conference room and get this meeting started."

"Yes, Cameron," Sara added, "we are very anxious to see the progress that has been made. With all the other diversions, getting these capsules properly managed and quickly implemented is critical."

POTUS nodded in agreement as the four of them entered the room.

"Good morning and thanks for clearing your respective schedules for this important meeting."

Ernesto Suarez, the Foreign Affairs Chair, uttered, "There is nothing more important, Mister President, than completing these tasks."

The President introduced everyone, and the reports began based on progress versus timelines.

After the first round of updates, several capsule projects were stalled due to one explanation after another. Sara felt no sense of urgency, mostly blaming other people for lack of participation. She looked at her notes…

General Patrick – still vetting key positions for recruiting.
General Grant – hasn't yet established a baseline from which to determine future state.
Doctor Griffith – doesn't have a coordination of academia and corporate expertise.
Frank Polansky – struggling to verify certain elements of the alien's evidence.
Suarez – on schedule and making progress on international liaisons.
Don Meacham – slightly behind schedule, but still his first priority.
RJ and his dad – no problems and on track.

An extremely irritated Echo jumped to her feet, and Sara and Pulse both knew what was about to happen. Echo scowled, "Enough!" After a three-second pause, "This is bullshit!"

The President felt her pain and anxiety, and stepped in. "I understand your concern, Echo, but sometimes these things take time to get traction."

"Traction, hell. This lack of focus in unacceptable… I'll show you what focus and urgency look like." Echo was communicating telepathically as she spoke.

Almost in mere seconds from her statement, Echo was having Aeon, the leader of the *Greys*, appear in the conference room.

"You all know Aeon from our meeting at your Congress. She has brought you a visual aid."

Aeon nods at Echo and instantly creates a large cage in the middle of the long, elliptical conference table. The members sitting around the table jump out of their seats as a hideous creature appears in the cage, and Pulse and Sara realize that the creature is one of the evil alien Dracs' fearsome warriors.

For scary and dramatic effect, Aeon tases the creature, who then morphs into a human-like male form… another tase and the creature takes on a female form.

One last tase and the large, foreboding creature, smelly and dripping with a green slime, wraps his clawed hands around the metal caging and lets out a terrifying shriek.

Aeon and Echo now have the absolute attention of everyone in the room… even the President is aghast.

With a nod from Echo, both Aeon and the immense creature are gone, but the disgusting physical mess left by this visual aid left no one thinking that this was a hoax or *special effect*.

Echo's last words to the committee were, "Do you want us to protect you…
or are you going to commit to protecting yourselves?"

The committee members just lived a *nightmare in Maryland!*

As Sara, Echo, and Pulse observed, President Sullivan immediately addressed
the group; and new, and very short, timelines were established.

Echo met with the President one-on-one before she left to discuss the incoming magnetic wave.

"If you can't get this done… I will!"

90

UTAH COMPLEX

West of Provo, Utah, Scott Woods had undertaken the job of directing the construction of a hardened underground compound, designed to withstand future disasters, alien infiltration, and life-extinction catastrophes. With extensive help from the President's enormous resource base, this complex would likely become the most impenetrable facility in the world, eventually housing key American military assets.

Scott invited the newest citizenry and resident guests, Mike and Christine Stevenson, to a presentation of their new home.

"Good morning, folks. Y'all getting settled in?"

Mike was excited. "Absolutely, this place is awesome and so full of high-tech gadgets that even I'm overwhelmed."

"It's not very pretty," a frowning Christine offered.

"Okay," Scott commented politely, "most of this will fall into Mike's wheelhouse. Sorry, Christine."

Scott began his Power Point slide presentation, "Let me start by saying that we can withstand a near direct hit from a thirty-megaton nuclear bomb."

Christine grimaced.

"This complex was built under granite, two thousand feet below the Earth's surface, and on an area of approximately five acres."

Mike was visioning a tip-of-the-iceberg coming from Scott.

"It contains five hundred thousand square feet of office, R and D, lab, manufacturing, and communications, and with a command center that would rival NASA." Pausing, "Fifteen three-story buildings are protected from movement, say explosion or earthquake, by a system of giant springs that the buildings sit on and flexible pipe connectors to limit the effect of movement."

Now, Christine was beginning to become impressed.

"As you can see by this diagram, an elaborate system of tunnels 'spider-web' into the adjoining mountains. There is an access tunnel with North and South openings, side tunnels to the main chambers and support areas, and the vast main chambers themselves."

"What about the 'people-friendly' stuff?" Christine asked.

Smiling and looking directly at Christine, Scott replied, "This complex has family-type housing for one thousand residents, suites for the leadership cadre, a huge medical facility, two stores, four pharmacy locations, two cafeterias, a movie theater and an incredible array of recreational amenities."

Scott continued to show details of the complex, but Christine was busy trying to send out text messages… to no avail.

Scott concluded with a statement that was both reassuring and scary, "This will become the largest private-shelter community on Earth… ten thousand people could survive here for at least a year."

Scott," Mike inquired, "where would the spacecrafts be built?"

"Spacecrafts?" Christine wondered.

"Fremont would be the location for building my Galactic Voyager spacecrafts, and manufacturing sites in Alabama and South Carolina would build the fleet."

Mike thought to himself, *"Scott doesn't cut corners."*

Scott was thinking, *"I'm glad we are on a government contract!"*

Christine just shrugged and had been drained by all this data and could simply add, **"Oh my!"**

91

CARPE DIEM

The day had finally arrived for Echo to meet with the members of the U.S. Defense Department at the Pentagon. As was expected, the Pentagon's own think-tank had their views, but late demonstrations by Echo and her alien friends had convinced the American establishment to take a back seat... at least for now.

General James Patrick introduced the now famous and most intimidating alien figure to the assembled Pentagon Brass, which also included Lieutenant Baker and Commander RJ Baker.

Echo began, "The origin of the wave was an electro-magnetic pulse machine created by the Draconians and launched from an asteroid named Apophis, a relatively small asteroid but capable of being the base for this power surge."

There was obvious respect for Echo, as she was so calm and direct.

"The intention was to evaluate the capability of Earth to withstand a medium-strong assault from somewhere in your solar system to see what the Draconian strike force would be dealing with in terms of Earth's defense. The scope of the Mars lunar base annihilation was the first indication of the severity and likely destruction from the surge, and the ability of mankind to communicate in quantum space."

A raised hand and voice from the front row broke the silence, "Echo, do you have a sense of the destructive capability of this wave?"

"Yes. The destruction would be similar to a Neutron Bomb, which was a type of enhanced radiation weapon, or ERW, that, as you know, is a low-yield thermonuclear weapon designed to maximize lethal neutron radiation in the immediate vicinity of the blast while minimizing the physical power of the blast itself."

General Grant added his expertise, "The thermal pulse, if unchecked, would cause third-degree burns to victims, kill thousands, and destroy all electronic capacity worldwide... a global disaster."

Echo added to the General's input, "The idea is to destroy the infrastructure, stop daily life in its tracks, and then invade and occupy Earth... we believe. Billions of elements of food, vis-a-vis, humans, would remain."

Echo raised her voice noticeably, "The defense systems presently on Earth are minimal and ineffective against this type of unconventional weapon. You have no defense... zero defense, right now."

Some of the old guard's male ego was waning.

"Our strategy was to destroy the machine at its source," Echo added, "which we did rather easily. However, the wave itself cannot be stopped, only minimized in its destructive capability."

Commander Baker asked, "What is the countermeasure, Echo, which you would and could employ?"

"We will erect a partial dome or shield to meet the incoming wave, Commander Baker. It will minimize the destruction, but not totally prevent it... a mitigation."

President Sullivan recapped Echo's prognosis again for those who may have missed her point, "This dome defense will mitigate the intensity of the impact, but not completely eliminate it. As the power is turned off, the wave is still in route."

"That is correct, Mister President."

Echo thought to herself... *"Three steps forward and two steps back."*

General Patrick thanked Echo for all that she and her team had done and wished them well in their efforts to minimize the damage.

"The wave is three days out... we have three days to plan and execute our dome strategy."

Looking directly at President Sullivan, Echo simply stated the obvious, **"We must *seize the day*... and we will!"**

92

BREAKING NEWS

President Sullivan went back to the Oval Office, from where he would speak to the American people. He intended to keep his speech short and to the point, as he would not be able to answer the many questions asked.

He got the latest info from his Chief of Staff, Ruth Baker Eisenberg, and had Mara Wallace prepare his address to the Nation regarding the pending wave that is about to hit North America.

"Mara, is this the text for my teleprompter?"

"Yes, Mister President."

"And you and Ruth have confirmed that my story will coincide with the other world leaders' account of the incoming wave?"

"Yes, Sir."

"Okay. I'm ready."

Looking into the camera, sitting behind the impressive Resolute Desk, President Sullivan began as the prompts wind down... five, four, three, two, and go.

"Good evening, my fellow Americans, and from the White House I bring you information and hope..."

He clears his throat.

"We on Earth are about to experience a 'natural' phenomenon from the Sun... an event that only happens once in a couple of thousand years."

He hopes Americans buy his little white lie.

"Fortunately, the people of Earth have the good fortune to have the peaceful Arrans alien race, who have saved us from several calamities in the past, working hard for us again today."

He cuts to a hastily drawn chart of the wave from the Sun.

"As we are speaking, the Arrans are installing a defensive shield that will protect Earth from the serious damage that the wave could do if not for this countermeasure."

Scientists and astronomers are quickly responding on social media that the Sun is not the origin of the wave. Fortunately for POTUS and the world leaders, no one knows what is real and what is fake news anymore on any social media sites, so it's *press on regardless*.

President Sullivan continues to follow his teleprompter.

"There may also be temporary power outages and the electrical grid in your particular area may be down. We anticipate this and will work to have everything back to normal as soon as possible.

"Good night and may God Bless the United States of America."

Before the President left the Oval Office, he got assurance from his Chief of Staff that the ISS2 and as many satellites as possible would be positioned on the far side of Earth, to avoid any major contact with the magnetic wave.

As President Sullivan left, he was told by Mara Wallace that Echo was waiting in the Situation Room. He hurried to meet her.

"Well done, Mister President."

"Thanks, Echo. I hate to lie, though."

Echo smiled as a nervous President had a very important question to ask, "Echo, do you have the simulation results back on the collateral damage from this wave?"

"I do, Sir."

"And?"

"There will likely be casualties… many casualties."

93

STORMY

The very next day, a similar global announcement, fabricated as an alternately sourced explanation, limited the event to a fake news story about a rogue Rossby wave. Those waves typically govern the Earth's jet stream and had resulted in a magnetic solar storm that was predicted earlier but thought to be mild.

Headlines throughout the World were consistent with either the world leaders' accounts or the many random global explanations, even though social media had conspiracy theories exploding in every corner of the world and blame being decided indiscriminately.

The entire Galactic Force realized that they had to avoid hysteria and widespread panic on Earth. Sara had the ETRT create some bullet points for easy transmission via several media that would get the word out quickly.

- *Verification of the Arrans dome installation*
- *Exact time of impact*
- *Precautions for thermal radiation exposure*
- *Immediate medical care for possible third-degree burns*
- *Duration of the wave's destructive life*
- *Degree of electrical grids down was estimated*
- *Impact of grids being down for citizens to prepare*
- *Shelter options and locations*
- *Food and water distribution sites*
- *Medical emergency locations*
- *Everyone must take cover, underground if possible, to avoid exposure.*
- *Emergency contact personnel, if connectable*

As the number of casualties, key essential shortages, and daily disruptions would be assessed by the President and his staff, it was now known that the major impact would be North America, likely by intention of the Dracs.

Pulse, Laser, and Vibe were going over their check list for both North America and the Arrans Moon base shields via their dome technology.

Precautions were limited to coordinating efforts of state and local governments to begin the repair and restoration of services, as soon as possible.

Hospitals were bracing for heavy volume of sick and dying… almost like the worst of the Coronavirus Pandemic of 2020 and 2021.

Medical first responders knew that triage was back in play.

Echo had Vibe do a fully detailed simulation of the Arrans' shield defense and it was promising. The Moon base shield was successfully activated, and the Earth's shield was in final countdown to deployment.

Everyone now was preparing for impact. Sara checked in with her parents, who were hunkered down in a massive complex, free of any impact concern, which Christine told Sara was, "just fine with me!"

A pensive Sara thought, "*What the hell is next!*"

As the entire Galactic Force waited for impact, Pulse leaned over to Echo and said, "I have the results back from Sara's before and after DNA that you asked me to check."

"And what did you find?

"Echo, this may surprise you…"

"I doubt it, Pulse."

A bewildered Echo was stunned by Pulse's remark, **"Sara's DNA taken now is exactly the same as when she was injured at the cabin blast."**

94

AFTERSHOCKS

At 3:15 pm, the massive magnetic wave struck the dome with reverberating shock waves that could be felt primarily in the Northern Hemisphere. As was expected by Echo, this enhanced radiation weapon produced a large blast wave and a powerful pulse of both thermal radiation and ionizing radiation in the form of fast neutrons.

From the Situation Room, President Sullivan received an early assessment of the damage from the Chairman of the Joint Chiefs of Staff, General Arthur van Buuren. "The blast was significantly minimized, due to the aliens' dome. There was a modified blast radius whereby unprotected civilians suffered minor burns, and blast pressures damaged many non-reinforced buildings."

"So far... so good, Art?"

"Yes, Mister President. Some very powerful winds, likely reverberating from the dome's surface, did inflict damage to structures, communication towers, and weak powerlines. The electrical grid, for the most part, was only moderately affected."

POTUS was visibly relieved at the early assessment.

General van Buuren continued his status report, "The biggest problem we face, sir, is that civilians will come out of their protected areas too soon. The radiation is not presently severe, thanks to the dome, but radiation will linger for hours... if not days."

"Thanks, Art. I will get the message out via all available media for people to stay in 'indoor lockdown' until told otherwise."

"That'll work."

"Anything more, Art?"

"Not for now. I will get with the proper military and admin personnel to address rescue, recovery, or repair. FEMA is already on 'high alert' and is 'on task' as we speak."

"Thank you. Talk later."

"Of course, Mister President. You know where you can find me."

With that, General van Buuren left the Oval Office as Mara Wallace stepped in.

"Good day, Mara."

"Good day to you, General."

"Mara, take some notes… you are as wise as they come. You'll know what to do with each issue."

Mara took her seat. "Of course, Mister President. Go ahead."

"I will need to have another address to reassure Americans and the world that all will be back to normal soon, and what diligence they must take. Etcetera, etcetera."

Mara put a check in one of her boxes.

"Get with my staff regarding planning our next steps and both short-term and long-term initiatives along with roles and responsibilities for same."

Glancing at a totally engaged Miss Wallace, the President continued, "I will need reports from both Provo and Fremont regarding any damage."

"Excuse me, Mister President, but I have already heard the 'all clear' from both facilities. No damage."

"That's wonderful. Just send my 'well wishes' and thoughts… yada, yada."

"Finally, let's look at my daily schedule and agenda items for the next month or so. Get back with me in about an hour, Mara, so we can re-allocate, if necessary."

"Will do. I'll take care of this short list and be back soon."

Mara left the Oval Office, and the President was left with a thought. "*What is the alien's end game… all of them?*"

President Sullivan contacted Echo and Pulse, via his personal link, and thanked them on behalf of the American people.

"Mister President, we are now… and have always been… a trusted ally regarding any issue that you and humanity will face."

"Echo, I need an education on all things alien and would like a tutorial from you soon that might explain all of the galactic forces and various alien cultures, and help me determine, or at least get some idea, on their 'end game' strategies."

"Pulse and I would be happy to do that, Mister President. Just have your aide, Miss Wallace, set it up."

"Will do, Echo. Thanks again."

As they disconnected from the President, Echo still had the Sara DNA report from Pulse on her mind.

Echo took Pulse's report and asked Pulse intently, "We still have some 'digging' to do into Sara's DNA, Pulse."

Pulse knew that look and it was the look of determination and resolve... a typical Echo characteristic.

"As Sara would say, 'Echo... A penny for your thoughts?'"

"Of course, Pulse."

Echo perused the DNA data file and simply drew an Echo conclusion.

"Sara's extraordinary skill set is as much 'supernatural' as it is natural!"

95

ALIEN TUTORIAL

Given President Sullivan's extremely vague question concerning various alien cultures and end games, Echo pulled Sara and Pulse together for a think-tank approach.

Echo thought to herself, *"How many different alien cultures are out there... which are friend or foe... and where are they?"*

As Sara and Pulse joined her, President Sullivan patched in on a video chat feed.

"Good morning, all. This student is ready to learn!"

"Good morning, Mister President, Echo said appreciatively. "Let's get started. This is an overview or info update... and nothing more."

"Understood," the President responded.

Echo began by speculating on each alien's home world location, "We believe that the Denon are primarily at the red dwarf star Gliese 667C, where nine planets exist and three of these lie within the habitable zone. Twenty-two light-years away in the constellation of Scorpius is where their leader took the name, Scorpio. There is a super-Earth in that system, an exoplanet with a mass and radius greater than that of Earth, but smaller than that of the giant planets Uranus and Neptune, and with an equilibrium temperature around forty degrees, Fahrenheit."

Sara thought, *"Echo can summarize so well... and she is just getting started."*

"The Draconian species are principally located near Thuban, also called the Alpha-Draconis star system, which is about two hundred and seventy light-years away in the northern constellation Draco. This system ranks among the brightest known eclipsing binaries where the two stars are widely separated, or detached, and only interact gravitationally.

"Thuban is considered historically significant for Earth since it was the North Pole star from the fourth to the second millennium BCE. It is a massive star and more luminous than the Sun... four-hundred times more luminous than the Sun.

"Draco contains several interacting galaxies, and sparing technical detail for now, this constellation likely has many inhabitable planets. This alien race is huge in size and dangerous for its scope and extreme colonization practices."

President Sullivan added respectfully, "I am overwhelmed... and humbled. And how do you define exoplanet?"

Pulse quickly offered, "Any planet outside this solar system."

POTUS thought sheepishly, *"I should have known that!"*

Pausing, Echo sternly advised, "Yes, Mister President, you don't want to mess with the Dracs... but now we must.

"Our friends, the *Greys*, have colonies and bases throughout the galaxy and are older, from the standpoint of an Earthly presence, than any other species. Their main home is on an Earth-size exoplanet about one hundred light-years away. It is referred to as TOI-700. With an abundance of water, it is orbiting a star that is about forty per cent of your Sun's mass and illumination."

<Pulse and Sara... put this exoplanet on our *Salvation List* for now.>

<Done, Echo.>

Nodding her head, <Ditto from me, Echo.>

"This exoplanet is one of three planets orbiting its star, and the planet's rotation matches exactly with its rotation around the star. That means the same surface always face its star, just like how the same part of your Moon always faces Earth."

Echo waited until POTUS was done taking notes and looked up at the screen.

"I will now just summarize the vast potential inhabitable planets that are fairly well documented, and many of which the Arrans have visited over the centuries.

"Kepler 22b, also known by its Kepler object of interest designation KOI-087, is an extrasolar planet orbiting within the habitable zone of the Sun-like star Keplar-22. It is located about six hundred light-years away from Earth in the constellation Cygnus and is likely inhabited.

"Kepler 1649c and 452b are exoplanets that are about six billion years old and very interesting, given that it takes about five billion years for intelligent life to form in our universe and beyond.

"1649c is an inhabitable exoplanet orbiting the M-type red dwarf star Kepler 1649, about three hundred light-years from Earth, and almost exactly the same size.

"452b is a rocky planet, likely inhabitable, orbiting a sun similar to yours, but about twenty per cent more luminous, with the same temperature and mass. It is way out there… about fourteen hundred light-years from Earth in that same constellation Cygnus."

"Way out there…," Sara thought, enjoying the tutorial.

Echo directly asked the President, "Are you familiar with the term 'Astrobiological Copernican Limit,' Mister President?"

"No. Sorry, I am not."

"Using the assumptions that intelligent life forms on other planets in a similar way as it does on Earth, researchers have developed an estimate for the number of intelligent communicating civilizations within your own galaxy, the Milky Way, which is one hundred thousand light-years across."

POTUS anxiously awaited her next point, expecting specificity.

"Today, they have calculated that there could be over thirty active communicating intelligent civilizations in this home galaxy."

"I bet you have a different number, eh Echo?"

"Well, you already know that we Arrans live in a seven-planet Trappist One system that is 'only' forty light-years away.

"Let me make two points, Mister President."

"Sara thought, *"I know what's coming… been there… heard that."*

"Point number one. The universe is fifteen billion years old, and this planet, Earth, is about 4.5 billion years old. Bacteria and fossils on Earth can be traced back to about 3.5 billion years ago. It is with inexcusably egocentric bias that one would conclude that we are alone in this universe."

Pulse thought, *"Echo should be a college professor."*

<Heard that, Pulse.>

<I did too, Sara. Maybe someday I will.>

"Point Number two. It is absolutely foolish to think that Earth was the only place in the observable universe with life… Among the hundred billion galaxies, each containing a hundred billion stars… orbited by a hundred billion planets."

"On that breathtaking reality check, I need to get back to my 'Presidential mundanity,' Echo," POTUS said, with a smile and slight laugh.

"Well, thank you for your time, Mister President. I hope this was helpful, and please let us know what we can continue to do to help."

"Will do. Bye."

"Sara?"

"Yes, Echo."

"I'm going to throw something out to you that was a shock to Pulse and me when we had this next item dropped into our massive data set."

Sara could feel that tension and anxiety in Echo's voice.

"Sara, we believe that there is a literal mirror image of your Earth and Sun about 3000 light-years away."

"And there is more, Sara," Pulse excitedly advised.

"Go ahead, Pulse," Echo replies.

"We have reason to believe that this mirror image is actually a parallel, or alternate universe. In theory, this universe is made up of worlds that don't necessarily act as we would call 'normal.' In a parallel universe, a totally different, sometimes opposite action occurs."

Echo quickly added, "And it could also be a hard indication of a multiverse that is literally in existence as we speak."

Sara recalled some very *long-term visioning* by her grandad, Pete Stevenson. "Very simply put... a multiverse is just a collection of parallel universes."

"That's right, Sara," Pulse confirmed.

"So, Echo, you said you had 'reason to believe' this theory?"

"Sara, I don't think it's a theory."

"We believe that this Earth-Sun system, 3000 light-years away, is part of a parallel universe that includes the evolution of Neanderthal-types."

"Echo, what evidence do you have? You must have some irrefutable facts that validates this theory."

"Yes, Sara. You know our alien friend, Aeon, of the *Greys?*"

"Of course. I call her 'the one,' for many reasons, Echo."

"Aeon has told us of her conversation with one of only two extremely powerful beings that traverse the multiverse using the power of unimaginable speed."

Sara was spellbound as Pulse knew what was coming from Echo.

"Yesterday, Aeon had contact with a multiverse time-space speedster purportedly from Exoplanet Earth Two."

96

ECHO'S ENERGY REVEAL

Echo could see that it was time to get Sara's cosmic education revved up even more.

"Sara, let's put Aeon's encounter with the time-space speedster on your 'back burner' for now. We will have ample time, I believe, to cross that alien 'bridge' soon enough."

"Fine, Echo. What's your present intention?"

"I want to discuss some methodology with you… that is, how you measure a civilization's level of technological advancement. Is that okay with you?"

"Of course. I can see just from the last few conferences that we have had, that this is a valuable metric. My learning curve is exponential."

"Yes, it is Sara. Pulse, pull down the Kardashev Scale."

"Will do." Pulse brought a three-dimensional holographic set of slides into view.

Echo, with laser pointer in hand, began.

"The Kardashev Scale is a method of measuring a civilization's level of technological advancement based on the amount of energy they are able to use. It was developed back in the 1960's by a Russian astronomer and is still used today."

Sara glanced up at the holograph and nodded.

"Sara, we can use this scale to determine the threat level that Earth is facing. The key… the common denominator, is energy and how it is contained and controlled."

"We need to make this info available to everyone as soon as possible, Echo."

"Yes, Sara, we will. But this will lead to something that has an immediate impact on you, and so it is for you alone… today."

Sara was getting a little nervous, given more unknown heavy stuff was coming.

"Sara, I cannot overstate the importance of energy and its power in your life… energy fields, both pure and zero-point energy… even the soul and human spirit.

Sara quickly asked, "Zero-point?"

Pulse informed Sara, "Zero-point energy fields are how thoughts become matter."

"Ohmigod!"

"There will be time, again I say, to get into details. Please be patient for now, Sara."

Sara gave one of her impatient sighs, and Echo continued, "There are four types of known Kardashev scales:"

Echo pointed to the four types on a screen.

Type 1 – Called a planetary civilization

"This civilization can harness, use, and store all of the energy available on its planet. So, Type One is a technological level of a civilization that is close to what is presently attained on Earth. Its energy derivation would typically be its Earth-Sun system, like here. If you can accept it, the current humanity has still not yet reached Type One civilization status."

Type 2 – Called a stellar civilization

"This civilization can use and control energy at the scale of its entire planetary system. In other words, it would be a civilization capable of harnessing the energy radiated by its own star. The energy use would then be comparable to the luminosity of its sun. The Arrans are working on this, and we are afraid that warring alien species may be further along than us."

Type 3 – Called a galactic civilization

"This civilization can control energy at the scale of its entire host galaxy. To put it in almost indescribable terms, it would denote a civilization with access to the power comparable to the luminosity of the entire Milky Way galaxy! To our knowledge, no alien culture in the known universe has reached this capability."

"Nuts, eh Sara?"

"Yeah, Pulse. Major nuts!"

Sara and Pulse chuckled as Echo mentioned an important fact, "Kardashev believed that a Type Four civilization was impossible, so he never went past Type Three."

Type 4 – Called a universe civilization or parallel universe civilization

"This civilization was deemed totally hypothetical at that time that Kardashev created his scale. It would suggest that beings could control or use the energy of the entire universe or control collections of universes. Recent conversations between Aeon and the multiverse time-space speedster may suggest otherwise,"

Sara thought, *"From perception to consciousness to evolution to spirituality…"* Sara's mind spun to the latter, the more spiritual.

"This would be an evolved mankind… or alien species becoming God-like!"

97

ECHO'S SPIRIT REVEAL

Sensing Sara's apprehension of both the literal and spiritual significance of those recent remarks, Echo took Sara aside for a one-on-one discussion that would have life-changing implications for Sara. Pulse joined them as he knew what Echo was about to reveal.

"Sara, we have had your DNA checked, due, primarily, to your extraordinary skills. I'm sorry to need to do this, but your skills are far outside the boundaries of any Arrans or human that we have evaluated and trained."

Sara could discern a sense of purpose and seriousness in Echo's manner.

Sara thought nervously, "*What the hell… that's pretty damn personal… and I wasn't even asked!*"

Echo sensed Sara's pissed-off mood.

<I'm sorry Sara… but you will see why we had to do this.>

Pulse interjected, "The DNA match itself was relatively easy. But first, we had to construct a simulation model that best fit the profile of a female warrior-type with exceptional physical and leadership skills." Pulse paused, "Then we ran tens of millions of simulations before we found the most likely matches. Further analysis placed the match in a fairly probable place and time."

Echo was pensive, but firm in her words, "We did a similar DNA study on Nikola Tesla many years ago, and it proved to be most enlightening."

Calming down a bit, Sara questioned, "What did you find?"

"Your DNA has traced back to ancient Egypt during the time of Pharaohs' rule, and we have a high level of certainty that one specific female Pharaoh was a match."

Sara drew a blank stare and was mystified.

"So, we had Spirit go to the Temple of Hatshepsut in the Valley of Kings in Luxor, Egypt, to extract a DNA sample, and when she returned, we had our conclusion."

Pausing, "Sara, your DNA is a perfect match with mythical goddess, Hatshepsut. Hatshepsut was the fifth pharaoh of the Eighteenth Dynasty of Egypt. She was the second historically confirmed female pharaoh, but the first female ruler of ancient Egypt to reign as a male with full authority of pharaoh."

Sara was stunned. Again.

"Her name means 'Foremost of Noble Women' or 'She is First among Noble Women,' and she ruled from 1473 to 1458, BCE. Queen Hatshepsut's bloodline was impeccable as she was the daughter, sister, and wife of a king."

"Are you okay with me going on, Sara?"

A most attentive Sara replied, "Yes. Please do."

"Her understanding of religion and alleged spiritual ties to Egyptian Gods allowed her to take measures to protect herself as a ruler in a man's world, so she chose to depict herself as a daughter of the god Amun, the most popular and powerful deity of the time."

"Was her rule a good one?" Sara was very interested after hearing the story unfold.

"Sara," Echo offered warmly, "she was a compassionate ruler and a great one. The reign of Queen Hatshepsut lasted twenty-two years; and during that time, she was responsible for more building projects than any pharaoh in history."

Pulse was aware of other accomplishments of this pharaoh and added his facts, "Queen Hatshepsut was the only female pharaoh to launch a successful sea voyage to the land of Punt, on the northeast coast of Africa, and bring back to Egypt precious minerals and godly 'marvels' indicating a connection with cosmic angels and Gods." Pausing and glancing over to Sara, "And she loved to wear black and red nail polish."

"Oh my God," thought Sara, excitedly. *"So, do I!"*

Echo continued, as Sara was fully engaged, "Spirit also found in Hatshepsut's tomb an artifact that drew Pete Stevenson to his alien research mission and involved his granddaughter Sara… the Saqqara Bird!"

Sara was speechless and overwhelmed with the info and the implications.

"Sara, it's time for you to understand the true meaning of life."

"What are you alluding to, Echo?"

"We are going to take you on a life-changing journey."

"When?"

"Now."

"Where?"

"To a place and being who will open up a spiritual world that will astound you."

"You said a being. Who?"

"You will be meeting with Trinity, one who represents our true spiritual being."

"To discuss what, in particular, Echo?"

"Trinity will explain many questions of a spiritual and consciousness level, but one in particular will hit home with you, given this latest revelation."

"Which one, Echo?"

"Reincarnation."

98
TRINITY

Echo described a place and an individual who would bring meaning and purpose into Sara's life. They hugged and Pulse gave Sara a gentle kiss, and Sara was joined by Spirit and Peace.

In an instant, Sara was transported to Machu Picchu, Peru, with Spirit and Peace. The three embraced and the two aliens departed. Sara was left alone.

Machu Picchu is the most historical site in South America, if not the World. It is also the location of a very powerful energy vortex, one of the strongest in the World.

Sara had been placed on the section of Machu Picchu that the locals called Intihuatana, or the Temple of the Sun, associated with the astronomic clock and dedicated to the Sun God and the Incas' greatest deity.

The Nazca Lines, ancient geoglyphs, were nearby and gave the entire region a balance between the cosmic and the spiritual.

In a magical encounter, Sara was approached by the lovely and petite Trinity, enveloped in an angelic pink haze. The aura around Trinity was a surreal mix of fact-of-the-moment and fantasy-of-the-spiritual.

"Welcome, Sara. I am Trinity. I am very close to Echo, and her suggestion that we meet means that you are an important piece to humanity's existence puzzle going forward."

"Hello, Trinity, I am so happy to meet you… and overwhelmed with questions and apprehension."

"Yes, you have many questions, Sara, and I will answer them. But first, I would like to explain and clarify myths and legends as they apply to the heavens, ancient astronaut aliens, and the Anunnaki."

Sara smiled as Trinity took her by the hand and they slowly walked amongst the physical and spiritual beauty.

"The Anunnaki were actually an advanced humanoid extraterrestrial species from an exoplanet who came to Earth about five hundred thousand years ago and remained here until the Great Flood. They were treated like Gods, because they came from the 'heavens' and many statues were created in their supposed likeness."

Sara was relaxed in Trinity's presence.

"Anunnaki were thought to be ruled by a group of eight deities, and if you wish, you can obtain divine perspectives from someone who studied that group of eight… your friend, Echo."

Sara thought to herself, *"Echo's eight capsules and her eight leadership team members: Echo, Pulse, Laser, Spirit, Peace, Vibe, Vigor, and Aeon."*

Sara recalled, *"And she even understood Tiffany's 'Power of Eight Intentions' process."*

As Sara was thinking about all that Echo had done for her, Trinity stopped and they both sat on a table rock. Now, physically close to Sara, Trinity softly spoke, "Echo gave you the gift of the cranial transplants, which signified how much she respected you and what she believed could be your galactic accomplishments."

Sara was getting a little misty eyed.

"As I stroke your forehead, I am transferring many items for you to consider and discuss with your friends… not now and not with me."

At that time, Trinity touched Sara's forehead and Sara could see and feel many thoughts and issues that have confounded mankind for an eternity: *the origin of the universe, creationism, the afterlife, heaven, and the theory of evolution.*

"Sara, the human body is mortal… but the spirit or soul is immortal."

Trinity stepped back from Sara and spoke in a quiet and soft manner while handing Sara a special gift. "Take this sacred 'dream catcher', which is considered the 'space-time web of life' and is meant to filter bad ideas of humanity and the bad dreams that you will encounter. It will help you to guide the people within your reach to achieve your mission and ultimate vision… both on Earth and beyond.

"I gave a dream catcher to your friend, Michaela, to help ward off the demons of her bad dreams with the Dracs."

"This whole experience is an awesome responsibility for me to take on, Trinity. Why me and why now?"

"Your soul will live forever, Sara Steele."

Sara gazed into Trinity's eyes as Trinity calmly explained, **"Sara, you are the reincarnation of the Egyptian Pharaoh Hatshepsut."**

99

SOUL SISTERS

Sara, Echo, Spirit, and Aeon met as soon as Sara returned from Machu Picchu, having been teleported directly by Echo, apparently on Trinity's command, to Echo's Starship Destiny, on the far side of the Moon.

As Echo led them into her office for some privacy, she spoke in a very quiet tone.

"Sara, I have never seen you so quiet. I am sure that your time with Trinity was as thought-provoking and surrealistic as any experience that you have ever had."

"Echo," Sara began, "it was the most bittersweet time of my life. This revelation, or expose, that I am a reincarnation of an Egyptian pharaoh, is still making me numb all over."

<Let's talk.>

<Yes, Aeon, we shall.>

Following that mental exchange between Aeon and Echo, Spirit offered a suggestion, "Can we talk through the telepathic issues that Trinity provided to steer Sara's psyche and give our newest disciple the benefit of our experience and perspectives?"

"Yes, Spirit," Echo offered, "that would be wise."

As the four began to think of what and how they would proceed, Pulse entered Echo's office, knowing that Echo had a do-not-disturb aura around her.

"Sorry to interrupt, but we are getting some interstellar 'noise' from the near-galaxy that is yet undefined."

"Very well, Pulse. Keep me posted when you have additional data."

"Will do, Echo," and Pulse left the room.

✦ ✦ ✦

"Sara, Trinity installed several 'thought portals' into your consciousness. Are they clear and distinct in your mind at this time?"

"Yes, Echo. I must confess, there is so much data that I have a fuzzy series of images that I am having trouble processing."

<Let's just take them one at a time, as Trinity downloaded them, Echo.>

<Yes, Aeon, we will.>

"Sara, Aeon suggests…"

"I picked up her thoughts to you, Echo."

Somewhat startled, Echo replied, "Well then, let's just do what our *Grey* friend suggested. I'll start. The origin of the universe, Sara, is as the best-supported theories suggest. Our universe originated about fifteen billion years ago as a dense, hot globule of gas expanded rapidly outward."

"Of course," Sara replied impatiently, "'the Big Bang Theory.'"

"Yes, Sara, but there is more… much more and it will lead us to our next topic."

Echo smiled at Aeon before continuing, "At that time, the universe contained nothing but hydrogen and helium… there were no stars or planets. The first stars probably began to form out of hydrogen when the universe was about one hundred million years old."

"I know that, Echo, and that is how our Sun originated about five billion years ago."

<Patience, dear Sara.>

<Sorry, Aeon.>

Echo winks at Aeon and continues with the detail that Sara needs to hear, "That takes us to what is called Creationism, or the religious belief that nature, and aspects of the universe, Earth, life and humans, originated with supernatural acts of divine creation. Much of that is true."

Sara listens for the *yes, but* that is about to come.

"There is a fine line in what it took to make the Sun and Moon and planets and galaxies, etcetera. Electrons, protons, atoms, subatomic particles called quark, and even bacteria, had to be specifically created, or developed, in order for the universe to have been born."

Echo looks at Sara as she provides one example, "The remarkable fact is that the values of all of these variables and their numbers had to be very finely adjusted to make possible the development of life. For example, if the electric charge of the electron had been only slightly different, it would have spoiled the balance of the electromagnetic and gravitational force in stars, and either they would have been unable to burn hydrogen and helium or else they would not have exploded. Either way, life would not exist.

"Think about this, Sara, if the exact composition of those physical matter particles was left to randomness, life would not exist."

Sara is now beginning to understand the complexity of creation as Echo continues, "Time and space are not absolute, and God simply created this universe from others using the same theory of relativity. Time is a curvature or warp phenomena, and God enabled our universe to develop over billions of years in the same way faraway galaxies and universes have been developing before... timing irrelevant."

Spirit sent a thought to all,

"But do not forget this one thing, dear friends: With the Lord, a day is like a thousand years, and a thousand years are like a day."

"Thank you, Spirit. Sara, have you heard of the Pillars of Creation?"

"Yes, my dad explained them to me. They were so named because the gas and dust were in the process of an active star-forming region within the Eagle Nebula and held newborn stars in their wispy columns."

Spirit added, "Stretching roughly four to five light-years, the Pillars of Creation are a fascinating but relatively small feature of the entire Eagle Nebula, which spans seventy by fifty-five light-years in size."

"So, Echo, the rapidly growing and expanding galaxies and universes are, in fact, under God's creation."

"Yes."

Sara offered her perspective, "And this is also known by the pseudoscientific argument for the existence of God called Intelligent Design, an evidence-based theory about life's origins."

<Very good, Sara.>

<Thank you, Aeon.>

"The afterlife, Sara, is both simple and complicated. You and I can discuss this at greater length in the future, as you can decipher much from your 'Trinity touch.' The fact that you are a reincarnation kind of makes this a moot point."

"For now, Echo, but later is good for a deeper dive."

"And, you have already come to a conclusion regarding Heaven, given the Trinity divine interjection?"

"Yes. Heaven is a place on Earth, awarded, for lack of a better term, to those souls who have either gained grace with God, and moved up... or did not gain grace with God, and moved down the 'soul train.' Yep, I got it."

<That was very good, Sara.>

<Thank you again, Aeon.>

Sara added one more interpretation from her new *mental log*, "Darwin's Theory of Evolution was flawed… divine intervention didn't alter evolution. Alien intervention did."

"Bravo, Sara." Echo was pleased with her young warrior princess.

As the meeting was wrapping up, an excited Pulse barged in. "I am truly sorry to break up this 'Oprah Winfrey book club' meeting, but we do have a serious issue."

<Oprah Winfrey book club, Echo?>

<Aeon, it's Pulse and his fancy assimilation of all things in American culture.>

With all looking at the serious alien with an off-the-cuff humorous remark, Pulse continued with his announcement, **"Massive alien pods have just landed in three locations on Earth."**

100

SPACE ODDITY

As Pulse was walking over to the small meeting desk where the four females were seated, he added some detail to his remarks, "At precisely the same time today and even the same minute… three huge black egg-shaped pods 'appeared' from the sky in a reddish haze."

Echo was immediately concerned as she glanced over to Aeon.

Pulse continued soberly, "These 'pods' arrived in three locations on Earth: in North America, in Europe, and in Asia. Their locations did not appear to be random. In fact, they were extremely strategic locations, as was determined by U.S. President Sullivan moments ago, selected to be at the very lifeline of global technology and communication."

Sara thought to herself, *"It is as if a science fiction movie was literally defining the roller-coaster ride that Earth was now experiencing."*

"One pod is in Redwood City, California, in the heart of Silicon Valley, and the cornerstone of all things innovative and AI related."

"That's right in our back yard, Pulse."

"Yep. One pod is in Stuttgart, Germany, the manufacturing hub of Europe, and the country that is deemed the leader in all things being built for worldly consumption."

Sara thought about issues her grandad mentioned, *"Germany is also the country that the Dracs hooked up with in the 1930s to develop space warfare equipment."*

Pulse added with a sigh, "The third pod is in Shenzhen, China."

"That makes sense," Sara uttered, thinking about the economic implications, "linking the vibrant city of Hong Kong with mainland China, which President Sullivan has been saying has now become the newest center of financial strength."

Echo added her observation, "Yes, that powerhouse country is now driving the global economy, a pinnacle once enjoyed by the United States, Sara."

"Pulse, what more can you tell us?"

"Well, Sara, literally within seconds of 'landing' at their respective locations, each pod opened, and their human-like visitor forms disembarked their spacecrafts with exactly the same messages."

Echo's wheels were spinning, as she had seen this before on the planet in the Kepler 22-star system.

Pulse continued sharing the facts as they were known, "These aliens resemble humans in every way… the look, dress, mannerisms, and even their speech, covering all three languages of their respective locations."

"And what was the common message, Pulse?"

"Sara, it is what you would call, transparent."

We come in peace and bear gifts.

Do not believe what you have been told. We are your friends.

We dissipated the destructive magnetic wave before it could cause significant damage and loss of life.

✦ ✦ ✦

Global security and civil defense warnings were immediately broadcast throughout the world, and citizens were instructed to stay far away from the strange pods.

The military of each country that was directly impacted by pod landings raised their warnings to the highest levels. President Sullivan immediately put the United States on alert, as all six branches, including the Space Force, were now in ready-to-respond mode.

The President contacted Sara, who was still on the Destiny, and the Arrans patched the feed from POTUS to watch the on-site events unfold.

Echo was sensing another alarming déjà vu. Everything on the screen was unfolding in the Arrans' purview, and Echo's alarm at this new incident became obvious among her fellow Arrans.

From each pod, small groups of the *visitors* were now slowly walking down a ramp to ground level. They walked out and placed a large variety of gifts of food, local currency, and devices that they claimed would benefit mankind.

At the Silicon Valley pod, Vice President Samantha Worthington was with that particular alien group and identified herself as a friend to the visitors.

The vice president, who was still perceived to be a legitimate U.S. leader, announced that they had the vaccine for Covid-19 and had enough doses for the entire world; and unlike with the Arrans' claim, there was no need to validate the vaccine… it had already been tested on humans and was ready for global vaccination.

The American VP advised that distribution centers would be set up, once each country provided the aliens with the plan for roll out.

As POTUS and the other world leaders were sounding many alarms, the citizens of Earth, he was told, were becoming immediately comfortable with their newly arriving guests.

Sara sent Cameron a text.

> "It is a distraction to get us 'off of our game.'
> We need to talk."
> "Agree, Sara.
> I will have Mara open a line ASAP."

Many original *alien skeptics* now believed that, like the Arrans, they were from our galaxy and were friendly aliens that were *here to help*.

World-wide alliances were getting a little soft, hoping that this *new reality* was *indeed heaven sent* and needed to become embraced.

Echo, Sara, and POTUS were extremely worried that Earth would let its guard down.

Even the U.S. Congress put out an unsubstantiated announcement, without Presidential authority, apparently coming from the office of the American Vice President.

"An invasion is not likely. These extraterrestrials come in peace."

101
ALIENS END GAME

Echo was patched into a video chat with President Sullivan and the ETRT.

Cameron began by stating his immediate concern, "This was obviously unexpected and, frankly, difficult to understand."

A somewhat distracted Echo replied, "Yes, I agree. And is this just the Dracs or a joint strategy by them and the Denon?"

Sara interjected worriedly, "The world has no idea what we have experienced to understand how vicious and deceitful these evil aliens are. If nothing else, look back at Michaela's abduction."

An agitated Cameron snapped, "The fact that the Vice President of the United States is giving credence to these aliens is scary. The majority of the population, not knowing that she has been transformed, will accept all that is being offered."

"And that freaking vaccine," Sara added; "what the hell is in it?"

"Sara," Echo replied as she looked directly at Sara, "I didn't even think of that. This vaccine could be the worst part of their insidious strategy. And, with their shapeshifters amongst us, we have no idea if anyone in authority can be trusted."

With an impatient sigh, Cameron blurted, "Simply put, how do we protect the unknowing citizenry around the world right now and defend this planet from whatever attack is coming? We must take both the offense and defense here... and soon!"

"We must take aggressive action," Echo recommended. "Mister President, could you pull your cabinet, the Galactic Committee, and the top world leaders together and, along with the ETRT and my team, to have a Summit Meeting as soon as possible?"

"Yes, Echo, I can and will. We will need comprehensive action plans developed that are implementable quickly. Sara, get your Utah compound ready and see what Scott Woods has up his sleeve regarding his starships or warships or whatever his 'skunk works' is working on."

"Will do, Cameron."

"Not only will we need implementation plans developed," Echo scowled, "but we will need a seriously detailed account of resources and their allocations. We don't have much time!"

Michaela chimed in, "I will get a simulation team together with ETRT members and Vibe and his team to try to get a handle on the various scenarios that make sense to these invaders, and our best course of action to take them on."

"Great idea, Michaela," Echo added, noting how good it was to have Michaela back.

Cameron muttered angrily, "My biggest concern right now is that we may not have the support of people of Earth, if they believe the newly arriving aliens are similar to Arrans and mean them no harm... only to help in whatever way possible."

"Yes, Mister President. I totally agree." Echo's demeanor was noticeably serious. "My expectation is now quite dark."

Picking up her tone, Cameron replied, "Echo, what is your current expectation?"

"Best case scenario... they are fishing."

"Worst case scenario, Echo?"

"Planet Earth could become a battlefield!"

102

TRIANGLE OF STRENGTH

With that remark, Cameron drew a logical conclusion… at least logical to him.

"Echo, I need to speak with you and Sara. We need a strategy to address this clear and present danger, and right now!"

<Sara, are you available?>

<Yes, Echo.>

Echo advised POTUS, "Rather than go to our secure chat line, Sara and I will teleport to coordinates that you provide. We are ready now, Mister President."

Moments later, Echo and Sara were in the Situation Room of the White House, and President Sullivan was eager to proceed.

"Thanks for getting here so quickly," Cameron quipped.

Sara replied with a smile, "Glad to see you haven't lost your sense of humor."

"Apparently you have an agenda, Mister President."

"Yes, Echo, I do. Let me check to make sure we are secure. Be right back."

Sara and Echo gazed at each other, realizing that a course correction was coming.

"Echo, what do you think he is thinking right now?"

"I know exactly what he is thinking… I am Echo and even now you should have this power."

"Sorry. You're right. I have been preoccupied with my parents' current situation and their safety."

"I'm the one who should be sorry, Sara. Of course, that would be your priority. I know what he is going to ask, and I already have a 'game plan' in mind."

"I would suspect so," Sara murmured with a head nod to her mentor and friend.

Cameron returned to the room in a more serious mood than earlier.

"Shit, the whole world seems to be leaning in favor of believing these alien invaders… we must move swiftly."

"We're ready, Cam," Sara quickly replied. "What's your plan?"

"Ladies, we need to take control of everything going forward now… just the three of us. Screw the damn committees and Congress. Even the wishy-washy world leaders can't make up their goddamn minds."

Echo immediately chimed in, "If you are comfortable with taking charge now… we are totally ready to do what is necessary."

"My grandad used to say," Sara snapped, "to ask forgiveness… not permission."

"Well, young lady, your Grandad Pete was a wise one," Echo replied. "We don't have time for either!"

Echo took the opportunity to start the strategy session, as she knew exactly what the President was going to say.

"I have an idea that we can implement immediately."

Cameron responded intently, "Let's hear it."

"We need intelligence info and we need it now. I have several advanced AI metahumans that represent the absolute pinnacle of technology and subversive capability. I would like to get three of them inside the three alien pods."

"Incredible," POTUS reacted excitedly.

Sara chimed in, as Echo had expected, with an integrated addition to Echo's suggestion, "We have three metahumans that could assimilate into the human crowd at each pod site to gather info and to be used as 'dummies' for the vaccinations, which worry the hell out of me!"

"That would be fantastic," Cameron added, nodding his approval. "Infiltrating those pods seem like our only option to get an understanding of what they are up to and what kind of timing is involved for us to react."

"Mister President, I am considering putting together three distinct teams that could deploy as soon as possible to these three sites and start our counterterrorism activity immediately."

"Counterterrorism, Echo?"

"My team tells me there is a one-in-fifty chance that the Dracs have a quasi-friendly intention with their presence on Earth. Our data and my intuition told me that they are planning an assault on Earth, and their presence is to either buy them some time, or totally distract us."

Sara interjected, "So, Echo, the teams?"

"Yes. We need joint teams combining the skills and expertise of human, metahumans, and Arrans."

"I like that idea, Echo. You have those team members grouped?"

"Yes." Pausing, "I see one team of Michaela, Commander Baker, the Arrans' Vibe and Laser, and the metahuman Valos, if Sara agrees."

"Yes. And Valos will be a good fit with that team."

"Team two would be Sara, Jeremiah, Pulse and another strong meta, Torin, again if Sara feels that they would be well suited."

"Absolutely, Echo."

"Team three would have the hacking capability… Connor and Justin, along with our Spirit and Vigor and the strong metahuman Elonis."

POTUS was smiling and much more relaxed as Echo laid out her plans.

Echo continued firmly, "I have three advanced AIs, Ava, Eva, and Ivan, ready to send into the pods, once we have an infiltration scheme."

Sara was impressed… and growing more assured.

"I would occupy my Destiny's Command Center with the ETRT's Tiffany and our Spirit and Peace."

Sara nodded as Echo continued, "I will determine roles and responsibilities for Laser, Spirit, and Peace once we get our resources aligned with countermeasure needs."

"I will do the same with the ETRT," Sara concluded emphatically.

"We may be faced with a very uncomfortable decision."

"What is that Echo?"

"Not doing what we want to do… but what we need to do!"

103

INSIDE LOOKING OUT

Once the meeting with the newly formed task teams was concluded, POTUS, Echo, and Sara moved swiftly to begin their required tasks.

Intel from various credible global sources indicated the likely strategy for the Dracs' geographic targets. Germany was currently the world leader in technical and weaponry manufacturing, California housed the innovation centers, and China had become the world's economic engine.

<Echo, those locations were not chosen randomly.>

<I agree, Sara.>

<It's like these pods are expected to be sponges for the Dracs and allow them to absorb all of humanity's technology.>

<Sara, we have seen them do this before. Not surprised.>

It was agreed that everyone had 24 hours to get their obligations in order, before heading to their assigned sites.

The Arrans team members were responsible for getting their respective teams assembled, and then teleporting them per Echo's logistical plan.

Team One, the Michaela and Commander Baker team, would teleport to the pod in Germany, where Echo was told the advanced technical and manufacturing hubs where targeted. AI metahuman Ava would attempt to infiltrate here.

Team Two, the Sara and Pulse team, would arrive at the California pod, assuming that this location would house the Dracs' innovation, AI, and military communication centers. AI metahuman Eva would be the infiltrator at this pod.

Team Three, the Connor, Justin, Spirit, Vigor, and Elonis team, would teleport to China, thought to be the pod of IT, interstellar transportation, and all things related to global finance. Joining them would be AI metahuman Ivan.

Once on site in Palo Alto, Sara announced the implementation plans to the ETRT, "Team one will have Ava, Vibe, Laser, and Valos in place and integrating into the civilian crowd that has gathered. Ava will make her way to the pod doorway, awaiting a physical distraction to gain entry. Valos will allow herself to get a vaccination, since it would have no effect on a meta, and Laser can analyze it immediately."

There was no pushback. All members either knew their roles or were developing them based on the intel.

"Team two will have Eva, Pulse, and Torin in place. Eva will follow Ava's script, and Torin will be receiving the vaccine. Pulse can also validate the formulation of the vaccine."

Pulse was excited and thought, *"This is the kind of battle I am prepared for and eager to begin… revenge for Ceria!"*

"Team three will be Ivan, Spirit, Vigor, and Elonis. Ivan will be the infiltrator, and Elonis can both obtain the vaccine and analyze it."

Commander Baker quickly inquired, "What will Michaela and my roles be, Sara?"

"I was just getting to that, RJ… Hell, you're more impatient than I am," she said with slight laugh.

"I will be the link to POTUS and keep him in a real-time update throughout the exercise. Michaela will be the contact with which-ever world leaders that the President deems trustworthy and helpful."

Sara was saving the best… that is the most important… role of all for Commander Baker.

"RJ, you will be in contact with a military liaison… one that Cameron selects, and you will be feeding him or her the up-to-the-minute status of all things deemed to be a military threat. You will also be patched into the communications center of the Space Force, via Echo's totally secure telecommunications."

"Cool," Commander Baker replied with a large grin.

"RJ, there is one more thing. It's kind of a 'mission impossible' thing."

Sara paused, "This task will include you and Michaela. It's one of the reasons Echo put you two together."

Michaela was thinking half-seriously, *"Yeah, I didn't think Echo was in the matchmaking frame of mind."*

"The most important issue for us to be successful," Sara advised her two friends, "is to determine what the Dracs are planning. But beyond that, we need to know where they are vulnerable… what is their Achilles Heel?"

Both RJ and Michaela were getting mentally pumped.

"Where is their weakest link?" Sara continued. "Where is the one spot where we can take down the Dracs?"

Pulse, who had been listening... as he usually does, provided his observation, "Like the Death Star was the Empire's ultimate weapon in the movie series, Star Wars, we need to find what it would take to destroy the Dracs, or at least send them off forever."

"Star Wars... really Pulse?"

"No Sara, I understand Pulse," RJ offered. "They may be vulnerable in high-tech equipment or high-tech operational software. It doesn't have to be a moon-size space station."

Pulse went on with his sidebar offerings "There was another movie, I can't remember the name, which had a similar military situation occur. It was a good flick. It had to do with humanity's independence."

With that comment, Echo scowled with her marching orders to the three teams, **"Enough of that talk. You all have a job to do. Just do it!**

104

ASSESS THE
ALIEN MESS

Following several hours of frustrating and intense communication around the world, it was time to provide an initial assessment of the pods and alien landing event. POTUS had his group together, including his Cabinet, the Galactic Committee, and various Congressional members.

Sara had the ETRT assembled, and Echo had every resource of the Arrans available.

With this record-setting leadership video meeting about to begin, a physically exhausted President Sullivan was about to turn the benchmark meeting over to Echo.

"Ladies and gentlemen, you all know by now, the Commander of the Arrans race, Echo, who is in the best position to give us an assessment and begin to compile an action plan going forward."

"Thank you, President Sullivan. The arrival of the pods here on Earth has rapidly pushed our plans for building a stronger planet to the side for now. We have two different, yet deadly, evil alien cultures to deal with, and the vast majority of Earth's population are now judging these visitors as friendly and benevolent."

The assorted galleries were silent… listening… processing.

"The scope and scale of this preliminary invasion has been well calculated by the Dracs, the reptilian humanoids, who we believe are in charge of the pod strategy. The Denon are an entangled race with morphing capabilities, and hellish creatures would be my description of their composition."

Echo was thinking strategically, *"I need to dumb-it-down, as Sara has taught me."*

"In our opinion, the Dracs are the high-tech, space-time invasion planners and creators, and the Denon are here to carry out whatever is the intent of the Dracs."

The German chancellor, looking at a pod in their backyard, asked, "Do we have a plan to counter... this menace?"

Echo replied slowly and methodically, "Let's look at what we know and what we don't know regarding these threats and form logical battle plans accordingly. Available resources will be key and must be deployed perfectly... but that is still to be determined."

No additional questions were coming, as Echo had established a reputation amongst the world leaders to date, as an adroit and extremely capable leader that was as focused and skilled as anyone in the galaxy.

"My team has run millions of simulations with the data set given to us today, and if you can accept our results, I will be willing and pleased to continue."

POTUS advised immediately, "Echo, we trust and respect you and your team. You have proven again and again that you only have our best interest in mind."

"Thank you, Mister President."

The Chinese ambassador likewise having an alien pod in his country, asked a question that many must have had on their minds, "Echo, what is the likelihood that these pods are here, in fact, as friendly aliens to help mankind?"

"Mr. Ambassador from Shenzhen, your question is very relevant and very important. The Dracs are a galactic presence that have been here for hundreds of thousands of years and have two main castes."

Echo was thinking distractedly, *"Again? I need to tell them again?"*

"One is a dangerous warrior caste, eight to ten feet tall, weighing six hundred to one thousand pounds, and are super-psychic and super-fast. From reptilian origin, they can best be described as upright- walking alligator lizards, with both mouths and gills, having steel-tipped claws on hands of long arms and with toxic tails."

Those remarks gave the entire audience the chills, as body language didn't lie.

"The other caste is the highly advanced and intelligent race that has thousands of offspring here on Earth and are indistinguishable from humans. This caste is the master of 'mind games' throughout the universe and most difficult to analyze."

This alien *education* was making the audience more scared with each comment and more hopeful that the aliens were, in fact, peaceful.

✦ ✦ ✦

Echo asked for a brief pause as she consulted her team and Sara's colleagues. It was obvious that Echo was connecting the dots for an aggressive plan to meet this challenge.

Ten minutes later, she was back hosting the epic global meeting to discuss the likely survival of humanity, "Thank you. I will now provide what our joint teams have concluded is our first step... I repeat, our first step."

Echo waited a moment to get everyone's attention. "First, we will place three metahumans of Sara Steele's determination, into the vaccination lines at all three pods. They have human anatomy for vaccine-giving, but these doses will then be immediately analyzed for ingredients and expected results."

Sara noted who would be selected.

"Secondly, I will have three of our most advanced AI creations assimilate into the alien contingent at each pod, by infiltrating as citizens of their respective countries. They will analyze every aspect of our visitors' composition and their thought patterns."

Echo paused, "If possible, we will abduct a sample alien body from each pod to return to my ship for determination as to which caste we are dealing with."

Cameron uttered a thought that had to be on everyone's mind, "You can do that?"

"Yes, we have been doing that with galactic species for centuries."

Sara had many questions of her own that were just answered with Echo's startling revelation.

"Finally," a very confident Echo advised, "we will put Arrans recon starships in place to launch into the near-galaxy and determine what, if any, alien battle equipment is in route to Earth. This will determine intention."

<Echo, why didn't you mention this to me earlier?>

<Because it is a lie, Sara, meant to give the President and world leaders the impression that we are fully engaged in this possibility as well.>

<But, Echo, it sounds like a good idea.>

<Yes, but we have already done that recon. It is our first step when meeting this kind of insurgence.>

POTUS had another question, "How will we know what you find amongst your captured pod-aliens? How will we know what we are seeing and dealing with?"

"Mister President, I assure you I will have clear, physical evidence of your visitors."

"Evidence?" POTUS was on the edge of his chair. "Will we be able to see these aliens in their actual bodies?"

"Yes. They are only now morphed into human-looking beings."

"Then, Echo, you'll be able to show them as they really are?"

"Yes," Mister President.

Echo glanced over to Sara before concluding, **"I will have visual aids unlike anything this world has ever seen!"**

105

STAR TECH

POTUS disconnected his feed from Echo and the Arrans team and the ETRT to address Echo's remarks with his contingent. This gave Echo the opportunity to display for the ETRT the vast array of weaponry at Earth's service.

She wanted to install a feeling of absolute confidence in the Arrans' capability for the ETRT to move forward with conviction and purpose.

Echo assembled a list with graphics that replayed several high-tech items and advised, "We have already demonstrated the prismatic refractor, the extrapolator, the antimatter microreactor, the battle sabre, the wrist-mounted lasers, and the neutralizer. You have seen us time travel and execute the mirrorverse. In literally each case, we demonstrated the 'tip of the iceberg' in your terms. There is far more capability here."

Vibe chimed in with those issues concerning his special skills and implementation techniques, "We have an extrasensory perception, or telepathy, that gives us the ability to distinguish between human, humanoid, metahuman, and alien. This can happen through touch or even close proximity. And our advanced AI is what Echo is putting in place right now."

Echo nodded affirmatively, "Yes, Vibe, those advanced AI 'plants' that I was referring to for the pods are like nothing the Dracs have ever faced. We partnered in a very critical venture with the Teslites, who possess the pinnacle of technical innovation prowess, and brought back from the future a diagnostic tool unmatched in the universe."

Sara interrupted Echo to provide some clarification for members of the ETRT, "The Teslites, as I recall hearing, are the highly evolved future alien race resulting from continual bundling of bio-technology, robotics, artificial intelligence, general AI, and advanced weaponry."

Connor and Justin smiled, as their *hot button* had just been struck.

"But, Echo, you said that there was a downside working with them."

"Yes, Sara, there was and still is. The Teslite race has become neutral when it pertains to one side versus another. Their entire culture and existence is based on two edicts."

The entire ETRT was focused on yet another potential threat.

"One, to constantly use every technological upgrade to improve their capability... And two, to execute any and all actions to benefit themselves. They can be ruthless, especially when you consider human life a non-consideration in any strategic plan rollout."

Echo paused, noting a sense of uncertainty from the group. "But the Teslites can be extremely helpful if there is a 'quid pro quo' that benefits them. They are truly a transactional culture."

Michaela flicked a gaze at Echo and asked, "What may I ask, Echo, was the transactional item that the Arrans gave to the Teslites?"

"History."

"What?" Sara uttered confused.

The ETRT was so engaged, waiting for an element of cosmic importance that this mention of history literally came out of nowhere.

"The Teslite race only began long after 'these days.' They have no grasp of what came before them... not thousands of years... not millions of years... not billions of years. So, we created a 'cosmic library' for them to have and to study."

Michaela asked curiously, "Echo, do you have any idea why this history issue was so important?"

"According to their leader, who we call 999, those who don't seriously heed lessons from the past are doomed to repeat them. Very philosophical for that species."

"Echo," Sara inquired, "why the name 999?"

"The Teslites consider themselves gods and angels, albeit artificial ones. The number nine, as you might know, is associated with the ending of one thing and the beginning of the next."

Another space-time lesson was unfolding for Sara.

"We Arrans view the number nine as having inner wisdom and strength. Its spiritual component focuses on humanitarianism and consciousness. I truly believe that the Teslites believe that they are the ultimate deity."

Echo added, "They always believe that whatever the problem or puzzle... they are 'right' 999 times out of one thousand."

Sara was impressed with the journey from technology to spirituality... but knew there was more to come. At that pause, Pulse prepared his virtual presentation of all weapons, large and small, and had his adrenalin pumping, big time.

✦ ✦ ✦

"Fasten your seatbelts, boys and girls… this will be intense. We have weapons that are as far advanced as our time travel will take us. From individual weapons, to starship weapons, to battle star weapons… we are well prepared. We have phased-array, pulsed-energy, projectile weapons, simply called phasers, in a wide range of sizes and power, ranging from small arms to starship-mounted weaponry. Our phasers on our larger warships are often used as an anti-missile defense system to destroy incoming projectiles."

RJ was feeling goose bumps from Pulse's deep dive and knew that Pulse was just getting started.

"Our energy-beam cannons are a form of directed energy weaponry that fire a plasma discharge in the form of a beam or a burst similar to plasma bullets fired by handheld plasma weapons, but much bigger in size. These are simple, particle-beam weapons that are easy to install or retrofit.

"Photon and spatial torpedoes are fairly conventional weapons, and standard on all ships. They can be launched at sub-light velocity and deployed as missiles, with antimatter warheads, and are programmed on our fleet using both voice-commands and heat-seeking devices for attacks."

Sara thought intuitively, *"I can only imagine our Federation Starships so equipped."*

"We also have the capability to engineer projectile and radiation rifles and handheld weapons, given the technology I just mentioned, for close combat or small-group defense. We also use it in tandem with our micro-transporter and a visual-scanning headpiece for a potent sniper rifle."

"I'd love close combat," a truly engaged Sara uttered.

Pulse took a momentary pause as he transitioned to a darker subject.

"Our arsenal of biological, chemical, and radioactive weapons is vast."

Michaela was getting a little nervous, in anticipation of Pulse's next remarks.

"Reflective assimilators are used to absorb energy from a variety of sources and then re-structure the compounds and redirect it back to its original source as hazardous radiation… most effective.

"We have a biogenic weapon that affects the nervous system. It is composed with a measured blend of nitrates and resins that can be fabricated to legal doses on a specific enemy species, but harmless to most other humanoids in its saturation area. This is scary stuff and used very sparingly."

"Good news… bad news," pondered Sara.

Pulse took a deep breath and continued, "Artificial Intelligence has a place… a big place in galactic warfare. Our tactical, antimatter missiles are nuclear weapons capable of destroying everything in a 500-mile radius. Each one of these small units has its own AI-controlled, target matrix, possessing total shielding, warp drive of indeterminate speed, and are programmed to do whatever is necessary to reach their targets and detonate. They cannot be stopped."

Pulse stopped for a moment, sensing his last revelation would be frightening and chilling.

"Our future weaponry has as its pinnacle, a weapon of mass destruction that is only to be used in dire circumstances… as in the world-ending."

Sara now knew what was coming…

"It is a multi-kinetic, neutronic missile with a yield of ten million of your atomic bombs, producing destructive shock waves throughout a galaxy, dispersing matter-eating organisms over a radius of ten light-years, affecting entire star systems."

"Pulse, we need a 'whatever' statement," Sara thought uneasily.

"This is a weapon that you hold over your opponent or enemy species' head, knowing it has end-of-all-life consequences."

"Thank you, Pulse," RJ thought.

"So, the question becomes, how do we assimilate the right combination of these weapons and align them with our expected needs? How and where to use and evolve this technology is of the utmost importance and moral responsibility."

As the audience became limp and totally drained, Pulse concluded, **"In our opinion, technology will rule… not just spirit and determination."**

106

POD CASTE

Less than 24 hours later, Echo pulled the team together with Sara and the ETRT for a debriefing on the logistics of the pod strategic engagement mission. Several assignments had been made, so report-outs were in place.

President Sullivan patched in as the teams were getting organized, "Hello, all."

"Hello, Cameron," Sara replied, as Echo noted the closeness of their relationship.

"Echo, where do we stand right now?"

"Well, Mister President, our first priority is to determine which caste within the pods that we are dealing with. It is much more likely that the barbaric warrior Dracs caste is in charge, but the enormity of their operation could have put the less warlike and far more intelligent cerebral caste in charge."

Sara asked curiously, "Wouldn't either caste be incredibly dangerous?"

"Yes, Sara. Yes, of course. The latter caste would be far more likely to persuade a nervous citizenry to trust them… that vaccine trick is an early indication of their plans."

RJ added with tongue-in-cheek, "So, we probably should assume that the 'barbarians' are at the door."

"Precisely, RJ."

Michaela harshly reminded everyone, "It would appear that we will need a detailed strategy to make our case to the world's population that all isn't what it appears to be."

Echo nodded and replied, "Yes, and we should have our assets in place now to get to the truth… whatever that may be."

A noticeably nervous President uttered, "What is the status of the asset base?"

"We have AIs Ava, Eva, and Ivan now in place at the entrance to each pod. Once we create a good distraction, we will signal the AIs to move inside with the Dracs, likely unrecognized."

"They can do that, Echo?"

"Yes, Mister President, this is… how do you say… this is not our first rodeo."
Sara smiled noticeably, as that remark was so un-Echo-like.

Echo added an unknown and critical fact that was chilling to all, "The biggest upside with these or any AI humanoid or robotic devices is their artificial intellect. They are designed to constantly update their coding or software improvements. In other words, as they proceed into any engagement or mission, they assess their capabilities versus their goal and re-write or upgrade their skills immediately."

"That's why this innovation can be scary as well."

Echo replied in a softer tone, glancing at Commander Baker, "Yes, RJ, you are absolutely correct."

Michaela changed the subject back to the issue at hand and asked Echo, "What about the vaccine program?"

"As we can determine right now, Michaela, that program is waiting for enough human volunteers to show up. Our projections tell us that it won't likely begin for at least forty-eight hours."

Sara added firmly, "Our teams of metahumans are already in place and integrating into the citizen crowds that are starting to gather."

"Yes," Echo continued, "we will be able to determine the composition of the vaccine formula almost immediately after they are harmlessly injected."

The President, referring to his notes, advised, "We understand from each site that the aliens will be presenting their case from one main pod very soon… we just don't know yet which one."

Echo kept on point, "Well, Mister President, we have Arrans positioned at each site, so our assets can begin the 'deep dive' on actual words and diagnosing speech patterns, inflections, key words, and timing issues to further discern the actual intentions of the Dracs."

With an impatient sigh, President Sullivan uttered a worrisome thought, "It appears that a majority of the world's population are supportive of the pod aliens. Our data has that majority number at roughly sixty-five per cent."

"That number is 'par' for the course," Echo remarks.

Again, Sara smiled.

Echo added her observation, "Typically, leaders say one thing… and the people believe something else. It's both political confrontation and human nature."

"Well put," Michaela murmured.

"And, Mister President, this is not the time for exercises in democracy. You make the decisions that are best for the survival of the world."

"Yes, Echo, you are right. That's why we, the leaders, are listening to your advice and for your guidance.

<Echo, it seems like the vaccines are on board the pods and will begin at all three sites as soon as local health and home-land security give the okay.>

<Thank you, Pulse. What is your hunch?>

<Ask Sara. I think we have a slight reprieve here.>

"Sara, Pulse…"

Interrupting Echo, Sara snaps, "I heard."

"Of course, you did, Sara. Sorry."

"No problem," Sara begins. "Everyone… Pulse informs us that the vaccine is now available at each of the three sites, waiting for the 'all clear' from local authorities to commence with the vaccinations."

President Sullivan immediately chimed in, "I'll take care of that. I can get us 'five days', I'm sure."

"Thanks. That will give us plenty of time to analyze the situation and plan a countermeasure."

"Done, Echo. Now, what's your plan for the distraction, so we can get your AIs inside?"

"Done, Mister President. We are going to create a diversion to enable Ava, Eva, and Ivan to slip inside the pods at that moment."

Pausing a moment, Echo continues, "We will set up a one-on-one… face-to-face meeting with your vice president, who the world still sees as a legitimate, high-level authority."

"And who would be our representative at the one-on-one, Echo?"

"That would be me!"

107

PODCAST

*C*itizens of Earth. We are the Devonians, and we come from the Alpha-Draconis Star System, some two hundred and fifteen light years away. Like the Arrans race, which has established themselves as a friend to Earth, we are a friendly alien species intending to bring help to your world. We will begin with the vaccination from the Covid-19 virus that has plagued your world for a decade.

A pause was taken.

Then, we will provide your world with "eight capsules" that will show you how to desalinate the oceans to provide fresh water for everyone, how to ionize the atmosphere to eliminate hurricanes, how to use the Earth's resources to eliminate worldwide hunger, how to manufacture the drugs to cure the world's illnesses, how to manufacture the strongest metal from elements in our universe, how to take your current AI technology to a level that will benefit mankind, how to accelerate worldwide solutions to climate change, and a blueprint on how to defend your planet from alien invasions.

Sara looked at Echo. "Do you believe what we just heard?"

"Yes, Sara. I now know which caste is in charge."

"And?"

"We are likely screwed!"

Thank you for listening. We will begin your vaccination process as soon as we have confirmation to proceed from your respective governments.

With that, the air went out of the balloon back at the ETRT. Even the Arrans were very concerned about what perception was forming with the world's population.

Pulse made the first conclusion to the combined teams of the ETRT and Arrans.

"We have had shape-shifting moles in our key restricted sites for a very long time. The exposure of our 'eight capsules' was a brilliant tactic by the Dracs and one that I am very disappointed that we missed."

"Yes," a perturbed Echo added, "With all of the leading indicators, a covert approach wasn't on my radar screen. Are you on it, Pulse?"

"Yes. I have Laser and an expanding intel team scouring every aspect of our implementation work."

Sara nodded nervously, "I have contacted Cameron and he is running extensive post-vetting on cabinet members and the Galactic Committee as well."

Sara was referring to an exchange of text messages with POTUS and continued, "The President believes that the overview exposure of the eight capsules came from VP Worthington."

"Yes, Sara, I'm sure, "added Commander Baker. "But, she would not likely be privy to details of the projects, as would be necessary to take the next viable step in 'helping' roll out the execution of same… she can't walk-the-talk."

RJ also advised, "I have contacted all of our sites, especially the Utah compound, to be on high-alert. We don't know their next move, but catching us being complacent is certainly in their best interest."

"Thanks, RJ," Sara replied with confidence in his role.

"I also contacted your dad, Mike."

"Thanks, RJ," Michaela added with a wink to Sara.

At that point, POTUS patched in with his latest update, "We now have the latest opinion poll numbers on the credibility of the Dracs."

Sara said, "Let's have the likely bad news."

"Yep, it's bad. The poll reads: Are the aliens friendly and believable? *Seventy-seven* percent. Are the aliens unfriendly and not believable? *Twelve* percent. Unsure is at *eleven* percent.' We have a serious uphill climb!"

"Yikes," Sara quipped. "This is not good."

"One more thing," POTUS muttered. "We have a meeting set up with Echo and VP Worthington for high noon tomorrow."

"Which pod, Mister President?"

"The one in Redwood City, Echo."

✦ ✦ ✦

Echo finished her leadership meeting with the Arrans team and contacted the AI Eva. Echo, Pulse, and Sara would teleport to California the next morning.

With Pulse and Sara standing out of sight, Echo approached the entrance to the pod precisely at noon. The VP was amongst many alien observers, which was exactly what Eva needed to infiltrate, once the two women began their meeting.

"Hello Echo. It is good to see you and thanks for coming."

"Hello Samantha. I am pleased to be here and I thank you for this meeting."
Echo extended her hand in greeting, but the VP declined.

Echo knew that the VP was no longer human, and just a touch would have confirmed that.

"Samantha, your *Citizens of Earth* announcement stated that the alien species was the Devonians. Is that to distinguish one part of the race from the less superior Dracs?"

"Yes, Echo. On top of their 'food chain,' excuse the pun, is the elite Devonian species… the smart ones… the leadership council. For now, you will be dealing with their galactic warriors, the Dracs, and me."

With an impatient sigh, Echo asked a simple question, "What do you want… what do you really want?"

"We believe there is a place for both the Dracs and the Arrans on Earth."

"Both?' Echo was waiting for clarification, inasmuch as the vicious Denon were actively involved.

"All right… We believe there is a place on Earth for all three alien species, and we just need to explore ways to make it happen."

<They want to preserve the planet for whatever reason.>
<Yes, Pulse. That is relatively good news.>
<Is Eva on board?>
<Yes, Sara.>

"Are you the spokesperson for the Dracs, Samantha?"
"Yes."
"Can you tell me what the Dracs' intention is?"
"Yes. We have a five-phase plan for humanity to consider."
"Go ahead."
"*Phase One* is to shape the scope and scale of our presence."

<Sara, patch this back immediately to POTUS and the ETRT.>

"*Phase Two* is to eliminate any negative impressions that humanity has.
"*Phase Three* is to take an initiative that fulfills Earthly needs.
"*Phase Four* is to stabilize the working environment amongst the cultures.
"*Phase Five* is to enable a civil authority, or socialism, that we can all live with."
"You can make those available to the U.S. President, Sullivan?"
"Yes, Echo. I assumed you already did."
"No, Samantha, I am just listening. Are you ready with your vaccine?"

"Yes, Echo. It's the same as the Arrans' vaccine, but not caught up in government red tape."

"When will you start?"

"Well, Echo, as soon as Cameron stops the regulatory bullshit, we will begin."

"Fine. I'll see what I can do. Would you like to meet again tomorrow?"

"No, Echo, that won't be necessary. Once the vaccination program is underway, we can meet again."

"Very well, Samantha. Until then…"

As Echo turned to leave, the VP raised her arm into the air.

"Wait, Echo, I have one more question."

"Of course. What is that?"

"How is Michaela doing?"

Pausing for several seconds, Echo replied, "Fine. Why do you ask?"

"We almost had her!"

108

VISUAL AIDS

With that comment, Echo knew full-well that the Dracs were blowing smoke up humanity's collective ass, and she was livid. The Michaela incident could have gone so wrong, if not for incredible skills, equipment, and luck.

As Echo walked over to Pulse and Sara, who had heard everything that was spoken, Echo's wheels were already turning.

"That BITCH!" Echo was using some of Pulse's human descriptions and Sara could feel the anger and resolve in her mentor.

"She knew that I knew everything that the VP said was a lie… almost defying me and us to do anything about it. Damn it, I'm pissed!"

Sara gazed at her friend and offered some additional info.

"I just spoke with Commander Baker, who was taking in all of those strategic comments and hyperbole."

"What was his input, Sara?"

"According to RJ, who lives and breathes this stuff, this is in-your-face shit. Their five phases are directly from US military ops manuals for occupational takeovers: shape, deter, seize initiative, stabilize, and replace civil authority!"

Echo immediately responded with a laser focus, "It's time for the ultimate show-and-tell!"

✦ ✦ ✦

So, Echo contacted Sara, who got in touch with POTUS for what Echo had described as the ultimate show-and-tell. Echo wanted a meeting with the Congress and the President's cabinet, as well as the Galactic Steering Committee, named *Operation Cosmic Storm*, as soon as possible.

Patched into the same Zoom chat, Echo laid out her needs.

"Mister President, were you able to assemble the body of people I described?"

"Yes, Echo, with the exception of a couple members who are otherwise unable to attend, we are good to go. House Speaker Elinor Gifford will preside."

"When, Mister President?"

"Tomorrow at 10:00 am."

"Good. Thank you."

"Pulse, have you identified a candidate from this body for our purposes?"

"Yes, Echo, I have."

"Excuse me, Echo, what is Pulse referring to?"

"Mister President, you need to trust me. We think we have found one of your moles."

"Oh. In that case, thank you."

"No problem." Echo asked Sara, "You and Pete ready?"

"Sure are."

The President asked, "Pete, the hologram?"

"Yes, Mister President, Pete, the hologram."

POTUS was both baffled and impressed with Echo's role as champion and the doer of all doers.

✦ ✦ ✦

At precisely 10:00 am the following day, Speaker of the House, Elinor Gifford, called the hastily assembled body together.

"Please welcome President Sullivan. Mister President, the floor is yours."

"Thank you, Madame Speaker. I won't waste another minute."

President Sullivan rose from his chair and walked over to the podium. "First, let me say that the vice president who you saw, our Samantha Worthington, is not one and the same person. She has become an ally of the Dracs, and how and why remains a mystery. We are only in contact with her as their ground spokesperson, since the Dracs have not provided anyone from their leadership ranks."

The President then looked directly at Echo. "Please welcome Echo, the Supreme Arrans Commander and someone that we all know and trust."

"Thank you, Mister President. I will explain where we are in terms of what we know about the alien pods. Sara Steele's ETRT and my leadership team have been combining our investigative resources."

Congress was patiently awaiting Echo's report. "First, our starship fleet has completed our recon sweep efforts and have found no sight of any incoming alien crafts. We will continue to monitor any changes and all activity within the near-side of this galaxy."

Slight mumbling could be heard within the chamber.

"Regarding the pod infiltration, we have our three best AIs inside now, having successfully assimilated into the alien population. They will provide highly valuable intel regarding the inside operations."

No questions were asked, so Echo continued, "Along with help from the ETRT, we also have metahumans placed within the groups of citizens outside each pod awaiting vaccinations. Once these metas are vaccinated, we will immediately analyze the vaccine formula to discern its componentry. Although the aliens claim that this vaccine is for the treacherous Covid-19 virus, we have our doubts. Sara Steele now has someone she wants you to meet... Sara?"

"Thank you, Echo. Several years ago, my grandfather, Pete Stevenson, was killed by an entangled alien species, the Denon, who have been on this Earth for hundreds of thousands of years. They were trying to silence the one human being that was cognizant of alien presence on Earth."

Sara and Echo could see a sense of bewilderment growing in their audience.

"Through the incredible three-dimensional holography of Doctor Matthew Palmer's advanced I.T. lab, combined with the Arrans' super-cognitive re-creation, I would like to introduce you to my grandfather, Pete Stevenson, in hologram."

Immediately, hologram Pete appeared on the floor of the chamber.

"Hello, ladies and gentlemen... It is indeed me, the late Pete Stevenson, and I am very happy to be here."

There were actually cheers that could be heard in the audience.

"Sara has already gotten me 'up to speed' on what you are faced with. My contribution here is simple. Several weeks ago, Echo, Sara, and I took an advanced virtual-reality trip into the future, as I have that prognostic capability and they had the technology that enabled us to travel."

Pete was animated, both literally and figuratively.

"What we saw was the destruction of Earth... an apocalyptic future awaiting this planet. It was very real... only we could not determine when this would happen."

With an impatient sigh, Sara continued.

"Thank you, Grandad. I need to ask you a very difficult question."

"Yes, Sara bear."

"Who killed you?"

"I was murdered by a man who called himself John Smith."

"You said he called himself John Smith?"

"Yes, before I 'died,' he, or it, morphed into an enormous creature, likely eight or nine feet tall, greenish with claw-like hands. I was never able to warn anyone… until right now."

"Thank you, Grandad. Echo, you're up."

"Many thanks for Pete's tremendous recall and for setting the stage for a life-changing moment for each and everyone in this room."

Winking at Sara and "Pete," Echo summoned Aeon, who appeared next to "Pete."

"Joining us is my second-in-command, Pulse, and you may remember our *Grey* alien friend, Aeon, from our last meeting. Aeon will now help us with a 'visual aid' that will take your breath away. Aeon?"

As Aeon approached Pulse, Pulse interjects his contribution to the developing drama.

"This shape-shifting capability of the Denon is part of the Dracs' strategy, and one that they hope will confuse us and buy them some time. I would like to invite Senator William Barnes to join us at the lectern."

Senator Barnes immediately bolted toward an exit.

Waiting, per Pulse's request, was the House sergeant-at-arms, who grabbed the senator. Echo had him placed on the floor below the Speaker with Pulse holding him in a chokehold.

Echo nodded to Aeon to take over, and Aeon placed a ten-foot-tall cage around Senator Barnes, who appeared to be a helpless, older person, clueless of what was about to happen.

With a shock prod from Aeon, Barnes transformed to another senator's image in the audience. With another prod, he once again transformed into another totally different senator.

The audience was beyond disbelief. Echo motioned for Aeon to pause.

"You have now seen the morphing capability of this evil alien species… but you have yet to see them in their actual bodies. Aeon, please?"

Aeon drifts over to Senator Barnes and touches *him,* without using a prod.

He transforms *hulk-like* into a nine-foot-tall, greenish reptilian creature with gills on its massive head, a long tail with an arrow-like tip, enormous arms and legs, and claws for hands. The creature lets out a long and powerful shriek!

With all in the chamber standing, Echo snaps at them almost like a mother scolding her child, **"These are the disgusting aliens that are now intermingling with your citizenry and giving your wives, mothers, and children vaccinations!"**

109

GALACTIC SUMMIT MEETING

With that startling exhibition and image of the alien Dracs, Echo says to her team, "We're going to reconvene in my office."

President Sullivan asks, "Where is that Echo?"

"On my starship, Destiny."

"On the Moon?"

"Yes, Mister President, on the Moon."

Echo called for a meeting among the Galactic Civilization, which included the *Greys* and the Teslites from the future.

> <Echo, would this be the time to have Cameron and his most trusted colleagues meet on the Destiny?>

Thinking for a moment...

> <Yes, Sara, I think it would.>
> <I will ask him.>
> <Go ahead.>

"Cameron, Echo would like you and your closest advisors to meet with her on the Destiny. You game?"

"Of course. Can you give me, say, an hour?"

Echo chimed in, "That would be fine, Mister President."

> <Great idea, Sara.>
> <Thank you.>

✦ ✦ ✦

Except for Sara and members of the ETRT, this would be the first time that humans were brought to Echo's cosmic warship, the Destiny.

President Sullivan selected two cabinet members and two Galactic Committee members and contacted Sheikh Mohammed bin Saeed al Nahyan, the Prime Minister of the United Arab Emirates in Dubai. The Sheikh was the most respected world leader and the President's choice to make the trip to the ultimate Summit Meeting.

It was decided that Sara and Pulse would teleport everyone, except the President, to the Destiny.

Echo understood the President's logic and quickly offered her help.

"I will take the President to meet with Sheikh Mohammed bin Saeed Al Nahyan, and when the Sheikh is ready, the three of us will join you on the Destiny."

Meanwhile, Echo conferred telepathically with Aeon, and they agreed that the leader of the advanced alien race, the Teslites, would need to be brought in.

The Teslites were the futuristic species, created by bundling biotechnology, robotics, AI, and advanced weaponry. They didn't even exist in the 21st Century.

Their leader, called 999, was very hard to *read*, as they existed solely to evolve their species, and human life did not factor into any strategic decisions. As was mentioned before, the self-aggrandized name was to connote that he was always right, 999 times out of 1,000, regardless of the issues. This was a massive ego taken to the nth degree...

As Echo was preparing to teleport the President to Dubai, he was handed a note from Mara Wallace, his chief aide.

> *The Dracs want one week, seven days, to prove that they are friendly and will help humanity with the eight capsules.*

"This is good news and bad news, I'm afraid," the President offered.

"Why is that Mister President?"

"Well, Echo, the good news is we now know that we are dealing with a time-sensitive ultimatum."

"And I know the bad news, Mister President."

"Yep, we likely have less than one week to decide the fate of the planet!"

"Echo?"

"Yes, Mister President?"

"Please call me Cameron. I don't refer to you as the Supreme Arrans Commander!"

Smiling, Echo nodded, "Yes, Cameron."

With that comment, Echo reached into to her hilt, removed her latest Battlestar Sabre, and handed the sabre to the President.

"What is this, Echo?"

"It is my second favorite Battlestar Sabre, the Valiant, and I want you to have it as a gift from me and the Arrans."

"Who, may I ask, has your favorite Battlestar Sabre?"

Winking at Cameron, Echo had an air of peace and closure as she responded, **"Sara Steele has sabre number one… Destiny!"**

110

MIDNIGHT MOON
MAYHEM

Echo and Cameron headed back to the Oval Office with Mara Wallace and the President's security detail. Echo would teleport from the White House with POTUS to pick up the Sheikh for the quick celestial journey to the Moon.

Sara and Aeon teleported directly to the Destiny and set up the Pete hologram once they got there. Pulse gathered the remaining four dazed Moon travelers, assured them that they would be safe, and *zap*, they were gone.

Within the hour of announcing their plan, all attendees of Echo's Summit Meeting were in place on the Destiny.

"Pulse," Echo ordered, "please take our guests, minus the President, on a tour of our base and a brief circumnavigation on your Star Runner Falcon."

"Falcon, Pulse?"

"Yes, Mister President. What can I say...? I'm a big Star Wars fan."

As Pulse took his group to the Falcon, Echo talked to Sara and the President concerning a couple revelations, "Review of the data from both inside the pod surveillance and the assimilation outside, reveal some critical and dangerous likelihoods."

"Like what, Echo?"

"Well, the Dracs haven't shown the softer caste at any point, so I'm quite sure the 'barbarians are at the gate,' Cameron."

"Movie buff, eh Echo?"

"Well, I'll admit, Pulse has that engaging 'look what I found' side."

Sara was puzzled with the somewhat humorous slant on the day's developing events, but she recalled Pulse's comment about the importance of humor when faced with dire consequences.

Echo, getting her serious face on, continued, "Cameron, we know the pods that we see are only a fraction of what is physically there."

"How do you know that Echo?"

"This isn't our first 'rodeo' with the Dracs."

"Love it," Sara thought fondly.

"What else, Echo?"

"Our deep-space galactic recon is now seeing very long-distance radar disturbances that are meant to deceive us, and that's alarming."

Sara was surprised, as the initial Arrans' recon showed nothing.

"Let me now engage 'Pete' and use his extended virtual reality."

As Pete joins them, the President now knows why the rest of his ensemble was, *exit, stage left.*

Echo nods to Sara to take the lead with the hologram. "Grandad, what do you see on the Earth's immediate galactic horizon?"

"Sara bear, I see devastation and death. Without humanity's intervention, the end of Earth's days is likely... and with the wrong countermeasure of retaliatory means, the known universe could possibly be damaged, altered, or destroyed."

As Pete's apocalyptic vision statement concluded, Echo voiced another concern "That vaccine is likely to have a horrible consequence to those that take it... and I don't see any way to stop the doses until we have the formula diagnosed."

Sara advised with her own laser focus, "Once Pulse has returned with his group of leaders, we should prepare a plan for how to address these and other issues in unity... we need to have a consensus on what to do going forward."

"I agree," added President Sullivan. "I have a suggestion, once we are fully assembled."

✦ ✦ ✦

Pulse returned from the mini-tour.

"That was awesome... best thrill ride I ever had!"

"Glad you liked it, senator."

"Yes, Pulse," added Sheikh Mohammed bin Saeed Al Nahyan, "that was truly remarkable. Gives one pause under these difficult circumstances to enjoy what life has to offer."

Echo smiled briefly, understanding what a bittersweet moment this was. She glanced at Sara and Pulse, who both were as focused on the scope of the meeting as ever.

"We are going to be seated in our War Room," noted Echo. "Please follow Pulse into the meeting room, where refreshments will be served."

Once seated, seeing her team fully in place, Echo turned the meeting over to President Sullivan.

"We need immediate plans as well as Plan B or C contingency plans."

Echo leans over to Vibe, who apparently has some breaking news.

"Mister President?"

"Yes, Echo."

"Sorry to interrupt, but we have a disturbing report from our AIs inside the pods that needs to be heard… and right now!"

The seriousness of the meeting became as stark as the midnight sky on the dark side of the Moon.

"Go ahead, Vibe."

"Thank you, Echo. We have just heard from the AIs, and they reveal that the pods are merely a global anomaly.

"What is that Vibe?"

"Mister President, a global anomaly is the quantum violation of a static, global, symmetric and current conservation. A global anomaly like this means that a non-perturbative loop calculation cannot capture its true size, scope, and definition."

Sara asks, a little annoyed, "In terms we can understand, Vibe?"

"Oh, yes. Sorry. Each pod is part of a larger quantum, displaced structure, and we are only able to see what the Dracs want us to see… they are literally controlling space-time."

"Eva," Echo asks, "what is the actual size of the pod's host?"

"It resides in what quantum physics calls 'imaginary time,' the time that is perpendicular to the present and is open only to those who have created it. It is separate from our space-time."

Commander Baker, understanding in concept what the Dracs are employing, offers his opinion, "This had been an extra dimension of time that minds like Stephen Hawking have lectured about for years. We are apparently seeing a purely hypothetical theory prove to be real."

RJ glances at Eva. "In your calculations, how big is the pod's host?"

Without hesitation, Eva replies in a stunning announcement, "Each pod host is approximately 12.5 cubic miles in size. And the pod itself holds warrior eggs in an area that is protected by a telemetric firewall. Therefore, I cannot estimate the number of eggs."

Echo quickly asks, "How many, based on the size of the egg area, would you estimate?"

Eva consults with Ava and Ivan to get a total figure from all three pods as everyone holds their breath.

"The total number of alien warrior eggs is at least three hundred thousand."

111

EDGE OF DARKNESS

Given that scary scenario from Eva, Sara took charge of the meeting and offered an agenda, "Let's look at what we know as baseline facts regarding the Dracs."

Echo smiled and nodded her approval.

"One, they unleashed a destructive magnetic pulse that allowed them to analyze our defense preparedness."

"And" added RJ, "their wave did not result in large human casualties."

"Which means they would be in need of worker bees... or a food source," exclaimed Pulse.

That remark from Pulse created a sobering thought amongst the group.

"Two, they will attempt to infect many of Earth's population with a so-called vaccine, to achieve some sort of controlling mechanism."

"We should know the results soon, as vaccinations are due to begin today at the site in China," responded Ivan.

"Three, we know that the barbaric caste is in control, inasmuch as VP Worthington has become their spokesperson."

<I am certain, Echo, the warriors are in charge.>

<Thank you, Aeon.>

"Aeon confirms that the warrior caste is in charge," Echo reported.

"Is there anything else that we know to be true?"

"Sara," Ava responded, "there is one thing that is now clear to the AIs that wasn't within our surveillance data earlier."

"Please, Ava, tell us."

"A large ocean four hundred miles below the Earth's surface is the likely home of the Dracs' reptilian colony on Earth that has been here for tens of thousands of years. It has been dormant for those tens of thousands of years... but now has become active."

"Ava... active? How?"

"Well, Sara, there is considerable movement in that ocean below, and it appears that there is matter consolidation occurring in ten separate locations."

Echo responded harshly, "This is bad… it means that they are planning a coordinated effort."

"We need to ramp up our sweep of the near galaxy."

"Yes, Pulse, we must do that," Echo replied.

<Sara, watch this.>

<Pulse… watch what?>

<Your E-watch screen. A sidebar. Lunatic cool.>

At that moment, a simulation of a winged starship with the Arrans' glyph is flying in a nosedive directly toward an ocean impact. Just prior to impact, the wings withdraw, and the vessel takes on the shape of a rocket or even a submarine. It enters the ocean surface at rocket-speed and is clearly designed to be submersible.

"Holy crap!" Sara shouted, with no one in the room aware of what got her juiced up.

President Sullivan glanced over to Sara, winked, and spoke as the group digested the additional bad news, "We need a consensus from world leaders as to what action we must take now. Sheikh Mohammed, could you chair the roll call, say tomorrow, as we provide these details to the major decision bodies, the G-Twelve, NATO, the World Council, and the six major economic powerhouses worldwide: China, Japan, Great Britain, France, Germany, and the United States?"

"Yes. Yes, of course, Mister President."

"Very well, we will provide each of these bodies with the info that we have and get a 'yeah' or 'nay' regarding the seven-day waiting period that the Dracs have requested."

"I don't like giving the alien bastards their one week. All hell could break loose."

"I agree, Sara," replied a determined Echo. "But we need to at least see what the consensus tells us. When it comes to resources required and additional allied strength, we will need all capabilities at our disposal."

<Echo, I am concerned about additional reptilian forces from space arriving on Earth as we wait. They are clever and resourceful.>

<I agree, Aeon. We will sweep, as Pulse suggested.>

<Echo, do you know how long it will take for a hatched warrior egg to become a fully weaponized warrior?>

<No, Aeon, I do not. How long?>

<About thirty minutes.>

112

THE FINAL FRONTIER

Following Aeon's chilling revelation, Echo bade farewell to the Arrans' guests and they are transported back to their respective locations.

President Sullivan and his contingent are returned to Washington D.C.

Sheikh Mohammed bin Saeed Al Nahyan is returned to Dubai.

Sara, Echo, and Pulse huddle to discuss immediate strategy and contingency plans.

"What do your instincts tell you, Sara, regarding the consensus of world leadership?"

"Echo, my gut tells me that the consensus will be to give the Dracs their seven days. I am almost certain that no group majority will decide to attack this alien species based on intel from another alien species and some young 'know-it-alls' with only limited credibility."

"I'm afraid I agree with you, Sara, and we need our own back-up plan."

"Yes, Echo," Pulse responds quickly, "and I think I know where Sara's head is right now."

"Damn right you do, Pulse. I will be returning to Utah to bring everyone there up to speed and then meet immediately with Scott and Matt."

With a clenched fist, Pulse snaps, "Project Zeus?"

"Damn straight, Pulse… Project Zeus!"

"Pulse, determine where our forces are regarding the Arrans' galactic fleet."

"On task, Echo."

Pulse gave Sara a warm hug, as he was off to get a report from his military leadership.

"Goodbye, warrior princess. We will talk soon."

Sara gave Pulse a long and passionate kiss, as Echo smiled lovingly, and then he was gone.

"It has now come to this, Sara."

"Come to what, Echo?"

"This could become an extinction-level event."

Echo moved over to Sara and put her hand gently on Sara's face and added, **"Beautiful Earth will likely become... Battlefield Earth!"**

113

BATTLESTAR EARTH

Arriving back in Utah, Sara assembled the entire four-hundred-person compound workforce together and provided the overview of what she knew,
skipping the dark and foreboding details that would likely cause severe panic.

She pulled Scott, Matt, and Mike aside and gave them those dramatic details.
"Okay, guys, where are we on Zeus readiness?"

"We still have a ton of bugs to work out, Sara." Scott was surprised at the
unfortunate timing that the Dracs' ultimatum had caused. "I will get an update
right away."

Matt chimed in, "I'll see how the technical integration is coming. Jeremiah
and Tyreek had several packages that are close to implementable."

Mike added his summary, "All management and admin policies and procedures are in place."

"Great, guys. I'm headed to the main conference room with Dad. The roll
call by Sheikh Mohammed will be starting in less than an hour."

"Honey, I'll meet you there later. Gotta give your mom an update."

"Sara, Scott and I will meet you there."

"Fine, Matt. I will have everyone on that feed."

Matt, Scott, and Mike shook hands and gave each other a "thumbs up."

Sara glanced at a very pensive Michaela and murmured, "What cha
thinking?"

"Just when we as a team, and I as a love-starved, single lady, were getting our
shit together, we are now facing end-of-world stuff."

"Yeah, Michaela, it's been 'par' for the course ever since Kat was killed."

"You don't look so good either, my friend. What's up with you?"

"I just don't feel like my usual self these days. Kind of tired and dragging ass
in the morning."

"Well, Sara, it's not like you have a life of leisure!"

Both had to laugh at the stark realization of what was pending.

"Let's go up to my quiet office and break open a good scotch... what do you think?"

"Great idea, Sara... lead the way."

✦ ✦ ✦

Walking into her office, Sara glanced again at the carved wooden bird that her grandad found in Saqqara, one of Egypt's oldest burial grounds. Thinking to herself, "*This bird and the cabin in the woods are what started the whole damn alien-search thing.*"

Following Sara into the office, Michaela walked over to the wet bar and asked, "Which glasses?"

"Get the Macallan Signature glasses... we're gonna open up the good stuff!"

Sara reached down to the bottom of the liquor cabinet and pulled out a bottle of Macallan Anniversary 25-Year-Old Single Malt Scotch.

"Whoa, girl, that's absolutely top shelf!"

"Yep, Michaela. No need to save it, eh?"

"Guess not."

Sara opened the bottle and gently poured the two ladies their neat scotch, giving her friend the largest amount of this expensive liquor. "Cheers, Michaela."

"Cheers, Sara."

Sara removed her denim jacket, rolled up her shirt sleeves, and proudly displayed her *"I Am the Storm"* tattoo.

"So, how are you and RJ doing?"

"I'll tell you what, girlfriend, he is Mister Dreamy. I pinch myself every time I see him to make sure he's not a man-hunk of my imagination."

"Fantasies?"

"For sure. Every time I take a bath, I have an image of him, along with my power bullet, making me hot and getting me off in record time!"

"Way more info than I need, sweetie, but I'm happy for you."

"Thanks, Sara. What about the man or men in your life? You don't need to go there if you don't want to."

"Oh gosh, not a problem. I know I can share anything with you. After Kat was killed, I figured life is short and we have friends to share our innermost secrets... that's why they are friends."

"So, give us a re-fill and let it rip!'"

Pouring another round of the Macallan 25 just for Michaela, Sara, with a warm sigh, began to open her heart to Michaela.

"I love Matt as a dear and wonderful friend. He is the kindest, gentlest, and most thoughtful person I know. I trust him, respect him, and thank him daily for giving me my life back after the cabin attack."

"Do I see a 'but' coming?"

"The only 'but' is that Matt is a very serious and committed physician, with such a focus on helping people and 'giving back' to the community, I'm often on his 'back burner,' and I get it."

"And the sex, Sara?"

"Ah… it's good."

"Just good?"

"Yeah, he really tries to make me happy in bed."

"You have a problem with that?"

"No. No, of course not. He's just so damn serious."

"And Pulse?"

Sara smiled, and gave a deep and resounding sigh. She raised her glass. "Ya wanna talk about fantasies?He's nearly seven feet tall, broad ass shoulders, big and gentle hands, and when his manhood goes erect… it's a damn moonshot!"

"So, the sex is good?"

"Oh no, not good… great. Out-of-this-world great. I mean literally, out of this world."

"Details?"

"We have made love on Earth, the Moon, and at the bottom of Tranquility Lake on Trappist One. He can create an actual sexual scene or fantasy of my choice, and then he completely takes control."

Michaela was beginning to perspire as Sara gave vivid details.

"Michaela, we can make love for hours and have multiple orgasms simultaneously. And his sense of humor! Damn, he is hot when you want it hot, cool when you want it cool, and funny those times when you want some relief."

"Bottom line?"

"Duh! I am so physically attracted to him. I just want to jump on his bones and never let go!"

"Congrats, girlfriend. Looks like we both met our match."

"Yep. Definitely our highlight reels!"

Both girls laughed as Elonis poked her head into the room.

"Hi Sara. Hi Michaela. The patch to the consensus meeting starts soon. You two coming down to the conference room?"

"Go ahead, Elonis. Michaela and I will be on our way."

"I do have an early evaluation of the vaccine from our metahuman insiders."

"What is their preliminary determination, Elonis?"

"Michaela, it appears to be either a mind-altering drug or even worse... a memory eraser of all human consciousness, making those vaccinated become literal vegetables."

Sara scowled, "Memories and human function lost!"

Michaela thought, *"What else are these dastardly aliens capable of doing to the human race?"*

◆ ◆ ◆

As an even more somber Sara and Michaela walked into the conference room, the big screen was already booted up for the Sheikh's consensus report.

President Sullivan had Zoomed in, as was Echo, Pulse, and the entire Arrans leadership team. Sara saw Matt and Scott on the other side of the room but stayed with Michaela and Elonis.

Sara waved to Matt, who was speaking to three company associates in the far corner of the room. RJ motioned for Michaela to join him and she did, leaving Sara and Elonis to await the results.

"I will now call the roll of our distinguished leaders and countries," Sheikh Mohammed said. "The response will be 'yes' or 'no' to the question of giving the aliens in the three pods one week, seven days, to prepare their assistance plan."

"The World Council?"

"Yes."

"The G-Twelve?"

"Yes."

"NATO?"

"Yes."

"China?"

"Yes."

"Japan?"

"Yes."

"Great Britain?"

"Yes."

"Germany?"

"No."

"France?"

"Yes."

"The United States?"

"*No.*"

As the President cast his *no* response, the Sheikh wrapped the brief meeting with his summation, "The vote is not unanimous, but the consensus is clear. Our world will allow the alien visitors one week from today to demonstrate their friendly intentions. If, at that time, we need to re-convene, that is what this global body of world leaders will do."

<Sara, we are now at Plan B and it is totally in our hands.>

<I agree, Echo. We are much weaker without the support of our allies.>

<We must do what we must do.>

<Yes, Echo. Did Elonis tell you about the vaccine probabilities?>

<Yes, she told Pulse and me, what she had learned and passed on to you and Michaela.>

Sara called for a meeting with the ETRT in the War Room, where she now needed to make a major announcement, given the results of the roll call.

Once the team was fully assembled, Sara took a deep breath, knowing that the reptilian alien invaders known as the Dracs are now on Earth and starting a sub-ocean consolidation.

"The ruthless and malicious aliens are here, and we believe that their intentions are either total annihilation or to take over the human race and occupy our planet."

Sara glanced over to Michaela and RJ and continued, "They have both a surface and sub-surface battle contingent, and we just learned that their vaccine is likely a memory eraser.

"Unfortunately, the consensus of world leaders is to allow the Dracs a full week to convince mankind that the Dracs are a benevolent species, like the Arrans."

Many hands were raised as panic and concern took over the otherwise calm and collected Utah workforce.

"I know what you are going to ask," Sara continued, "and the answer is that we will not stand by and let this charade force us to wait until it is too late to react. We don't have an immediate plan right now… but together we will prevail!"

Sara couldn't help but feel worried and stressed out… even given her newly acquired superhero skills. "*I need a little calm after this latest storm,*" she recognized.

Sara turned to her long-time and trusted metahuman friend Elonis, as they both observed smiling ETRT member faces turn to the dreadful reality of the moment, and Sara sent a telepathic thought just to her and her alone.

<I have something to share with you, my friend.>

<Yes, Sara. What is it?>

<On top of everything else, Elonis, I'm pregnant.>

Elonis responds, <I know.>

Sara advises wistfully, <I just don't know who the father is.>

Elonis thought to herself, *"But I do!"*

Then, materializing suddenly in an apparent teleportation from an unknown origin, in an eerie purple haze, was a battle-dressed alien warrior princess, nearly six feet tall, wearing a black uniform with silver trim and a black cape. Her silver helmet had a crested visor which immediately enveloped a darkly shaded face shield, and her blonde hair shown out the back of her helmet.

The warrior princess wore a necklace with a black and white cross and was holding a gleaming black light sabre pulled from a silver hilt and had a distinctive glyph on her breastplate. Her aura seemed supernatural... and surely not of this Earth.

The intimidating cosmic visitor looked directly into Sara's eyes, raised her light sabre firmly in her right hand, pointing her left hand at Sara, and made a stunning announcement...

"I am Aras, daughter of Sara Steele, and a time-space speedster from Exoplanet Earth Two that is the mirror image of this Earth and Sun, some three thousand light-years away."

Never had a room been so quiet. Sara gasped.

"The pods are a Dracs' Trojan Horse. They are a global anomaly. Each pod is in a third-dimension time loop and is the size of an American city. The evil Dracs control time and space and have your world in a closed-time loop."

A thousand thoughts raced through Sara's mind as Aras continued...

"There are ten million warrior eggs in each pod that will hatch in SIX DAYS. They will quickly destroy humanity using humans as their food source!"

COMING IN 2021...

Book four in the Stargate Earth series:

BATTLESTAR EARTH

ABOUT THE AUTHOR

Garry J. Peterson is the author of several books, both fiction and non-fiction, following a successful career in international corporate management. His most recent non-fiction book is a *how-to* business book, **Who Put Me in CHARGE?** Garry has also completed a companion Implementation Guide for this book, **Getting to the NEXT LEVEL.**

As a former consultant and business coach, Garry now spends his time writing science fiction thrillers and conducting both motivational and subject matter speaking engagements.

Garry has written over 300 trade journal articles, white papers, client presentations, and website content. He has given commencement addresses and public service keynote speeches.

He has a passion for hard science fiction and weaves personal stories, humor, and visionary spiritual thinking into his writings. His current writing project is a five-book science fiction thriller series, **STARGATE EARTH.**

WARRIORS OF THE GALAXY is book three in this series, following **SHATTERED TRUTH** and his recently published book two, **ALIEN DISRUPTION.**

STARGATE EARTH is a visionary series that gives the reader an alarming apocalyptic future; and then, despite evil aliens, Garry creates a unified and holistic transformation of aliens and humans into an alliance to save humanity.

Garry follows a writing principle to guide his creativity via a quote from Tom Clancy, *"The difference between reality and fiction is... fiction needs to make sense."*

Garry lives in Florida with his lovely wife Vaune. He plays in a competitive softball league and is an avid scuba diver and kayaker. Their daughter, Sarah, lives in Los Angeles.

Visit his website at www.garryjpeterson.com.

You can also follow Garry on Facebook, Twitter, and LinkedIn.